I0562027

i

THE ORIGINATORS

Other Books By Charles Schwartz

POETRY MOMENTS
[Collected Poems]

BETWEEN THE SHEETS
[Selected Poems]

UNDER MY SKIN
[Selected Poems]

THE ORIGINATORS

A NOVEL

By CHARLES SCHWARTZ

NOTE•WELL•PUBLISHERS™
HIGHLAND PARK, ILLINOIS
USA

Copyright © 2005 by Charles Schwartz

All rights reserved.
No part of this book may be reproduced in any form,
without permission in writing from the author or publisher,
except for the inclusion of brief quotations in a review.

Library of Congress Control Number: 2005902116

ISBN 978-0-9744793-2-2

For additional copies of this book,
Order directly from Amazon.com/books
Booksurge.com
Or contact Charles Schwartz's publisher:

Mail: Charles Schwartz
             c/o Note•Well•Publishers™
             1001 North Avenue
             Highland Park, IL 60035

Phone: toll-free: 866-741-9908
Local Phone   847-432-3736
Fax: 847-432-3272

Email: notewell@sbcglobal.net

Enclose Payment of $20.99
Free shipping within USA

This is a work of fiction. Though some characters,
incidents, and dialogues are based on historical record,
the work as a whole is a product of the author's imagination

Published by:
Note•Well•Publishers™
Highland Park, IL 60035-1129

First Printing: May 2005

The Originators

444 Pages /6x9 format / Perfect Bound

Smooth opaque off-white pages 50#

10 Point 4-color Paper Designer Cover
Printed in the U.S.A.

ACKNOWLEDGMENTS

This is my first novel, and fourth book with. *NOTE•WELL•PUBLISHERS.* The other three were books of poetry.

Once again, Mary Ber proved herself to be the confident, assuring editor she was with my poetry books. Her support and encouragement was generous with wise critiques and suggestions, most of which I adopted. Her ability, I suspect, is not common among editors.

At home, my family, my wife Toby, my daughter Ellen, and my son Rob, showed me what really matters by being natural editors of encouragement. Our cat also knows what matters—her bed.

DEDICATION

TO THE SANCTITY OF THE INDIVIDUAL AND HIS RIGHT TO HIS OWN LIFE.

they mutilate they torment each other
with silences with words
as if they had another
life to live

they do so
as if they had forgotten
that their bodies
are inclined to death
that the insides of men
easily break down

ruthless with each other
they are weaker
than plants and animals
they can be killed by a word
by a smile by a look
                    —Tadeusz Rozewicz
(Translated from the Polish by Czelaw Milosz)

"*To know that a question is an answer in disguise is a minimum of wisdom.*"
—A. J. Heschel

The Originators

a novel

Part I

Prologue

Paris, 1884

Three darkly clad figures stood around an empty field next to the river on the *Champ de Mars*. The cold was bracing, although the wind had died down since dawn. They paced the field, looking for something that would tell them that this was the right spot.

The tall one looked up at the sky, noting the cumulus clouds that floated past and bumped into each other. He bent down and picked up a handful of dirt, then poured it into a small glass case. He lifted the case full of dirt up over his head into the air. Ten seconds later, a fork of lightning streaked down through the sky and struck the box. The impact made the tall one stumble backward. The glass case glowed a metallic blue, the dirt having been blasted out by the electricity. The other two figures, who had been watching this scene, briefly nodded to each other as the third regained his footing.

A little to the east, German and Austrian engineers tinkered with their gasoline-powered carriages. A little to the west, Americans and recent American immigrants tinkered with their understanding of electricity.

Chapter 1

New York, 1889

Hyim Hopewell never knew his father to be a meticulous man. Ezra Hopewell's drawing room was usually cluttered with papers, opened and unopened packages from all corners of the globe, and all manner of new-fangled gadgets. Ezra's first love, his late wife Harriet, had introduced him to his second love, the new and sometimes unbelievable world of electrodynamics.

A diamond merchant by trade, the elder Hopewell kept track of new developments in electrical phenomena by way of various scientific journals, published in French, Swedish, and Hungarian. Although he could read French and Swedish, Hungarian was still a mystery, so his subscription to *Mathematikai és Természettudományi Értesítő* was a source of private amusement to the son, who didn't tell his father that this journal had little to do with electrical experiments.

Hyim sat at the other side of his father's desk, eyes fixed on a small gadget that sat on top of a stack of papers. Aside from the danger of such a device that spontaneously produced a spark every now and then being among paper and wood, Hyim had little desire to disturb it, but merely watched for its effect like a cat watching a moth flitting around a gaslamp.

Already an accomplished physicist, having received what he called his "first" advanced degree from Harvard by the age of 20, Hyim was the first Hopewell in the sparsely documented 3,000 year history of the family to get an advanced degree from a university.

"Harvard, at that," his father would say proudly. "A Jew at Harvard! Hah!"

Ezra was fond of saying things like that, about being a "proud

Jew" and his son being a "brilliant Jew." But Hyim knew better. His father was not a religious man—their family had not been what anyone would call *devout* since great great great grandfather Hiram L. Kovacs fought on the American side in the War of Independence. This history had been told to him from early on.

"Son..." the elder Hopewell began. This made Hyim even more bemused than he already was.

"Son, you're getting married tomorrow," he continued, "and there are a few things you should know about being married. Now... this is difficult for me to say. You know that I approve of Leah. She *is* proper wife material..."

"Dad..."

"Nevertheless, there are a few things you should know about women..."

As his father went on, Hyim found his attention slowly turning toward that small sparking gadget sitting on a pile of papers. It was an enclosed, oblong piece of glass with dark metal squares at either end, probably magnets. There was no source of power, as far as he could see, but it managed a spark all the same. The first time he saw it, it startled him.

"... when your mother and I were married. She was from a good family, you know. They were Sephardic Jews from Portugal by way of Brazil and the Netherlands..."

After the spark, some kind of gas inside the glass oblong slowly changed from a blue color, the color of the spark, to completely transparent, at which point it would spark again, filling the oblong once again with a bluish haze.

"... the marriage bed, I can tell you. That got me in trouble the first time. It's just not polite, apparently."

In his reverie over the gadget, Hyim became aware of a palpable silence.

"Are you listening to me?"

"Of course."

"That young Leah of yours. Are there any illnesses that run in her family?"

"Come on now."

"I'm just concerned for the grandchildren. It's not every day that my only son ties himself to a woman. The family, they aren't from money, are they?"

Hyim exhaled audibly. He loved his father, but there was always something about the father that was too practical and analytic, almost cold. "Not as such," the son said. "You've met them; they're nice people."

"Oh, yes. The *Sterns*." The father said their name with emphasis, not quite derisively, but with just enough of an effect to give the son something to think about. "He's, what, a grocer?"

"He sells lamps," Hyim laughed. "Oil and kerosene."

"Yes, the lamp peddler," the father said sarcastically. "I suppose his family went to the CC's?"

"It's not *old* money. They're not wealthy perhaps by your standards..."

The father put his hand up. "But this is not a conversation about money. I really don't care where this girl comes from. All I want to ask you is if you are happy."

Spark.

"I am."

"I see. Well, she's a capital girl. A nice, proper girl. Treat her well, and... and, uh... well, you'll be happy, I suppose."

"All right, Dad," the son said, still bemused. He often wondered what his mother and father's relationship was like, what their lives had been like before he was born and shortly afterward. Many families he knew had six or seven children or more. Leah herself had two sisters and four brothers. Why did his parents decide to have only one son? Or did his siblings all die at a young age? It was something that he had always wanted to ask, but it

5

seemed to be a sore point, so he never pressed it. The father never seemed to have gotten over the death of the mother, always having a wistful expression whenever she was mentioned.

"There's something I've been meaning to ask you," Ezra said suddenly. "Why France? Why not San Francisco or Siam?"

"I want to see this tower they've put up along the Seine. It's supposed to be very impressive and very controversial, a real feat of engineering. I want to see it up close. And, of course, I've managed to convince Leah. She wouldn't mind visiting, either."

"Capital! Capital!" the father said, a little dismissively. Then he paused and sighed, choosing his words carefully. "You must be cautious in Europe. They're not as tolerant of us over there as they are over here. There's a lot of... hatred in the world. We're blamed for a lot of the world's problems. You don't know what it means yet."

"We'll be fine. Don't worry so much."

"Just be careful. Make a promise to an old man."

"If it will make you feel better. But I'm not sure what I'm promising."

The father smiled. "Oh, and one other thing. I got you a present. I wasn't going to tell you this until later, but I might as well tell you now. When you get back, you'll have a house to come back to, fully furnished, fully paid for. I spent months looking for a place that had enough room for a laboratory."

"I don't know what to say."

"Somebody, one of our American presidents, once said, 'I study war so that my son can study architecture so that his son can study poetry.' Well, I'm almost done with my studies. And I've got more money than I know what to do with. I don't want you to have a vocation, Hyim. You're too smart for that. You're smarter now than your father ever was. But we live in a fine country. The finest in the world, in my opinion. All I want is for you to make this country better. So I'm giving you access to my personal accounts.

"Your name will be right under mine."

"That's awfully generous of you, Dad. But I thought I was going to make my own way in the world."

"If you like. But I wanted to give you the comfort of not having to work in order to live. And you need the trappings of... of comfort. I'm recommending that you take Li-Yan's son into your employment."

"Li-Don? What do I need with a manservant?"

Spark.

"You would be surprised how often one comes in handy. Besides, you can afford it now. I can't tell you how much I appreciate having a butler like Li-Yan. You'll understand it one day. For now, I would like to encourage you to employ Li-Yan's son as a favor to me."

Li Yan's son, Li-Don, was Hyim's same age. They grew up together and knew each other well. Although they were expected to have—and had—different circles of friends, they were always great friends at the house. Li-Yan was always very protectively secret about his family to the outside world. But his wife, Mei-Gao had been like a second mother to Hyim after his own mother died. He and Li-Don were very much like brothers.

It would be very strange to order around a family friend like his father ordered around Li-Yan.

"I don't know what I'm going to do with him," Hyim said.

"Don't dismiss having a traveling companion."

"I'm going to be with my wife!"

"Now, now. Don't take this too seriously. Li-Don is a very intelligent young man and can do things that... you don't—let's say—have an interest in."

Having a third party along wherever he went made Hyim nervous, although if it had to be someone, Li-Don would be pleasant enough to have around.

7

"You wouldn't be trying to spy on me, would you?"

"Come on now. I may have a rich son, but I'm not worried about how he spends his money. Speaking of which... Have you made any, um... work commitments?"

The son relaxed. "No. Nothing yet. I understand Princeton is looking for young people like myself, physics professors for the tenure track. But I haven't even made inquiries."

"Princeton, eh?" Ezra smiled. "That's in New Jersey, as I understand it. Oh, well, I guess you can't live your children's lives for them." The father held his hand out for the son. "I'm a lonely old man, Hyim," he said. "Don't tarry too long overseas."

Hyim was feeling a bit sorry for his father. He had made untold millions of dollars working as a diamond broker; he had more money than he knew what to do with. But he was truly alone. Of course, there was Li-Yan and his wife, Mei-Gao. But they were more like family friends. Ezra never remarried after his wife died, for reasons that Hyim could only guess.

Hyim's mother died years ago, when he was only five. Hyim remembered her like she was etched in glass. First standing in front of him with a cup of hot cocoa, then lying down, in bed with a sallow fever on her face. Then, nothing. Her death didn't mean that much to him when it happened. To a young child, she had only left the house. She had left hundreds of times before that—to the store, to her sister's house in Rochester, to many different places.

But when Hyim turned six, he was still waiting for her to come back, still waiting for his cup of hot cocoa. The memory was so real, and he could see her even now, could smell the kitchen and the faint scent of burnt sauces on the stove.

Spark.

"What is that little thing?" Hyim said, pointing to the glass oblong.

Ezra picked up the glass oblong, surreptitiously wiping a tear from just under his eye. "I haven't the faintest idea. A colleague of mine sent it to me a few weeks ago. He said he found it in Budapest. I don't know who made it or even how it works. But every five minutes and 38 seconds, it makes a little tiny electrochemical pulse. Fascinating little object. You can have it if you want it."

Hyim picked it up, expecting it to be heavy. But it was lighter than

a fountain pen, despite being many times larger. The gas slowly changed from the thick blue smoke inside the glass to transparent. While he was mesmerized by the process, the father handed him a sealed envelope.

"Are you going to Amsterdam?" the father asked.

"I hadn't planned on it. We were just going to stay in Paris for a while."

"Well, if you would, I would like you to make a special trip to deliver this message for me to a colleague. It's important that you deliver it in person. It involves some crucial business."

"Why don't you just use the telegraph? It would be there in hours, not weeks."

"This is much too important to let it be seen by anyone else. *Anyone* else. Do you understand? Now, the man's name is Brightferry. Sylwyn Brightferry. It's very important that you deliver it to him by yourself."

"By myself? Well, what's all this? Why all the intrigue?"

"There's no intrigue here. Well, not much anyway. But my competitors would love to get hold of my information. It's very new and speculative. They would gladly bribe the telegraph operators to get what I have here. I hate to involve you in my business, you know that. But you're going anyway."

"All right. If it's that important."

"And Hyim," the father said with a sudden seriousness. "Take care of yourself. Promise me."

"Yes, father."

Chapter 2

Leah Stern was a bright, attractive Radcliffe girl. Passing her on the street, however, one might not guess she was the most intelligent person within shouting distance. She had a prim and prudent air about the way she conducted herself, and her choice of fashion might give the impression of upper-class snobbery and closed-mindedness. Nothing could be further from the truth.

Her family came from the distressed Polish farmers who had fled one of the waves of anti-Semitism that swept over Europe. She was part of the first generation of Poles born in New York, and her father was fortunate enough to have invested in a small and modestly successful metalworks, though he still sold lamps and lanterns on the street because he loved working with people. All of Leah's siblings had graduated from the free CCNY system, but she insisted on going to Radcliffe. It was something that a father could not deny his youngest daughter.

She was a paradox to Hyim. She was a very proud woman, yet her humility was endearing. She was a tenacious debater when it came to politics, yet she was gracious in social situations around people who—in his opinion—did not deserve such treatment. She studied French without a real desire to go France. They met at one of the various cotillions between their two colleges, and continued to meet in gradually more and more informal settings. Leah liked to say he would have been expected to wait for her in her father's sitting room, discussing the wholesale lamp oil trade, had they not been away from home together.

She stood at the railing of the *Rotterdam II* with her new husband (Hyim liked hearing that word, *husband*, more than he thought he would), looking out over the calm North Atlantic, the hair underneath her hat blowing every which way in the wind. The frantic wedding was behind them, their families had finished exchanging stilted and uncomfortable conversation, and everyone was now back at home, safe from each other until there was another reason to get together.

"It's strange for me," she said. "When I was a girl, all I heard was how terrible it was in Europe, how awful the people were."

"We won't go all the way to Warsaw."

"It's not just that. It's Europe. It's the Old World. The people there don't care if you think you're a person, they only care if you're the right sort of person. Your family has been in America for generations; you don't know."

"I read the newspapers."

"Typical American response."

She had no trace of a Polish accent. As her parents explained to Hyim, she had started affecting a "theater-style" American accent after seeing *H.M.S. Pinafore* at the Odeon when she was 12. It had affected her deeply in ways she couldn't quite explain. What she did understand, however, was that the American language spoken on stage was nothing like the American spoken in her neighborhood in lower Manhattan.

"She walked around like little Miss Pinafore," her father said. "Showing how much she could speak like those spoiled little *shiksas* uptown. No offense."

Her family spoke Yiddish to each other, often loudly. Hyim knew some of the vocabulary, but their conversations were a mystery. They were very polite to him, but they didn't care for his father, who seemed a little too much like the off-putting nobility who forced them out of Poland.

But though Leah's father liked Hyim, no one was more shocked when he showed interest in her. Hyim could see it on the old man's face and the way he shook hands a little too vigorously and a little too long. Leah was the youngest of seven children, the rest having been married off long before. She was the precious baby, arriving unexpectedly after her siblings were already grown and were contributing to the workforce.

11

Hyim was struck by her independence and fiery spirit, qualities lacking in other girls who had given him attention. He first noticed her at a mixer while she was just outside the front door of a church hall, giving a small lecture to a group of girls about how to behave around "those Harvard boys"—so that they wouldn't be an embarrassment to the female gender. She didn't see him smiling at her juxtaposition of classical rhetoric and modern behavior.

He was a fresh graduate with his Bachelor's degree in his back pocket. Literally. He had been carrying the sheet of paper around for weeks. He had come with some of his school friends, taking a good ribbing because he didn't participate in their drinking games—although alcohol was not allowed at the event, that didn't stop them—a seventeen-year-old among men in their 20s.

When she dismissed her classmates after her Stern lecture on males, she stayed outside, alone, breathing deeply.

"Excuse me, Miss," he said, coming out from behind a column.

"Yes? Oh, I didn't see you there. You shouldn't be sneaking around a place like this; people will think you have dishonorable intentions."

"Not... not at all, Miss. My name is Hopewell. I wasn't sneaking around. I just heard your speech. I thought it was very well contrived."

"Well, Mr. Hopewell, I would thank you if I didn't know you were spending your time eavesdropping on innocent girls."

Little did Leah know she would fall helplessly in love with him because of his inquisitive nature and his appreciation for intellect. And, much as she wouldn't like to admit it to him, the cut of his figure—fit from years of competitive crew and fencing—and to his bright smile made her legs feel weak.

Here it was, three years later, and she was with him, next to him, *being* his wife. "I can't believe we're actually here," she said. "Sometimes you plan for something and it seems so far off that you start to make the planning a part of your life. And when you reach the goal it's just so... unreal."

12

Hyim knew that they were on their way to the part of the world that had essentially thrown her family away. He felt this apprehension in her. His father's admonition about the way Jews were treated had affected him more than he realized. Before this, never thought of himself as a Jew unless someone else pointed it out to him, and now he was sure that they would.

They watched New York fade into the morning mists of the Atlantic, then spent a few more hours on deck watching the sea until they couldn't resist each other anymore. Decorum dictated that they do little more than hold hands in public, but the night before, in a hotel room in New York, they had each discovered new worlds with each other. A normally impatient woman, Leah kept still while Hyim's hands trembled unlacing the back of her honeymoon gown, she let them fumble and slip—stopping and starting—with the patience of a mirror, reflecting his own love back at him.

That first night they were both filled with nervous energy, but despite the conscientious efforts of their parents and friends to educate them about *intercourse,* they discovered that they knew next to nothing about the mechanics of how it worked. They sat apart on the bed, looking at each others' naked bodies, expecting something to happen. Leah was a strange land of beauty, with a beguiling topography that Hyim didn't quite understand. They touched each other hesitantly and offered their own theories about what might be the best course of action. But then something did happen; it was organic and smooth—all too quickly and with very little fanfare, but it happened nonetheless. And then they understood.

Hyim was a little queasy at the sight of blood and was unable to speak, but Leah comforted him. "I've been told my whole life that being with a man is illicit," Leah told him. "That I should guard my chastity with my life. But now I see what this marriage business is all about. We've been sanctioned to satisfy each other's lusts. Encouraged, even. This is how society can manage its civil exterior. This is how we give in to our desires without fear of retribution or shame. It's a *monde á deux.* We are free to be

13

ourselves behind our doors, regardless of what society expects in front of them."

"Our animal selves," Hyim said, finally.

"This is the secret of the subjugation of women," she said. "Not out there, but in here, where men actually start to believe in their superiority."

"Or inferiority."

Regardless of how much his wife tried to make sex political, Hyim couldn't restrain himself around her.

On the eve of their voyage to Europe, Hyim's recurring nightmare appeared. *He is alone, standing in the middle of a forest in an lightning storm. Trees are struck by the lightning and fall around him as he tries to run away. But the storm follows him, striking down parts of the forest. The noise is deafening, but he can still hear the crunching of his running footsteps on the forest floor.* That's the sound he remembered vividly, the leaves underneath his feet. He couldn't remember how old he was when it started or why. The dream haunted him his entire life and he woke up sweating and exhausted many times.

"What is it?" Leah asked, waking up next to him in the middle of the night.

He was sitting up, his palms sweating and clasped together behind his head. He was in an unfamiliar place and the room was moving slightly, the walls making tiny creaking noises. He realized he was aboard a ship... headed for Europe. It was the beginning of their married life. And though they had known each other for years, there were still many things they didn't know about each other. He looked around. The darkened room, with a tiny bit of light from the stars coming through the porthole, was altogether unfamiliar, though he knew what it looked like and could picture how it looked during the day. Then the figure of Leah, holding his shoulder with a look of genuine concern on her face.

"It's just a dream," he said. "A childish nightmare. There's no need to worry."

"I'll worry when I want to, Hy."

"It's nothing."

"I watched you sleep. It's not nothing. You're not alone anymore, so there's no reason to dismiss me like that."

"Listen. I have a certain dream from time to time. It's very childish, really. Just myself alone in the forest in a lightning storm. It's just something that happens."

"All right. As long as you're all right, that's all I care about."

He kissed her on the forehead. "This living arrangement is going to take some getting used to," he said. Then he smiled and they both went back to sleep.

Though Hyim and Li-Don were the same age, Li-Don seemed younger to people who saw them together. Maybe because it was difficult for people to gauge the age of someone of a different race—but it was probably because he was only five feet tall. Hyim attributed a quiet dignity to his friend that he might or might not have had.

Li-Don had been on the boxing team at Harvard. It took a while before the other members on the team warmed up to the idea of a Chinaman in their midst. Li-Don, however, was the only one who could qualify at featherweight, and this alone made him quickly popular with the team. The strings that Ezra Hopewell pulled for his son he also pulled for his butler's son—and everyone seemed to know this, which kept Li-Don from demonstratively celebrating his wild success in the ring.

Many of the undergraduates in Li-Don's class refused to talk to him or even associate with him. He once confided in Hyim that he did not know if it was because he was a Chinaman or because his ticket had been punched.

But regardless of anything else that might have distracted him, he gained his bachelor's degree in world history. And even though the provost refused to shake hands with him during the graduation ceremony, Li-Don Wei proudly received his diploma, which he carried with him wherever he went.

Hyim thought it was not only odd to be telling Li-Don what to do on the trip—carry luggage, make reservations, keep the accounts in order, etc.—but it was also odd that his manservant held such a distinguished degree. His childhood friend, who now knew more about classical civilizations than anyone he knew, was now his secretary.

In truth, Li-Don liked just being around Hyim because of their philosophical discussions. They were both outsiders in society, in a way, and it was comforting for each of them having someone else who knew what that was like.

Standing on the railing with his bride gave Hyim some comfort on the second day out, but the thick clouds overhead reminded him of his recurring nightmare.

The seating for breakfast was almost over. They had awakened up early but couldn't make it out of the room without reminding themselves why they were on a honeymoon. Hyim's nightshirt sustained a rip up one of the seams.

They quickly made themselves presentable and headed for the dining room. On the way, they met Li-Don, who was coming back. He gave them a small smile. Li-Don had been giving them knowing looks since Hyim had asked him to accompany them to Paris.

"Come join us for breakfast," Hyim said cheerfully.

Li-Don chuckled as he passed them by. "I've already been and gone. You had best hurry, Mr. Hopewell. They will be closing the kitchen in a few minutes." He headed back for his room, next to theirs.

16

Leah had been wary of Li-Don, at first. She had never seen someone whose family was from the Far East, and his angular face that held rounded eyes and nose made her feel uncomfortable in a way she couldn't explain. Later, she met his family, and as they got to know each other, they became friends also—although in a more formal sense.

"You must join us sometime for a meal," she said to him.

He touched the bill of an invisible cap and politely walked on.

The Hopewells made it in time for breakfast and were one of the few people left. Leah was out of breath. A waiter was pouring their coffee when Hyim felt a slap on his shoulder.

"Well, if it isn't Pliny the younger," said a familiar voice. Hyim turned around to see Jimmy Primerhaven, one of his Physics colleagues from Harvard Arts & Sciences. His hair was a little longer than before, and he was dressed better, but otherwise he looked exactly the same—an inquisitive pointed face. He, like Hyim, kept no facial hair, which made him look younger than he actually was.

"You old dog," Jimmy said. "Or should I say, *young* dog. But, lo! What is this beauty braving the seas with this old dog? James Harrison Primerhaven of the Middlebury Primerhavens, m'lady." He affected a false aristocratic air as he took Leah's hand.

"Imagine us meeting on the same ship," Hyim said. "I'd like you to meet my wife. Leah, this is Jimmy, a fellow student."

"Please," Jimmy said. "Fellow student hardly covers it. Mrs. Hopewell, this man is a genius. Your husband is practically a legend. I can only hope to grasp the things his mind has already put together."

"What takes you across the Atlantic, Mr. Primerhaven?" Leah asked.

"I'm going to Germany to see if they'll take me at the Heidelburg Institute."

"Jimmy here wants to be the next Isaac Newton," Hyim said.

17

"Yes, you know, the seventh one, the one after Faraday." He sat down at their table, grabbing a biscuit from Hyim's plate. "This man," he started, pointing at Hyim, "this *young* man, this *boy*, is the reason that I graduated."

"Is that a fact?" Leah said.

"I figured that if a strapping young man such as this can slog through the horrendous swamp that is the Harvard Physics program, then certainly *I* can do it. You see, I was inspired by example. Do you know what your husband's doctoral thesis was on?"

"I must say I have no idea," Leah said. "Nor would I understand it if you told me."

"It's not incomprehensible at all, my dear. The laws of thermodynamics are readily absorbed by a ready populace."

"Please," Hyim said. "No thermodynamics before breakfast."

"Do not worry, Mrs. Hopewell, five out of six graduate faculty couldn't understand it either."

"Fortunately for my doctorate, the sixth faculty member was my graduate advisor," Hyim said. "He was more open-minded."

"Consider your cup of coffee my dear," James went on, grabbing another biscuit from Hyim's plate. "Thermodynamics says that there is no chance of keeping it hot indefinitely without doing something to it, like getting more hot coffee or putting a flame under it. But imagine if we could build a coffee cup that has no opening, but contains this very same coffee, and is airtight and perfectly insulated. Then we can keep it hot indefinitely."

"But we can't construct something like that, can we?" Leah asked, playfully.

"No. Sadly. There's no such thing as perfect insulation. But imagine if there is some way that we can build it. Now imagine that the coffee grounds that invariably occur at the bottom of your cup are arranged in a certain way, let's say in the shape of the letter 'W'. Thermodynamics says that those coffee grounds will likely be in every other conceivable combination between 'W' and randomness—except 'W'—before coming to an ideal state. But, hold up now, not so fast. Our hero here says that in a perfectly insulated environment, there is no such thing as an ideal state. Instead, the randomness will cause the 'W' to appear again and again. In fact, entire alphabets will appear from time to time, even recurring with numbers and symbols and other patterns."

"But, like you say, there is no such thing."

"Well, sure. But that's neither here nor there. Now imagine that we are inside your open-mouthed coffee cup again. We put the cup on top of a flame to keep it hot. That is, as heat escapes into the air, we replace it with the exact same amount of heat from the burner."

"That makes sense."

"Of course it does. It takes a genius such as myself to explain this. Now, this heat escapes in a random way—out the top of the cup, or through the porcelain—into the air. But we are replacing the heat in a very controlled manner. Our hero here argues that we can not only simulate the conditions of our previously mentioned perfectly insulated cup—allowing the grounds to change their positions into the various letters—but we can also influence which letters the grounds make. We can even control how the heat escapes, making the air itself create those same letters for us."

"You just lost me, Mr. Primerhaven."

"This is where we lose our faculty also, as it were."

"Besides," Hyim said, "the whole thing is finished anyway. I understand Poincaré is going to publish his own volume about *recurrence*, which will trump mine when it comes out in the fall."

"Bad luck, old boy. But at least it validates your point. This can only make you more popular."

"I don't know, Jimmy. It's all so theoretical. Mathematics. Vectors. Molecules. Atoms. Every time I think about my studies I come back to how much I really want to do experiments."

"You can't mean *chemistry*! My God, man! Chemistry is more

art than science. You want to see pretty colors and strong smells, you go to a chemist." Jimmy couldn't help laughing at his own joke.

"I was thinking more of electromagnetism."

"Once again, your head's in the clouds, old boy." Once again, Jimmy unsuccessfully forced back a laugh.

"Don't you have a lady waiting?" Hyim said, feigning exasperation.

"Don't be rude, Hy," Leah said with a smirk. "Mr. Primerhaven is just enamored with his own voice."

"Much like a foxhound," Jimmy said. "You've got a live one here, uh... *Hy*. All right. I'll leave you two to too much honeymooning all on your own. But I'll check back with you later. Where are you staying in Paris? I can give you the good or the bad news from Heidelberg."

"At the *Hôtel Bourdonnais*. We look forward to hearing from you."

Jimmy made his graceful exit, doffing his hat and bowing.

"He's quite a character," Leah said as breakfast arrived.

"He's one of a kind all right. Or, we can only hope."

As they ate breakfast and remarked on the other passengers, Hyim slipped his hand into his jacket pocket absentmindedly, and his finger found a small slip of paper. He didn't remember it being there before, nor had he recalled anyone giving it to him. He unfolded it with a deft movement of his fingers and glanced at it under the table. On it was a series of numbers and letters on three lines.

He recognized it immediately as *FC Code*. And the only one who could have given such a note to him in that code was Jimmy.

While graduate students, they were a part of a semi-secret society called The Freecobblers. It was largely a joke—supposedly founded after Catholics were banned from Freemason membership by the pope in 1738—and its only goal seemed to be perpetuating itself. More than one rumor had both John Adamses as members. But, having little in the way of written records, its true past was lost in the clouds of time.

The FC Code was developed who knows how long ago. It was based on a 36-letter alphabet (26 letters and 10 numerals) that shifted positions based on different numbers depending on who was sending the message. Glancing for a few seconds, the message was too complicated for him to work out entirely in his head, although he did recognize the first two words, "Meet me," the words "the", "on", and "are" and a time of day. Jimmy almost always gave messages that started with "Meet me".

"Is something wrong?" Leah asked.

"No. Just good old Jimmy being peculiar." He smiled and slipped the paper back into his pocket, out of view. They finished breakfast and went for a walk. The air was crisp, and the banners and flags flapped loudly above them. Their full stomachs gave them a short respite from their physical longing for one another.

"You know, Leah," Hyim began hesitantly, "you don't have to apologize for not knowing what it is that I study."

"Pardon?"

"Your remark about not understanding the concept. You don't have to be politely demure about things like that. Especially around my friends."

"Oh come on, now. I wasn't being demure. It's just small talk. Your friend seems harmless enough."

"It's just that I want people to know that you're an intelligent person."

"You're making too much of this. Your friend was just trying to be charming."

"I didn't marry a demure girl, Leah. I could have, you know. There were many girls who were after my father's money and would have happily been shrinking violets if they could have had their own new wardrobe every year. I married a girl with her own mind, Leah. You're very smart—it's one of the things that I married you for. I know I don't take the time to talk about my work with you, but it's not because I don't think you won't understand it."

"Well, isn't *that* very nice of you to say. If we weren't already married, I could slap you silly, you old fool."

"I don't understand."

"Come now, Mr. Hopewell. You don't have to be demure with me. Just because I don't explain it to you doesn't mean I don't think you'll understand it."

Hyim smiled sheepishly. He knew when he was beaten. "All right, I give up. You can do what you want. All I meant was that I didn't want you to think you had to be... well, you know... the *female* in the discussion."

"I won't take that personally, either."

"I can't win with you, Mrs. Hopewell, can I?"

"I don't know why you bother trying."

It was useless to argue with Leah. She invariably won all arguments. It was endearing, in a way. He found himself wondering if he should even bring up the cryptogram that Jimmy had slipped him. It's possible she would have something to say on the subject. On the other hand, it was a *secret* society—in theory—so would divulging any information about it be a betrayal of that?

Of course, the entire subject of the argument was silly. But Hyim took this step in their relationship very seriously. He could have kept it a secret or told her with an equally clear conscience. He decided that because he fell in love with her for her mind—one reason, if not the only reason, mind you—that he should share as much as he could with her. And not just to share it with someone who was his chosen life companion, but because she might have something useful to say on the subject.

After he showed her the code and explained what it was all about, he was surprised to find her more excited about it than he was.

"Well, crack it, Hy," she said. "Don't just carry it around like a pebble in your shoe."

"It could take a while."

"Longer than it took him to come up with it? We've got nine more days on this trip, how long could it take?"

It took all of 10 minutes. His first attempt didn't make any sense. It took him a second try after he figured out that Jimmy was using *James* as his first name.

```
meet me on the aft deck at eleven tonight
there are enemies on board
bring beer — j
```

"What does he mean by 'enemies'?" Leah asked.

"It could be anything. It could be his debtors. It could be Cornell graduates. You never know with Jimmy."

Jimmy was one of those characters who was always leaving without telling people where he was going. Then he would turn up somewhere as if he had never left. Wild rumors floated around about him, which he did nothing to discourage. Hyim was never too curious about his schedule, though, which Jimmy seemed to appreciate.

"Well," Leah said, "how am I going to get through the day knowing that there is some secret meeting tonight?"

Chapter 3

Possibly against her better judgment, Leah was very excited by all the intrigue. Secret societies, strange codes, enemies—and all on board a ship. "It's like being in the middle of a Stevenson novel," she said.

"It's just Jimmy," Hyim kept saying, to no avail.

They discussed whether Leah would accompany him, but finally decided against it. Jimmy would be more apt to speak freely without a lady present. So Leah stayed behind with a book, her travel journal, and Li-Don.

"The course of world history has been changed by such meetings," Li-Don warned facetiously.

Hyim went out into the chilly air with no expectations.

The ship was different at night. The noise of the ship's engines seemed quieter, yet closer at the same time. Strictly speaking, passengers were discouraged from being up on deck after nine, but no one paid attention to that. He walked past people looking up at the stars, holding each other close in the cold night air, some with glowing pipes or cigars, the orange glow moving around with their gestures. Jimmy stood, alone, leaning on the railing on the aft deck, gazing out over the ship's wake. Hyim handed him a bottle of beer and then they shook hands.

"I have to congratulate you on your choice of mate," Jimmy said. "She's quite pretty."

"Thank you. I wish I could take credit for that."

"Oh, but you can. She was beautiful all by herself, but you're the one who chose to marry her. She's much too good for you."

"Her family's from Poland."

"Well," Jimmy said. He started to say something, but then stopped. "I bet your father had something to say about that."

"Repeatedly."

They stood for a while, Hyim waiting for Jimmy to speak. But his former classmate was still watching the wake of the ship. "I'll bet there's an equation to describe the way a ship cleaves the ocean," he said finally.

"I'm sure there is. Probably some lost Archimedes script."

Jimmy smiled. Then he got serious, looking back up at Hyim. "The world is changing, Hyim."

Jimmy almost always used the English pronunciation of his name, with a soft "H". But this time he used the guttural, aspirated sound. It was startling, to say the least. It was like Jimmy had suddenly decided to become a polyglot.

"The world used to be full of science," Jimmy continued. "But now it's all about engineering. Technological developments are all well and good, but how can we *use* it, how can we make it *serve* us? Pure science is on the wane, my friend."

"I don't believe that."

"Look at this ship. First it was paddlewheels, then it was screw drives, now it's propellers. Who knows what they'll have in another twenty years."

"First of all, sir, this ship is a screw drive. Only the newest ships have propellers. Second of all, what harm does that kind of innovation do? Faster ships mean less time between points. That's progress. That's mankind moving forward."

"Progress, yes. But for whom? Sure people move across the ocean faster. But guess what? Now they're *expected* to move across the ocean faster. It used to be that a transatlantic voyage took three months. If the winds are right, you get there early or you get there late. Now it takes just ten days. Ten days. Leave 9:00 AM New York, get to Boulogne at 6:00 PM. We're becoming as mechanized as our machines."

"That's an awful lot of pessimism, isn't it? I mean, look what we're doing. Instead of leaving in early December the previous year, we're leaving in March to get to Paris by that same March. We've gained those three months before we leave to spend as we wish. Not only that, but we're not subjected to shipboard life for nearly as long."

"Yes, but look *why* you're doing it. You're going to see a monument. A *building*! Would you have gone had the trip taken three months? Would you have paid the ferryman just to see a building?"

"The *tallest* building."

"I'm trying to tell you something, and you're completely missing the point. Progress doesn't mean scientific inquiry anymore. Progress means innovation. It means getting people places faster so they can spend more money on either side. That innovation on this ship was made under the auspices of the shipping company. That magnate is making the money for the innovation."

"Why shouldn't he? He's providing a service, not just for the people on his ships, but for the engineers who have a viable idea but no means to carry it out. He gives them the means."

Jimmy scowled and looked directly into Hyim's eyes, but he couldn't keep that look for long without breaking up. "I give up, Hy," Jimmy said, laughing. "We are at an impasse."

But Hyim wasn't ready to stop. "Why didn't you say to me that this is a false dichotomy? A business magnate doesn't just *give* the means to engineers, he *demands* the results."

"Do I even need to be here to argue my side?"

"Jimmy, you bring me out here to debate technological progress, then you give up? What's going on? Who are these enemies?"

"Look, Hy, there's a lot here that I can't explain to you right now. I don't even think I could explain it if I wanted to. Some of it I don't understand myself." Jimmy looked genuinely shaken. He paused to collect his thoughts. "Something happened to me about a month ago. I was in Ontario, riding in the country. It was just coming to twilight and I was heading back to my uncle's farm from a half-day's ride. Now, I've seen the northern lights a few times in my life, so I can tell you that what I saw was not the northern lights. It wasn't an electrical storm, nor was it lightning bugs. I don't know exactly what happened, but I was suddenly in a... a *beam* of a strange light. It didn't seem to come from anywhere. I looked around me, and I appeared to be surrounded by this light—or maybe it was a group of lights. I believe that my horse was in it also. I could see her head and ears, but nothing past her. It was so bright. I remember I could smell something like— you're going to think I'm crazy—like metallic eggs. I'm afraid can't describe it any better than that. "

"Maybe you were too close to Tesla's laboratory."

"Laugh at your own peril, my friend. I felt the... light, the electricity pass right through me. It hit every sense in my body. For a moment, it felt like nothing and all I could see was a strange light. I could hear the light, I could taste it, it was palpable like a... cage of fire. No, not fire. The way electricity passes from one wire to another, like I was the gap, the conduit, the commutator."

"You know that all this sounds crazy."

"I've thought that. What if I've gone around the bend? But I don't seem to have any ill effects from it. To the contrary, in fact. Ever since then, I've felt better than I have in my entire life."

"All twenty-three years of it."

"Scoff if you will, but something happened to me. My uncle wrote to me later and asked what I fed his horse, because she seemed to have buckets and buckets of energy after I left."

He took a big swig of his beer. "I'm not really going to Heidelberg," he said ruefully. "I'm just leaving New York. Maybe I'll end up in Heidelberg. But I just needed to get out of the country. Tell no one this... I'm a stowaway on board this ship. Well, not really. I paid, but I'm not on the manifest. You see, I'm being followed."

27

Hyim suddenly realized why Jimmy had asked him out there in the middle of the night on the aft of the ship where their voices would carry out to sea under the din of the engines and the wake. Jimmy was telling him he feared for his life, but for all his bizarre honesty, he couldn't bring himself to say those words out loud.

"There is someone or something that is just on the edge of my perception. I can feel it... him... it watching me. I can sense something out there. I don't think it's on the ship with us..."His voice was quavering with paranoia and the beer shook in his hands.

Hyim put his hand on Jimmy's shoulder.

"I brought you out here," Jimmy said, "to tell you this and also to tell you to watch out for yourself."

"Myself? What have you got me mixed up in?"

"It's not my doing."

Just then, Hyim remembered his father's message and his almost dismissive attitude about his "competitors." Could it be that it wasn't Jimmy that was being followed, but himself?

"Do you believe in God?" Jimmy asked, incongruously.

"I don't know," Hyim answered, a little bewildered.

It was a stock answer to that question, which he had been asked many times. The truth was that he didn't want to think about it. If he started thinking about God, he assumed that he gave up a little bit of himself as a scientist.

"I never did, myself," Jimmy said. "Until that moment. It wasn't just that I saw a 'bright light' and all that rubbish. It was this *thing* that happened to me. Me. James H. Primerhaven. Do you know what that does to someone? I was singled out for an effect. And for what reason?"

"It could have been anything, you know. It sounds like you might have been struck by lightning. Maybe ball lightning was involved."

28

"And maybe I was caught up in the electromagnetic polar effect. Yes, I've thought about these things. But I can't explain how it all relates to me. Why did it happen to *me*?"

"Come on, you were there when the effect happened."

"Just like that? It was coincidence that there was this effect that struck right as I was going by?"

"You probably saved some poor tortoise on the ground from the experience by intervening."

Jimmy fell silent. Hyim realized that he had been questioning and perhaps making light of his friend's perceived religious experience. There was so much that Science didn't know and was just beginning to find out. It would be all too easy to explain unexplained effects by a supernatural occurrence. But it happens. People want to believe in these kinds of things to make sense of them.

They parted amicably. They were cordial through the rest of the journey, but Jimmy was not nearly as friendly as before. When Hyim told Leah what had happened, she thought Jimmy needed to be alone for a while. "He knows how you feel," she said. "And he'll come to you when he's ready."

But now Hyim could not shake the sense that someone was lurking in the shadows, watching him and his movements. There were a few people on board the ship who could have fit the description of a spy. One was a tall, craggy man in perhaps his forties who sported a gray riding cap and could be seen above deck with a silver muffler. Another was a young man who was suspiciously unremarkable except for his thick dark-brown mustache and darting eyes. Still another was a boyish man who features were so soft and rounded that it appeared as if he might have been a woman in disguise.

If Jimmy's paranoia were founded, there was no lacking for people who would fill the role of antagonist. If unfounded, there was certainly enough evidence to give him the benefit of the doubt. As Hyim walked back to his cabin, his father's message audibly crinkled in his inside jacket pocket. He found himself wondering if he had been followed because of that message. He thought he saw the soft-faced man hurriedly look away as he walked past. Whatever reason Jimmy had for making Hyim aware of a possible antagonist, it was done. Hyim walked faster.

Leah didn't know what to make of Jimmy's story. They agreed that Jimmy was peculiar.

The faces aboard ship appeared more suspicious than ever. Hyim was beside himself with distrust of his fellow passengers.

The rest of the voyage was pleasant enough. Li-Don was given very little to do, and he often stayed below deck, reading. Jimmy's unofficial suspects seemed no longer suspicious during the cold light of day (and besides, a true spy would not even *appear* suspicious). Hyim and Leah spent most of their time either in their stateroom or out on deck, often taking meals in their room. They explored each other further both physically and emotionally, gaining new knowledge every day.

But there was still that lurking doubt in the corner of Hyim's eye; the doubt and suspicion that there was some malevolent force just behind him, ready to strike at any time.

Chapter 4

The ship made a short stop in Portsmouth on the last day. It was not on the itinerary, and they lost a few hours because of it. Leah had spent the better part of the trip trying to calm her husband down and ease his fears. When they were back out at sea, in the English Channel, Hyim and Leah went above deck to watch the sunset.

"The first thing I'm going to do when we get to Paris," Leah said, "is buy a hat. One of those fashionable ones you see in magazines. I've never had a fashionable hat."

"You've never needed one," Hyim said. "There shouldn't be anything to hide that lovely face and head of hair you have."

"I always knew you were attracted to me because of my hair. What if I should lose it or sell it? I wouldn't think your friend Jimmy would approve."

"I don't know that he has a valid opinion on this. I don't care what your hair looks like."

"How very romantic, my dear."

Hyim brought a hand to his eyes. Beaten again.

All at once, they heard a scream. It was very nearby. Hyim ran around a corner and down a corridor to find a woman lying on the ground, her maid's clothing torn, her breathing heavy. Standing over her was a man of medium height in a non-descript white sailing shirt and tan pantaloons. In the dimness of the ship's electric lights, Hyim couldn't quite tell what was going on. But he knew it was malevolent.

He started toward the other man. The woman on the ground looked up at him, which caught the other man's attention. He turned his head to see that Hyim was coming toward him, then

31

spun his whole body around to face him.

"Mind your own business!" he growled. The accent was English.

Hyim turned to the woman. "Is this man harassing you?"

She nodded with wide eyes.

Hyim suddenly realized he was unable to muster the necessary strength to do anything. It wasn't that he lacked energy or strength, *per se*, but he found that he was unable to comprehend what he was supposed to do in this situation. Some kind of instinct told him that he should intervene in this situation—find out if the woman was OK, stop the man from doing anything harmful, etc.—but this same instinct had nothing to say when it came to actually *how* he was supposed to accomplish anything.

"This is none of your concern," the man said. He shifted something in his right hand, it was something light and metallic that flashed in the meager light. Hyim realized it was a knife.

"There's no reason to threaten me," Hyim said calmly. "Me or anyone else. We're all civilized adults, here. Surely we can hash out a..."

"Stuff it!" the man said. Clearly, he was a threat. Though no taller or larger, and less physically imposing than Hyim, the other man would win a fight. If for no other reason than he might have known more about it than Hyim did. Now, if they had had swords, Hyim could have taken care of him. Maybe. Being a fencing champion with *epées* was different from actually fencing with the genuine articles.

The man took the front of Hyim's shirt in his fist. "You bloody Yank! Sticking your nose in business where it doesn't belong. This tart and I had a deal. Now she's going back on it. As *civilized adults*."

What happened next had to be explained to Hyim later. After the other man released Hyim's shirt from his grip, he stumbled back and only managed to avoid hitting the floor by spinning and breaking his fall with his hands. Other noises behind him suggested a struggle.

In the intervening instant when Hyim had been released and had fallen to the floor, Li-Don had come charging in, silently, and had caught the other man with his hand exposed. Li-Don dispatched the knife with one kick, and it went flying harmlessly to the far wall and the floor. The surprise gave Li-Don the advantage in the fight, and he punched and swatted at the other man until he went down. It was over by the time Hyim got to his feet.

"Oh God! Oh God!" the woman said. She was still on the ground and had seen the whole fight.

Li-Don stood with his foot on the other man's neck. "Are you all right, Mr. Hopewell?" he asked.

Hyim, amazed at the sight of this small man victorious over a larger opponent, nodded. Li-Don had always been physically gifted, but this was more than he'd ever seen out of his friend.

The woman got to her feet. "Oh, Eddie!" she said. "What have you done?"

Five minutes later, a couple of the ship's crew bound the other man's hands and dragged him off.

The woman could not be consoled, despite Leah's best efforts. Hyim got the impression that the woman and the man had known each other, but something had gone wrong.

It did not escape his attention, however, that this man with the knife, this *Eddie*, could have been the enemy that Jimmy was talking about. Obviously a disagreeable, if not outright violent man, Eddie fit the role of a suspicious character right away.

"He looked familiar," Leah said. "I only got a glimpse as they led him away, but there's something about him that I recognize."

"Of course you recognize him," the woman said. "He's the bloomin' Prince of..." she stopped in mid-sentence, then brought her hands up to her lips as if she had said too much. Then she ran out of the passage.

When they finally arrived in Boulogne, Li-Don once again seemed more comfortable with his role as personal secretary— which is what Hyim began calling him, *manservant* being so *bourgeois*, for lack of a better term. They said good-bye, good luck, to Jimmy.

Three gendarmes came up to them just as they were boarding a carriage. "*Pardon, monsieur*," one of them said to Hyim.

"Yes?"

"We wish to extend our thanks for capturing this criminal."

"All the thanks go to my personal secretary."

"Yes, quite. *Monsieur*, there is a delicate matter of secrecy we wish to impose upon you. We ask that you do not reveal this incident. It is for the sake of international relations."

"Say," Hyim said. "Who was that gentleman?"

The gendarmes looked at each other. "We believe he is a notorious criminal. This is all we are prepared to say *au moment*. Please forget the entire incident."

They bid their farewells and left Hyim, Leah, and Li-Don to continue boarding the carriage.

"My goodness," Leah said.

They took the carriage to a railway station and by the middle of the next day, they were in Paris.

Chapter 5

The city was alive with a buzz about the tower. It was crowded beyond anything Hyim had ever seen in New York or Boston. The sidewalks were packed with people chatting and smoking and laughing and drinking. Everyone wanted to not only see Mr. Eiffel's tower, but also talk about it. And there was no missing it, even from a distance. Although it was not due to be opened for another three days, it was unapologetically in full view from the steps of the *Hôtel Bourdonnais* as well as from almost everywhere in western Paris. There were several other buildings around its feet, but there was nothing quite as spectacular as its topmost spire.

Hyim remembered what Jimmy said about engineers. Mr. Eiffel was an engineer by trade. He had been a structural designer, mostly, having completed rail bridges and other mundane buildings. He designed the structural support for the remarkable lady who enlightened the world in the New York Harbor, but the design of the statue itself was done by another French gentleman. And there was that business with the Panama Canal company bankruptcy.

"It takes your breath away, doesn't it?" Leah said as they climbed out of the hansom. They could hear the noise of the workers preparing the exhibition site.

"This is what the *inside* of a real building is supposed to look like," Hyim said. "Look at that latticework. That's a supporting structure. But there's no skin. It's an amazing example of utility— function dictating form. It's skeletal nature allows wind to pass right through it. You couldn't do that with a *real* building."

"For God's sake, Hy. Must you analyze everything?" Leah said playfully.

The Hopewells were met by an overly solicitous hotel staff. Li-Don looked pleased that the bellboys were deferring to him. He was all too happy to direct them when they took the bags up the stairway. Leah spoke to the staff.

The hotel itself was an impressive building if not a picturesque one. It might have made more of an impression had it not been a neighbor to such a grand tower. Even the typical opulence of the lobby was overshadowed by the newness of the form.

There was a message waiting at the front desk.

Mr. Hopewell,

Please allow me to extend my hospitality to you and your wife on Saturday evening. i will send a coach round for you once you arrive by train.

Lord Sylwyn
Brightferry, Amsterdam

"*Lord* Brightferry," Hyim said aloud. His father never mentioned anything about nobility.

When they were situated in a suite on the third floor, and the hotel staff had gone, Li-Don felt free to speak to Hyim..

"You speak of the tower with the mind of a scientist. I ask you to consider the political implications of the tower."

"Political?" Hyim said. "It's a structure. It's an edifice."

"Yes, but what is its use? Buildings ought to be useful in addition to being visually appealing."

"What do you mean?"

"It's an amazing feat of engineering, as you say. But why build it? Will there be offices? Residences? Will it be a watchtower for the army?"

Leah looked uncomfortable with this abrupt philosophical exchange, but Hyim was all too pleased to have someone challenge him intellectually.

"It's for the Universal Exposition. It's an observation tower.

You could see all Paris from up there. It's a showpiece."

"Ah, yes. It is a commemoration of 100 years passing since the French Revolution. But also consider that it is an assertion by the French body politic that France is still a great country in the world."

"You mean, the tallest building in the world is somehow tied into the national consciousness. This is just an example of engineering, not just French engineering."

"I have to say that perhaps France is feeling a little nostalgic for its days as an Empire. It is no longer an Empire. It has been many decades since all of Europe quaked with fear over a Frenchman. This tower brings them that kind of prominence."

"But that's the people who commissioned the tower. I was speaking of the tower as a work of technology."

"With all due respect, you cannot separate the two. It is not only a symbol of prominence in the world, it is also a symbol of exactly what it is, a feat of engineering. *French* engineering."

"Quite true, I must admit."

"My father, Li-Yan, has said to me before: Things are built because there is a need."

"Li-Yan is a wise man."

Leah stood up. "Myself, I thought the tower was a clever visual pun. It's a giant letter 'A', isn't it? In French, it means, 'at'. Very thought-provoking."

It was almost impossible to leave the hotel on the morning of the *Exposition Universelle* opening. The Boulevard de Bourdonnais was packed with pedestrians, and there was general confusion as horses and carriages were trying to navigate around and through the crowd. Hyim, Leah, and Li-Don made their way through the crowd and across the *Champ de Mars* to the tower

Leah had brought a dress especially for the occasion, green and pink. She bought her hat the day before, however, from a milliner who was nearly out of stock. Hyim thought she looked more elegant than he could ever remember, but he didn't say so.

Banners that had been hung from each railing flapped and fluttered wildly. It was spring, but the air had a cold bite to it, and the wind was incredible and unpredictable. Hats flew off of heads and longer beards shifted over some shoulders. Above them, an observation balloon floated by.

They toured the grounds around the tower, visiting the garish, bronze-colored *Dôme Centrale* and several of the participating nations' pavilions. Li-Don spent some time looking at the Javanese, Siam, and Cochinchine pavilions. He had never been outside of the United States before, and though there was not a Chinese display, he sought out nearby parts of the world.

They passed a number of acrobats, jugglers, and impromptu performances by musicians of all sorts, including young women who seemed to do little except bare their legs as they paced back and forth.

Hyim and Leah continued on until they reached the *Galerie des Machines*. Hyim was awestruck. As impressive as the Eiffel Tower was, the *Galerie* was truly astonishing. It was like a market of mechanical devices, enclosed by a row of archways on either side and a massive sloping glass and ironwork roof; more remarkable, it covered 15 acres and did not appear to have any supporting columns. The entire structure was supported using a system of bows and arches that left the interior open. To Hyim it did not look real.

At the front was a passenger elevator, similar to the ones in the Eiffel Tower, except this one was electric instead of steam powered. Inside the gallery were hundreds of mechanical exhibits, including a moving walkway that ran the length of the building.

Leah seemed amused by Hyim's interest in this great hall of metalworking. Hyim had to admit he was fascinated by it. He spent a great deal of time at the Thomas Edison display.

They lunched on pickle and lamb salami sandwiches in a less crowded street café.

"Dad would have loved it here," Hyim said. "Except for all of the rabble, I mean. I don't know why he didn't want to come here himself."

"He has enough to do," Li-Don said. "Your father has a complex business."

"You're certainly enamored with all the mechanization," Leah said to her husband. "Perhaps you haven't realized how much those machines are taking the place of actual workers."

"Those machines are creating more positions for workers. Construction, maintenance, design, selling."

"I'm afraid I have to agree with Mrs. Hopewell on this," Li-Don said. "For every maintenance position created by these machines, as many as ten laborers are displaced."

"Ten!" Hyim almost shouted.

"Sewing machines are faster than manual sewing. You only need to employ ten people who will do the work of a hundred in the same amount of time."

"And what about the phonograph?" Leah said. "Instead of attending a concert, you can play the roll over and over again. If enough people did that, the musicians wouldn't have people to play to."

"All right, all right, you two! I admit that progress isn't perfect. But doesn't the inner workings of such things fascinate you?"

Leah and Li-Don looked at each other, "Not really," they said in unison.

Chapter 6

They could still hear the commotion of the *Exposition Universelle* from across the street, even from inside the hotel. The sun was going down, and the Tower was in the process of being lit up with tiny electric lights. It was something to behold. The gaslamps in the street were outshone entirely by the giant sloping triangle of light that pointed to the sky. Or, rather, to the many threatening clouds that obstructed the sky.

They decided not to attend the official "unveiling" because Hyim was feeling nervous with all of those people moving swiftly around him. He did not like so many people or things moving around him—he liked calmness. Slow, deliberate movements. He was not above running, himself, if the situation called for it, but he did not like being in fast-moving crowds. Li-Don did attend the opening, by himself.

The couple sipped champagne in the lobby. Leah had perhaps a half-glass too many and started to giggle at the slightest provocation.

"Hy," she said, throwing her arms around him. "You *are* a funny man. The man who likes machinery but not people. I don't know why I love you, I really don't. But of course I do. Like a partridge on a fencepost, I love you."

"What in the world does that mean?" Hyim asked, laughing.

"I don't know. I don't care. I'm in love with the least romantic person on the Earth. It's a burden I must bear, mustn't I?" she fell into a short fit of hysterical laughter.

"I think I'll take you upstairs before one of us gets arrested."

They made their way up the stairs. Hyim helped Leah get her footing.

"I never knew you were such a drinker," Hyim said.

"It's a special occasion. Besides, I believe in suffrage, not temperance."

"I must admit, I feel a little clipped, myself."

"Oh, yes, we're learning quite a bit about each other, aren't we?"

They reached their room, which, unfortunately, did not have a view of the Champ de Mars. Instead it had a view in the opposite direction, a partial view of the *Palais Archépiscopal*, and the rest of northwest Paris. They made love jubilantly under the window, then retired as the sky turned dark blue, feeding each other small blocks of cheese.

They were sober now, and something was bothering Hyim. Leah had called him the least romantic person on the face of the Earth. As much as she was teasing him, it wasn't altogether untrue. He had very little experience with what other people might call *romance*. It was one of the things that Leah said she found refreshing in him. That he didn't pursue her with the formal and complicated manners required of a Victorian courtship. He was awkward and made too many honest remarks for that. But she found his lack of charm very charming, especially for one so handsome.

Still, he could think of a dozen times when she had made a similar remark.

Around ten, Li-Don popped into their room—knocking first— to tell them how amazing and frantic it all was. "Mr. Eiffel is quite a showman," he said. "And for some ungodly reason the Prince of Wales was there to do the honors. Imagine Britain and France being so friendly!"

The noise never really died down until midnight. Leah fell asleep quickly, as she always did, but Hyim couldn't sleep. Maybe it was the excitement of the day, maybe it was her comment, and maybe it was the sounds of thunder rolling in the distance, but he couldn't put the Tower out of his mind. It was both structurally impressive and terribly romantic. He sat for hours, staring at his sleeping wife, and thinking.

At three-thirty in the morning, he shook Leah awake.

"I have an idea," he said. "A crazy idea."

"What? What on Earth...?"

"Let's go to the Tower."

"All right. All right. We'll go," she yawned. "Right after breakfast."

"What? No! Now. Right now. Get dressed. Put on a coat or something."

"My God, Hy. What time is it?"

"Who cares? It's time I took you on an adventure."

"Couldn't we have an adventure in the daytime?"

"Too many people, Leah. Come on, let's go!"

Leah looked at her husband like he was a madman, but she did what she was asked. She refused to wear her good dress, however, putting her heavy coat on over a more conservative blue frock. Outside, the lightning crackled.

A quiet knock at the door was followed by a whisper. "Is everything all right in there?"

"Yes. Yes, Li-Don, we're fine. My husband has just gone insane is all."

Hyim opened the door.

"We're going to the tower, Li-Don. Don't tell anyone."

"I'm coming with you."

"No, no. This is supposed to be romantic."

"Forgive me, but it's not safe after dark. The Ripper has been quiet of late and he might have got across the channel by now. I'm going with you."

"Fine thing to say!" Leah said. "You think he would mistake me for a common harlot!"

"I mean no disrespect."

Leah composed herself. "Oh... don't mind me. I haven't had enough sleep yet."

"Very well."

The three of them snuck out of the hotel. It was easy enough because the staff went home before eleven. But it was an old house and creaked in many places that they hadn't noticed before.

Once they were outside, the cool, electric air felt good on their faces. The darkness and stillness of the city was eerie, but it felt liberating to be outdoors with no one around.

They came to the stairwell at the base of the Tower. There were chains across it, but they were not impassable. They were designed mostly to discourage people. Hyim and Li-Don helped Leah up and over the chains to the stairwell. They stepped carefully because the noise seemed the echo up through the tower. Li-Don had heard rumors that Mr. Eiffel was currently using the top level as a second residence, and they wouldn't want to disturb him.

The Tower was no longer lit with its tiny lights. The swiftly-moving clouds passed over and around the almost-full moon, brightening the sky, then darkening it again. There was more than enough light for them to see their way upwards while it shone. The stairway kept on going.

Hyim's heart beat heavy in his chest. Not because of the climb—although that was enough, and adding to his heart rate—but because he was trying to impress Leah with his impetuousness. He felt giddy with his nervousness, like he was a schoolboy trying to impress a girl; like Tom Sawyer.

The lightning was a small worry, but not really. The conductive metal was dampened by its attachment to a natural grounding. It was startling more than anything else, briefly strobing them and everything around them.

They reached the first level, breathing heavily, but it was worth the extra effort. The view was incredible. Individual lamps across western Paris looked like fireflies. The moonlight gave a shadowed outline to the buildings and streets.

"I can only imagine what Paris looks like from the top level," Li-Don said. "You would be able to see the roads and circles like it was a map."

They could not see the entire first level because of the darkness and because it was so huge. They walked around it, Leah taking Hyim's hand. She was smiling, though she looked tired, too. They came to a corner and watched the moonlight dance along the Seine. They kissed.

"You're mad," she said. "Completely mad. You are no longer the least romantic person on Earth."

"Not even if the police find us and put us in jail?"

"As long as it's the same cell."

They kissed again, then resumed walking around the platform. The wind produced a harmonic tone in the girders that was just barely audible. Their footfalls echoed back down to them from the floor of the second level. They seemed to get louder. And then they seemed to echo from different places around them. Leah's hand rested on a section of the guard fence that surrounded the first level, which rattled just a little bit. Sudden light shows all around them of forked lightning gave them brief shocks, but soon they expected it.

Suddenly, Hyim felt what can only be described as a *presence* behind him. He was used to such feelings. He was unusually aware of the people around him. At first he thought it was Li-Don. But Li-Don was up ahead of them, trying to see an exhibit of French writers in the moonlight.

As Hyim turned around, he somehow knew that he should lean out and down. It was almost an unconscious action, like his body knew what to do before he did. As he fell and his head swung around behind him, he saw the figure coming at them quickly and silently. What followed took only a few seconds, but it seemed to Hyim like it was drawn out over several minutes, in slow motion. The large, dark figure was amorphous at first, then he could make out a hand, a head, feet, a hat. The figure grabbed his shoulder, but because Hyim was falling to the ground, the figure tripped over him and fell into Leah, who was up against the railing. She was completely helpless and breathless, tipping over the railing, her face dark, but her hands flailing. She did not scream. *Why didn't she scream?*

The figure, who could now be clearly seen as a man dressed in black clothes and coat, briefly looked into Hyim's eyes. The moonlight was just right for Hyim to make out a face and empty, dark eyes. That face... that face. No, it couldn't be. That face was on the ship. Yes, it was. He was sure of it. That face had been walking around as he and his wife were walking around. It wasn't any of the three faces he thought of before. It was a different one, one that had been with a lady friend, lighting her cigarette with a phosphorous match that lit the first time it was struck. The two men's eyes locked in that moment up on the dark tower, each recognizing the other without the time to analyze the implications of their meeting. Then, the other man leaped up, and was gone without making a sound. It all happened too fast for Hyim to do anything.

Hyim held out his hand for Leah, but it was too late and he was too far away from her. He could do nothing as she went over the edge.

"NO!" Hyim shouted. Instinctively, and in the same motion of holding his hand out for her, he jumped to the edge of the fence and saw his wife falling, her arms out, her legs kicking, and then...

..and then...

Hyim couldn't quite believe his eyes. It appeared as though a bolt of lightning shot *from the ground* and hit Leah as she was in mid-air. She was now engulfed, brilliantly illuminated in a pool of bluish light and Hyim could see her face contorted in a soundless scream, her eyes wide.

Hyim shielded his eyes from the light and then saw another figure on the ground, where the beam of light was coming from. She stopped falling and hovered gently over the ground until she was on the ground, completely unhurt, but crying silently with terror.

Then the bright glow stopped. She was lying on the ground almost completely in shadow, but he could see her moving. He shouted her name. She had fallen over two hundred feet down. His eyes adjusted quickly back to the darkness. He thought he saw... yes! he did see another figure on the ground fleeing, running under the Tower. This figure was not all black but had what appeared to be a blue suit and vest underneath a straw boater. It left Leah behind. quickly as she touched her own face, like she as trying to make sure it was still there..

Over his shoulder, Hyim heard a commotion. He quickly ran towards it and found Li-Don facing off with the man in black. Li-Don had just landed a blow to the man's midsection, but the man seemed unfazed and shot a fist to Li-Don's head, which sent him reeling. Then the man raced for the stairway. Hyim wanted to follow him, but couldn't find the will within him. What would he do when he caught him? Fight? Hyim had never thrown a punch in his life. That man had just tried to murder his wife, had just assaulted his best friend, and he could do... *nothing?* He didn't accept that. He raced down the steps as fast as he could, but the man was gone. Disappeared. He had hesitated too long. He went to his wife, who was completely unhurt. He checked her head first, feeling the back of it for any sign of injury or blood. There was none. He then checked her arms and legs, but they were fine, too.

The figure on the ground had also disappeared. It had all happened so fast. *Think, Hyim, think!*

Hyim wrapped his arms around her, thrilled that she was alive yet confused that she wasn't dead. His mind raced. *What could possibly be going on?* The noise of Li-Don's steps on the stairway were funneled down to them.

Leah slowly sat up and pointed toward the center of the tower base. She tried to speak, but did not have the air. The face of the Man on the Tower was burned into Hyim's memory, and he could see it even as he helped his wife to her feet.

But the man below in the blue suit and incongruous straw hat had not shown his face.

"Can you walk?" he asked.

She nodded.

They headed for the ground beneath the center of the tower. There was a metal door in the cement that led underneath the tower. Hyim pulled it open noisily and stepped down into the darkness.

But the steps led only to a small room with controls for the elevator, no other exits besides the door.

And no one was in there. Hyim stepped back up and came back to his wife.

"I don't understand," he said. "What happened here? Why aren't you dead?"

Chapter 7

Hyim knew it wasn't a dream because Leah and Li-Don also remembered it. Li-Don had a shiner around his left eye for his trouble. They each helped Leah to get back to the hotel, where they snuck back in without much difficulty. They knew where the floor creaked and avoided those floorboards.

Leah was still weak when they set her down on the bed. Her face was flushed and her hands trembled when she tried to use them. She reached out for Hyim's shirt, trying to bunch the fabric in her fingers, but they wouldn't close into a fist.

When they had arrived at the hotel four days earlier, Hyim set the glass oblong from his father's study on the nightstand. He didn't know why he set it there; it was purely on impulse. Leah had not mentioned it, although she could not have ignored it if she tried. If she was annoyed by its constant pulse, she didn't say anything, although she didn't bring it up, either. It sat behind her head next to a hurricane lamp.

"What do you remember?" Li-Don asked her. She tried to speak, but still couldn't.

"I... I'm not sure what I saw," Hyim said. He turned to Li-Don. "Did you see it?"

"See what?"

"The... the light."

"What light? Which one?"

"The light... around Leah... She fell over the edge."

"Slow down, Hyim. I'll be right back." Li-Don brought each of them water in glasses. For Leah, he also brought a warm wet towel. Hyim sat next to her in a chair, holding her hand. She took a glass and held it in her shaking hands. The water seemed to make her feel better.

To Hyim's eyes, she had more hair than before, or maybe it was just arranged differently. It seemed lighter in color, too. The redness in her cheeks and the sweat around her neck made her appear healthier, although the rest of her body wasn't acting quite as healthy.

He went over the scene in his head. The line of electric light that ran from the blue-suited figure on the ground to the figure of Leah made Hyim feel petrified as a husband. But as a scientist, he found his mind racing over the possibilities.

It was distinctly possible that his mind had wrapped the experience the other way around—that his wife had been hit by lightning and, for some unknown reason, had been interrupted in her fall to the ground. But such thoughts were beyond his perceptions. He had to go on what he saw, or remembered he saw. The beam of light came from the ground, at exactly the point where the man in the blue suit and ridiculous straw hat stood.

Suppose for a moment that the light coming from this man in the blue suit was mechanically generated electricity. It follows that there must be some kind of mechanical contraption that could produce such electricity. For decades, people have known about the power of magnets to produce sparks and to generate AC power. But there always needed to be a conduit, a material that allowed the energy to pass through it. This line of light was passing through the air itself, through the aether of the atmosphere. Was it possible that the substance of the air was organized in such a way as to produce a plasma discharge of that magnitude? Or maybe there was an unseen strand of metal, an un-insulated wire that was somehow suspended between the blue-suited figure and his wife in just that instant. Either way, how was the descent of the falling object halted in an instant and the quality of levitation achieved?

The man on the ground was an unknown quantity, as was his mechanical electricity device. But what was even more maddening a mystery was the Man on the Tower. Hyim had seen his face clearly, it was the man on the ship with the phosphorescent match.

And the worst part of it all was that it could have meant anything. It was a multiple variable problem: $x + y = z$. Where x=the Man on the Tower, y=the man on the ground, z=whatever it all means.

There must be some relationship between the two, he reasoned. The Man on the Tower had a specific intent in mind, following them for some reason. He had followed them (not Jimmy) all the way from New York to that Tower. Why? Had he meant to kill Leah? Hyim's foot had stumbled at just the right time (another coincidence), and the man had tripped over him and forced Leah over the edge. Was that his intent? Or was the fact that he grabbed Hyim's shoulder an indication that Hyim was the target and Leah was just in the wrong place at the wrong time? What kind of terror was this man trying to inflict?

Assume for the moment that the Man on the Tower was trying to murder Leah, regardless of any coincidences or happenstances that might otherwise affect this condition. He succeeded in getting her in the air, where she would most certainly fall to her death. Except for the variable of the man on the ground. Next, assume for the moment that the beam of light actually did originate from some mechanical device operated by the man on the ground. However fantastic that machine might be, assume that it exists, too. Might as well also assume that the electric field generated by the machine did not harm Leah in any way, or at least was not *meant* to harm her.

In this set of assumptions, the man on the ground was an ally. He was somehow in the right place at the right time to activate his electric field and prevent Leah from falling to her death. This would mean that the man on the ground was not only a variable to Leah, but also to the Man on the Tower, i.e., he wouldn't have known that the man on the ground would save her.

But what if the Man on the Tower was trying to save Leah from getting caught in the terrible electric field—whatever it might do—from the man on the ground, and somehow Hyim interfered and caused exactly the opposite situation of what was intended.Hyim quickly drew up several cases based on his set of assumptions:

Case 1: The Man on the Tower is an enemy, the Man on the

Ground is an ally, the electrical phenomenon was benevolent. Entirely possible. The Man on the Tower fails to murder Leah— requires that the two other men were enemies of each other. Probability: 60%

Case 2: The Man on the Tower is an ally, the Man on the Ground is an enemy, the electrical phenomenon was harmful. Possible, but not likely. If so, the enemy had succeeded in "infecting" Leah with his electrical device. This requires that the Man on the Tower was foiled by chance and also that his sneaking around was intended as guarding instead of stalking. Probability: 15%

Case 3: The two other men were working together as friendly forces. Not possible. They could not both be working for the benefit of Leah or else there would not have been an incident. Probability: 0%

Case 4: Both other men were working together as enemy forces. Entirely possible. Both succeeded in what might have been a plot for exactly what happened. It requires that electrical "infection" was the goal and that Hyim's distraction was necessary. But why was the plan so complicated? Probability: 25%

And this was only if Leah was the intended victim. What if the man in the Tower had been targeting Hyim? The most likely scenario, however unlikely, was the first. It was the simplest and most logical solution. If Leah was the target, then this was the case that had the least amount of complications in it.

However, if Hyim had been the target, then Leah was merely hit by chance. The fact that she was spared from death shows that the man on the ground knew that something was going to happen. The fact that he was on the ground and not up in the Tower with them shows that he probably didn't know exactly what was going to happen. Case 1 still applied if Hyim was the target. This, of course, neglected the other important questions. Who were these two people? What was the goal of the man in the Tower? What was the electrical phenomenon? Why had that man in the Tower followed them all the way from New York? Was he really one of his father's enemies? And how was Jimmy involved?

"Hy..." Leah said quietly.

"Yes? Can you speak?"

Leah nodded. "I feel fine," she said. "Just tired." Her speech was a little garbled, sounding like she had chestnuts stuck in her mouth.

"We'll get a doctor to come around sometime tomorrow," Hyim said.

Leah nodded.

Li-Don motioned to speak with Hyim in private. "What exactly happened to her?" he said in a low voice.

Hyim paused. "You wouldn't believe me if I told you."

"She fell over the edge and she wasn't killed. That is fantastic enough. Tell me and I will believe you."

Hyim related his story, mentioning the man on the ground, but not his theory of what was going on. When he was finished, Li-Don sat down. "Are you sure that's what you saw?" he asked, wiping his forehead.

"I told you. I don't quite believe it myself."

"But the electric field. It could be a coincidence. It could be a trick of moonlight."

"I would think so, too, if Leah wasn't lying over there alive. The fact that she is alive is the puzzling part of this. I can imagine all sorts of atmospheric phenomenae that would have produced that effect, but because if affected her that way..."

Hyim stopped. He suddenly remembered the dream that Jimmy had recounted to him on the ship. About being surrounded by a strange light. He went back over to Leah's side.

"There is something I want to ask you that is very important," he said, stroking her hair. "Do you remember what happened this night?"

Leah shook her head. She spoke slowly, as if she were trying to remember, but also as if she were trying to choose her words carefully. "Parts. Pieces. I remember being up on the first level of the Tower with you. The next thing I knew I was on the ground, lying on a stack of mattresses."

"A stack of mattresses?"

"It was soft on my back. But I think they were old mattresses. They didn't smell very good. How did you manage to get them out there? Or were they there before?"

"Do you remember the light... lightning?"

"Lightning? What do you mean? Was there a storm? I am so tired," Leah said. "Could we do this tomorrow?"

Hyim nodded. But he was not going to get any sleep. He spent the rest of the night and early morning watching her and the night sky, wondering if he would be able to see that effect once more. He saw a few flashes of lightning, but they were of the normal variety. The storm quickly passed with just a few drops of rain.

It could have been the result of an increase in electromagnetic activity. The wrought iron they used for the new Tower was a known quantity, but no one had ever constructed such a tall structure with it. Iron, silicon, nickel, and a small amount of carbon from charred wood. Of course it was magnetic, but could the height of the Tower have somehow tapped into the Earth's electro-magnetic field? The way the lattices were joined with cast iron rivets and the way that the magnetic (or possibly conductive) properties of iron interacted with the Poles could have caused any sort of effect.

But an effect that demonstrative at exactly the right time? It was too much to believe. No. The effect had to have been intentional. And the man on the ground was somehow responsible.

It was more likely that the man on the ground somehow tapped into the electrical powers of the Tower in order to produce the effect.

Ah, but what of the man in the Tower? Hyim poured a glass of water from the pitcher that Li-Don had brought in. The sun was just beginning to color the sky. The man in the Tower was most undoubtedly malicious in nature.

Hyim's mind drifted around why anyone would want to kill Leah, but the only conclusion he could make was that someone wanted to get to him. It was close to impossible that someone would want to murder her. Leah was merely accidentally pushed over while Hyim was the real target. But was the aborted mission to murder him?

It could have been to warn him of something, like the man on the ground. But, again, if the Man on the Tower was friendly, why the stealth and why the brusque introduction? There had been enough inertia in the Man on the Tower to have pushed a 115 pound woman (give or take) past a metal barrier that hit her roughly around her fulcrum. He must have had some sort of forceful intent.

Maybe it really did have something to do with the diamond business, and, if so, probably with his father's message.

When Leah woke up at about eight-thirty, she sat bolt upright with wide eyes. "What a night!" she exclaimed. Hyim, who was bleary-eyed and already dropping off in his chair marveled at her energy.

"Why husband," she said, "why are you as dour as a shepherd?"

"I didn't get any sleep."

"Well, sleep now. I'll have breakfast for you when you wake up."

"We need to call a doctor."

"*On n'a pas besoin de medecin*. No doctors necessary."

Leah ran around the room, humming and prancing like a little schoolgirl. Just watching her made Hyim tired.

"What about the police?" Hyim asked.

"Now what would you say to a policeman? He would think you were insane."

"Why don't you get some sleep," he said, crawling into bed. "You look tired. I'll go get us some breakfast."

Leah laughed him as he fell asleep.

He awoke to the sound of Leah and Li-Don coming into the room with sandwiches. They were chuckling at something as they opened the wax paper.

"What time is it?" Hyim said.

"It's nearly sundown," Leah said. "Not only did you miss breakfast, you missed lunch as well."

"It's two-thirty," Li-Don said.

"We met the most disagreeable man today," Leah said. "We were at the foot of Mr. Eiffel's tower when a wildly bearded man came up to us and scolded us for gazing up the structure like it was a Roman statue. He said we should be facing the other way so we could have an unobstructed view of Paris—without the Tower getting in the way."

"I think it was Maupassant," Li-Don said.

Hyim stretched and yawned. He felt a little better. But that was nothing to how Leah looked. Even through his blurry vision he could tell that his wife looked as vivacious as ever.

"No ill effects from last night?" he asked her.

"Nothing," she said brightly.

"She's in better shape than I am," Li-Don said. The skin around his left eye was dark blue and his temple was swollen. It looked worse than the night before.

"You let her go out?"

"I couldn't stop her."

"Oh, piffle, you two," she said. "I feel fine. Better than fine. I feel marvelous. I'd like to try scaling the third tier of that Tower out there."

They sat down to have a short lunch after Hyim cleaned himself up. A knock at the door interrupted them.

"Message pour Monsieur Hopewell," a voice from behind the door said. *"Un télégramme."*

Li-Don opened the door, took a piece of paper from the porter, then tipped him. "It's from your Mr. Brightferry," he said. He read the note aloud, "Change in plans. Still sending coach around. Will meet in my château at Argenteuil. Shorter trip for you. Longer for me."

"Well, we can't go," Hyim said.

"Why not?" Leah asked.

"Because we don't know what is happening to you."

"Tant pis. Cela ne fait rien. Since when did you become such an expert on electricity and the human body? We can't refuse a invitation like that, especially since he's making the trip especially for us. Besides, I feel fine. I'm alive."

"For reasons no one understands. And, in case you've chosen to overlook it, an attempt on your life was made not twelve hours ago."

"Seventeen," Leah said brightly. "All the more reason to get out of the city."

Hyim once again realized that he could not win an argument with that woman.

The coach came for them that afternoon. Hyim wasn't feeling

up to meeting people, but Leah had insisted. Besides, there was the message to deliver and a little matter of a honeymoon taking place, during which Leah was to be treated as the field marshal she had always appeared to be.

He wondered if he should ask how Brightferry not only knew that they were there, but also knew enough to make it easy to meet him. But Leah told him that would be improper.

"Besides," she said, "it's not unreasonable to assume that your father mentioned to a business colleague the wedding of his only son."

"I don't think we should mention the events of the night before," Li-Don said.

"I quite agree," Leah said. "The whole thing is just too outrageous to make of a civilized story. Let's try and be personable."

"Like my father says," Li-Don said, " 'Only tell stories of which you know the meaning.' "

The bumpy, noisy ride took about an hour, but it seemed longer. The coach had clearly been designed for smooth, plain dirt roads of the countryside and not the cobblestone streets of Paris. To make matters worse, one of the horses was having intestinal problems, which combined with the industrial smell of burning coal to produce a truly nasty experience. The three of them held handkerchiefs up to their noses and mouths. Li-Don had to lend one of his to Hyim, who hadn't brought one. When they finally arrived, it was a true relief to be out of the closed space of the vehicle.

Chapter 8

The château was a marvel. The stonework looked hundreds of years old, as did the landscaping. The drive up to the front door was at least a quarter of a mile long, with towering oak and cypress trees on either side. A circular fountain with winged horses graced the entrance and was the centerpiece of a meticulously trimmed garden.

"This is a colleague of your father's?" Leah asked in wonderment.

"I believe he's a wholesaler. I can't say for sure."

A gaggle of servants led them into the foyer, which was a towering, dark room with only stained glass allowing sunlight in from high on the walls. It was so far above them and recessed into the stone that they couldn't tell exactly what the design was.

"This is early Renaissance architecture," Li-Don said. "You can tell by the buttresses on the ceiling. But the work is entirely stone. This building has probably been here since the 16th century."

To their right was a steep wooden staircase that arched over them onto the second and third stories. To their left were double-height doors with thick ironwork. They entered through these doors to a room lined with bookshelves and a small fire in a large fireplace. It was a good deal cooler inside. It was a lovely April day, but that wasn't evident from the dank interior. Additionally, the lack of windows made Hyim nervous.

"*Monsieur Brightferry ne fait qu'aller et venir*," one of the servants said.

"He'll be with us shortly," Leah translated. They sat down on *au courant* furniture that seemed out of place in the dank stone room. After a few minutes of scanning the bookshelves, Leah could no longer stay in one place. She got up and perused the collection, pausing now and then to take one down.

"*Agricultural Methods of Byzantium in the Macedonian Era,*" she read from a spine. "They all appear to be cut," she said, leafing through it. "These books aren't just for show. Our host has probably read most of these."

"That's not possible. There must be five thousand books here," Li-Don said from across the room.

"Six thousand twenty-eight books, to be exact about it," came a voice from a small doorway in a far corner. Hyim and Li-Don stood up abruptly. Leah quickly put the book back on the shelf.

Sylwyn Brightferry was not what Hyim had expected. What had he expected? Maybe with these Medieval surroundings, he had expected someone more Gothic and imposing. But Brightferry was neither striking nor imposing. His face was as close to being completely free of character as was possible and yet still retaining a humanity about it. It was entirely forgettable. He could get lost in a crowd very easily. Hyim had a staggering memory, but he wondered if he would be able to remember this man's face after it was out of view. Not at all like the face of the man in the Tower.

"Good evening," Brightferry said in a warm voice. It echoed as if he were on stage in a theater. His black clothing and topcoat gave him a Shakespearian quality, though only slightly so. "I trust your journey here was not too unpleasant."

"Perfectly fine," Leah said quickly.

"Please, sit down. Can I offer anyone a Cognac or a Muscat?"

Hyim felt his father's letter in his coat pocket make a rustling sound as he turned around. He took it out and held it with both hands. Suddenly, he realized he should say something. "No, thank you," he said.

Leah cleared her throat.

"Um..." Hyim began. "The lady will have a... a Cognac?"

Leah nodded.

"Dry sherry, if you have it," Hyim said. "Two."

"Dreadful, dreadful ride from Paris, isn't it?" Brightferry said. "Still, I love it here."

"Did you take the train this morning?" Leah asked.

"Oh, no. God no. I dislike trains in the morning. You always feel like the day is lost. I came in last night. At least I could have the first half of the day to myself." He brought their drinks over.

He was about the same height as Hyim, with much the same complexion and coloring. He appeared perhaps twenty years older, perhaps a little more. Maybe a little older than he looked possibly because of a clean, trouble-free life. If that was true. He held up his glass to propose a toast.

"*Biz hundert azoi ve tsvantsik*." he said, then tipped the crystal goblet towards his mouth.

Leah turned her head. "You speak Yiddish?"

"I speak a great many languages, my good woman."

"Dinner shall be served in a short while. Please take this opportunity to have a look around."

Hyim whispered to Leah, "What did he say?"

"It's an old Yiddish expression. It means 'May you live to 100 as a twenty-year-old.'"

"May I ask about this building?" Li-Don said to their host.

"But of course." He walked the length of one of the walls, pointing out some of the features as he went. "It was completed in 1530, built by King François for his courtesan Louise of Arles. Thus the lack of windows on the east side. He did not want anyone who happened to be arriving unexpectedly to accidentally see his mistress. But he quickly sold this palace to my family. He was trying to finance his war with Spain—and on top of that, he was getting married. Louise fell out of favor. I think she ended up in Malta."

"That's quite a story," Leah said.

"There are many stories here," he said cryptically. "Personally, I think it's a wonderful accident to not have such windows. Very little of the industrial particulate matter from our neighbor to the southeast gets inside the walls.

"You mean Paris," Li-Don said, joining Leah at the bookshelves. Hyim took the opportunity to give Brightferry the envelope.

"I presume you know that my father is Ezra Hopewell. He has asked me to carry this message to you in person."

Brightferry carefully unsealed the envelope, then read the contents. Hyim had not expected him to open and read it right then and there.

Brightferry seemed intrigued by the letter. He looked up at Hyim, then back at the letter, then up again. Then he held it up to a light high on the wall, presumably looking for a watermark. Hyim recognized his father's script, backwards through the paper. He accidentally saw the word *uaeniloM* before he turned away.

"This is good news," he said. "Very good news indeed. We'll have to celebrate." He stepped over to the fire. "Your father is a very clever man." He gently set the letter down on the fire, where it was consumed quickly by the small but hot, glowing logs. The wax from the seal sizzled for a moment, then died down. "A very clever man."

He pulled a loose rope that hung from a garishly decorated hole in the wall, a signal to the servants. Hyim knew it would be impolite to ask about the message. He probably wouldn't have known its significance had he read it. He didn't know his father's business very well. He felt awkward standing there, watching the letter burn brightly, without anything to say. He kept thinking of that word, *Molineau*. He was intensely curious now, for reasons he wouldn't be able to explain. He wasn't generally interested in his father's business, but that word seemed to have some resonance for him. Was it a name? A place? A mineral ore? A government regulation?

61

He also had a strange feeling about the whole situation. This Brightferry character was not a known quantity. It made Hyim nervous to have such a variable in this situation. He was to bring the message to the recipient, but instead the recipient came to him. But it was more than that.

The movement of the message from Paris-Amsterdam was reduced to Paris-Argenteuil, but to what purpose? Hyim found himself thinking in terms of friends and enemies once again. It was something he was not used to, as if his entire life had been either positive numbers or unknown quantities; now all of sudden he was trying to factor negative numbers, irrational numbers, the variables of which he couldn't begin to fathom without enough information. This man standing before him could very well be an impostor, but to what end? And what was there to do of it now?

"Do you have a residence in Amsterdam, also?" Leah asked.

"In a way," Brightferry said wistfully. "The city used to be a wonderful place, full of artistic and scientific vitality. But I moved out of the city proper years ago. It's a filthy little place, let me tell you. They say the city was founded by two fisherman and a seasick dog, who vomited on the future spot of the city center. Well, that's what the place smells like, old fishermen and dog vomit. The best thing about Amsterdam is the *spoorweg* that takes you out of it."

"Is your family Dutch?"

"Sort of. A little of everything, if you know what I mean."

A silence followed. Brightferry smiled at Hyim, who wondered if he was indicating the dubious legitimacy of his ancestors, or perhaps a motley pedigree that was not worth mentioning. Leah turned away, refusing to comment. The silence was broken by the sound of a muted bell that came from the doorway.

"Dinner is ready," he said with a short bow. He led them out of the room.

"What did he mean, 'a little of everything'?" Hyim whispered to his wife.

"I think he meant there were a number of illegitimate children."

"Oh, really?"

"I thought he meant that his family were wanderers, or Gypsies or such," Li-Don whispered.

"You could both be right," Hyim said.

The dining hall was the most ostentatious room so far. It was clearly designed to impress guests. Gilt-lined frames on the walls housed pastoral scenes of central France. Silver candlesticks peppered the table, which could be set for thirty people or more, but was instead set for only five. Two enormous arched windows were at either end of the room, bringing in the light from the waning hours of the day. Two huge chandeliers hung from the ceiling, each having at least fifty candles, which were being lit one by one by four servants with long, thin iron torches.

The walls and ceiling were lined with stone and metal panels, some with intricate designs, others with impossibly smooth surfaces.

The four of them sat down to wine and bowls of pine nuts.

"Are we expecting someone else?" Leah asked, indicating the fifth place setting.

"Oh, yes. You people are from out of town, aren't you? It's a custom here. A quaint little tradition, or superstition as you might call it. You set an extra place just in case one of your enemies shows up. Then you can invite him to your meal and make him a friend. Very charming, if you ask me."

"You speak as if you're an outsider to this custom," Leah observed.

"The servants do it without my asking. Or without asking me either," he chuckled. "In any event, it's harmless."

"It's like setting a place for Elijah."

A couple of the servants looked over at Leah in surprise.

"Sorry?" Brightferry said.

"Elijah, the prophet. Jews set a place for him at the table for Passover."

"Do they really? Fascinating. Tell me, Madam, are you, yourself of the Jewish persuasion?"

She looked over at Hyim, who didn't know if this was a breach of social etiquette or not.

"I am, just like the other Hopewells."

There was an uncomfortable break in the conversation.

"So they are! So they are!" he laughed. "I had nearly forgotten. Old Ezra doesn't mention it much, you know." He turned to Li-Don. "You're not Jewish, are you?"

"No, sir. I am a follower of the Buddha. Loosely, as it were."

"Ah, yes. Old Gautama. Is that so? Tell me, how do you reconcile working for the deists at the table?"

"The Buddha does not preach prejudice, sir."

"Hm. Quite true, quite true."

The soup arrived in a porcelain tureen with a giant silver ladle, which Brightferry took to serve everyone. It was a tart onion soup, very salty, with enough white wine in it to make Hyim a little dizzy just by smelling it.

"But I didn't ask you to come just to talk about religion," said Brightferry as he poured out the soup. "Mr. Hopewell, I understand you are interested in electricity."

"Yes. I am."

"Well, I have a little story I want to share with you. I realize that none of you here know anything about me. Well, that's understandable. Your father doesn't talk much about his personal life, and I don't talk much about mine. We're private people. But let me tell you something about me now. I am what you might call a well-traveled man. I have been all over the globe, in fact. Several times. Just a few months ago I was coming home on a caravan through Turkmen territory."

"My father mentioned you were in Budapest."

"So I was. Yes. Anyway. When I was in Java a few years ago, I saw the most amazing Buddhist tower. Fascinating, fascinating structure. Very simple, yet very complicated. And very old. Over one thousand years, they say."

"The Chandi Borobudur," Li-Don said.

"You've heard of it. Excellent. Well, they've been doing some excavation there, and it's all very exciting. It's a step pyramid rising out of the ground, but the base of it has been buried by years of overgrowth and volcanic activity. I met the man overseeing this operation, a Mr. Izjerman—an excitable fellow Dutchman. He said something remarkable to me. He said that they found a completely separate building underneath the top. Almost as if the base of the pyramid was built before the rest of it was even considered. They found something like one hundred-fifty scenes of what they think are the life of the Buddha. I imagine you've read a little about this."

"What is available," Li-Don said, rapt with attention.

The servants took away the soup bowls and presented several smaller platters of olives, bread rolls, spiced oil, almonds, and chopped capsicum.

"I spoke with some of the natives there, doing work for Mr. Izjerman clearing away the overgrowth and the soil. They told me of an ancient legend about the place. Something that I had not heard about from the white men there. A story is told that the place has healing powers. And not just your run-of-the-mill miracle cures. It is said that a sick or injured man who is pure of heart can go to the temple and be cured by the god of the moon. More specifically, by the god of the moonlight. Details are sketchy at best, and no one there had seen anything like it personally. It's more like the Babi-Yar story in Poland, passed down orally with perhaps a genuine origin that has been lost through generations of retelling. Many of them said that the old story tells of the temple as if it were a lost city, a fabled city, like we in the Occident have our Atlantis."

"Or Troy," Li-Don said.

"Quite. But these people had their lost city revealed by white men. It is no doubt that this structure was their fabled temple. But they were sanguine about the whole thing. They knew there was *something* there. A part of it was always visible, even before they unwrapped it of jungle. But they didn't know what exactly it was. When it was finally revealed, they didn't know quite what to make of it. Should they treat it like a holy site? A true temple? A tourist attraction? What do you do when one of your childhood stories suddenly has a real-world context? It's a tricky business.

"They first discovered it almost eighty years ago, I think. Their culture has had time to digest it. Many of them tried to be healed at the site, but without success. In any event, there is one story that I uncovered about the recent history of this healing phenomenon. About twenty years ago, it seems there was this old man who had some kind of chronic intestinal illness. He also, apparently, had a deformed leg from a fishing accident years before. I won't horrify you with the details, suffice it to say he was going through a bad time. This man claimed that he sat at the foot of the temple and meditated for twenty days, taking only water. And on the 20th day, there was a storm. Lightning struck trees around him. It hit the tower several times as if attracted by a lightning rod. One of these strikes was somehow diverted from the top of the tower and struck him full on the head. This is a very important detail. He claimed that this lightning bolt first struck the temple, then was *directed* towards his head. And you may guess the rest of the story. He was completely cured of his illness, and his leg was somehow miraculously healed.

"I went to see this man, but he has since gone senile. Completely incoherent to the point that he no longer forms words. The bloke who told me the story said that the old man was fine for the first year or two, but then started to go slowly insane. Perhaps he was insane all along and made up the story, or perhaps his experience caused some sort of delayed dementia. Now, storms are not a rare occurrence in this part of the world. And it's not unreasonable to expect that people will be hit by lightning on an island of that size—many people know someone who has been struck, quite frightening but not fatal—and the cure of this man's illness is not unexpected after fasting. But his leg being completely healed is an amazing story. The story suggests that this man's leg was almost at a right angle in the wrong place, having healed incorrectly, yet the man I saw was clearly upright, with no leg injury at all—albeit standing with a cane, having the appearance of a man of a hundred years old."

"Is it real?" Leah asked.

"It's not for me to say," Brightferry said.

The servants came back and replaced the small platters with one large plate of small smoked fish, each on the end of a wooden trident. Wine glasses were refilled and more bread was brought.

The three guests looked nervously at each other. They were all thinking the same thing, Hyim could see it in their faces. The electrical phenomenon. It was almost too much to keep silent about, but no one said anything. The silence had become uncomfortable when Leah excused herself from the room and got one of the servants to escort her outside. "It's not quite that exciting of a story," Brightferry said with a laugh.

Chapter 9

The main course at dinner was quail, broiled with tiny potatoes, carrots, and celery. By the time the quail came, the room was subdued.

"Come now," Brightferry said. "I can't have violated some law of table manners. After all, I'm the host."

"Your story is quite remarkable," Hyim said. "A little fantastical is all. Who would believe it to be true?"

"I would, for one. I don't really expect you to believe it, Mr. Hopewell. You do not need to believe in such things in order for them to have happened. Besides, it's just a story. Told secondhand to me." His eyes darted back and forth to gauge reaction.

"You must forgive me for changing the subject," Li-Don said. "But I must ask what the scenes in the temple depict."

Brightferry exhaled audibly. "I must confess that I didn't see them, nor did I inquire. But you might be intrigued by the top of the monument. The top of the temple is a series of circular terraces with these small cone-shaped structures—not unlike stone tents— set at regular intervals around the circumferences. Inside these little tents are life-size statues of the Buddha. There are holes large enough for a man to reach into and touch the statues, but the lighting is such that you can only see them if you look into them. That is, you can only see Buddha if you look for him. Quite effective and ingenious. There are about 500 of them, I think, and there are different versions of the statue inside the tents depending on which direction they are facing. Wonderful, wonderful place. Dreadfully hot and humid, though. A sweaty business, that."

"Life is suffering," Li-Don said.

"Quite."

Hyim was practically bursting with suspense about the electrical phenomenon, but he dared not say anything. After all, Brightferry's story was just that, a story. It had happened to someone else with no witnesses. A perfectly acceptable apocryphal tale. But Leah's experience was immediate and personal. It was, of course, improbable that the two events were related. And yet...

And yet...

Two towers in different parts of the world, each with its own strange electrical phenomenon. One using the power of electricity in lightning, the other using some kind of device that possibly channeled electricity somehow. Hyim had read of miracle cures derived from electrical shocks, but they were always unproven and ultimately fakes.

What if it were possible that there was a man at the top of the Borobudur temple who had been the commutator of electricity towards the old man at the foot of the temple? Perhaps using some kind of device?

Alternatively, what if one tower were constructed for one purpose of channeling electricity, and the other for another purpose? Two civilizations, separated by thousands of miles and hundreds of years erect monuments for similar purposes.

Still further, what if the two towers somehow acted on the electricity beyond being lightning rods. There was a lightning rod at the top of *Tour Eiffel*, but what if there was something about the construction of the tower itself that altered the electric current somehow? If true, the question would be, *Was the construction intentional or an accident of design?* It was well known that Eiffel did not trust the new methods of making iron into steel, favoring the older methods of rending iron for his girders. What if he knew something about the construction that he did not reveal, that was somehow related to the construction of this temple?

But why would one electrical phenomenon be curative and the other act as a levitator? And why would one need a man with a device while the other did not?

Hyim's head swam, and he wanted to ask questions. But now was not the time. It was important they all keep silent about the events of the night before. But now, Hyim wasn't sure exactly *why* they had to continue to keep silent about it. It had been to avoid giving the impression that they were all lunatics. But after that story?

"There's something that I should explain," Leah said. "Something about our behavior just now. Your anecdote has resonated with something that happened to me."

"Leah!" Hyim half-whispered, half-shouted. But she waved him off.

She told Brightferry about what happened. Hyim noticed that she left out the part where Li-Don had been flattened by the strange man in the Tower, out of decorum, no doubt (although Brightferry seemed to have taken in his shiner and analyzed it as they were talking). She explained the sensation as being in a limelight or a Bude light, with the brightness in her eyes, but with the heat absent. She thought she was dead and was moving on to the afterlife.

Hyim realized they hadn't discussed how she felt during the experience, and that she initially had not recognized the light or its effect. These words were as new to him as they were to their host, who listened with the patience of a clergyman. Hyim had been so caught up in the theory of what happened that he had neglected what had actually happened.

When Leah was finished with her story—including how they had all agreed not to talk about it—Brightferry stood up and went over to her. He knelt down next to her chair.

"I'm so sorry," he said. "You poor creature. You have gone through a great deal."

"I feel fine. I feel wonderful, in fact."

"True, but the mind is not as resilient as the body sometimes."

Hyim felt a pang of jealousy. These were the things that he should have been saying.

"Please," Brightferry said. "Each of you. I do apologize for going on about all this. Be my guests tonight. I insist. In fact, please feel free to stay here as long as you like. You have all been through a great deal."

They had their belongings gathered from the *Hôtel Bourdonnais* and brought to the château. They set up rooms on the second floor. Despite being unused for several months, the dust was minimal, and everything seemed fresh.

"Why did you tell him that story?" Hyim asked Leah as they unpacked their things. "We don't know anything about him."

"We know he works with your father."

"He could be a spy. He could be a business rival. He could be behind whatever happened last night."

"In which case he would already know."

"I'm being serious. We have to be careful."

"I'm being serious, also, husband. It happened to me. To *me*. Not you. Let me appear the loopy one if I like. You think I'm not worried about it? About what it might have done to me? Well, I can't do anything about that now can I? So allow me to appear unstable if I wish." She spoke matter-of-factly, in contrast to the nervous energy that was in her eyes.

Hyim impulsively kissed her. "God, but you're beautiful when you're independent."" What a thing to say."

Chapter 10

The Hopewells were awakened in the middle of the night by a rustling at the door. It was locked with a bar across the middle, but it quickly unlocked from the outside and flew open. One of Brightferry's servants stood in the doorway with a candle.

"On doit quitter! Quittez maintenant!" she shouted in a high-pitched voice.

"What's she saying?" Hyim said after waking with a start. His heart was beating fast. He had been in the middle of his nightmare in the forest. He usually didn't have it more than once a year, but this was twice within a two-week period.

"She wants us to leave," Leah said in a groggy voice. *"Pourquoi?"* she asked the servant.

Then they heard the sound of a small metallic explosion, a popping sound, then a scream. The servant left, hysterical, leaving them in near darkness. A small window at the top of the far wall let in starlight, but that was all.

They quickly put on topcoats over their pajamas, and shoes over bare feet. It was the closest that Hyim had come to regretting their lovemaking—they were ill-dressed to go out into the night air. The popping sounds were coming from the stairway. Hyim fought the impulse to yell. Clearly the direction of the stairway wasn't safe.

They met Li-Don in the hallway, who was almost fully clothed. "Follow me," he whispered hastily. They ran down the hallway, made several turns and came to a false wainscoting, which Li-Don hit deftly with his fist. A secret panel pushed back, letting in some additional light to the dark hallway.

"Wha..." Hyim started to say, but thought better of saying anything. When they were in a well-lit stone tunnel, Li-Don relaxed and re-closed the trap door.

"I found this while I was exploring earlier," he said. "I never really went to sleep. I noticed that the downstairs floor plan didn't quite mesh with the upstairs. It took me a while to find the secret, but here it is. I doubt many people know about it."

"Let's hope," Leah said.

They walked down the hallway, which was lit with small torches every so often. Upon closer inspection, Hyim saw that they were gas-powered lamps made to look like Medieval torches. The walkway was sloped downward and spiraled slowly to the left, seemingly away from the house. They came to a dead end.

"Watch this," Li-Don said. He ran his hand along the wall and found an indentation, which he pushed with very little force. The dead end became a swinging doorway and they passed through. The lights in this now wooden hallway were clearly electric, still sloping down and to the left.

"This is as far as I got," he said. "These buildings were all constructed with secret doors and tunnels for just such a time as this." They walked on.

"A time as what?" Hyim said. He still didn't know what was going on.

"I'm not sure. I don't speak French very well. But I gathered from the conversations among the servants that there were three intruders in the building. They began shooting up the place, but I didn't hear if they killed anyone. I don't know where our host is or even if he's still alive."

"Do you know who they are or what they're doing here?"

"Sorry. That's all I could understand."

Hyim discovered he was shaking.

"That woman may have saved our lives," Leah said. "I can't believe this is happening."

"I can't believe that this kind of violence comes from the diamond business," Hyim said.

"Diamonds are very profitable, with very little investment," Li-Don said. "There's a great deal of money to make in diamonds."

"This could have something to do with last night. These men who invaded our host's home might be associated with the Man on the Tower."

"Or the man on the ground," Leah said. "Maybe they were trying to protect us from Brightferry."

"You can't think that he's in on this somehow."

"Or even your friend from the ship," Leah added. "I don't know what to think. I don't know if there is anyone we can trust anymore. God, but I detest guns."

They walked on, noting that the lights were getting brighter. "I hope this leads somewhere safe," Leah said.

Li-Don seemed to sense where he was going. The air got colder and noticeably damp. "We're below ground now," he said. "This is a very long escape tunnel. Longer than is normal for these things."

"I wonder where the source of power is for these lights," Hyim wondered aloud.

They continued on until they reached an underground chamber. A wooden frame opened into what appeared to be a natural cave. The irregular ceiling and walls were natural stone and earth. The ground was paved with small stones and sand, packed in from years, perhaps centuries of use.

"Louise must have taken this path in and out," Leah said.

On one end of the cave was a metal rail that came up out of the ground on pipes. There was also a wooden stall for horses. Nearby were the skeletons of small animals. The inside was lit by the same small lights running across the ceiling.

"These rails are probably replacements for the original wood," Li-Don said. "You wouldn't see these in 16th century France. In fact, they are probably fairly recent."

There were three wooden doors in the wall of the cave opposite the entrance they emerged from. Somewhere, steady drops of water hit a small pool with a noise that was louder than it should have been.

"The lady or the tiger," Leah remarked. "One of these might lead back to the chateau. Or all of them."

"Or none of them," Hyim said. "Where are those lights getting their power? Do you see a wire going anywhere?"

Li-Don traced a line in the air with his finger, roughly along one of the strands of lights. "I can't tell," he said. "The walls are too dim behind the lights. The power cable might be coming from up above."

"Well, then. Let's try one of the doors, shall we? We can't stay here and expect to be safe for very long."

Li-Don brushed by them, holding up his hand to let them know he was their protector. He put his hand on the first door. "Cold," he said. On the second door, he said, "Cold as well." On the third door, he said, "This one is warmer. Also, something is vibrating it."

"That's the one," Hyim said.

Li-Don pulled on the iron ring, but the door wouldn't budge. Hyim helped him, and they got it to shake a little. But, clearly, it was locked. The entire cave echoed with their grunts and the sound of the ring clanging back against the door.

"Is there a secret to that door, like the others?" Leah asked.

Smart girl, Hyim thought. He and Li-Don ran their hands across the rock face around the door. Hyim was doing it rather hurriedly. He was thinking that he might have missed something, but he kept going. Suddenly, one of the other doors opened—the first one. Leah gasped.Out stepped Brightferry in his nightshirt and sleeping cap. "Terrible disturbance," he said. "Oh, well. Some things can't be helped. I expect they'll be tearing up the place by now."

Charles Schwartz ~

"Who..." Hyim started to say.

"You'd best leave while there's still time."

Brightferry took a key from a chain around his neck and unlocked the third door. "When you get above ground, take horses from the stable and ride to Brussels. It'll be about a four days ride, but they'll be expecting that you're headed to Marseille, so you'll have plenty of time."

"You mean they're after *us*?" Leah asked.

"There's no time to explain. I'll have a message waiting for you at the train station."

"What about you?" Li-Don asked.

"I will delay them as much as possible."

"That's madness!" Hyim said. "Surely you're in danger!"

"Just go. You must trust me. And you must trust your father. Know that he is on your side and that whatever he does is because he loves you."

"What's that supposed to mean?"

Brightferry did not answer. He quickly left by the same door. The sound of the lock clicking shut filled the cave before it once again fell silent. Hyim was now less frightened than he was angry. He wanted to shout, but found that he didn't have the vocal power. His anger quickly diminished to mere annoyance.

His mind, momentarily clouded by emotion, was suddenly cleared as if by a spring rain. *Why would he tell me that?* he thought. *He's either being a martyr or he knows that he's in no danger. He either really believes that he can throw these people off the trail or else he's collaborating with them, in which case they really are after Leah and me. Or else he's lying, in which case he's undoubtedly collaborating with them.*

As he opened the now-unlocked third door and led Leah and Li-Don through it, he said, almost under his breath, "We can't go in either direction."

The third door led to a room filled with giant wooden casks for winemaking. It, too, was lit with small electric lights. The acrid odor hit them as soon as they stepped in. The ground, paved with pebbles and stained with smashed red grapes and stems, was wet and murky. Leah stepped lightly in her cloth slippers. Li-Don was barefoot.

"This wine isn't going to be very good," Li-Don observed. "It's too warm in here."

Hyim headed for higher ground. "How far underground are we?" he asked Li-Don.

"It's impossible to tell. At least thirty feet."

"Is this a natural cave?"

"Hardly. The previous one looked natural. This one, however, was carved out of limestone, probably part of the same igneous tube system, but enlarged for storage space.."

"Storage space," Hyim said to no one in particular. "Why isn't it colder in here?"

They kept on against the slope of the room, hoping that it would lead outside. "Something doesn't smell right in here," Leah said. "At first I thought it was Bordeaux wine, but now I'm not so sure."

"What do you mean?" Hyim asked.

"While it's fermenting, Bordeaux smells like old books, sugared tea, and... well, a used water closet, if you'll pardon the expression."

"That pretty well explains this place, then."

"No, there's something else here. Something different."

"What? Do you mean like a Cabernet?" Li-Don said with a smile.

"No. It's... I don't know. It's difficult to describe. Almost like mustard, but more smoky than that."

Hyim didn't know what she was talking about. He didn't take much notice of it, either, mostly because he couldn't smell anything stranger than the wine and the wet gravel. Their crunching footsteps were getting softer as their slippers became damp, and finally sopping wet.

When they reached the main entrance, Li-Don made sure the way was clear to the stables. Hyim took one last look back, lamenting that

he could not find the source of power for the electric lights. *If Brightferry really does survive this*, he thought, *I'll have to ask him what's going on.*

Out in the night air, their wet feet became colder and uncomfortable. It was a relief to be out of enclosed spaces, though. The main building was a good distance away. He hadn't realized just how far they'd traveled underground.

There were a number of horses sleeping. They would have to be ridden cold, with harnesses but no saddles. Leah was an expert equestrian, having ridden most of her years in college, but Hyim had never ridden without a saddle. And Li-Don had never even been on a horse.

"We should be one rider each, and bring an extra if we can," Leah whispered.

Li-Don picked up two handfuls of hay. "Use these to dry the soles on your feet," he said, and handed them off.

Leah chose four horses and led them out. She came out with three leather riding jackets also. "Strange that they leave the harnesses on overnight," she said. "Almost as if they were expecting a midnight ride."

"Which way are we headed?" Li-Don asked.

Hyim pointed to the northeast. "That's Brussels," he said. "Where our host told us to go. To the south is Marseille, almost three times as far, where he said he would tell them we're headed. I don't trust him."

"They might look for us in Boulogne," Li-Don said. "We should get to Germany."

"No. We're going the quickest way out. Due west. We shouldn't stay in France any longer than we have to."

Just as Leah had mounted her horse and Hyim was trying to help Li-Don, they heard a violent commotion behind them.

"Where do you think you're goin'?" came a rough voice through the night air. It was a man's voice, someone who had been through

many trials and whose voice had been scratched by many attempts to forget about them. Hyim turned to see five men in the moonlight, each with a rifle pointed directly at him.

Chapter 11

"Get away from those horses, you anarchists," said one of them through a thick mustache.

"What is this?" Hyim said.

He squinted through the darkness to try and get a better look at their faces. They were a group of rough-looking men who appeared the same as the pictures of the Western territories in the newspapers back home.

"We've been looking for you folks for quite a while now," the mustachioed man said. "We've been instructed to get some information out of you."

Hyim saw that Li-Don and Leah were not moving, silent. He motioned for them to dismount the horses. It was apparent these men had some kind of tactical plan in mind when they arrived, else why would five of them (if more were present somewhere, or if this was all) be meeting them at just the right place. Another minute and they would have escaped.

Whatever the case. There was no escape. They were, perhaps, American Civil War volunteers or conscripts, seeming of about that age.

"Who sent you?" Hyim asked.

"That's not a discussion topic right now."

"You're Americans."

"Yes, sir."

"Are you going to kill us?"

"Depends on your answers. First off, what's your hurry?"

"I think we are justified in running when we see guns," Li-Don said.

"Tell your Chink to shut the Hell up when I ain't talking to him."

Hyim nervously turned around to indicate to Li-Don that the men with the guns made the rules. Li-Don's scowl was palpable.

"What are you doing here in the land of the French?"

"My wife and I are on our honeymoon. This is my personal secretary, Li-Don."

The mustachioed man seemed satisfied with that. He pulled a slip of paper out of his pocket, momentarily letting his gun down.

"Now then," the leader said. "Where is your daddy?"

"My father? In New York."

"*Where* in New York?"

"He's not hard to find. It's not a big secret."

"The address, you uptown wattle-brain!"

"210 Park Avenue."

"You're trying my patience, Jew boy. The *new* address."

"What new address? You mean my brownstone? Sixty-four, Fifth Avenue. But I haven't... that is to say, *we* haven't..."

"If you don't tell me where he is, I have been instructed to shoot you full of this here buckshot until you do. We'll find out eventually, but I have been instructed to find out sooner rather than later."

"He could be at the warehouse."

"Don't you think we've checked there?"

That made Hyim's blood go cold. Not only had this man indicated that there was an effort to find his father, he said *we*. Like it was a concerted effort. Implying some kind of *we* that went beyond these five. What else did it mean? His father was in hiding, if this band of ruffians could be believed. And someone on a higher level was looking for him. If the diamond business really was this dangerous, it's no wonder his father had not encouraged him to follow.

Another one of the men whispered into the leader's ear. "Oh, I get it," he said. "I have a special surprise for you, son. Your daddy is a criminal. There's a passel of people looking for him right now, and no one seems to know where he's at. My job is to get you to tell me."

"I don't believe that. Any of it."

The other man raised his gun so that Hyim could see the end of the muzzle. "You see this here shotgun?" the man said. "This here's a Remington double-barrel 16-gauge. Do you know what that means? It means that my friend here can make your entire right foot disintegrate into a fine ash. We're the ones with the guns, son. It's the only truth I'm offering you. So unless you don't want all your parts put off one by one, I suggest you tell me what you know."

The other four men made a half-circle around him. "This is entirely unnecessary," Hyim said. "I would tell you anything if I knew anything."

"We know he sent you a message."

"You're joking."

"I'm a serious fella, son."

"I couldn't have received any messages from him. He would have sent them to the hotel, and we weren't there."

Hyim looked him right in the eye over the barrels. He was surprised to discover that although he did not wish to die, he was not afraid of it. It hurt him to think about the sadness that would overcome his wife, his father, his friends. But they would be able to go on. *World – Hyim = World*. It disappointed him to think that he would not have a life's work of research at a major institution or to help benefit the world, as his father had always wanted. Most of all, he felt pain for the children that he and his wife would never have; those that would be leaders of their generation, those that would be scientists, poets, social progressives, architects, or maybe even lawyers.

After short silence, the man said: "OK boys, hold his leg in place."

Three of the men quickly restrained Li-Don, correctly guessing that he was the biggest threat. Leah made a noise behind him, which indicated that she was being restrained also. One of them grabbed Hyim from behind, wrapping an arm around his throat roughly, with no attention to whether or not he would be able to breathe. Another one held his leg in place. Gradually, he felt himself slip toward the ground, where he was forced to sit with his outstretched foot as a target for the described shotguns.

Hyim was preparing himself for the pain. "This is ridiculous," Hyim said, choking the words out over his assailant's arm. He forced his mind to think about his other foot—the awareness of the hay that at one point had lightly tickled his arch, but was now just so much straw compost held in place by a fraying slipper. He tried to think what it would be like to lose a foot, to have any feeling stop at the end of his ankle. Perhaps it would burn, but like any wound, it would heal. He wondered if he would forget it wasn't there once it was gone, accidentally stepping hard on it and falling over. Or, just like the way Mei-Gao had taken up the limited emotional space he had available for a mother, would he be able to feel that part of a future wooden prosthesis? *Hyim – right foot = Hyim.*

The men's guns clicked, and for a moment, Hyim thought they had misfired. He did not have much knowledge of guns, other than the fact that they were horrible destructive machines designed specifically to kill things. But the probability of both guns misfiring was extremely high. It was more likely that this was some kind of mechanism for the preparation of firing. The metal sound of it was less sudden and more spring-like, so the most likely situation was that there was a firing mechanism that required the immediate release of the spring for metal to strike metal.

Gunpowder needed fire, so the backward action indicated by the clicking must release the spring that released the metal to strike another piece of metal to create the spark that set the powder off, containing the explosion and insulating the operator and the surrounding air from the effect, therefore propelling the pellets (or whatever kind of projectile was in there) in the only available direction. And then...And then...

He heard the explosion, he was sure. It was unlike anything he had heard before. Oh sure, he had watched hunters practice with clay pigeons and rifles, and he had seen the discharge of civil war weapons that the Dean of the college of Arts & Sciences had acquired (for no particular reason). But the sound did not bear any relation to any other rifle or pistol shot in his experience. He heard it from about five feet away. And in that moment of the flash of the gun, he was partially blinded by the sharp light and blinked. He felt the force of the pellets and for a moment, he thought he felt pain. But there was no pain. In fact, the pain of his feet from walking all that way in unsuitable footwear was also gone.

When his eyes opened, he saw the man standing over him with their guns pointed at him, wide-eyed and frightened like squirrels. But his vision was clouded by a filter of blue light that shimmered like water around him. He was no longer being held down. Out of the corner of his eye and through the pool of light, he saw the two men who had been holding him down—they were backing away, as terrified everyone else. He heard a humming sound, like being on the other side of a door from a steam generator.

He could barely breathe, but for some reason he did not need to. He tried to speak and shout, but could not get the air to do so. In an instant, the pool of light was gone. He was still out of breath, as if he had been running wildly downhill like he used to when he was young and Li-Don's parents took them to a waterfall park in upstate Connecticut. His sight was distorted because of the change in light, but he could clearly see his wife standing over him, reaching out to hold his face as he tried to speak. Then Li-Don came into view, saying something that was garbled as if he were underwater. And then, the plainly, smirkingly placid face of James H. Primerhaven, III.

Chapter 12

At first, the historical enormity of what had just happened to Hyim had eluded him. He was mute, deaf, partially blind, and could no longer feel pain. But that only lasted for an hour or so.

He was now deathly afraid of what was happening to him. He was helpless to warn them that the men with guns might be coming back, probably would be. Then again, they may have figured that out on their own. Even his thinking was muddled and unformed.

After a few minutes his mind cleared, although he still was not entirely aware of what was happening to him. But this much was clear: the lightning effect that had enveloped Leah—and the one that had been described by Jimmy in his forest—was the same as the effect he had just now experienced. He remarked to himself how accurate Leah's description of the experience was. He would have to trust her more, if that were possible. The light, the sound, the smell. There was no doubt that he had just gone through the same thing that she had. And now he knew that it was not just benign, but protective.

As he began to sort things out, he realized that rascal Jimmy was nearby, perhaps the whole time. That could not have been a coincidence.

He wasn't sure what happened next. He found himself inside a coach next to his wife and across from Li-Don. He felt lucid, but his tongue was heavy and his mouth felt filled with cotton.

The face of Brightferry was peering through the window.

"What...?" Hyim managed to say.

"All's well that ends well, eh?" Brightferry said.

Hyim tried moving his mouth to form more complicated words, but all that came forth were a few misplaced grunts

"Don't worry, my friend," Brightferry said. "You're in good hands now. It's a hidden blessing that they followed you here instead of trying to ambush you in Amsterdam. Suddenly we know they don't make a habit of intercepting our cables."

Hyim tried reaching out to Brightferry -- perhaps to make him stop and answer questions, or maybe it was enough seeing his face again that would make him want to use physical violence against him. Instead, the coach started moving, and Brightferry fell away into the distance, waving.

After a couple of minutes, Hyim regained his ability to speak. "What's going on?" he bellowed.

"You should ask your friend," Leah said.

Li-Don and Leah exchanged glances. "Your friend Jimmy just saved our lives," Li-Don said. "It's the third time that someone intervened to do that in the last three days."

"I wonder what will happen tomorrow," Hyim said, still with a thick mouth.

Li-Don smiled.

"So Jimmy has one of those electric devices?" Hyim asked.

"You really should talk to him about that," Li-Don said. "You are probably the only one who would be able to understand him."

Li-Don shifted uncomfortably in his seat. The ride was rough and made Hyim's head hurt.

"He's the one driving," Leah added.

Leah brushed some stray hairs from out of Hyim's face. "It didn't hurt, did it?" she said, seeking confirmation. "It wasn't entirely unpleasant. That is to say, I was terrified at the time, but the bubble I was in—that's what Jimmy called it, a *bubble*—gave me a strange sense of peace. Did that happen for you?"

"I... I don't know." Hyim was still shaken by the experience. He had been bracing himself for the pain of metal on bone, and instead had received a tremendous shock of current.

Li-Don looked contemplative. Having appointed himself the protector of the Hopewells, he was no doubt feeling the failure of that mission. Hyim felt bad for him; nevertheless he was sanguine. Little by little, he began to feel more and more grateful for the incident. That is, the electric pool of light that had surrounded him at exactly the right time was not just a fortuitous turn of events, but an astounding occurrence that he had been a part of.

His senses quickly returned to normal, and then went beyond normal. Though he had not been acutely aware of his surroundings before, he was now immersed in a sensory experience unlike anything else he had ever been through. He felt refreshed, strong, directly energetic, and, curiously, as magnanimous as a benevolent lord (not to mention a little randy in the presence of his wife).

"I'm going to have a word with that coachman," he said. Then he climbed out of the cabin and stepped up on the roof, steadying his balance for a moment as it moved over the rough road. He sat down next to Jimmy, who held the reins for three horses in one hand, smiling. It was too loud to have a conversation. He would have to wait for the next stop.

Hyim looked around and took a deep breath. The world was a beautiful place. Colors had more color, sounds had more sound, and smells... well, that may have been a downside. But he drank it all in, looking around in wonder.

His eyes then fixed on a bracelet that wrapped around Jimmy's left wrist. It was a streamlined shape, metallic, and had two points that stuck out away from his arm, at right angles to one another. Completely incongruous with the prissy blue suit Jimmy was wearing.

This had to have been the device. It was a marvel of design, but its secrets lay hidden. Hyim couldn't get over that it was such a small thing, about the size of a stirrup. But he had seen the power it could generate and manipulate.

"What is that thing?" Hyim shouted over the crunching of the wheels and stomping of the horses.

Jimmy's reply was unintelligible. Maybe it was the register in which his voice was located, or maybe it was the unfamiliar words Jimmy was using, or maybe it was just the din and racket of their vehicle. Hyim held a hand up to show that he couldn't hear anything.

Instead, he contorted himself back into the cabin. Li-Don still looked downcast. He looked up. "I am concerned about what those men said about your father."

It was jarring to hear this kind of talk after the physical trial that Hyim had just been through. He had almost forgotten.

"Mr. Hopewell is very dear to my family," Li-Don continued. "If it is true, if he really is missing—or worse—they will be in great pain. Your father saved my family from deportation. I would be driving spikes and splitting rails for the *chemin de fer* if it were not for him. My mother and father would have been thrown out of the country by now. I can't imagine what my life would be like if it had not been for him."

Hyim didn't want to think about that.

"I'm sure it's all right," Leah said, though not convincingly.

"I think we should get back as soon as possible," Li-Don said.

Hyim nodded. He might even cable back to New York to let them know—if there was time.

"If those men are related to my father's disappearance..." Hyim said, and trailed off. He couldn't think of what he might do. The truth was, he didn't think he could do anything. Had he been able to wrestle one of the guns away from them (an unlikely event in the first place), not only would he not have had the knowledge to know how to operate it correctly, but he didn't think he would have had the will to assassinate any man, regardless of the circumstances. He did not think he could even cause injury to one of them with a fist or a foot. The world was full of such brutality, and it made him almost physically ill to think about it.

Surely it was physically possible to project one's closed hand towards another man's jaw or abdomen. The force of such a blow would be akin to the dropping of a woodsman's axe or a blacksmith's hammer. Force, after all, is only the result of the motion of a mass-bearing object. But the particular type of force required behind the actions of such a fist required first the actions of the mind, which Hyim had no concerted wish to apply, let alone will.

Li-Don was the fighter. He could send his fists, feet, forehead flying at a moment's notice, bested only by much larger opponents. Hyim thought he might have been relying too much on Li-Don's protection to get them all through this. But Li-Don was no match for five men, no matter how well he could fight. They were all amateurs at this espionage business. And surely it was now espionage; however it started out, it was now about gathering enemy information.

There was that word again, *enemy*. It was a concept that rose in Hyim like a tide punctuated by waves. He did not like the idea that there were people working *against* him. It didn't make any sense. Even if this was about his father's diamond trade, how could anyone put that sort of effort into something so ephemeral as monetary trade? What purpose does money serve? Material gains could not compensate for the kind of satisfaction that came with completing a task, resolving a quandary, bringing a mystery out into the open.

Spoken like a true rich man's son, Hyim, he told himself.

It wasn't until that night, when they were safely at the port city of Le Havre, that Hyim was able to hear anything Jimmy said to him. Leah's burst of energy had subsided somewhere between Rouen and the coast, and she was fast asleep when they pulled in at dusk. It was approximately 30 hours after her electrical experience, and her extra energy appeared to have completely worn off.

As Li-Don and Leah slept, Jimmy and Hyim went for a short walk, always careful to keep the coach in view in case anyone decided to come upon them. They sat down on a fallen log, the air between them more serious than it had ever been.

"That was you at the foot of the tower, wasn't it?" Hyim said. Jimmy nodded.

"Why were you there? How did you know you would be able to do something about Leah?"

"It's complicated," Jimmy said. Normally loquacious, Jimmy seemed reluctant to talk further, which only made Hyim more anxious. Hyim had so many questions he didn't know where to start, but he saw the far-off expression in Jimmy's eyes and knew he would have to be more politic in his questions.

"The device on your wrist," Hyim said. "May I see it?"

Jimmy held out his arm to show it off.

"What is it?"

"It's called a projected-emission particle and ether amplification generator. I just call it an *emitter*."

"...particle and ether amplification," Hyim said, thinking. "The *particle* being an atom, and the *ether*... I'm afraid to ask. I don't really believe in the ether theory of physics."

"Wrong on both counts," Jimmy said. "What is called *ether* is not what you think it is. No doubt another word will describe it at some point in the future. But for now, it's the best word we have. And the *particle* is not the atom, but the result of the cleavage of an atom."

"So Plucker and Crookes were right. Dalton's atomic model is wrong. Cathode rays *are* charged particles. The fundamental units of electricity."

"You're on the right track, but that's not exactly true."

"What do you mean?"

"You have to let your knowledge catch up with your understanding. That is the key."

"What does that mean? What are you on about?"

"The vocabulary for how this device works isn't in existence yet."

Hyim exhaled loudly. He did not get exasperated very often, but this was very close. "Don't take this the wrong way, but you're not as good a physicist as I am. How is it that you know how this contrivance operates and I don't?"

Jimmy laughed. "In some ways, that's true. I would no more know how to put something like this together than a common macaque. But the knowledge I have about its mechanism goes far beyond what our university brethren would call *part of the canon*."

"Jimmy, if you didn't assemble this thing, then where did it come from?"

"I can't tell you that."

"What is this, a state secret?"

"Very much so."

"All right, fine. Which state?"

"I can't tell you that, either."

"Why were you following us?"

"For your own protection."

"My... our... protection? Look, Jimmy, do you know what has happened to myself, to Leah, these last couple of days? It's fairly obvious that not only are we in danger, but my father is also in danger. And somehow you knew that. Yet you didn't prevent the danger from happening, you only mitigated against its effects. With that device, you could have made our trip completely painless and danger-free. Now you're going to tell me some things. 1) Why haven't I heard of this device and why hasn't it been in any of the literature? 2) Why hasn't the physics behind this device been in any of the literature. 3) Why are people chasing us with guns...?"

"I can't answer any of these questions."

"Why not?"

"I can't answer that one, either. I have a lot to tell you. But not yet. You must trust me. Certain... situations prevent me from revealing to you what I know. I can tell you this: you must get back to New York as quickly as you can. There was a plan for you to remain in France, but that situation has changed due to forces beyond my control. You must go back. And you must have patience."

"I know we have to leave, but I don't know why. I want to know why. I want to know that we will be safe. I want to know how my

father fits into all of these things. We've known each other for, what, five years? I am searching and thinking about what I know of you and your character. I don't believe anymore for one second that you are James H. Primerhaven, III—at least not the one you pretend to be for the rest of us. And I want to know who you really are."

Jimmy stared right at him for a good long time before he answered: "Everything will be explained in due time."

"You're asking me to trust you, whoever you are, and whoever you are working for."

"You should trust no one else."

Hyim took a deep breath. "You think your answers will make me somehow unable to function as a human being? Will I be rendered mute, deaf, dumb, blind, nonsensical? Since when has knowledge been so strong an offensive weapon and destructive force? The little I have grasped will drive me to distraction enough, but more information from you will only lessen that effect."

Hyim was breathing heavily now. He rarely became so agitated. He could barely control what was coming out of his mouth. He didn't feel good about it at all. His questions were legitimate, he reasoned, but his demands that they be answered were less politic.

"These are the effects of the emitter," Jimmy said. "They will wear off, and subsequent exposures will be less traumatic." He put his hand on Hyim's shoulder. "I'm a friend," he added.

Hyim held his head in both hands and nodded. "I trust you, Jimmy," he said. "I don't know why, but I trust you."

Chapter 13

The cargo ship, *Juventus*, pulled out of port and the mouth of the Seine in the early morning hours before dawn. They were lucky. The ship had been scheduled to depart several days earlier, but the threat of a possible *mascaret* between Caudebec and Jumieges kept it in port downriver until the tide changed.

"Over a hundred ships have been destroyed by it in the last eighty years," Li-Don said with too much glee than the information required. "The *mascaret* is a fascinating and unpredictable phenomenon."

The three of them were placed in a room normally reserved for the illicit transportation of alcohol from the West Indies. It had the faint stench of the sweet oils derived from sugar cane, which Hyim found distracting, but which Leah and Li-Don did not notice. Leah was still a bit fatigued from her experience, but she was none the worse for it in any other way.

The captain was a surly fellow with a thick moustache named Gaillard. He was genial enough, but had clearly been coerced (somehow) into smuggling these three individuals back to America. Or perhaps bribed. Bribery was more likely considering his geniality.

Leah tried to translate the captain, but was having difficulty. "He mumbles," she said. "In general, I think he's telling us to stay in the room until the voyage is over, unless absolutely necessary. What he said exactly, I'm not actually sure, but I think he said that the lavatory is to the left, and through the first hatch."

"What about food?" Li-Don said.

She turned to the captain and asked him. Gaillard mumbled something, spitting a couple of times.

"He says we'll be brought whatever they have after they have their fill. He also bothered to... shall we say, *compliment* me on my cosmopolitan dialect, expressing his... *sympathy* for Americans who learned Parisian French."

The captain grunted and slammed the hatch door shut. There was also the sound of the hidden panel put in place. There were no windows in the room, and the burlap and wool they were given was little better than the hard, wooden floor. Hyim dreaded the twelve days they would be spending in that room. It might have been possible to get Li-Don out of the room for an hour or possibly a bit more, but it was just as likely that Leah would not be willing to make love in such a location. They would have to wait.

Both Leah and Li-Don brought books they were now reading. Jimmy had provided them with a number of pieces of reading material, but Hyim didn't feel like reading. He had a new problem, now, to work on. In addition to the true and perceived identities of everyone they had met up until then, there were the technical aspects of the phenomenae they had been subjected to, the introduction of their enemies, and that fateful encounter on Mr. Eiffel's Tower; but now he had to worry about his friend who was not quite his friend.

Jimmy's device implied a fundamental knowledge of particle physics that Hyim was not aware of, and because Jimmy had been exposed to the same teachings and learning the same ideas—more or less—he could not have had the knowledge or acumen to fit it together (let alone into such an aesthetically pleasing shape and functionally convenient form). This knowledge was not available—apparently—at Harvard.

Assume some years of development, some years of research, some years of inspiration, trial and error, and finally—going back further in time—some years of theory. The most recent date that this device could have been conceived was around 1843; the science had to be developed by 1840 at the latest. And it had to have been done in secret and held in secret for at least forty-five years. Because the effects of the device violate the laws of many natural forces, it would have to have been thought up either deep inside a private institution or else a government—in either case, again, in secret.

Secrecy would not have been difficult. Few people in the world would have been able to understand even one or two aspects of the device (Jimmy, himself an operator of the device, confessed to his ignorance of its inner workings). However, the rush to publish such a breakthrough as cleaving an atom—preposterous as it sounded, and surely a potential subject of ridicule—would have strained the muscles even in the most egg-headed neck.

This is not even to consider the manufacture of such a device. Hyim now regretted not asking Jimmy if there had been more of them produced for other people (for why waste such a momentous technological treasure on a gadabout pontoon-footed ludicrant such as Jimmy. Unless, of course, he was merely acting that way and was, in fact, a hyper-brilliant scientist slumming with the graduate faculty at Harvard. In the five years he had known Jimmy, he had neither known nor suspected that Jimmy could be anything other than he was. He was always a bit mysterious, with his departures from time to time, and his attitude towards his studies was always a little inuring and insouciant. But he always seemed a natural character and never gave any hint that he was anything else.

Jimmy would have to have been as skilled and brilliant an actor as he might have been a scientist to pull off such a long-term prank—which was to say it was impossible. For all of his mysteriousness, he was an entire character as he presented himself—if he had a large secret it would sooner have been that he had no vices and that his regular disappearances were jaunts into the country where he would have been a Presbyterian minister, chastising his flock for talking too much.

The *James Conundrum* could not be explained by the romantic notion of personality alone; there had to be a clue of science—technological engineering of which he was not a member, but merely a minion.

Suppose Jimmy were exactly as he said, a protector. The only conceivable protector would have been his father, which meant that his father was somehow a part of the beginnings of the device. Hyim's father was certainly within the timeframe and had the general knowledge of particle theory to pull it off. It was plausible that the seeming tangential interest his father had in physics and physics

theory was, in fact, a vocation rather than an avocation. Hyim didn't have the knowledge of his father's business to be able to understand what happened beyond what appeared to happen, nor did he have the curiosity for retail and wholesale trade practice and theory to allow him to even speculate on whether it was a front for such technological progress that would dumbfound the best minds in science.

Such an undertaking—his father's secret particle physics organization—would require not only a vast amount of accumulated knowledge, but also an enormous testing area, designed, possibly exclusively designed, to produce enough energy to create the effect. Such energy was unknown on the Earth— perhaps it could be found in the sun or the Earth's clouds.

"Outwardly," Hyim said aloud to himself, "the effect is so similar to lightning that one might expect that lightning was involved in the energy gathering process. But that is only speculative and could very well be a superficially derived canard."

Leah and Li-Don looked up from their books. Leah was visibly tired, her eyelids drooping.

"Is it possible," Hyim said, "that there is a different source of such a vast amount of energy, a voltaic pile the size of Long Island?"

"What is lightning?" Li-Don asked. "What is it made of?"

"Electric current," Hyim replied, "with no commutating material. Extrapolating from Coulomb, electrostatic charges accumulate in the air and on the ground, and at some point the force that unites the two charges over a given distance becomes greater than the force required to hold them from each other. Electric current with a large enough force needs no conductor to allow it to pass through."

Li-Don gave him a blank look. "Somehow," Hyim said, "I think an analogy could better make this clear if it came from our mysterious friend James."

"What is current?" Li-Don asked.

"Electricity moving from place to place."

"What is electricity?" Li-Don asked.

"It's the result of... the result of... static charges accumulating..." Hyim stopped. "Maxwell said that light is an electromagnetic phenomenon."

Li-Don persisted, perhaps sensing that Hyim needed an extra push into parts unknown. "If electricity is the effect of two opposite charges, what are its constituent parts?"

"The ancients thought lightning was fire."

"That only deflects the question into what fire is. Assume that lightning and fire are the same thing. But by our own eyes they are expressed in different ways. Does that not imply that there is a common substance that makes up the two that has its own properties which can be measured?"

"They must be different then. Two different effects in two different situations."

"Why can they not be the same? Rain and the ocean are made of the same common substance, but to our eyes they are different. Man and mud. Hydrogen and helium."

"Is this science or philosophy?"

"Scientists merely discover that which philosophers have known all along."

"Or poets," Leah said suddenly.

"Science is just the expression of proof," Li-Don said. "So prove that lightning and fire are different and they shall be different."

"All right... all right. I don't approve of the ether theory, but let's say that light is merely the effect of ether waves on our eyes. Different kinds of light produce different kinds of waves, like the different colors emitted by different burning substances..." Hyim stopped there. His mind wasn't working like it usually did.

"What rot!" he said after a moment. "This is getting us nowhere. I can't think in this enclosed space." He started to pace. It had been almost six hours since they left port. They would be in view of the mouth of the English Channel by then. Already he was feeling like a caged animal. His logic was failing him and he didn't know why.

Just then, they heard the engines stop. "What's this now?" Hyim said, annoyed. He increasingly felt the warmth in the air—it seemed exaggerated from what he remembered.

"There are only a few reasons why they would stop the ship," Leah said. "None of them are good news."

After hearing some unidentifiable muffled noises, both metallic and human, they heard the panel being slipped off, then the bang of the door latch opening. Gaillard poked his head through the hatchway and mumbled something to Leah. Then he disappeared, latched the door again and slipped the false panel back on.

"He says they've been stopped by what he termed some kind of... authority. There are some loose planks there and there," she pointed to the wall at two places. "We can hide behind those."

"But surely this room is secure," Hyim said.

"We should take no chances, according to our captain."

Li-Don immediately set to work to remove the two planks on the walls, each of which had handles on the interior side for just such a purpose. He ushered Leah and Hyim into one of the small spaces and re-attached the plank, then stepped into his own space and sealed himself in.

Hyim and Leah had just enough room to stand front to back, with Hyim in back because of the sloping angle of the ceiling. It was very dark and even more cramped—the space was big enough for one person to stand in relative comfort, or for two smaller people, perhaps if they knew each other very well. Where board met board, they could see the interior of the room, but they were well hidden.

None of them had taken a proper bath in days, and Hyim could smell the sweat on the back of Leah's neck—not altogether unpleasant, but he would just as soon not be this close to her in his current state of irrationality. He tried not to think about her feminine form, which was, of course, impossible in those close quarters. He could not help the images that came into his mind, but he tried as hard as he could not to consciously touch her in any way, lest one of them cry out (probably him) in some kind of unrestrained passion. Hyim didn't think he could keep himself from making a sound, so he kept himself from making a move.

After about twenty minutes of standing over Leah's neck, they heard someone pounding on the walls. The noise was close, but not near the room. Then the noises got louder as the pounding got closer. The noise changed as the pounding came to the wall on the other side of the room. The sound was more hollow when it reached the room. Whoever was knocking on the wall could hear the same noise that they did, and knew that the room was behind a false panel. Whoever it was, was specifically looking for that room. And had now found it.

Hyim heard Leah gasp. She knew what was going on also. He leaned over to see the door through the gap in the wood. They heard the panel come off and get set aside. Then they could hear voices. *Oh no!* Hyim thought. *The books!* They were still on the floor, perhaps lying face down to save their places. But maybe it was all right. They were possibly looking just for the alcohol. That made the most sense. The presence of the books would be odd, but surely the captain could talk his way out of that. In any event, there was no sign of humanity other than that, so they would have to continue to search the ship if they thought people were on board.

The hatchway unlatched and flew open. A dark-bearded man in a white cap stepped forward, his hands behind him, looking authoritative. He spoke, then a series of interpreters spoke, then the captain spoke, and then back again.

"Interesting nook of this iron heap," he said with a stiff British accent. Hyim took him for a commissioned naval inspector. "Why are these lights on in here?"

A mix of murmured and mumbled dialects of swallowed French followed, then the English interpreter said, "He says that the previous owner of this bucket of bogwater ran rum and what'all. But he's a legitimate pusher of fruits and the like, if you get my meaning, sir."

"Tell him we're not looking for spirits, but for stragglers."

The various interpreters talked among themselves. Hyim could not make out the captain's voice, but his ears were attuned to anything that might have to do with the "stragglers".

"They had a couple of stowaways when they left port," the interpreter said. "It was a bit of a row, but they was tossed overboards."

"That would explain the peculiar odor," the inspector said. "Have him describe these stowaways."

The interruptions in English conversation made Hyim more nervous. It was not a sure thing that the captain wouldn't give them over if pressed. Finally, the interpreter said, "It was a young married couple. They was a little prissy like they was putting on airs, if you get my meaning, sir. And it was also a Chinaman, a little bloke, looked very young. The captain thought he was some kind of indentured servant, if you get my meaning."

Then, another voice, "Did you say *Chinaman*?"

It was a voice that Hyim had not heard before, but he instantly recognized it. And when the man stepped into view through the hatchway, Hyim had just enough time to put his hand over Leah's mouth before she gasped.

The face that was burned into his memory had not come with a voice, but for some reason, he knew that the voice was from the Man on the Tower. Those sunken eyes darted around the room, looked briefly at the floor, then around the walls. They briefly lighted upon the two Hopewells before moving on around the room.

"Did we ever get a good answer about why the lights were on in here?"

The interpreter line spoke, then answered, "Sometimes the previous owners smuggled plants, and they need the light."

"Hm."

"The captain wishes to know if you require him to turn round and head back."

"They were here," he said quietly, almost to himself, with his nose in the air. "Tell the captain he can get moving if he wants. We're done here."

His voice was measured, calm, like a priest on a cloudy day. His accent was flat American. Hyim could not tell where exactly the man might have come from. Nor did he know why he wondered where the man might have come from. The Man on the Tower looked around a little bit longer, then left, and the room was sealed again.

Chapter 14

It took a while for the three of them to get their breath back. They stayed in the hidden compartments for a good thirty minutes after the inspector's party left. After composing themselves as best they could, they were silent, not wishing to make sounds to possibly give away their position and existence—but also because they didn't really know what to say. Hyim noticed that his fear about the books had been unfounded. Resourceful Li-Don had brought them into his own hidden compartment with him. How he did it without making any noise made Hyim respect his physical abilities all the more.

In another hour or so, the engines started back up again—coughing—and they were on their way. They read until they were tired, and then, one-by-one, fell asleep.

Throughout the trip, Hyim would silently comfort his wife, who was seized with a sadness and depression she couldn't explain. She didn't have to. There was too much they had been through to not have had an adverse reaction. She was also not used to being on such a ship that was not meant for the comfort of the passengers, and suffered from seasickness on the first couple of days. It subsided, however, and she was able to eat and drink without becoming sick on the third day.

They ate like the rest of the crew: thin soups, hard bread, salted fish and pork, and dried fruits. Li-Don was particularly interested in the dried figs. He had never seen such a thing—a fruit with all of its water let go like so much hydrogen from a balloon.

"I've read about these, but this is the first time I've seen one," he said. "Or tried one." He was hooked, and grateful for his introduction to this particular delight, despite the circumstances.

The effects of the emitter were wearing off on Hyim, and he

found that he was falling into the same depression, as if the high of the effect was now responsible for the low they were falling into. A wholly not unreasonable explanation.

The face of the Man on the Tower, and now the voice, filled Hyim's mind like mineral oil. The mouth was much less cruel than he remembered, the features much more ordinary. He had a perfect picture of the man's face in his mind, but the attributes he interpreted as malevolent in memory simply were not evil, in person, in full lighted view. It was a peculiarly plain face, with the exception of those eyes.

Either his father's enemies were very persistent, or... or what? Still more questions. He had a long time to think about it.

He kept thinking about Jimmy and his *enemies*—the man who had been aboard their ship who suddenly showed up in the middle of the night on the Tower trying to... trying to do what? *Enemies*. The word sounded so strange to him. The concept itself didn't make any sense. Someone working against someone else. Usually for access to or possession of something.

The experience of hiding in such a small space left them all a bit dizzy.

"Why are people enemies of one another?" Hyim wondered aloud.

Li-Don sat up. "Antagonism," he began, "is as much a part of the human condition as anything else, as much as love. The Iliad describes rivalries between countries, between countrymen, between generals in the same army, even between the gods. Vanity, lust, power, greed. People seek pleasure through perceived satisfaction, and will use force to get it if they think someone else prevents it."

"Surely there are better ways than force to settle disputes."

"Surely there are. But none more effective. Diplomacy only works when both sides are diplomatic. My mother used to tell a story to me about two poor farmers, Hai and Sai, who constantly argued over a plot of land. It was the best, most fertile land in the valley, but they could not agree on who should till it. Hai and Sai were not enemies at first, but because each wanted the entire plot of land for himself, each would not let the other have one inch of it. Both of them could make

more money than they could use if they were both to plant on just half of it, but they would not allow the other to make use of any of it. If Hai tried to plant corn, Sai would plow it under overnight and salt the ground. If Sai tried to plant cabbage, Hai would release rabbits into the field to eat up all the seedlings.

"One day, their wives could take no more. 'They will surely destroy the land between them,' said Hai's wife. 'Then no one would benefit from it,' said Sai's wife. Behind their husband's backs, they decided with each other to build a wall that split the plot of land in two. They both convinced their husbands to go to into the city to search for livestock, which they knew would take many weeks. Hai's wife and Sai's wife built the wall, stone by stone, pike by pike, working every day until it was finished. Finally, both Hai and Sai returned, but they returned together, and without animals.

"They had met at a market in the city and it came out what their wives had told them. They figured out the plan and came back, taking the road together. The two men stood before their wives. Hai said to his wife, 'How dare you split this land with our worthless neighbor that was to provide for our children and their children's children.' Sai said to his wife, 'You foolish woman! You have given half the land to our enemy without regard to our family!'

"Together, Hai and Sai pulled down the wall, stone by stone, and pike by pike, until there were only the weeds and the dirt. The wives could do nothing about it. Many months passed and finally the field was ruined forever with salt and vermin. Their wives berated them for being so stupid as to have ruined the plot between the two of them. But the husbands said, 'at least the enemy does not have it.'"

"That's a terrible story," Leah said. "Both families stayed poor."

"It is a terrible story, and that is the point. But each had the solace that the other was poor and would always remain so. They each successfully held their own envy of a richer neighbor at bay by making their neighbor un-enviable. This is the ultimate reward for antagonism."

"They were both acting irrationally," Hyim said.

"That is also the point. Humanity is full of such nonsense. We are the only ones who can keep ourselves from it, but we are pulled in many directions because of our conflicting internal forces. Greed made them try to till the land, and greed made them destroy the other's attempts to do so."

"Piffle," Leah said. "Greed had nothing to do with it. They weren't striving for the pleasure of money, they were pushing against the fear of poverty. Each one of them must have imagined the great wealth they would accumulate if they could have the entire plot for themselves—they would have no fear of being poor ever again, probably in only a few years."

"Begging the mistress's pardon," Li-Don said. "But half the plot would have given them that wealth. But they were so blinded by hate that they could not condone the other having the same success."

"I imagine that if one of them had a culverin, he would be the one to control the plot," Hyim said.

"No doubt."

"I don't like this talk of violence and farming disasters," Leah said. "We're in direness as it is."

There was a silence between them.

Finally, Li-Don asked Hyim: "Do you believe the alchemist stories about the regenerative powers of electricity?"

"I used to dismiss such tales. But I have to wonder just how much of the stories I've been told are true. Jimmy's forest ride nightmare, Brightferry's preposterous drama at a temple on the other side of the world. And what happened to Leah and now myself. If that even *was* electricity."

It had not escaped Hyim's attention that Jimmy's story of being in an electrical storm in the middle of a forest was similar to his own nightmares. Up until now, he dismissed it as happenstance. There was not even enough quality relevant data to make it a coincidence. But Jimmy had mentioned God.

God was a wildcard in Hyim's universe of understanding.

Or, rather, *Understanding*. According to the religion of those around him and his father, God was the original scientist and artist. Sculpting Man out of unformed clay, which he had previously created. The electricity of lightning may have been involved, was probably involved. What other tool would God need than that force?

Hyim remembered his first demonstration of electrical power. An arc of light between two metal rods. His father had taken him to a traveling show of "man-made natural wonders", where there was also a steam engine and some very heavy and powerful magnets. It was thrilling. And it was science.

But the mention of God made him feel hollow inside and he would start to sweat. God was always the end of the conversation. "It's all a part of God's plan," was enough to end an argument for some of his colleagues at the university. It was maddening; almost as if they were using this idea of God as a crutch for their own will to understand.

The three of them fell asleep quickly while trying to continue a serious conversation.

Chapter 15

The captain never let on what persuaded him to take the Hopewell party from Le Havre to New York, and he was much too gruff and otherwise disagreeable to even think about asking. Besides, Leah was the only one who could speak with him.

If Hyim had ever thought he could somehow fumble his way through French (because of its Latin roots—visible if not audible), Gaillard was more than enough assurance that he could not. The man's mouth barely moved when he spoke—in fact his ears moved on either side of his black-mopped head more wildly than his mouth did in the middle of it.

The captain did not see his smuggled passengers off when they arrived in New York. The *Juventus* did not even come into port. A small sailboat came up alongside the larger ship to pick up Hyim, Leah, and Li-Don, just out of sight of land. The boat's pilot, a tall, grizzled captain—who looked like what Hyim thought a New England captain should look like—did not exchange pleasantries, he merely helped his passengers with their footing from one vessel to the other, grunting and clenching a cigar in his mouth that may or may not have been lit.

This seemingly imperceptible transfer of non-existent passengers by more than one unknown transmitter gave Hyim a more defined sense of intrigue than he already had. He and Leah had since fully recovered from their electrical experiences and were now just tired. But the enigmatic nature of their voyage— both to anyone who might have been following them, and to themselves—gave them a strange sort of alertness to what might happen next. They watched the fog-shrouded harbor come into view in the early morning light as the small boat sailed closer to the mainland.

"Don't ask me no questions," the pilot said. "And I won't ask you none." He kept himself busy at the wheel of the boat while they stayed near the bow. They had nearly nothing of what they brought almost two weeks before—the travel papers in a sling underneath Li-Don's shirt, were the only tangible things that they came back with—but they were grateful to be coming back at all.

Li-Don was fidgety, like a young officer before a battle.

"After all that, what I really want is a slice of cheesecake," he said. "And perhaps some dried apricots."

Hyim smiled for the first time in a long time. He was using muscles that he hadn't used in a while. His nervous energy was gone, his accumulated anxiety was subsiding, and now he couldn't stop himself from smiling at his friend.

"I just want to get out of these clothes," Leah said.

They had borrowed clean clothes from the crew of the *Juventus* on their first day, but had not had a change since then—twelve days.

When they got to the harbor, the pilot swiftly executed a hard turn to starboard and headed for the fishing docks. As they sailed in closer, the pilot slid some fishing gear across the deck to them, meaning for them to look like fishermen as they came out of the ocean and were back on land. Leah wrapped her hair into a ball and stuffed it under a cap. From a fair distance away, she might have looked like a small man—as small as Li-Don—but anyone with eyes from closer than thirty feet would have seen that she was clearly female.

No one bothered them when they disembarked, however. The pilot tied up his boat and waited, as if waiting for more crew or for someone to help him unload his catch. But no one need have helped him unload his real catch, as they were under their own power, passing by the port authority and obtaining a ride from a commercial buggy toward midtown Manhattan.

In the back of Hyim's mind, he was terrified about going back to his father's house because of what he might find—or not find—

there. Logically, there was a good reason to be afraid of what might await him—and there was also a good reason to not be afraid of what had happened over a week ago half-way around the world. Desperate people, *enemies*, liars, common thieves, uncommon thieves—whoever those men were who caught up with them in the French countryside, there was no more reason to believe them than to disbelieve them. But Hyim's logic was disintegrating under the pressure of his fear. And when the buggy turned the corner onto Park Avenue, Hyim's fear almost took over.

The neighborhood was still there, but the house in which he had spent most of his life was gone. It was an empty space between the two houses on either side. Instantly, he knew what had happened. The houses on either side: the Mackay family home and the Hendeman family home, were both streaked with angular soot marks, betraying the fire that had consumed the Hopewell residence.

It all came crashing down on him: the men with the guns, the letter that Brightferry had carelessly tossed into the fire, the whereabouts of Li-Yan and Mei-Gao. The black streaks were longer on the first floor of either house, and as they stacked one upon the other on the Mackay house, which had been painted white and cream two years earlier, they presented at more and more acute angles of incidence from the perpendicular. On the Hendeman house, a brick building with a less flat and more customized façade, the streaks were not only closer together, but rose at less of an increase in angle. The only obvious conclusion was that a part of the house had exploded near the Mackay house, possibly on the second of three floors. That room was, of course, his father's study.

The fact that an explosion could have happened in that room was not surprising. There were many strange pieces of electrical, mechanical, and chemical flotsam that came together in that room. And because his father was an avowed amateur at how those different pieces interacted with one another, it was quite possible that he had left one electrical device too close to a chemical device. It could be argued that it was puzzling that such an accident had not happened sooner.

But that was the problem that was making its way around Hyim's logic (eluding it at every turn). It was the timing of this particular accident that caused his mind to race through the possibilities. This much was true: 1) his father was not at the house, and 2) there was no house. But as for the rest...

Was his father missing as the men with the guns had said? Hyim's heart sank. It was quite likely that he was incinerated. He fought back the feelings he did not want to feel. He did not believe for a second that his father was dead. Old Ezra could have made such a serious error as exposing some kind of pitch compound to electricity—that was very likely—but the men with the guns assumed he was missing, despite the fact that his house had burned to the ground. That was inconsistency #1. It was entirely possible that these two incidents were completely separate, but not likely.

Inconsistency #2 was the fact that the Mackay house, the Hendeman house, and every other house on the street was still standing. A fire that had been started by an explosion (or an explosion that would have been exacerbated by a pre-existing fire) would surely have caused adjoining houses—with their dry wood and other flammable materials—to catch fire. Which would then cause their adjoining houses to catch fire, and so on. And it is was quite likely that there would not have been a response from the fire department in time to keep the entire block from being destroyed. Yet the houses stood, almost as if a fire department—with a highly efficient water engine—had been at the scene when the fire happened; or as if the house had been insulated on either side.

As the buggy came around the corner, the driver whistled. "That's not the place you wanted to go, is it?" he said.

"Oh, Hy!" Leah said. "Oh, no. Oh, Hy."

Hyim remained motionless, looking at the empty space between the Mackay and the Hendeman houses. Li-Don stood up in disbelief as the buggy pulled up to the side of the road.

Li-Don jumped out and helped Leah step down. She surveyed the empty space, then quickly stepped over to the Hendeman house and knocked.

111

Hyim stayed in the buggy, studying the scene.

"That your house?" the driver asked.

Hyim nodded without looking at him.

"That's a real shame, that is. I guess you can say you were lucky you weren't in there when it happened."

"My dad may have been in there when it happened."

The driver said, "My God," then stayed quiet.

Slowly, Hyim stood up and made his way down the short stepladder to the street. "Stay here for a bit, will you?" he said to the driver.

"Whatever you need, sir."

He stepped around the stone entranceway, which was still partially standing, but had clearly been disturbed by all of the activity around it. The space itself was covered with charred wood and ash in a rough outline of the house's footprint. If there had been anything standing after the fire—which was unlikely, but not out of the realm of possibility—it had been demolished afterward, either by weather or the hand of man for reasons of safety, secrecy, or scavenging.

He stood roughly in the location of the kitchen on the first floor, where Li-Don's parents might have been but most likely were not. His donated fishing boots—slightly too big for his feet— crunched and popped over the detritus of the ground. The houses on either side towered over him like gentile church spires. Despite his deduction that his father had not been killed in the fire, he could not help thinking that he was stepping upon his cremated remains.

Leah came into view from out in front of the Hendeman house. Her posture indicated that she did not have good news. He slowly made his way toward her, both wanting to know what the Hendemans had told her and not wanting to hear it.

Leah shook her head. "I spoke with Jules and Edith," she said.

"Tell me," Hyim said. "I have to know."

"Jules told me that they had just left Ezra in his study not ten minutes before they heard the explosion," she said.

"What? Why were they there?" Hyim asked quickly.

Leah was a little taken aback. She was by now used to her husband's dispassionate manner in virtually all things, and it always seemed a surprise to her when he showed his emotions, despite the situation.

"He was showing them one of his new toys," she said haltingly. "An electrical gadget of some kind. They said nothing but good things about Ezra. He was in a very good mood."

Hyim looked at the sky.

"The good news is that the Weis were not in the house at the time. Li-Don is going to see them now."

"Thank God for that," he said.

"Hy, I'm sorry."

Hyim looked into her eyes and remembered why he had fallen in love with her. Sensing his vulnerability, she went and retrieved the information he would be too preoccupied to seek himself. Then she told it to him in the most direct and delicate manner she knew he would accept. And now she was trying to comfort him in her own way just by looking into his eyes. In her gaze was all the comfort he would ever need for any ill that might befall him.

But despite her transferred comfort, he was still bothered. His preoccupation was not—as would have been humanly appropriate, he guessed—with the idea that his relationship with his father was now fixed, immutable by any further interaction between them; but instead with the idea that his father had not died at all, that he was not in the house when it exploded, and (most curious) that he had not yet come around and told everyone that he was OK. That would most probably affect their relationship once the father was found and would be forced to provide some sort of satisfactory explanation.

113

"There's something else," Leah said, reaching into her handbag.

Hyim watched as she pulled out an earth-colored cloth sack. Carefully, she unwrapped it around her hand to reveal a wide, gold ring with a red stone. Hyim recognized it as his father's. Then he tried to imagine how the Hendemans had taken possession of it and came to only one conclusion: the explosion had blown apart his father corporeally enough to send this ring—perhaps with a finger attached, perhaps not—into an area that would have protected it from the heat of the initial blast and ensuing fire.

"There were some... remains," Leah said carefully. "The Hendemans aren't Orthodox, but they realized what had happened. They took care of the burial."

"What remains? Was it the finger on the ring? The whole hand?"

Leah shifted uncomfortably. "They did not volunteer any additional information of that type, and I did not pursue it."

Chapter 16

Leah and Hyim told the driver to take them to the burial site near the temple on 25th street. Hyim did not remember ever going there.

Ezra's memorial was remarkably unostentatious for such a wealthy man. Just a stone with his name and the two individual years that marked his passages of life. It was markedly similar to his mother's stone, which was in southeastern Massachusetts among her family. Perhaps the Hendemans did not know this. It would not be proper to move the remains, as Leah continued to say, but the stone was somehow out of place near a religious building.

He thought that going to the marker would remove his doubts about his father's true whereabouts, but it did not. If anything, seeing the grave with his father's name on it seemed like a prop in a theater production. It was all that was required to convince anyone who did not suspect anything.

After about twenty minutes, they had the driver take them to the residence that Ezra said he would be setting up for them. It was just a short distance towards Central Park, with a small bit of land on either side of the house, unlike the crowded buildings in the rest of the city.

Hyim was feeling more and more paranoid about people following him, though he didn't say anything. He hadn't told Leah anything about his suspicions since they had arrived in the city, which was unusual. But he didn't know if he could successfully convey to her the exact nature of his gut feeling without sounding like... well, like Jimmy.

There was just too much happening all at once, and he couldn't sort it out, and he couldn't find the time or the peace to get it sorted out. The gravesite was not even a sanctuary. He had to sit and think somewhere less theatrical, perhaps with a small stack of paper, and work it all out. He could feel his mind trying to bend itself around the facts to create a coherent, plausible narrative, but he, himself, could not tie everything together.

It was always possible that not everything fit together neatly; but there were too many coincidences, and they were happening all at once. It would be an emotional time for any man: a wedding, personal attacks in a strange land, a father's disappearance. But his attitude was less one of emotion than it was of intellectual frustration—he recognized this as he saw Li-Don's wordless countenance react to the empty space where his parents' residence had been. He recognized it in Leah's eyes, which seemed to be searching for something in him that needed to be solaced. Had she found it? He couldn't say.

He could say he aware of a here and now, and this was it. Leah was sitting next to him as they came up to their new house, and for that he was grateful. Li-Don would be by later, perhaps with Li-Yan and Mei-Gao back from the hotel. And perhaps not. But the house was there, Leah was there, he was there.

After paying the driver with borrowed coins and sending him on his way, the two Hopewells stepped into their new house with the spare key that the Hendemans had been keeping for them.

Instead of being a chaotic setup of dust-covered chairs, tables, and other objects d'art, the entire house had been set up with an unseen decorator's hand as if Hyim and Leah had been living there for years. Hyim recognized some of the furniture from his father's house, but most of it was new. They toured the house in open-mouthed silence until they got to the top floor, which was all one room. To his astonishment, Hyim saw that his father—or an agent of some kind—had paid meticulous attention to obtaining and placing various pieces of lab equipment, the crowning jewel of which was what appeared to be a small-scale replica of Tesla's alternating current induction motor, one of the displays at the Universal Exposition.

But the object that kept his attention was sitting on a roll-top desk in one corner. In the center of a small, crumpled sheet of packing paper was the sparking glass oblong, the object which had captured his attention on the last day he had seen or spoken to his father. He had thought it was lost forever in the move to Argentueil when all of their packed possessions had been left behind.

It popped blue as if acknowledging his presence, then became gaseously ghost-like. Next to it was a folded letter from the *Hôtel Bourdonnais*.

"The hotel sent this," Hyim said. "Probably on the day we left."

"It couldn't have arrived more than two days before we did," Leah said.

"Dad put this here, I'm sure of it."

"But the fire was over a week ago. Li-Don's parents could have received the package and then put it here."

Hyim relaxed into submission. "That's true," he said. "They do have a key, and they would be authorized receivers for packages addressed to... to Dad."

"I don't mean to imply..."

"I want him to be alive, Leah. I can't accept... there are too many loose ends. There may be witnesses to the accident, but there were no witnesses to his death."

"There does not have to be a witness to the actual... death. The remains..." Leah's voice trailed off. It was clear she did not want to give bad news, but it was also clear that she felt she had no other choice. "Hy, you have to concentrate and listen to me. Listen to me carefully. The burial has been done in the traditional manner. Perhaps if we had been there you might feel differently. But we still must have a *shivah*. Your father wasn't a regular visitor to Temple, but you still have to do what's right."

"But I don't believe..."

"Concentrate!" Leah shouted. She rarely raised her voice, so Hyim was surprised. She walked over to a narrow table along one wall, pulled off her borrowed jacket and hung it around the small mirror that was attached to the wall. "Ezra would have wanted you to memorialize him, not just to help him convince people that he was a good Jew, but because he would have wanted his death to be a source of knowledge for the world."

"But we have to find..."

"We have to find a way to mourn him."

"We have to leave..."

"We have to leave him behind and get on with our lives. What would he have wanted?"

Suddenly, in Leah's open and deviously simple Slavic face, he saw what she was trying to tell him. The idea came to him like a kite in the rain. Once again, he was grateful for the intelligence that had cemented and verified his initial attraction for his wife. She had realized that—whether or not it was true—Hyim thought his father was alive, and if that was true, it was dangerous knowledge. If it appeared that they thought he was alive, it was a virtual certainty that the people who were their antagonists would be back and do something antagonistic. This, despite the fact that the origination of the idea was the result of the antagonists' blunders.

The fact that she was trying to inform him of this in such a circuitous fashion meant that she thought someone was listening to them, which was, of course, ridiculous. And yet, it was not out of the question that their correspondence was being monitored and their movements were being recorded somehow. It was very likely that the men with guns had thought they were going through a true Jules Verne moment, and had explained the previously science fiction experience to their employers, whoever they may have been. So the curiosity and awe to which the employers must surely have been subjected would only have added to their ardor.

This Leah had communicated with just a look; and some logic.

Li-Yan and Mei-Gao had confirmed the story that Ezra was in the building when it exploded. Hyim searched their faces for any signs of irony or the comfort of a noble lie, but found none. The Weis tried to help set up the house for *shivah*, but they did not know any more about it than Hyim did.

"It has been eight days," Li-Yan said. "We did not allow a memorial service until you arrived."

"We will not have a formal memorial service," Leah said. "All we will need is an acknowledgement of the passing of someone close to us."

Leah made all of the arrangements, with help from Li-Don, who was more useful than Hyim was, despite the distraction of having his parents around. They received some of Ezra's acquaintances in their home over the next week, allowing people whom neither one of them knew to pay their respects.

"If there is anything that I can do..."

"He was such a generous man..."

"He loved everyone..."

"I never heard him say an unkind word..."

"There is a hole in the world..."

Most of them either worked with Ezra or worked in the business. A man named Doyle with a small face and large hands shook Hyim's vigorously.

"Guess you'll be taking over the imports?" he said, soliciting an answer.

"I'm sorry?"

"Ezra was the real brains of this operation."

Leah stepped in. "This is neither the time nor the place to talk business."

"Sorry, ma'am," he said sheepishly. "But we will need an answer." Then he disappeared into the crowd.

Neither Jimmy nor Brightferry showed, although some people who worked for the Hopewell diamond "empire" did show up and say nice things. Leah's parents also came for a short visit and asked some uncomfortable questions about their time in France.

"Just lovely," Leah said. "But I'm afraid we didn't get to see as much of it as we would have liked."

"Maybe someday we'll go back," Hyim added. But he secretly started to despise the place.

Mei-Gao wanted to make food for the guests, who sometimes stayed for two hours, sometimes just for a few minutes. But Leah didn't want any refreshment for the guests, so she only cooked for the close family. Hyim asked Li-Don's entire family to move from the hotel into the house. Leah added that they could be the house staff, just as they were for Hyim's father.

Once again, it was strange for Hyim to have his surrogate mother figure be his employee. He let his wife handle those matters.

When Hyim was growing up, Mei-Gao had been as loving as she could be, under the circumstances. The Weis were suspicious of people outside the family—Ezra Hopewell being the exception because he had proven to be worthy of loyalty—and Mei-Gao was generally frightened of much that went on outside the house. Li-Yan or Li-Don, when he was older, usually went to the market to get food and other necessities. Hyim remembered Mei-Gao as helpful and loving, but not saying much because she was shy about her English with such an amateurish but enthusiastic orator as Ezra Hopewell in the vicinity. Through her wordless encouragement, she gave Hyim the model for patient observation and understanding that, in some ways, led him to his love for science, cause-and-effect, and the insight of logic. She was also a prototype for a hypersensitivity to outsiders which Hyim expressed through his fear of crowds. They had a close relationship that was not so close that she became his mother, she was more like a favorite aunt—who treated both boys the same, but clearly favored her own son.

The Weis—all three of them—were the most loyal people Hyim had ever encountered, something he did not appreciate until he left for university and saw how cold-blooded academic life was by comparison. Li-Yan tolerated his father's occasional ravings with the patience of a saint. There was no one else in the world (not even Hyim) who could have done so with as much grace.

In short, his relationship with the Wei family was complicated; by the time he was ten years old, at the age when children realize the effects they have on others, he did not know how to act around them. He observed them as one might observe a reagent, interacting within a solution. They were a discrete family unit.

As the well-wishers moved in and out of the Hopewell house, Hyim could still see this unit behave altogether differently from the time he remembered. Li-Yan and Mei-Gao exchanged furtive kisses when they thought no one was looking. Li-Don would receive playful swats on the head from his mother when he was being facetious (which was often). They worked separately, but together as a team, pulling each other along, helping whenever it was needed (swatting whenever *that* was needed).

Hyim's relationship with his own father was far simpler. Ezra was more like a benefactor than a father. In truth, if Mei-Gao was like a favorite aunt, Ezra was like a rich cousin. Hyim found himself thinking all these things, idle as his mind was while strange and polite people visited and watching everyone's behavior. He understood Leah's compassion and persistence as having come from a large family—her contradictory nature was suddenly understandable.

And despite the world falling apart outside of their house, inside their house he became organically comfortable—all that other stuff, the bizarre intrigues and the scientific improbabilities, didn't matter a whit. The feeling washed over him like oil. This was love.

Chapter 17

After seven days of mourning, the household gained a sense of day-to-day normalcy. Hyim was still haunted by his father's disappearance—if not death, which time and reflection had presented as a possibility. He wondered what might have happened that would make Ezra want to disappear. But it was very easy to settle into the routine that might await him for the rest of his days: using, testing, and experimenting with the equipment in his third-floor laboratory. With the bulk of his father's fortune—minus some sensible and seemly, if out-of-the-way contributions to various religious and social institutions—he did not have to worry about making a living for his family. The events of the preceding weeks became more distant and more vague. Though a definite threat, the outside world was still *outside*.

During the *shloshim*, approximately two weeks later, Doyle came back for an answer to his question. He stood in the doorway uncomfortably, his fedora in both hands, as Hyim held the door open and kept his hand on the handle.

"I am trusting that the organization can run itself," Hyim said.

Doyle's smile widened. "But you'll be the head of it in spirit, no?"

"I never thought about it. I suppose I'll just own it and leave the running to you and the rest of the board."

"Very good, Mr. Hopewell. I'll send over the necessary papers."

They shook hands too vigorously for Hyim's taste. Doyle disappeared down the street. No sooner had he gone that a man in overalls and working cap came to the door, saying they were activating electrical lines throughout the neighborhood. "It's a bit exciting to be a part of the great experiment, isn't it?" he said. He had on overalls with the name "Pearl Street" stitched onto them.

"You mean Edison's direct current wire," Hyim said. "Tell me, my good man, has he solved the signal degradation problem?"

"Beg pardon, sir?"

"The one-mile problem. Has induction been achieved with direct current, or are the magnetic poles of the wire too ephemeral?"

"I'm just here to inspect the wires, sir."

"I see. Well is there any way I can talk to the man?"

"I would think he's a bit busy for that, sir."

Hyim thought for a moment. Far be it from him to stand in the way of progress. "Very well," he said. "If you must. But don't enter the house for any reason. Just attach the wire to the outside of the house and we'll take it from there."

"If you'll notice, sir, the lines are already attached to the house. I just need to make sure it's all set up right."

"No need."

The man seem confused. "The power has not yet been directed to this part of your neighborhood, so it may appear that there is no problem, sir. But I assure you, these lines are a very complicated business, sir. And if I may say so, it requires a knowledgeable hand."

"I'll manage."

"Beg pardon?"

"I'll inspect them myself."

"I don't think you'll understand..."

"I have a Ph.D. in physics, my good man. I'll be able to look at them."

The man exhaled loudly. "You'll have to sign a waiver."

"Whatever it means. Just don't come inside the house."

"Begging you pardon sir, but I must see those wires!" the man said, trying push past him to get in the door.

Hyim froze, not allowing himself or the man to move an inch in either direction. "You will not enter this house," Hyim said calmly.The man stepped back, a little stunned. He smiled only briefly and tipped his cap. "I see, sir. Of course. Well, uh... the power will be coming within the week."

As the man went down the steps, Hyim shouted after him. "It's about time you people did this part of Manhattan."

He slammed the door and returned to his wife in the drawing room.

"You were awfully rude to that man," Leah said.

"I still don't trust anyone. And you shouldn't either. I just wish there was some way I could get back in touch with Jimmy. He has the answers, but I have to find a way to get him to tell me."

"Jimmy doesn't strike me as someone who can be tricked into revealing a secret."

"Perhaps not, but..." he stopped in mid-sentence. He turned to Li-Don, who was sitting at a table in the corner, poring through old Ezra's accounts. "We already have electric wires?" Hyim asked him.

"Yes. Your father made sure of that. They are not active yet, however."

"Hmm. I should speak with that man Edison."

"What do you hope to gain by this?" Leah asked.

Li-Don, who had been listening in, spoke up spontaneously for the first time since they had established their household roles. "Mr. Edison is going about his strategy all wrong," he said. "He is trying to conquer New York block-by-block with an inferior technological idea. It has only one true public positive, which is safety. But markets don't worry themselves with safety when cost is a consideration. Like my father says, 'You do not choose a cow over a bull because it has no horns.'"

"I'm not sure I understand that," Hyim said.

"I've never said that!" came a yell from down the hall—Li-Yan overheard and denied the knowledge and wisdom of the remark with one blow.

"But your point is well-made," Hyim continued. "If there were a more cost-effective way to deliver direct current, perhaps through higher voltages... I don't know. Tesla's electrical solution is just too wild and dangerous and unpredictable. I prefer Edison's more sedate one-way magnetic fields."

Li-Don, who might have continued to press his point further, instead kept quiet. His protective failures continued to weigh heavily on him, and having his parents in the same house made him feel a particular humility that Hyim recognized but did not understand. There were only two limitations of his lifelong friend and personal secretary being a protector: 1) that he was not more than one person, and 2) that his fighting skills and protective instincts were not quite enough to overmatch a better prepared and/or equipped opponent.

Hyim sat down in frustration. There were so many things he did not understand and could not prepare for. He had a future family to think about, to care for, to provide for, if it ever came to that—if not money, then a coherent world view. He knew his father had always wanted him work toward a cause that would make the world a better place. But *what* cause? And what did *better* mean? Who was to say which type of world was better than any other type of world?

He looked over at Leah, the mother of his future children. One of the few things he was sure about in the world was her and her place in his life—and his place in hers. She did not yet know what she wanted to do with her life: mother, teacher, rabble-rouser, lab assistant, what have you. He had come to find out that his life was not quite an open book to himself, either.

Before their trip, he might have said to anyone who would have asked, that he was planning on becoming a professor emeritus of electro-dynamic physics, that his plans would not have ceased until he was put out to pasture by the new crop of students. His time was just beginning, but it would end someday. And between the two points was no longer a straight line. He could not imagine being an academic for the rest of his life having been through an ordeal for which he had no explanation, about which there were only a few missing people he could ask.

The three of them: he, Leah, and Li-Don had not spoken about their adventures, not even to Leah's and Li-Don's parents. The less their friends and family knew about what happened, the less likely they would be accosted by some pernicious stranger who wanted information, or worse.

Failing a visit from Jimmy for a complete demonstration and dissection of his *emitter*, there was only one thing that was stopping Hyim from creating a similar device to protect his house and his extended family: Empirical knowledge. Protection had to be the goal.

"*Shloshim* is over," he told Leah abruptly. Then he headed up the stairs to his lab. If the *emitter* wasn't going to come to him, he would have to go to it.

END OF PART I

~ The Originators ~

Part II

Prologue

Somewhere in Pennsylvania, 1904

As the gray-suited men were ushered into a dimly lit room on the *Georgia Mae*, a stern-wheeler on the Susquehanna, a five-piece band played an up-tempo type of improvisation that many of them had never heard before. They could hear the faint chugging of the steam engine, although being in that room gave them no sensation of movement.

They all sat down in a small theater normally reserved for showing Vaudeville and dance revues. There were twelve of them, and none of them knew why they were there. But the invitation was intriguing, and their dislike of the current American President coupled with the greed of their profession (not to mention the threats of being put out of business) brought them to Harrisburg, where they boarded and were led either upriver or downriver, none of them could tell which.

Some of them recognized each other, and though they were filled with an antipathy that is reserved only for generals that had been outmaneuvered, they resisted the urge to throw their fists around for the sake of the occasion.

Somewhat anticlimactically, a figure of average height and features stepped out onto the stage. What impressed the audience was not his peaceful countenance nor his simple costume of a brown friar's robe and hood; it was the way he stepped down the stage, taking his steps slowly and carefully, seeming almost to stop, but then continuing on, impossibly slow—though the stage was only thirty feet long, it seemed like his entire movement to the edge of the stage took five minutes. They could not tell if he was barefoot, but some of them suspected as much from the sound of the footfalls.

"Gentlemen," he said. "Thank you for coming." His low and measured, but unprojected voice echoed in the small hall more than it should have.

"Where's the women!" one of the suited men shouted. Others guffawed.

"In time," the host said. He held up a hand to bring silence to the room, which, as the suited men were astonished to discover, it did. Some of them shifted uncomfortably in their seats. More than one of them began to suspect this was some kind of religious ceremony.

"I will not take up much of your valuable time," he said. "Let me only tell you this. many of you have lost a great deal of money in the last few years. Others of you have the lost a great deal of potential for making money that you once had. And almost all of you have at one time or another been antagonists."

A small rise of nervous laughter came from the audience, then died down dramatically in the host's subsequent pause.

"But I am not here to mediate your petty struggles with each other or with the Roosevelt administration. I am here to bring your attention to something much more serious. I assume you all know each other? In this room is represented more money than most of the great civilizations in history. And there will be yet more. Everyone here knows that oil is a growth business. But you should know something about your business that you do not yet."

A man at the back shouted, "what could you possibly know about the oil business that we don't?" This was followed by guffaws.

"I know more than you realize. Not only do I see what you are accomplishing now, I can see the future of your business. Gentlemen, I see five years of continued prosperity and then the bottom falling out. Your revenues are based solely upon the products that are manufactured by others. Remove those products and you remove your profits."

"What are you talking about?"

"Your president isn't interested in putting you out of business. He only wants to limit your reach. And if you look into the future at least thirty years, you will see that you can all coexist and flourish. Neither you nor your government are real threats to your livelihood. The real threat is far more serious and far-reaching. It's called *market forces*."

He waited for an objection, but there was none.

"Imagine for a moment that there is a source of energy more powerful, more plentiful, more populist, and more inexpensive than the one you are currently mining out of the ground. Do you think it will be a simple choice of the consumer to decide which source of power to use? Yours costs a hundred times the other, it constricts the airways of your customers, and it smells bad. Now imagine that there is only one company who knows how to produce this energy. Scary?"

He waited again for a stray comment, but again, there was none.

"There is a man living here, here in America, who is trying to put you—all of you—out of business. You have all made your money because you own the land on top of which are your oil resources. You hold all the rights to these resources in perpetuity. However, this man—and perhaps others with him—is now working on an energy source which cannot be owned, claimed, sold, bought, stored, or traded. It has a source that will never run out, a power potential greater than the sum of all your resources combined, and it is available to anyone who wants to take it."

"Preposterous!"

"Bollocks!"

"Impossible!"

"You talk like it is sunlight or water!"

The host smiled. He had them. "It is neither. And yet both are required in order to produce and process it. It must be processed, true, and that can have some potential economy of scale, but the process requires only a device like this one." Here, he held up a small metal object about the size and shape of a coronet, with a small intake pipe leading through a series of valves, curling back and forth and finally ending in a larger exhaust bell. Many of the suited men did not recognize the shape as a musical instrument. "This device costs five dollars to make," he continued, "and will produce as much power as twenty thousand of your oil wells in less time than it takes to fill up a glass of water from a well.

"This man," he continued, "who seeks to put you out of business is not interested in your business. He is not interested in competition. He is not interested in capital. He is not interested in profit, nor merger, nor partnership, nor any kind of economic theory to which you subscribe. He is planning to make these devices free to the public. He is a threat to your very existence."

There was a pause, and finally, from the middle of the audience: "How do you know this?"

"I was once a partner in his organization. And I used to make these devices." He held up the coronet-like device and placed a hand on one of the valves. "Still not impressed? I don't blame you. You need proof. Come out to the main deck and allow me to demonstrate the effects."

Chapter 18

New York, 1904

Hyim sat at the wheel of his two-year-old gasoline-powered Oldsmobile Curved Dash Runabout. His hair and beard were long and flowing in a mild breeze. On his way from his residence on Fifth Avenue to the block-sized warehouse in the Bronx he had purchased some years before, he encountered some folks by the side of the road, fretting over their own raggedy vehicles.

He knew his machine was imperfect when he bought it. And after carefully researching the technology, he recognized its limitations almost immediately. The combustion of petroleum products was inherently inefficient and unpleasantly pungent. There was little he could do about the fuel, which was little more than refined kerosene, but he did improve the intensity of the combustion by fiddling with the spark producer and adding a filter that forced in an oxygen mixture that was richer than that of the ordinary atmosphere. He also put in a more effective brake and tightened the steering mechanism. With the help of Li-Don, who was more familiar with the Medieval mechanics that the engine was based on, he improved the efficiency of the engine almost 300% (as far as he could measure it).

Unfortunately—or fortunately, depending on who you were at the time—translating the efficiency into the speed of the vehicle was not a priority at the time he tinkered with it. So, although he could toddle along for almost five times as long, it was still at the same 15 miles per hour. This was something of a relief to Leah, but at the moment, Hyim wished he could get from place to place faster.

It wasn't that he wanted to be anyplace in particular at a sooner time, although he was a little impatient to get to the converted warehouse, his staging grounds. Even after the fifteen years since he and his extended family had last been attacked—fifteen quiet years—he still had the feeling that people, persons unknown, were monitoring him, waiting for the right time to attack again. Out there in the street, he was generally helpless. He was without his father, without Jimmy, without any sort of protector.

In fifteen years, the Hopewell household had not changed much. The Wei family still served as housekeeping and bookkeeping staff. Leah was still trying to maintain a Jewish household despite the fact that she was the only one really practicing (Hyim tried but was not impressed with the reasoning of their rabbi). There were no children despite best efforts. Leah now thought herself too old to have children; the Hopewells resigned themselves to a childless life.

Li-Don had dated young girls within the tiny Chinese community that had sprung up but confided to Hyim that he had not been impressed with any of them. They spoke about it while working on the Oldsmobile.

"The Exclusion Act keeps them from coming. And the ones that are here are, for lack of a better term, stale. They are all very much old world children. I have a mind to marry a girl like Mrs. Hopewell. I see how much she cares for you, helps you. And she still maintains her own separate identity, which, I have to tell you, is rare and much frowned upon in my culture. Listen to me. My culture. What I should say is the *Chinese* culture. I don't feel that it's mine anymore. Those people... *my* people are as strange to me as your particle physics."

Hyim thought of his own *people*. He felt no more Jewish than Li-Don felt Chinese. He had gone with Leah to Temple occasionally, but it was more of a favor to her because he knew he had been spending less and less time with her. She had worked on the Roosevelt campaigns for mayor and governor, but was discouraged from continuing in that line of work by his campaign managers.

"You aren't of any use in a national campaign," one of them told her. "You can't convince anyone to vote, and serving as a Suffragist only hurts the cause you work for."

T.R. himself once called her a "busy little bee" who should be rewarded for her hard work. But he didn't follow up, and she never got her consideration. Though he didn't actively prevent women from working or campaigning or doing whatever they wanted in general, he also did not encourage their participation. She couldn't fault him for his politics, but he apparently didn't see how much power he was denying the Republican party.

Hyim, upon hearing this story, had to agree that her cause was not his cause. They had been steadfast Roosevelt supporters— although, to be truthful, Leah told Hyim how to vote, and he didn't disagree. Hyim was the only member of the household who could vote, and he was the least interested in it.

When Roosevelt became president—in such a shocking and head-shaking manner— to her surprise, she was offered an appointment to the newly created Department of Commerce and Labor. She had not heard from the man or his campaign staff in six years, but here was an invitation to join him in Washington (even if it was just as an assistant secretary). She reluctantly and politely declined, citing her work in New York, which, at the time, was almost exclusively as a suffragette.

When Hyim reached the warehouse, he was greeted by the apprentice architects he had employed to help him with his latest experiment.

Fred French was a young and brash engineering student at Columbia. His smile was as wide as the Hudson river, and he carried a small pad of paper with him wherever he went. All of 21, his designs were not so much unique as they were meticulous, which is what Hyim was looking for. They had a mutual friend in Leah.

Cass Gilbert had a great deal more experience designing and building structures in pre-defined styles. He was a large, friendly man—having learned to be friendly to offset his imposing figure.

"Morning, sir," French said as Hyim stepped out of his runabout. "Is today the day?"

"Today's the day."

"I hope you find what you are looking for," Gilbert said. "I'm afraid I won't be here to watch the festivities. I'm needed in St. Louis. Even so, I wouldn't want to watch. I'm afraid this is *adieu*."

"I should hope not," Hyim said. "My company has a need for people like you."

"I'm not interested in industrial design, Mr. Hopewell. This was a kind of fun distraction for me, but I really must put my mark on the world."

They exchanged pleasantries, then Gilbert took his leave, walking away with a flourish and an *adieu*.

French followed Hyim into the warehouse. It was a huge structure, not unlike the expansive metal and glass tent Hyim had seen fifteen years before at the Universal Exposition in Paris. It was the only building in New York City that was wide and tall enough to contain his experiment without exposing it to public view.

In the middle of the concrete floor were the exact replicas of the three houses on 5th Avenue which had been affected by the explosion that took his father's life (maybe). The Mackay house, the Hopewell house, and the Hendeman house. Every detail was copied. French had to research the original plans for the Hopewell house, since it had been destroyed. A four-story brick building had been put up in its place after Hyim sold the plot to a developer. It made the Hendemans and the Mackays more than a little irritated with him because the new building was designed to house three different families on three different floors.

What French couldn't interpret or have the knowledge for, Hyim directed and sketched from memory, such as the dull-brown painted shutters and the columned entrances.

"Seems a shame," French remarked as they paced around them. "Those are livable structures."

Hyim was a little nostalgic about the house. He, too, thought it was a shame that he was forcing himself to demolish it. But it was for science. Of the many questions he had about that short three-week window of his life when he first got married, this was the one he felt he had the most control over: how did the explosion that destroyed his father's house leave the two adjoining houses untouched?

After fifteen years, he thought he had finally come up with the answer. He had inserted a series of steel-plated ceramic panels inside the walls of the old Hopewell house. Rather, he had ordered it done by Gilbert's team of builders. They were five panels thick with half a millimeter in between. It was a little thicker than a normal wood-frame house, but did not exceed the specifications of the original structure.

Hyim theorized that the house would had to have been built with these panels in place from the beginning, or else installed before they moved in. This meant, in turn, that the Hopewells would have been expecting trouble.

He, himself, had set up the apparatus that would produce the explosion, based on the sparse reports of the neighbors of the funny gadgets his father had and the patterns of soot on the adjoining buildings. If the explosion had not destroyed the surrounding structures, it nevertheless left a footprint.

He said goodbye to French, who really wanted to stick around for the "festivities". But Hyim wouldn't let him.

"This is something I have to do alone," Hyim said. "If I need anything else, I'll knock on your door."

"It's been a pleasure, sir."

As the young engineer's footsteps lost their echo, from handshake to slamming door, Hyim walked over to one corner of the warehouse, where he had set up a small observation post behind a kind of thick glass that he had designed and forged. The curved glass had most impressed Gilbert, who asked how he was able to manage such a thing.

"Patience," was Hyim's reply.

He took his place and pulled the switch that activated the power into the middle house. He then pulled the switch that activated the Marconi. He altered the radio design slightly so that it would send switching data to a magnetic receiving unit inside the house (instead of telegraph or voice waves), which would then detonate the house in the way he wanted. It was hooked up to a button that he could press to get the desired effect. He stared at the setup for a good long time.

If he looked hard enough, he could almost convince himself that his father was in his office on the second floor. But not really. He could no more imagine that there was a shadow where there was clearly not than he could imagine that his father was actually in the house, waiting to be incinerated for the second time (maybe).

He pressed the button. He heard the click of the switch underneath his badly designed panel. Badly designed, that is, for the eye; it was well-designed for its function. Then he heard the faint click of the switch inside the house, having received its invisible instructions. It took another five seconds for the explosion.

In those five seconds, Hyim's heart raced. This was the reason he had wanted to be a physicist. He had set up an experiment—a very complicated experiment on a large scale. He would soon know if his theory was right, if it was wrong, or if he had been a fool to try to find out. The anticipation of the event was, in some ways, more satisfying than the conclusion. In those five seconds, the world compressed itself into that warehouse, into the rebuilt house, into the re-designed and re-manufactured studio office, and at the same time compressed itself into Hyim's narrowed field of vision.

The explosion itself was not nearly as intense as Hyim thought it would be. True, the initial blast was intended to be contained so that the primary impact would head directly for him in his observation seat (a move, which, in hindsight, he might not have attempted to make a second time). The force and heat were small compared to what he had been bracing for (although the noise was enough to ring in his ears for a good long time). However, the reinforced steel-ceramic panels within the walls of the office had clearly failed. The blast was more omnidirectional than it should have been, and the resulting fire quickly began consuming all three houses.

He watched as dispassionately as he could for a short while, then pressed the button that activated the overhead sprinkler system, which put out the fire in a matter of minutes, and got him soaked in the process (he made a mental note to himself that it was not necessarily bad luck under such circumstances to have an umbrella opened indoors), having first shut off both electricity sources.

When the sprinklers shut off, he began his visual inspection of the houses in their soggy, burned out state. Curiously, the steel-ceramic panels in the other parts of the old house had held their ground against he fire. It was apparent that the initial blast had damaged the panels in the office to such an extent that the flames could leak out into the Mackay and Hendeman houses. The fire had traveled from those points directly to the Mackay house, which took the greater damage of the two. The fire moving in the opposite direction had to breach not just one or two walls, but also a third, which was damaged enough by the blast to let a tiny sliver of flame through to lick the sides of the Hendeman house before it, too, caught.

The scent of charred and wet wood and plaster was very similar to the faint one present at the actual location fifteen years ago. But those houses were still standing. The middle one was just a shell, with all walls except the front walls intact. The exposed steel panels where the plaster and paint had burned off looked like the random patterns of some exotic animal. The Mackay house was somewhat less damaged, and the Hendeman house had barely been touched.

The structural integrity of the houses was admirable, especially wet. As Hyim walked around, his shoes stepped into and out of some running puddles, rivulets of which ran out into the streets surrounding the warehouse. Drops of dirty water fell from the structures onto the floor, staining it. He remarked how similar this was to the winery underneath the Brightferry estate.

The main door opened and shut quickly, briefly letting in light from the outside.

"There is something wrong," Li-Don shouted. "Something wrong with Leah!"

Chapter 19

Hyim sat at his wife's side in their bedroom as Dr. Merritt put his instruments in a flask of alcohol. He was a portly man with an upper New England accent that had a little gravel in it. His continued use of the word *however* set Hyim's teeth on edge.

"Mr. Hopewell," he said with an air of gravity, "you may wish to leave the room for this. However, you may wish to stay. It is of no consequence to me."

"I'm staying right here."

"It's a very delicate matter. We may need to discuss some things that a man should never hear. However, you may wish to hear it firsthand."

"We've been through a lot. You have no idea."

Dr. Merritt put his finger to his lips. "However, there is always the chance that you will lose respect for your wife for what you are about to hear."

Hyim grabbed Leah's hand, trying to show he was not leaving.

Dr. Merrit sighed. "Mrs. Hopewell, how long have you had this irregular bleeding?"

"Almost three years."

Hyim turned quickly to his wife. She looked back, almost defiant. It was a signal that she had told him something of this in the past and he hadn't been paying attention.

"But it hasn't hurt at all until a few weeks ago," she continued. "There was a... a time when it was watery. That was right before the pain started."

Another look came between them.

"Mr. Hopewell, Mrs. Hopewell, you should stop trying to have any children. It will not do you any good. I am afraid there are not many things that can be done."

"Not many..." Hyim stammered.

"Mr. Hopewell, this is not a simple dropsy. Your wife has a tumor. I must emphasize the seriousness of this situation. I am most expert in these matters, I assure you. These things start out as a harmless growth. Most often, they get rid of themselves naturally. However, sometimes they become attached and grow quickly. However, in the case of Mrs. Hopewell, they linger for many years until finally they end as a cancer. I have seen eighteen of these in my lifetime."

Leah gasped. Hyim fell into an introspective silence. His experiment upstairs trying to fuse atoms of Helium would be completed in four hours. His legs started to feel weak.

"Well, then, what can be done?" Leah asked gruffly.

Dr. Merritt cleared his throat. "Total uterine extraction and quicksilver therapy," he said, getting up and collecting his things into his bag. "It's really the only thing that can be done. It's not a certainty, but it's the best thing to be done now. However, there is a chance that the patient will not survive the procedure. And there is a good chance that the patient will not survive four weeks from the procedure. The survival rate is not good." he stopped.

Hyim put his head into his hands. He wouldn't let his mind comprehend what he was hearing. "Leah must live," he said simply.

"Of course, we will do whatever needs to be done. She will have the best surgeon..."

"Hy," Leah said. She had not called him that in a long time. "Hy, we all have our time. If God wants it, I will go to Him."

"I won't accept that," he said. "If your God wanted you to die, He wouldn't have allowed me to marry you, because I'm not going to let it happen."

Dr. Merritt collected himself. "There is something," he said. "It is experimental. Controversial. I hesitate to say anything about it, in fact. But there are some anecdotal successes."

"Tell us," Leah said. "I don't relish the idea of surgery."

"Yes, well, Mrs. Hopewell. I have been reading about a curious form of tumor therapy called brachytherapy. There are trials going on in only one place in the world."

"Where is it? We will pay anything, go anywhere."

"At the Radium Institute in Paris."

"Paris!" Hyim hissed.

On the deck of the *Rotterdam III*, the Hopewells and Li-Don stared out into the endless North Atlantic. It was less a happy occasion than their first transatlantic voyage, and they stood in silence, watching the fog roll by.

Hyim couldn't believe they were going back to Paris. He never wanted to see that place again. but, with the welfare of his wife foremost in his mind, he had no choice.

"Are you feeling any pain now?" Hyim asked his wife.

She shook her head. It was clear from her actions and gestures that the two had grown apart. Somewhere between his obsession over his father's possible death and her disaffection with politics, they had stopped communicating.

For Hyim, it had been a long time since he was not in the process of conducting one experiment or another. He had forgotten how to live with other people. His wife no longer bothered him with day-to-day concerns, such as what guests they might have on a particular night or when the Weis would have the day off. She did manage to convince him to shave his beard and cut his hair for this trip. The look on her face when he presented his naked face to her was one of surprise. He had aged rapidly. The lines around his eyes, the hanging jowls, the strange acid stains on his nose and forehead. He looked like a man of fifty instead of thirty-five. His hands trembled with inaction. Left with nothing to do, they worried about Leah.

Li-Don was silent for the entire trip. He and Hyim had not spoken like brothers in a very long time. His employer was distracted and unpredictable. He never lost his temper, only his reading glasses from time to time.

It was not a pleasant cruise. They jumped with unsprung tension every time Leah made a wrong move or paused in a conversation or coughed, however insignificantly.

Another thing that filled Hyim with tension was being out in a public place. Of course, he had been in his runabout now and then out in public, but he had a peculiar feeling of solitude, even in a crowd of other horse-drawn and horseless carriages. It was much different from standing or walking around with other people present. He was still hyper-aware of their collective and individual presences around him. So much so that it heightened his already wound-up defensive paranoia.

Li-Don, of course, made sure that they were among the least number of people as was possible under the circumstances. It not only made Hyim uncomfortable, but it took a lot out of Leah to have to speak to people. She refused to be pushed around in a wheeled chair like a wounded war veteran, but she found it difficult to wander very far around the ship.

He also brought newspapers from New York, Boston, and Philadelphia. He read out loud in their first-class stateroom as they fidgeted, relieved of the expectation of speaking.

"The Morning Journal," he said, skimming the front page, "is showing Hearst himself campaigning for president. It says here that he is the 'champion of the little fellow.'" He switched papers in front of him. "Then here in the World, on page 12, it says that Hearst is a dangerous radical who wants to turn this country into a socialist experiment."

"He'll never get past Tammany anyway," Leah said offhandedly.

Hyim briefly looked up at her while she sat up on the bed sheets. She was no longer the sleek, rounded beauty he had married. Did he just notice that? How long had she looked so sallow and thin?

"They can't stand the man," she added.

Li-Don quickly shifted papers. "Listen to this from the Philadelphia paper," he said, then began to read a short article from the middle of the front section.

Steamship Makes 250 Mile Journey in Five Minutes?

One might be forgiven for imagining that the happy stern-wheeling *Georgia Mae* could sprout wings and fly like some magnificent albatross. The very brothers Wright, looking down from their North Carolina flying contraption might tend to be skeptical about such a feat. But George Malleton, harbormaster of the tiny town of Grace, Penna, on the north shores of the Chesapeake, only has so many explanations for what may have been either the fastest navigation of the Susquehanna in recorded history or the most successful prank in riverboat lore.

Yesterday, at eleven minutes after ten o'clock, Mr. Malleton thought it strange that the *Georgia Mae,* normally a pleasure boat that runs from Scranton to Baltimore, but chartered for this occasion, would stop in his small town and not go on to the larger city. He decided to telegraph the harbormaster in Scranton, a Mr. Whalingham to see what was what.

"Imagine my surprise," he said, "when Mr. Whalingham said they had only departed five minutes earlier."

For the record, that is 250 miles from 10:06 am to 10:11 am. Despite the fantastic story, Mr. Malleton has a less fantastic explanation. "There had to have been two ships. I imagine the first one is still up around Wilkes-Barre or Sunbury, and this one just came around here. Either that or Mr. Whalingham is mistaken on a scale normally reserved for physicists."

Officials are still looking for the second boat.

"It doesn't really say that, does it?" Hyim asked.

"I made up the part about the physicists," Li-Don replied. "But the rest of it is true."

"I'm sure of it. If there is that kind of power in the world, what are we doing stuck on this rust bucket with four days left?"

Li-Don continued to read about the Russo-Japanese war, the presidential campaign, the Monroe Doctrine, the latest Panama canal news, and strange little items that were hidden away in the folds of various newspapers.

"The Manhattan to New Jersey underground railway is almost finished," he said, skimming the article.

"Is it going to run both ways?" Hyim asked, which made Leah break up in giggles for the first time in a long time.

"Oh, it hurts!" she said. "Don't make me laugh."

They were more at ease after Li-Don's daily readings, but it did not take long for their fears to come back once he was finished.

With a day to go on the voyage, Hyim asked Li-Don, "Who is aware of where we are going?"

"My parents, Leah's parents, Dr. Merritt, of course, and any of his colleagues and staff he might have told. The people at the Institute. Are you worried about being away from the house?"

"I'm always worried about being away from the house. It's the only safe place in the entire world for us. You know how extensively it's wired."

"I know that my parents and I can't enter or leave without telling you."

"I have to switch the electric fields on and off."

"I know. I'm as vigilant as you are about protection of the family." Li-Don paused. "But this anger you feel... Anger against a enemy. An unseen enemy. It is not unwarranted, but it is also not... helpful. Only a becalmed sea can stop an angry gale."

"I do not have anger, Li. There is only watchfulness. Alertness. I have my paranoia, and I have a right to my paranoia. I know it's been a while since we have been set upon, but think what might have occurred if there had not been any vigilance, if we had just left our fate to the winds. No. I firmly believe that it was my efforts that kept our house from being attacked."

"Begging your pardon, but I disagree. No matter how many electro-magnetic fields you set up around the house, they by themselves will not stop a bullet. True, the windows have been fortified, but they are not impenetrable from rifles or pistols, or even more primitive means of destruction. At bottom, the only thing that can be said is that there has been no attack. You have to allow that if someone truly wanted you to be dead, you would be dead, now, at this moment. Whether it's your runabout being sabotaged, your warehouse invaded, or what have you. Someone who knew your routine would have been able to get to you quite easily."

"That's very comforting, thank you. Remind me to raise your salary."

"My point is, *sir*, that your vigilance is consuming you. Leah sees it too."

"Has she told you?"

"She doesn't have to. I can read it on her face."

Hyim looked over at his sleeping wife: pale, clammy, red circles around her eyes. He turned back. "Enemies," he said. "They're all around us."

Chapter 20

Paris was much more sedate than he remembered. True, the last time he was there, it was a great city-wide party. But now the parties were confined to specific areas. He kept track of the *Tour Eiffel* from his third-floor Manhattan laboratory. It was intended to be knocked down until Eiffel managed to convince the authorities that the highest structure in Paris could be used as a radio tower for the military. So there it stood, to the consternation of many an architecture critic.

When they arrived at the Radium Institute, they were met with dour-faced scientists and hospital workers. Leah did most of the talking, since no one seemed to speak any English. *That* hadn't changed. Hyim did not ask her about what they were saying and she did not volunteer any information. He had done some research on his own about the Paris Technique, as that form of brachytherapy was called, and did not want to know any more.

What piqued his interest was not the procedure itself, but the application of radiation. Gold and radium isotopes were injected directly into the tumor, through the use of a tube, which managed to shrink and wither the tumor without affecting healthy parts of the body.

He found radiation and the fact of ions and isotopes to be fascinating. The free electron having been revealed by Thompson and Lenard—which he had guessed at—it was now apparent the atom, itself, was not a free-flowing plum pudding, but a universe of its own, with particles and perhaps sub-particles much like the Earth's solar system, with its own rules. And yet, some elements spontaneously turned into other elements because they shed their own power. Strange.

He thought radiation was too dangerous to work with, so he left it alone, but he read all he could about it: alpha particles, beta particles, gamma rays, x-rays, the quantization of light, the ultraviolet catastrophe in black body radiation, etc. He did not analyze this kind of information as he once did, so much as he took it in like sunlight. Analysis would require experimentation and hard thought, of which he had little to spare.

Leah would have to stay there for a couple of days for observation and suitability testing. He would stay at the *Maison de Sacré Cœur* nearby. Alone together in the room that would be her home for the next month, they stumbled through a conversation about hope.

"Everything is going to be all right," he kept saying. "I've read about the procedure, and it looks genuine. But I wish I could talk to the doctors here."

"Hy," she said. "We have to look at the probabilities. There is a good chance that I will be dead within a month."

"Come on, now."

"No, it's true. We have to accept the mortality of the species. We have to become aware that nothing lasts forever, that we all die, and that we cannot choose our date when we wish."

"Stop talking like that."

"I mean both of us, Hy. They're going to ask you to leave in a few minutes, but in that time, and in the spirit of this conversation, I have something I need to tell you."

"You don't need..."

"I love you, and that's why I'm going to tell you this. I'm very proud of everything you've accomplished, of everything you've invented or dreamed up. You vowed to protect us and you have. But as you've protected our lives, you've also stifled them. You lost sight of the goal of protection, which is to give us not just the freedom from enemies, but also the freedom to live a normal life. You don't have any real friends, Hy. Acquaintances here and there, but no real friends.

"I have you and Li-Don."

Leah smiled. "Your father wanted you to make the world a better place. And you've been trying, but really you've only succeeded in making your own house a better place. I am telling you this because I want you to go on with your work if I should happen to die. I want you to promise me."

The room smelled of rubbing alcohol and the soles of flat hospital shoes. Though it was not a *hôpital* in the truest sense of the word—something for which he was grateful—it was staffed by medical personnel as well as scientists.

"I... I promise," Hyim managed to get out.

Just then, a woman came into the room. She had a half-sphere of dark hair tied together in a bun, the usual school-marm look. "Good evening Mr and Mrs. Hopewell," she said. Her British accent was vaguely French at the same time. She was possibly pregnant—with a slight paunch—but it was difficult to tell, and Hyim wouldn't dare ask.

"How are you feeling?" she said to Leah, sitting down next to her on the bed.

"*Comme ci, comme ça.*"

Hyim tried to follow the direction of the conversation, but it was in French, which he still had not made the effort to learn. The two women spoke for a time and then the woman with the dark hair turned to Hyim. "You are familiar with Becquerel radiation?" she asked.

"Yes ma'am."

"So you know how this procedure is going to work."

"I'm a skeptic, ma'am, but we are at the end of possible therapies."

"I understand. You know, we are nearing the end of our trials with this procedure. The gents in Manchester and Stockholm have stopped trials altogether. But we soldier on I suppose." She turned

150

to Leah, "Please, don't worry," she said.

"I'm not the one who should be told not to worry, Nurse."

"Oh! I'm not a nurse. I'm just a scientist." She got up. "Someone will be by to give you more information. I just wanted to be sure you were all right." She left down the hall.

Hyim's curiosity got the best of him.

"I'll be right back," he said to Leah who nodded.

He stepped out into the hall and tracked down the woman. "Mrs. Curie?" he said.

"Yes, *Monsieur?*"

"I just wanted to shake the hand of a woman who won the Nobel Prize."

Madame Curie smiled demurely. "You are Hyim Hopewell, are you not?"

"Yes... I... I am."

"I read your paper on *recurrence*. It was very impressive."

"Thank you, but... I must say, I was not the one who came up with the word. I called it *hyper-insulation of static substances*." Hyim was caught be surprise, not realizing his paper had made it outside of Cambridge, let alone outside of the country.

"I think I remember that. Well, whatever the case, I looked for more papers from this Hopewell fellow. But none ever came. What happened to that fellow?"

"It's a long story."

"Not so long that whatever has happened cannot be overcome. I read your paper almost five years ago, now. It contains some wonderful insights on power sources and heat manipulations. You entered into a fine set of beginning points, but you did not carry them through. I am sorry for whatever may have happened to you in the time between then and now, but nothing must get in the way of science." She looked down at her belly. "There are people in this world who would prefer it if I would just shut up and raise my children, but here I am."

Hyim nodded.

"There's someone I'd like you to talk to. He's been hanging around my husband at the Sorbonne, trying to get a job. Very *egoiste*, very disagreeable, but I understand he has the ambition you lack. I hope you don't mind, but this is a very selfish act. I want to read more Hopewell papers."

"Yes, ma'am. Who... who is this man I should meet?"

"I don't know him, really. My husband says he's a Swiss secondary school teacher. I don't know how he could possibly expect to become an assistant professor. You'll find him at the *Café Soufflot*. It's just down the street. His name is Einstein. Say hello for me, will you?"

Chapter 21

Hyim, confused though he was about why he was going to meet this mystery man, nevertheless arranged for Li-Don to be in the room with Leah while she slept. Li-Don did not feel comfortable being alone as a protector, but Hyim expressed full faith in him. Hyim knew that he was the most likely target, not Leah. He guessed that Li-Don thought the same thing.

He headed towards the Sorbonne, fully expecting to be set upon by ruffians. He had no defense except his wits, which were not quite as honed as they used to be. But he found the *Café Soufflot* without being molested.

There was a man with dark hair and a modest moustache sitting in a window of the café, situated so that he could view the Sorbonne, possibly to make sure it wasn't going to move without him knowing.

"*Je m'excuse*," Hyim said clumsily. "You are Einstein?"

"Yes."

"I'm here at the advice of Mrs. Curie."

"Please forgive," the man said. "English of mine is none that good. *As-tu dit Madame Curie?*"

"She says you are a secondary school teacher."

"Teacher? No. At one time. No longer. I wish a lecturer... um, position. But I have not the most terrific respect for scientists. The Curies are different. They are good people... un... untarnished by fame. Please, sit down. I know them not personally, but I respect them."

Hyim sat down. "What are you doing now?"

153

He laughed. "Ask one person, you will get one answer. Ask another, there will be another. Ask me, and I will tell you I am a patent attorney, and I am an amateur physicist. Amateur, yes. No one is going to pay me for my papers."

"Your papers?"

Einstein smiled. "There are papers I have back in Bern. Essays." He motioned to someone behind the bar. "Tell me, how do you know Madame Curie?"

"She is treating my wife for a medical condition."

"I'm sorry for that. But why meet me? I know nothing of medicine."

"I have a degree in physics."

"*Ah, bon?* So you are familiar with mathematics?"

"Yes. But my field is electromagnetism."

"*Ah, bon?* Electromagnetism. Where have you studied?"

"Harvard."

Einstein laughed a little. "Harvard," he repeated, mocking Hyim's tone. "Let's see how smart your institutionalized brain is. You are familiar with Planck?"

"Sure. From what I understand, he's a mad genius. His theory of packet radiation is particularly interesting."

"Genius? The man is a charlatan. His scientific method is suspect, to say nothing of his mathematics. He is a faker. But, as it happens, he is right. Radiation waves and light waves arrive in... um, how you say, single packages with energy *porportionale* to frequency. But, then you say, how can this be? These waves should have any amount of energy, without regard to our frequency. Waves have their own energy, yes? So how come more waves have fewer energy? Hmm?"

Hyim thought for a minute as a young woman brought him a demitasse of thick coffee. "Why can't waves have their own energy?"

154

"Simple man! The energy of a wave is dependent on the energy of the initial... um, action."

"But it does not need to be a direct relationship. It can oscillate depending on the type of force in the initial action."

"Bah! You must be an Ætherist, Harvard man. Waves are waves. They do not think for themselves."

Hyim sipped the coffee lightly. It was just as bitter as he imagined it would be. "I am not an *etherist*, as you say."

"But you are clinging to waves like a life preserver. Planck says light is tiny little hunks of matter. Light is matter! What nonsense, your Harvard brain says. Now I want you to think very hard. But not too hard. No sense giving yourself a headache. Light is a wave *and* it is matter."

"Seems true," Hyim said. "That would explain the discharge of radiation from photoelectric plates and double-slit effects."

"It impresses me that you can hold both of these ideas in your mind at the same time."

"I suspected as much, but I never did any of the experiments. But I have an alternate theory that is completely unusable."

"Please. I am always interested in unprovable physics."

Hyim took another sip. "People are interested in whether light is a wave or a quanta. I say it is neither and both. I say it is something altogether so different as to be incomprehensible to our eyes or our measuring instruments. So it must be some kind of medium that gives us experimental results that are type II errors, except that they are not errors. By coincidence, perhaps, our concepts of light have been pigeonholed into the two very things that we are looking for."

Einstein thought for a minute, sat back in his chair, and pulled a cigar out of his jacket. "I was wrong about you, Harvard man." He stuck the cigar in his mouth, unlit and uncut, and put his hands behind his head. "A third way. Hmm. Preposterous, but interesting."

"But experiments and theory apply equally and equally rationally to the other two ways. So it can be both without being either."

Einstein looked back out at the Sorbonne. Several horse-drawn carriages went noisily by in different directions. Young students milled around on one of the corners, the brims of their hats angling and bouncing like the rings of Saturn. Hyim wondered what they were talking about.

Einstein indicated the façade with his head. "We should both be in there," he said. Then he turned back. "I assume you are married."

"Yes."

"Hmm. We do things because of the women in our lives, do we not? Still, we try."

Hyim did not quite understand what he meant, but said nothing.

"Tell me, Harvard man," Einstein said, suddenly brightening, holding the cigar out for the young woman to cut, which she did quickly (they were the only ones in the café). "What was the real reason the lady Curie send you to me?" he asked as he struck a match to light the cigar.

"She said you had the ambition that I lacked."

"Is that so? You have no ambition?"

"I have no wish to be an academic, if that's what *ambitious* means. I have things I would like to accomplish, but I have no need for accolades."

"That's an interesting answer, *liebling*. But still you experiment?"

"Yes. Now, may I ask you a question?"

"Of course."

"Why does an attorney wish to practice physics?"

"That sounds like the first line of a joke. But the truth is, I'm a physicist who practices law. Not even law, really. I'm in a perfect position to be... theoretical. I have no *departement* to answer to. If I can prove what I say, I can say anything I want. I can be a physicist without having to practice, as you say, academics."

"And yet you want in to the Sorbonne."

"Ah, yes. You've discovered my guilty secret. *C'est la vie.* People are funny that way, yes? We ridicule that which we can't have and justify that which we do have. I imagine if I was offered a professorship somewhere, I would not turn it down. As I suspect you would not."

Hyim nodded. The two men began to understand each other better. Hyim noticed a small, waving strand of gray hair on the head of his companion that ran from one side of his head to the other. They sat in silence for a short while.

Hyim poured a little bit of sugar into his *demitasse* and stirred with a tiny spoon, perhaps a little more vigorously than was called for. He tapped the spoon on the side of the cup several times, trying to knock a small drop of the viscous coffee off of it.

"Listen to that," Einstein said. "Your clinking spoon is descending musically down the scale. The pressure of the liquid on the cup is greatest when you stir it."

"Logical," Hyim said. "You put more energy into the system and the pressure increases. The cup is merely responding to the pressure. The coffee pushes against the cup and changes its harmonic properties."

"Hmm. The coffee atoms are bombarding the porcelain atoms."

"Coffee atoms?"

"I misspeak. I mean coffee *molécules.*" He lit his cigar. "Or do I? What is coffee but water and the oils and acids of the coffee bean? Is there such thing as a coffee molecule? Or is it just a *mélange* of chemicals that produce a singular effect on the tongue? Hmm. Curious."

Hyim smiled.

"Will you get to Bern on your trip?" Einstein asked.

"I don't think so."

"Terrible pity. We have a small group that discusses just this kind of thing. You might find it a good time. I think you might need a translator. How come so many Americans I meet speak less than one or two languages?"

"We do not come across people who do not speak our language very often. I imagine you could travel for a day and go through areas that speak three or four different languages. You could travel for a day in America and the people would all still speak English. So, practicality being what it is, we practice different forms of multi-communication techniques other than language."

"I'm sorry? What did you say?"

"The part of your brain *you* use for different languages, *we* use for other things."

"Ah. Fascinating," Einstein said, getting up and putting on his coat. He took special care not to allow the ashes from his cigar to spill onto his clothing.

"Am I that dull a companion?"

"Not at all, Mr. Hopewell. It is just time for my daily *promenade* towards the physics department. I have been there every day for the past three weeks. One of these days, lady Curie's husband is going to take pity on me and give me a job."

"Good luck."

"Luck is for fools and Greek heroes. What I need is charity." He extended his hand, which Hyim took. "I trust we'll meet again under dissimilar circumstances?"

"You never know."

The diminutive Swiss man took his leave, forgetting to pay for his own lunch. Hyim watched him stroll across the street and disappear around the left arm of the Sorbonne's façade.

Hyim stirred his coffee again and tapped the cup with the tiny spoon, remarking on the changeable tone. He thought about pressure and particles, heat and energy, waves and radiation. He sipped some more of his coffee. The sugar hadn't helped. He just wasn't used to that kind of bitterness. He left some francs on the table and stepped quickly out the door.

His sense of the people around him was particularly acute, perhaps because of his ruminations, perhaps because of the coffee. There wasn't a crowd, but the sidewalks were well populated with warm bodies who weren't paying attention to anything in particular (except for Hyim, who was hyper aware).

As he arrived back at the Radium Institute, he became aware of one of those warm bodies that was traveling faster than the others. He couldn't tell where it was coming from, but it was heading towards him quickly. This sense he had of the people around him was something he never really understood or even cared about much (although it generally kept him from being comfortable in large crowds), but this time he wondered about it. In the few seconds he had to think about what it meant to have this kind of sense, he postulated that his parents could have been the same way. He did not remember a time when his father was comfortable in a large crowd, and, of course, he did not remember much of his mother at all. His childhood could be characterized as depopulated.

The impact of the warm body on his own was not a surprise. Hyim felt the swiftness of the other person and had concluded that the impact (and theoretically measured the force) would, in fact, occur. But despite his anticipation of the incident, the force of the collision was supported by the other person's arm that hooked onto his own and half-pushed, half-pulled him up the steps and into the building.

In what was becoming a recurring phenomenon, Hyim was not surprised that his old friend Jimmy had grabbed him and pushed/pulled him inside (his subconscious mind—if he, indeed, believed in such a thing—had told him as much); he was surprised that Jimmy's face was twisted into an insistent scowl.

"We have to get out of here, now!" Jimmy whispered.

159

Chapter 22

Leah, alone in her room reading, at first did not realize that Jimmy had arrived. Hyim rushed over to her bedside and began pulling off the blankets and sheets that covered her.

"What in the world..." she began. But Hyim covered her mouth. He put a finger to his lips.

"We have to go," he whispered.

Leah, who was not used to such high-energy movements from her husband, was noticeably confused. She pulled her arms up and tried to free her mouth, but he wouldn't let her.

"I will carry you if you can't walk," he said. "But we have to leave."

Leah's eyes went around the room until they landed on Jimmy, over Hyim's shoulder. Then she looked back at her husband and nodded reluctantly.

"I can walk," she said.

"Can you run?" Jimmy asked.

Leah nodded, getting to her feet.

"Where's Li-Don?" Hyim asked. "Why isn't he with you?"

"I sent him to lunch," she said, grabbing her overnight bag, which Jimmy took from her. "I don't know where he went."

After she pulled a suitable frock on over her bedclothes, they ran out of the room and down the hallway towards the back exit. Hyim had not asked why Jimmy was trying to get them out of the building, though after seeing Leah's expression, he felt in himself the same type of doubt. Their footsteps together rang down the hallway like little cymbal slaps, which made him wonder just how far away their pursuers had to be in order for their noisy clandestine escape to do any good.

Searching for Li-Don, however, proved to be a greater challenge than trying to figure out who was after them and how far away they were.

Hyim suggested they split up to search for him, but Jimmy would not let anyone be alone. A three-person group that split up would necessitate at least one group of one member, which was not acceptable. Especially since Jimmy slipped his wrist emitter device from out of his sleeve to show him why they should not be separated.

As they rounded a corner to face a street that seemed too full of nothing but cafés serving *déjeuner*, Hyim asked, "Have you made any improvements on that thing?"

Jimmy looked back at him strangely. "What's to improve?" he said.

They scanned the sidewalk crowds for Chinese faces and found none. As a group, their progress was slow through the street, first checking the outside tables, then inside through the glass. They looked in this way for about twenty minutes.

"I have an idea," Leah said. She had not made any comments since they left the Institute; probably because she was too frightened of whoever was pursuing them.

She led them towards the *Boulevard de Montparnasse*, which they followed for a good ten minutes. Hyim had his doubts about his wife's ideas, but kept them to himself. In an hour, they would be able to find Li-Don either back at the Institute or in the custody of their pursuers, who would have wanted to display their catch to them for instructive purposes (so said Jimmy).

After a bend in the road, they came upon a small, cultivated forest with statues and headstones, surrounded by a Gothic iron fence. In the middle of the young forest was Li-Don, munching carelessly on toasted bread chips in a wax paper bag. When he noticed that Jimmy was with the Hopewells, he nearly dropped his bag, catching it in mid-air and spilling only a couple of pieces of bread.

They were separated by the fence, whose gate was on the other side. "What's going on," Li-Don said, with concern.

"We have to leave this place," Hyim said. "Get yourself out of there."

Li-Don looked up at the spires on the fence and the relative height of the crossbar, then thought better of trying to make the climb. He dashed off in the other direction towards the gate.

Without prompting, Leah said. "I knew he would be here because he had been talking about how cities were growing at the expense of the surrounding wilderness. There was a small notice in the paper about the *Jardin des Plantes*, which he listened to with great interest.

"'Listened to'?" Hyim said.

"I translated part of the newspaper aloud with him in the room."

Jimmy hailed a buggy as Li-Don came running around the block. They all hopped in and he muttered something to the driver that Hyim did not catch.

It had been a long time since they were in a hurry to go anywhere or do anything. It felt just as alien to them as the first time they had moved quickly to avoid capture.

"We're staying at the *Maison de Sacré Cœur*," Leah said. "Shouldn't we check out?"

"No," Jimmy said curtly.

"Are you going to tell us how, exactly, we are in danger?" Li-Don asked.

"No."

"We're not going to the Brightferry Estate, are we?" Hyim asked.

"No."

Hyim had a funny feeling about Jimmy. He couldn't tell if it was genuine or if it was useless paranoia. The last time they had seen him, he had given them a reason to distrust him. The fact that his entire life, perhaps, had been a complete fabrication was more than a little unnerving. But it was his face, more than anything else, that made Hyim more suspicious.

Leah's face had grown several prominent wrinkles, most notably around her smile and the corners of her eyes. His own eyelids were starting to droop like his father's had, his jawline had become less defined, and it seemed like his nose was growing. Even Li-Don, always child-like in appearance if not attitude, had begun to show signs of age. But not Jimmy. His face still retained the soft, short hairs of youth above his beard; there were no furrows in his brow, no alternate colors in his hair. His face was exactly as they remembered it.

Hyim might have let this go without a second thought. After all, it wasn't that unusual for someone to retain his boyish features throughout his life. And it wasn't all that out of the ordinary for Jimmy to be out of the ordinary. But there was something about the way Jimmy was acting—the lack of buffoonery, the stone-faced seriousness, and the laconic delivery. Jimmy should have been chatting up a storm. There was something wrong with this person who was hustling them out of the Institute.

"What about Leah's surgery?" Hyim asked. "Our doctor told us that she needs this procedure."

"She will be taken care of," Jimmy said.

That raised Hyim's alarm more than anything else thus far. He turned quickly to Li-Don, who was showing his teeth through pulled back lips and half-open eyes. A strange sense of shared strategy passed between them. Jimmy was busy looking out towards the street ahead. In what seemed like one motion, Hyim grabbed Jimmy's right wrist to immobilize it, and Li-Don flew out of his seat like a thrush, his open hand striking Jimmy (or whoever it was impersonating Jimmy) in the head. Leah gasped. Jimmy crumpled to the floor of the buggy under Li-Don's blow. It was one of the most well-placed, well-timed shots he had ever thrown.

"*Arrêtez*," Leah shouted to the driver, who pulled up on the side of the road.

Hyim jumped down to the cobblestoned road below and held out a hand. Li-Don grabbed Jimmy around the arms and shoulders and pulled him out over the side, where Hyim took him and dragged him to the sidewalk.

"I don't know who you are," Hyim said to the groggy man lying on the ground, "but stay away from my family."

Hyim jumped back into the buggy and patted the driver on the shoulder. "*Allons*," he said, using one of the few French expressions he knew. As they pulled away, the Jimmy-like man on the sidewalk was moving, but not very much and not very fluidly. The driver began shouting something that sounded like epithets.

Hyim and Li-Don turned to Leah. "Absolutely unrepeatable," she said.

Chapter 23

They headed back to the Institute. Hyim's foremost concern was Leah. She was clearly in pain now, holding her stomach, pressing on it with her fist. She needed at the very least the anaesthetic that a doctor could provide. Either that or she would need to drink herself into a medicinal funk or obtain one of the newer tropical substances from South America, which none of them had tried before.

Exiting the buggy at the Radium Institute's courtyard, Hyim helped Leah walk back up towards the office. He hoped that they would be able to convince the proprietors (maybe even Mrs. Curie herself) to forget the incident of their bolting from the building not one hour before. It was clear that Leah was now in pain—the excitement of the premature escape, no doubt—she could not be refused treatment just for being rude.

They probably would have been re-admitted to the radium trials, but they were intercepted by a small group of cloaked men who seemed to tower above all of them.

"Come with us," one of them said. He sported a van Dyke along with eyebrows that were much too bushy. "My name is de Meurre," he said. "I am knowledgeable of your situation and I can help."

Hyim was not about to let his paranoia drop just because they were outnumbered and outmaneuvered. "My wife needs radium treatments," he said.

"We can take care of her," de Meurre said.

Jimmy had said that. She could be *taken care of*. He didn't like the sound of that. What could he do? He now wished he had stolen Jimmy's wrist emitter. Despite his ignorance of its operation, he at least had a better chance of somehow getting it to work than of getting out of this situation.

"We're not here to fight you," de Meurre said. "In fact, we're here to help you. We can cure you, Mrs. Hopewell."

"How?" Hyim demanded as threateningly as he could.

"It's impossible to explain here. And I really must insist that you come with us."

Hyim's inner sense of danger was on full alert, but he could do nothing to prevent these people from doing exactly what they wanted.

"A part of what we have to tell you is about your father," de Meurre said.

That got Hyim's attention and perhaps also got his better judgment. Against all his initial instincts, he raised his eyes to meet this man, waiting for the next thing he would say. "Excuse me?"

"Please come with us."

The carriage they took was more lavish than anything they had ever been in. The ride was unusually smooth through the cobblestone streets. The interior of the cabin seemed cooler than the outside air. Hyim wondered if there were ice compartments in the walls of the carriage that helped cool down the interior air.

The ride took less than twenty minutes. During the entire trip, Hyim tried to comfort his wife, who was now unable to sit upright and leaned against him. Li-Don wanted to speak, was itching, in fact, to say something—no doubt about how recklessly dangerous this was. This de Meurre fellow is a complete mystery. And with Jimmy lying the gutter somewhere recovering from his own handiwork, Li-Don wanted to say something about who they should trust (no one), and who they shouldn't (everyone).

Hyim saw this all on his face. Or maybe it was that the two of them knew each other so well that they did not need to say such things out loud. Or perhaps they had simply gotten out of the habit of speaking frankly to one another.

The probability that de Meurre was a so-called enemy was high. The probability that Jimmy was a so-called enemy was low. And yet they had evaded the latter only to come into the camp of the former. Was he playing against the odds, or was there something more at a gut level at work? Jimmy was clearly acting unlike himself and was either an impostor or a crankier version of himself that had not been previously revealed. And yet this de Meurre fellow...

Had he been an avowed enemy, he could have simply had the three of them taken by force and thrown into this carriage—nothing could have been done. Instead, their new host had said almost exactly the correct things that would have made them go voluntarily. Was he trying to shorten the time that Hyim's own inner sense of danger could be overcome? Or was he merely trying to tell them what they wanted to hear in order to minimize the force required for their capture? *Hyim's father; Cure for Leah.* Those were two points worth of positive response right there.

This certainly was a different sort of capture (if that's what it was) than the clumsy and violent ruffians from fifteen years before. Had it been only fifteen years? The memory of those cowboys was still sharp in his mind. Out of all the things on that honeymoon trip, that was the incident they had spoken the least about. Had they spoken about it at all after arriving back in New York? He couldn't remember.

However, the pattern of capture was the same. Group of pursuers catches up to the pursued, tries to talk them into something before violence ensues. There was no threat of violence—perhaps the ham-handed nature of the first capture helped to set the stage for this one, i.e., no threat of violence was necessary because it was implied. On the other hand, if what de Meurre said was true, why have the threatening henchmen at all? Why not just have a carriage come around for the three of them like they were guests instead of wildlife intended as pets.

They arrived at a nondescript building somewhere in the city. By the traveling time and the turns that had been made, Hyim guessed they were on the eastern side of Paris, somewhere near the *Place du Trône* or maybe as far as Vincennes (there were no windows in the carriage).

Their escorts walked them inside. A wheeled chair was presented for Leah, and Hyim was allowed to push it up to the steps, where she was carried until they got into the ground floor. *Ground floor* didn't quite cover it. The scene they came upon was as incongruous to the outer appearance of the building as it could have been. There were potted palms arranged in a geometric pattern whereby the points (pots) radiated out from the center—a small waterfall over rocks that led into a pool—in slowly increasing distances. But the scale was incredible. There were at least a hundred of these plants, and he couldn't quite reconcile the outer appearance of the size of the building with this interior scene. People walked around between the plants and the pool very slowly. The humidity increased as they went further into the room.

"It's an Ottoman bath," Li-Don said in a low voice to Hyim.

They passed through a giant pointed archway to another chamber, which became gradually darker.

Leah, in much better spirits because she no longer had to walk, sat upright. Despite the circumstances of their escorted walk, Hyim could sense that she felt a relief from her pain, and that made him feel a little better. But he still had the feeling that he was rolling her towards some kind of terrible place.

"This is so familiar," she said. "This is like the escape tunnel at your friend's castle all those years ago."

Hyim had suspected that assaulting the false Jimmy was a mistake, and that he had perhaps been the real Jimmy, acting strangely because of the strange circumstances. But now he was sure of it. They were being led, not quite voluntarily, towards an unknown evil. And yet...

And yet...

His inner sense of danger was not giving him any more warning signals. Was it broken or flabby from inattention? Paradoxically, this made him feel more and more of a panic. With his hands on Leah's mobile chair and his feet moving them inexorably closer into the growing darkness, his lack of paranoia made him more paranoid. He felt sweat gather along the line of his forehead. Somewhere along the line, perhaps everywhere along the line, he had made incorrect decisions about who to trust and what was the most effective escape. Not even his own instincts were working correctly. Hopelessness filled him like powder in an hourglass.

He closed his eyes for a moment. he could sense the people around him: four behind him, two in front, Li-Don on his left, Leah in the chair in front of him. What was the probability that his sense of the others around him was working correctly, yet his sense of danger was not? He had always suspected they were linked somehow, that his dislike of crowded places was justified because of it. Even now he felt closed in by the people around him—and a growing sense of dread—yet did not have an instinctive reaction that he was in danger. Curious.

After a large door was opened at the end of the dark, dank corridor, the brightness of the final chamber was startling to their eyes. Electric lights hung from the ceiling in chandelier shapes. The walls were made of stone, as was the floor. Some of the covered lights were clearly aimed at one end of the room, where a dark open doorway gave the scene a pregnant sense of anticipation.

Two of their escorts took Li-Don by the shoulders and dragged him back towards the entrance. "No one will be harmed," one of them said.

Li-Don struggled and Hyim headed for him, unsure what he was going to do, but intending to confront them. Li-Don was pulled out of the room and the door shut before Hyim could do anything about it.

"What have you done with him!" Hyim shouted.

"Please be patient. No one will be harmed."

"Bring him back here!"

"That is not possible."

Another voice came from behind Hyim, "Nor is it advisable."

The man who entered from the showcased doorway bore a striking resemblance to someone Hyim remembered very well, someone who had been a question mark ever since he entered their lives, affecting them forever.

Chapter 24

For a short moment, Hyim's internal storage area of faces and overall countenances recognized the man as Brightferry. But there was something different about him, something that would not have been the result of age, lifestyle, or even scar tissue. This man standing before him, though in the same simple brown friar's robe with hood, and with essentially the same facial features and even a similar voice, was nonetheless minutely different enough.

This staged entrance was so artistically similar to Brightferry's, however, that it could not have been a coincidence. Maybe they were brothers.

"Welcome to my corner of the world," the man said.

"What have you done with Li-Don?"

"Nothing, I assure you. There is no intention of harming any of you here. But what I have to say concerns only you and your wife."

" 'What you have to say?' What will you do once you have said your monologue?"

"That is not the question, Mr. Hopewell. The question is, What will *you* do?"

Hyim thought a moment. He scanned the room as best he could. There were so many shadows. It was difficult to tell where the opposite end of the room began. The two *guards* (let's call them) who pulled Li-Don out of the room left four others, no doubt guarding exits. He could see two of them standing next to the door where he had come in and Li-Don had been escorted out. Then there was the brightly lit entrance. It was not a certainty that a different exit lay in the shadows. And it was highly likely that one of the guards would get to him before he moved ten feet. No. The time to have done something stupid was back at the Institute, in public. Now that he was here, he had to play the best hand he could. There was too much mystery in his life already. He had to concentrate on the things that would help him and his family right now.

"Your goons said that they can help my wife."

"Hm. And so that is true. But there is time. Please have a seat and listen."

"Bollocks!" Hyim shouted. "I'm done listening. I assume you know who we are. You've probably been spying on us for some time now. You know that Leah is sick and you know how to cure her. So take it upon yourself to ask yourselves how important it is that I listen to what you have to say. These are my terms."

"Mr. Hopewell... Chaim..."

"Hyim," he corrected.

"You are not dictating terms here. You will listen regardless of terms. Terms are irrelevant in this room."

Leah looked up at her husband. "It's all right," she said. "There is no choice."

"Pardon me for disagreeing, but we do have a choice. I can close up my mind to any verbal techniques you, sir, can think of. I presume you will be trying to convince me of something. Well, I can tell you right now that it will not work. There will be no convincing. There will be no exchange of ideas. You will be merely another crackpot to whom I have been subjected."

The man reflected on this for a while, pacing back and forth slowly. "Our research on you does not show this side of your personality. I trust you are well."

"I am not taking any of this without a *quid pro quo*."

The man looked right into Hyim's eyes. It was an intensity that revealed something about each of them. There was a time in Hyim's life where he would have backed down and accepted what was happening to him. But that time was well in the past. He was now pushed as far as he was going to go, and that limit had shrunk a good deal since he was a young man. He felt the mind of the other man shift under the weight of his persistence and will. He felt it. In the eyes of this stranger, he saw his own power grow.

The man unlocked his eyes, then nodded to one of his "goons," a larger man with a full black beard. The latter disappeared into a darker part of the room and came back with a thin metal ring that had several prongs on it. There was a small cylinder that opened into a bell on the top and had a small wire coming out of the bottom that attached to another, smaller, metal ring that hung loosely underneath it.

"Do not be alarmed at what you are about to see," the man in the friar's robe said.

Hyim opened his mouth to say something, but the other man cut him off. "You made your bargain, now live up to it."

The man with the beard approached Leah. He pulled the larger ring around her arm. His appearance suggested that his movements would be rough, but he was very gentle with her arm, rolling up the sleeve of her frock and lifting it carefully to wrap the ring around it and position the prongs at regular intervals around her upper arm. He then slipped the smaller ring around her thumb.

"I don't like the looks of this," Hyim said.

"I had rather hoped I would be able to give you the explanation of this before we actually used it," the man in the robe said. He pulled up the sleeve on his left arm all the way up to his shoulder to reveal three healed scars in roughly the same position as the placement of the prongs on Leah's arm.

"We've all been through this treatment," he said. "Many times."

The man with the black beard scowled and revealed his own set of scars from beneath his shirtsleeve.

Hyim's eyes came back to Leah's arm. "What does this thing do?"

"I told you to wait for the explanation. Now, Mrs. Hopewell. All you need do is twist that little canister there. Just one quarter of a turn. It may cause some discomfort. But the wounds are not as bad as the scars make them out to be.

" He turned to Hyim. "If you want your wife to be well, do not interfere with this process. Agreed?"

Hyim nodded, in a terrible state of mixed curiosity and terror.

Leah looked up at everyone in the room, in turn, then finally back at Hyim. She put her fingers on the cylinder, then backed off. "Oh, I'm not doing this. I can't."

He held her right hand and knelt down next to her. "I'm right here," he said. "I don't know about the reasons behind what they are doing, but I don't think we have a choice."

Tears came out of Leah's eyes.

"Think of what you were going to endure at the Radium Institute and ask yourself which procedure would have made more sense."

"This one doesn't make any sense at all," she whispered. "How is a three-part injection into my arm going to... going to cure me?"

"I don't know. But my instincts now tell me to trust these people."

"You can't be serious."

"I can't raise any objections to this."

"You're not the one who is about to do this."

Hyim moved his hand to her face and stroked her cheek where a curl of her hair fell. "I'm right here," he said. "I'll be right here. I'm not going anywhere."

She turned back to the cylinder. "Well," she said. "I don't seem to have a choice. All right. Everyone in this room with a conscience is a witness."

She took a deep breath, reached over with her right hand, and gave the cylinder a twist.

Hyim had expected the prongs surrounding her arm to move, to penetrate the skin like needles. But they did not move. Instead, there was a short hum that increased in pitch, during which time the smaller ring around her thumb glowed blue. After a few seconds, both the hum and the glow were reaching a critical stage that Hyim could feel, could feel in his bones. Then there was a sharp, quick flash from the prongs that made Leah jump in her chair and throw her arm straight up into the air. She audibly yelped.

A white smoke of some kind rose from the wounds that were now in her arm. Curiously, they were not the bloody red that Hyim expected. They were, instead, red-colored skin lesions that resembled new bruises, or perhaps burn marks. The ring around her thumb had fallen off in the process, and it hung down by her side, but there were no visible marks anywhere on her hand, let alone the base of her thumb where it had rested.

He noticed that Leah was breathing heavily, possibly more out of fright than anything else—although some kind of effect to her lungs was not out of the question.

"The cure is already starting," the man in the friar's robe said. "How long it will take to be completely cured depends on the size of the tumor and the patient's metabolism."

"Excuse me?"

"Metabolism. The speed of the patient's bloodflow. Now you must allow her to rest. It takes a while to recover from the first treatment."

Hyim hugged his wife around her neck. It had just then come home to him that he was about to lose her to either a disease over which he had no control, or to one experimental treatment or another. He buried his face in her hair and started to cry. "Leah," he whispered. "I will never leave your side."

"Now it's my turn," said the voice of the man in the friar's robe. Hyim rubbed his eyes, pulled a chair from the wall, and sat down to listen.

Chapter 25

"First of all, I have been rude, have I not? I believe introductions are in order, if not previously, then now will suffice. Hyim Theodore Hopewell, my name is Ptolemy. And I knew your father. But let's set that aside for just one moment, shall we? The story you are about to hear is one that you will not believe. It is possible that you will never believe it. It is also possible that you will someday discover its truth on your own. But I am gambling that you will believe it, believe *in* it right as I say it to you, almost as if your own mind were saying these things to you. But I don't wish to just tell you a story. I wish to make this a dialogue, a Socratic story, if you will. You may stop me at any time to ask questions. Mmm?"

Hyim glared up at this man who claimed to be called Ptolemy. There was nothing, nothing that this man could say that would be believable enough to justify what was happening to him and his family.

"Nothing just yet? Fine. Let me first say that I have always wondered what it would be like to reveal the truth to an individual such as yourself. Just your ordinary everyday brilliant physicist who wasted the best training years of his life trying to discover the secret to a riddle that has no answer. I find it difficult to know where to begin. But I must tell you, for reasons that will become clear as I continue. Where should I start? Let's start with your father's business. Yes. Diamonds. I was once in the business, myself. I know a little something about it. Very lucrative business. They say that an expert can tell where a diamond comes from by the alignment of the crystals. I, myself, cannot. However, I do know that it is possible to 'help along' the process of crystallization to match the alignments of various mining locations. It is even possible to add flaws to make them less suspect. This is not forgery or smuggling or fraud, young Hopewell. Your father was an honest diamond merchant. However, if you have a need for a great amount of cash with few questions asked, you need look no further than diamonds. To keep questions to a minimum, you must keep the truth as hidden as possible. Because you are now in this much farther than you know, I will tell you. The heart of your father's diamond operation is a mine in eastern Canada at Molineau. It is secret, well-protected, and yields, unfortunately, imperfect gemstones, normally unsuitable for distribution. However, using a process which you may or may not understand, it is possible to make them suitable enough for trade. Am I clear so far?"

At the word *Molineau*, Hyim's memory shot back to the letter that Brightferry had tossed into the fire. That one word shone through the paper before it disintegrated, and it shone through the muddle of Ptolemy's speech. He was determined not to appear interested, but his interest rose nonetheless. He hoped it didn't show on his face.

"So much for fund raising. Why the need for all this cash? Surely his company could gain all it needs just from wholesaling. Why produce synthetic diamonds to risk diluting and depressing the market? This is something that might surprise you. Your father's company was founded over a thousand years ago, over two-thousand years ago, back when its employees had to fend off attacks from Swedes and other primitives. The *company* got its start by selling precious gems to Egyptian pharaohs and Etruscan kings. Since then, we've taken care of our families. We put them on the payroll whether they worked for us or not. They therefore did not need to find gainful employment in order to live. This is your legacy."

"My *legacy*?"

"Of course. Your family is a key part of the company. Or, more accurately, this *part* of the business. The money part, I mean. "

"Why are you telling me this?"

177

Ptolemy let out a small laugh. "I've waited a very long time to find you. But that's not entirely accurate. I've waited a very long time to find someone *like* you. You are a member of one of the oldest families in the world, on Earth. The most recent member."

"What does that have to do with you?"

"I am a member also. Oh, don't worry, I'm not a brother or an uncle or anything. It's more like a society brotherhood than a blood family."

"What are you, a Jewish Templar?"

"Oh, Heavens no. We're much older than Templars. We pre-date the Jews also." Ptolemy paused noticeably. He had more to say, for sure, but it was only now that Hyim realized he was participating in the conversation, almost against his will, and certainly against his intentions. It made him annoyed to realize that he had been outmaneuvered in this way.

"There is no reason in the world that could make me believe something like that."

Ptolemy came closer, off the stage, as it were, and bent over a little to meet Hyim's face closer. He smelled of olives. He pulled something out of an unseen pocket.

It was the sparking glass oblong.

It still had the same hypnotic effect on Hyim. He stared at it as the blue smoke was turning clear.

"Have you had the dream recently?" Ptolemy asked.

"What...?"

"You're alone, lost in a dark forest. All around you is a lightning storm. You don't know which way to turn. Tell me, are you one of those who is on horseback, or are you on foot?"

Hyim fought his argumentative nature in order to stay silent.

"Hm. Yes. I thought so. Your father is from the pedestrian branch also. But your mother was from the equine, so I couldn't be sure."

178

"My mother..."

"This sentimentality of yours is amusing if not practical. This forest dream is common to all of us. Myself, I am a pedestrian as well. Interesting case of evolution, these dreams. In any event. Now then. Continuing on: outside of the dream world, in your everyday life, you have a sense that there are people around you, even if you can't see them, am I correct?

You have a tendency to internally analyze everything and have little capacity for emotion. You have little desire to be noticed, but a great desire to help society progress. You have absolutely no capacity for violence, and death seems unnatural. Ah, yes. Now I can see I've struck a chord with you."

Hyim felt his mouth drop open. Leah made some wordless sounds of consciousness, then became silent again.

"And so all of these are true with us."

Cheap parlor stunts, Hyim thought to himself. *He knows I am a scientist, he's done—or read—the research on me, and he's making suppositions about my character based on the profiles of other scientists or on interviews of people I've met.*

As for the dream. There were only two people in the world who knew about his dreams: himself and Leah. Leaving out the possibility, for the moment, that he might have said something to someone else about it—in a drunken-induced haze or a haze produced by another substance, that left Leah. Was it possible that she said something to someone else about this? Anything is possible, few things were likely.

More importantly, however, what was the reason behind the telling of these stories? What purpose could they possibly serve? Assume for the moment that Ptolemy was lying—everything out of his mouth was a deliberate falsehood. He could be trying to convince Hyim to do something. It would have to be something that he would not ordinarily do. Or, he could be trying to convince him to stop doing something. This was less likely. What would he possibly be doing that someone would want stopped?

Now, assume that Ptolemy was being truthful, that he was, in fact, reciting the history of Hyim's family and knew everything there was to know about him. As ridiculous as it sounded, it was possible. This was the more problematic of the two possibilities. Of the two people who gave him any sense of his own history— this creature in front of him and his father—his father had never mentioned anything like this. His father's recitation of the family pedigree was always very brightly drawn if not terribly detailed. What purpose would his father have for concealing this information?

Leah rolled her head around on her neck and opened her eyelids halfway. She was gradually coming back to consciousness.

As if sensing the opportunity, Ptolemy smiled at Hyim and crossed his arms. "Ask her if she feels better."

Hyim lightly shook Leah's shoulder and his hand on her cheek. She looked up at him, bleary-eyed but lovingly.

"How do you feel?" he asked.

"I feel fine," she said, as if his question were out of place or had been asked once too often. She seemed to be unaware of their predicament. She yawned, then stretched her arms high in the air. The ring that had been around her thumb hung loosely and carelessly as she raised, then lowered her arms.

"Are you in pain?"

"Oh, no, of course not," she said. "That is to say, *no*. That is interesting, isn't it? I no longer feel the pressure from inside either. It feels as if a great weight has been lifted from my... interior."

"Of all the hopes I have ever had..." he said, and he kissed her.

"She will be completely well in less than seventy-two hours," Ptolemy said.

Hyim carefully removed the ring from around Leah's arm and inspected it, turning it over several times. There were no seams in the material—which he had never seen or felt before— nor was there any indication of how it worked. Leah watched him. "What

180

does it do, exactly?" she asked Ptolemy.

"You would not understand if I told you."

"You've obviously been studying me," Hyim said. "What is the probability that I would understand your concepts? Rearranging diamond crystals, secret societies, common dreams, miracle medical cures—these are all interesting stories, but there is no proof."

Ptolemy counted out on his fingers: "No proof? What proof would you need in order to believe a secret society exists? What proof would you need in order to realize that the dreams of two people are the same dream? Ah, but we *can* prove the medical 'miracle', as you call it. We can also prove the rearrangement of diamond crystals. And many other things I could tell you. But I am afraid that there is only one piece of proof that you will need in order to believe."

"Proof does not define belief," Hyim said, trying to be argumentative. Leah seemed to be better—much better, but the reason might have been something other than curatives—it might have been mere stimulant—and Ptolemy was saying a lot that made sense, in a purely scientific way (not at the gut level, which is where Hyim found himself). "Proof removes belief," he continued. "If you prove something to me, then I have no more reason to believe in it because now I am convinced, and I know it. I don't know what you're up to here, with all this, trying to make me believe in something, but your faith in me is misplaced. If there is one piece of evidence you have for any and all of this mishmash of a quasi-religious and technological sect and somehow my lineage being affected by it all—or vice-versa—then I suggest you show me now."

Ptolemy stopped smiling. "Follow me," he said, stepping away and back to the brightly lit doorway. "You will have your proof."

"What about Li-Don?"

"He will not be allowed to see this. However, he is quite safe."

"I want to see him."

Ptolemy motioned to one of the guards, who opened the door behind them. A short while later, Li-Don was led back into the room. He didn't look any worse except for his indignation.

Hyim went over to him and the two spoke in low tones.

"You're fine?"

"Don't worry about me. What about Mrs. Hopewell?"

"She seems to be better. They did something to her that's supposed to cure her."

"Do you believe them?"

"I don't know. I have no reason to believe or disbelieve."

"You have got plenty of reason to disbelieve."

"This gentleman told me some wild story. And now he's preparing to show me proof that it's true. I can't say for certain any of it is true, but some of it made sense."

"This may be a new experience for you. You may have to rely on your instinct. You may also have to decide first if there is a choice. You should also be ready to instantly analyze the situation and act accordingly." Li-Don's voice was tense.

"I'll remember."

"Something about these people is different. They are very deliberate and don't take chances. The fellows escorting me are accommodating, if not polite. But they have an inner calm that does not match with being kidnappers. If their purpose is to convince you of something, I would be careful about being convinced. The snake always speaks the truth, but is not interested in justice."

They parted, Hyim now assured of his friend's safety. He grabbed hold of the handles on Leah's chair and pushed her along after Ptolemy, who had disappeared into the doorway.

"I feel just fine," she said. "I don't need to be sitting down any longer."

"It's just a precaution. No sense taking any chances."

They went through the artificially dark doorway into a small elevator cabin with Ptolemy. The door abruptly closed—before Hyim could turn the chair around to face forward, and they felt the slow downward glide.

Chapter 26

The elevator continued downward for a good while. Ptolemy did not try to engage them in conversation, instead merely looked at them from time to time. Hyim pictured the workings of the elevator beyond the cabin: the counterweight, the steam engine, the greased rails, the pulleys.

Hyim had a view of the back of the attendant's head, which did not move.

"Jews are a people who have a society that goes back over 3,000 years," Leah said without prompting.

Hyim did not know she was listening to the conversation, did not know she had the mental capacity for it at the time.

Ptolemy shot her a look that said he didn't know she had been listening either. "It's not exactly a secret, is it?" he said cheerfully.

"Do you mean to say that you aren't Jews?" Hyim asked.

"Some call themselves Jews. Most do not. There are no requirements. I think you'll find that our membership in most institutions mirrors the general population."

Our membership. Why did that sound so disingenuous and ominous at the same time?

The elevator slowed down, then stopped. "You should prepare yourself. What you are about to see may be a bit of a shock."

The attendant slid open the gate, then the heavy metal door. It was a large underground room with a gravel floor and a damp, carved-rock ceiling.

"That smell," Leah said. "That smoky mustard smell."

All Hyim could smell was the wet gravel. But he remembered

that well enough to send a chill down his spine. The air had the same consistency to it, but instead of the giant casks of fermenting wine that were underneath the Brightferry estate, this cavern had giant cylinders, twenty or twenty-five feet tall, maybe as wide, made of a material that looked like dark iron. There was some rust along the top and down the sides in streaks. It could have been pure iron.

The chair would not roll on the gravel, so Leah got up and walked. Hyim helped her to her feet and held onto her arm. Hyim's danger instinct was suddenly aroused when he took in the scene. The round towers of iron gave him an odd disquiet. They stepped closer to the giant structures, their feet sinking a little in the noisy gravel.

"How are you feeling now," Hyim asked his wife.

"I feel wonderful. A little strange. Like there is some extra activity going on underneath my skin."

They could now see that the giant cylinders had openings in them—tall and narrow windows, as such, ridged with glass and a regular pattern of iron latticework that gave the impression of a street grate. With Leah's arm in his hands, Hyim suddenly stopped, causing her to stop also. The resulting decrease in the noise of their footsteps caused Ptolemy, about ten feet ahead, to stop himself, and turn around to face them.

Whether it was Hyim's disbelief that caused him to misidentify the person behind the iron latticework—i.e., inside the cylinder— as Jimmy or whether it was just pure chance that the person looked a lot like his one-time friend, he audibly gasped. But almost immediately, he realized this was someone different. Someone he had never seen before. More, it was a female.

She stood behind the window and the dark metal crosshatching like a diorama. Her face was downcast yet virtually expressionless, revealing something beyond emotion and beyond circumstance. Briefly, she glanced up at them, then resumed staring at the floor of the cylinder. Her cheeks were sallow, her eyes sunken, her hair graying. She looked about 45 or 50 years old. But her older female face had several distinctive features that reminded him of Jimmy: the smooth, linear placement of the eyes, almost perfect ovals, the tapering nose, the small lips and angular jaw.

As the cylinders were arranged in rows and columns, the original impression was of the wine casks in Brightferry's basement. But when Hyim saw that another cylinder containing another person was across the aisle, he had altogether a different idea about what he was seeing. This one was a man of about eighty, seated, with the same expression on his face as the woman had.

"What is this, a prison?" Leah asked.

She did not get an immediate answer. Hyim looked behind them to see the guards following them down the row. One of them was de Meurre.

Ptolemy said over his shoulder, "It's more rehabilitative than that." But Hyim did not quite process those words before he saw the last thing he had expected to see in such a place. As they came down the row, his glances in at the people behind their respective grates became more and more furtive and strained until finally he saw the bearded face of his father, Old Ezra, eyes closed, face down just like everyone else.

Chapter 27

Hyim was unable to reason out what he was seeing. His original suspicion that his father was alive somewhere had not been a rational idea. He knew this, and it had helped him to get past that feeling. It was always in the back of his mind, but it wasn't in the back of his rational mind. It was just a speck of memory in the emotional part of his brain, the part he could easily dismiss. To see his father in that place, in that pose, even, was so untimely, unthinkable, unbelievable; and yet it was, in many ways, expected. Their steps on the graveled ground halted; he and Leah could hear a low hum quietly echoing through the cavern.

After a few moments of indecision, Hyim stepped toward the window and put his hand up to where his father's face was. The entire world seemed to slip away; Hyim's vision and focus narrowed and only his father's downcast face was visible, with the periphery of his vision just a blur.

Ezra opened his eyes, which startled Hyim out of his narrow vision. Hyim pulled away, now aware again of all the people around him. The father looked at the son, his gaze unwavering, his face unmoving. It was as if this moment had been predestined, and the father was just waiting for it. Not surprise, apprehension, pride, shame, terror, wonder, nor any kind of unease or disbelief showed. He turned away and closed his eyes once more.

Hyim felt a hand grabbing his arm and pulling him away.

"You are one of us," de Meurre said. "Just as everyone here is one of us. Well, almost everyone."

Ptolemy broke in: "I see the shock and confusion on your face, young Hopewell. This is not unexpected. This is a lot to take. But I must ask you to concentrate and to take in what you are seeing."

Hyim heard the words, but did not follow their meaning.

"There is a right side and a wrong side. I am now giving you a choice to decide on which side you wish to belong. It is the same choice I offered to everyone here. They have chosen incorrectly. But they will come around... eventually."

Hyim was led around by de Meurre to the back of his father's *de facto* prison cell. Leah was forced back into her chair, which could not roll because of the graveled ground.

When he had been led to the door of the huge cylinder, de Meurre inserted a small sheet of metal into a corresponding slot beside the door. It unlatched and fell open a crack. "Speak with him," de Meurre said. "We are not unfair. Listen to him and then make your choice."

Hyim could not possibly grasp what was about to happen. Even if he had known that he was going to face his father—regardless of the topic of the conversation—he would not have known what to say. He had spent almost half of his life trying to either prove or disprove his theory about father's death, but he had never thought about what he would say to his father if his theory had proven true. His most immediate question had been what exactly happened during those ten minutes he had been alone in the house before the explosion—and during the ten minutes afterward—had it been an elaborate ruse.

Now, confronted with his father, he felt the trepidatious resentment that is reserved only for children who have been abandoned by their parents. Much to his own surprise—and self-disappointment—he was actually angry.

"You look like Ezra," Hyim said after the cell door was latched behind him. "But there is no proof that you are him. I have seen strange, unexplainable things in my life. Forgive me if I do not believe."

"Skeptical Hyim," the father said. "You must remain so. I raised you as a scientist, or so I tried. You must keep your mind all the way open, like a dike gate. If you close the gate, your mind will flood with muck and sediment. You will have to make a choice. One which no one in the history of humanity has ever had to make.

And you will have to take in a great deal of data in order to make it. So prepare yourself as a scientist and make observations carefully."

The father was stone-faced as he spoke. There was something almost cruel and dismissive in his voice, as if Hyim had disappointed him somehow. It was devastating.

"You were not supposed to know this," the father said, sighing heavily. "You were supposed to live your life. You were supposed to grow old and raise your children and do your research."

"I don't understand."

"You were not meant to understand."

"Stop speaking in vagaries! Do you know what Leah and I have been through? For fifteen years I thought you were dead. I thought you were *dead*. But you know what? This little voice inside my head—a very little voice—told me that something didn't feel right about it. Something was wrong. The whole scene looked staged. Did you know that I tried to recreate the accident? I had the whole house rebuilt with..."

"Yes, I knew."

Hyim, frustrated, thought he had been misunderstood. "I staged the accident to see if you really could have survived. Do you know how much time I spent trying to understand what had happened?"

"I blame myself. I raised you to be too sensitive. I see that now. You were supposed to be one of our great scientists, perhaps the one that would complete our destiny. You were the great experiment for me. But I loved you as a son. It had been so long since I had had a son."

Hyim decided that the best way to get his father to talk was to stay silent. It was not a strategy that he had used before. His most favored way to cull information was to argue it out of people. They generally relented because he was so good natured and polite about it. But his father was now in a state somewhere between death and life. He seemed a specter, and yet he was real enough. It was perhaps the prison, but that wasn't all of it. The prison had its

189

effects, but the regret in his voice was not over his predicament; it was over his son.

"Things should be explained to you," the father said. "Things that don't get to be explained to very many people. My God. I only wish that I had handled this better." He sighed. "Where do I start? I've never really said all this before, out loud. I'll start with the most immediate. Hyim, you *are* my son, in case you had any doubt. Flesh of my flesh and all that. You are your mother's son. My father—your grandfather—is a... a functionary in government. Your grandmother was a microbiologist. Your mother's parents were farmers. Your mother... your mother was a research scientist. She was a brilliant lady. Her work was very important..."

Here he paused. Whether it was because he was thinking of his wife or because he did not know how to continue was not readily apparent.

"I assume that our captor has shown you this," the father said, rolling up his shirtsleeve, folding it into itself up his arm. Hyim recognized the three-pronged scar. "Your mother helped invent it."

"You're one of *them*."

"It's more like they're some of *us*."

"They used that thing on Leah."

"Leah? Oh, yes, I see. They told you it would cure her. Yes. I can picture the conversation. They must want your help with something. The only reason they would have to cure her would be to get your involvement. To explain that, I must explain everything. Everything, however, will sound so unbelievable to your ears. You've seen this little apparatus working?"

Hyim nodded.

"There is a flash and then the body tries to recharge itself. You don't have the vocabulary for a satisfactory explanation of how it works. But I'll try and summarize. Hydrogen in the air is collected, stripped of its negative particles, and then reconstituted with artificial negative charges. When there is enough aggregate meta-hydrogen, the resulting... This is beyond your capacity."

"I can learn."

"Yes. Quite. How to put this? The transfer infusion of meta-hydrogen into the body sort of replaces its normal energy consumption process. We discovered that the... consumption of energy provided by... uh, certain... uh... Tell me, how much do you know about cellular-level microstructures? Never mind. The energy normally produced by the body is abandoned in favor of the meta-hydrogen, and then a funny thing happens. The mitochondria—is that a term with which you are familiar?—the mitochondria alters its function so that it accepts only meta-hydrogen. The normal energy starts to behave like meta-hydrogen... its structure is similar to a simple sugar, did I mention that? But it breaks down quickly... This is too much. Suffice it to say that this halts the aging process by reducing the amount of normal energy consumed. Cells live longer and reproduce less often. The body's immune system operates at a high level of efficiency because it has more time to identify and destroy renegade tumors and outside germs and parasites."

Hyim suspected he had a blank look of misunderstanding on his face.

"Leah's immune system is already attacking her tumor and soon it will be gone. Now, this not a panacea or the fountain of youth. Neither. It's no panacea. There are no cures for many inherited conditions. And it won't put you back together if you've been... stabbed, say, or shot. I'm only talking about infections and cancers. And it's no fountain of youth either. More like the fountain of suspension. It's not that you don't get younger, you just don't get older. Still, it was quite a discovery for us. It allowed us to make new scientific discoveries in different fields. A single person could follow a line of reasoning and a scientific theory to its conclusion; and beyond that, to its application; and beyond that, to its fine-tuning. The original apparatus was a chair, and there were twenty-six points of entry. We've modified it since then."

"You say *we* and *they*. Ptolemy said..."

"Is that what he's calling himself now? The impertinent bastard... I'm sorry. You were going to ask me a question?"

"He spoke of a secret organization of diamond miners."

"Ho! But that diamond stuff is relatively new. Only since we needed money. It used to be there wasn't a need for it, you know. Barter and all that. But diamonds are only an ancillary part of the operation. Don't get sidetracked by the diamonds."

"But Diamonds were your whole life!"

"Not exactly. Diamonds have been a part of my life, but not all of it." The father stood up and began pacing back and forth. "Hyim, son, how old are you?"

"You know very well I'm 35."

"Yes. This is very difficult for me to say. You have to understand that I have not tried to explain this to anyone else, let alone a son of mine. However, logic dictates that I must. Our captor has informed me that either I tell you this truth or else he will. I am inclined to believe that if you hear it from me, you see through his demented version of it. Hyim, I, and now you, are a member not just of a secret society, but we are members and participants in the greatest scientific experiment carried out by humanity. And by *humanity*, I mean we bipedal creatures. And by *experiment*, I mean a work in progress, a work of both art and science. A work that has gone on for over ten thousand years. And your mother and I helped write it."

"Helped write *what*?"

"The outline for the original experiment. This is the part where you will need to keep your mind open. I—and many of my fellow originators of this experiment—have been alive for the extent of this experiment. I, myself, have been alive for 10,371 years. That is to say, Earth years."

Hyim's head was swimming. His doubt prevented him from accepting what he was hearing, but his curiosity could not help instantly exploring the possibilities.

"*Earth years?*" he suddenly asked.

Chapter 28

"Let's go back to meta-hydrogen transfer..." the father started to say.

"Hold on. Hold on. Now, I am perfectly willing to believe that there are these bizarre electrical devices that are somehow kept secret from the outside world and that are therapeutic in some way. That makes at least a little sense and can be proven scientifically, should we have the time. And I am perfectly willing to believe that there is this parallel society built on the economy of gemstones."

"Not quite parallel..."

"Let me finish! I can believe that you, my father, are sitting here despite having been incinerated in a very public flash explosion. And there are numerous other small details that I can probably accept given enough time and data. But I am not about to accept the fact that my father, my blood relative, is... is ten thousand years old. I'm afraid you've gone around the bend on this one. Those electrical fields have damaged your thought processes, surely."

"Hmm. This is disappointing. How can I prove to you that this is true?"

"You can't. There's no way to prove how old you are. People don't have tree rings."

The father thought for a minute. "No," he said. "But you can verify how old I am. I can tell you the exact location of a kauri tree that I planted over 2,000 years ago. 2,131 years ago, to be exact. I can tell you the geographic features around it, the rocks, the location of the sun at the spring equinox."

"That doesn't prove anything. You could be describing a location you saw a month ago."

"Well, if there's no way to prove it, then you'll just have to continue to listen. Why is it so frustrating talking to you? There's no point in arguing this. It is not logical to refuse to listen to what I have to say. Now keep your mouth shut."

The dark, circular chamber now felt a little smaller. Hyim became aware of his breath, the air circulated by a quiet (and very strategically secure) fan in the ceiling, maybe 20 feet above their heads. It was the first time he had really felt this person was his father. He kept his mouth shut.

"As I was saying... This meta-hydrogen transfer infusion effectively shuts down the aging process, causing you to age very, very slowly. This isn't immortality. After using it long-term, we have discovered that we age one normal year every 544 years, give or take. So, eventually, we will die of old age. Another thing. The effects on the mitochondria wear off after about two years. You can feel it, the way the energy changes in your body. It's not pleasant. It's happened to me a number of times, but I usually can catch it in time. You see, we have to take these transfers every two years or the initial effect wears off and we start to age normally again. I have aged probably an extra 5 weeks because of my failure to infuse in time."

"OK. OK. For the moment, let's say that you are telling the truth. You still have some problems in your story. Ten thousand years ago, there was no civilization, there were barely stone tools. There was hardly this kind of technology, let alone the knowledge and intelligence to process the results. If you believe the Bible—and that's a stretch anyway—humanity barely knew how to clothe itself."

"There is another piece of information that you don't know. But before we get into that, I have to tell you that we—*we*, meaning all of us in this society—are in kind of a crisis. It was one we expected, but it hasn't quite turned out the way we had planned. You see, over the centuries, we have had to keep our secret. But while our neighbors grew old and died, we did not. It made people suspicious to know who we were, and also that we didn't grow older. Some of us, in the earliest civilizations, were accused of witchcraft or sorcery—that happened a lot, in fact—and were either killed or exiled. So we decided to periodically kill off our old identities and assume new ones.

This was not difficult in terms of logistics. We could move from place to place, claiming to be from somewhere else, while our old selves were left behind as victims of various accidents, wars, murders, what have you. It was difficult in terms of leaving behind some people you came to know as friends, but we always knew— at least, I did—that these same friends would be the first to suspect that something was wrong with our ages. So it was necessary. And, as I say, it was easy. But recently, it has become more and more complicated to do this. We underestimated the hold that the occult has on people. With photography, telegraphs, radio—and the inevitable visual information transmitted over radio waves—it will be increasingly harder for us to maintain our lives of serial identity, and we will be accused of all sorts of supernatural happenings."

"Leaving aside the fact that you did not answer my question, why don't you just cloister yourselves in a monastery somewhere? Surely no one would ever know of your secret if you stayed out of all view."

"Unfortunately, we are not among the people of the world just for fun. We have a purpose. And that purpose is being threatened not just by our exposure, but also by a new group."

"Ptolemy," Hyim said.

"Yes."

"And this purpose?"

"Power. Energy. We are trying to push humanity towards the solution we came up with thousands of years ago."

"So you consider yourselves to be not a part of humanity?"

"Absolutely not. But back to the energy..."

"Your crisis, then, is that you will be discovered and persecuted. Is that it?"

195

"Precisely."

"So you must push humanity towards your solution without revealing it outright."

"Exactly."

"That's irrational. It's idiotic. It's beyond the pale. What you are doing is hiding this technology from a culture that badly needs it. You have had this cure for disease, this source of energy—which I'll get back to in a minute—and this secret formula for immortality..."

"Not quite..."

"Yes, yes, yes. But still, you are (claiming to be) ten thousand years old and you're not dead yet. So forgive me for approximating the philosophical hyperbolic function. Now tell me why you couldn't find it within your collective hearts—if not heads—to grace this, our petty civilization with your cure for most of society's ills."

"In a word, *superstition*. I already told you what has happened to us when we are revealed to be perpetually the same age. Persecution. Plain and simple. Man has not been ready for these kinds of technological revelations. A few would accept our gifts happily and without reservation, there are always a few. But the great majority would not be able to comprehend the workings of the gifts, and would therefore call them magic, sorcery, the Devil's work used to lull them into submission, or corrupt them with black magic, paving the way for evil to take over the world. A corruption of ethics and all that. Tell me it isn't true. Make a case. The fact is you can't. Humans have always been suspicious, aggressive, and destructive. They condemned and destroyed many of our initial attempts at revealing ourselves. They continue to have a hatred of the unknown rather than a curiosity about it. Finally, we just learned to hide."

Hyim did not have an argument against this line of reasoning. He still did not believe the story, but this particular part of the story made sense. "OK," he said. "Back to the energy."

"Very well. Let's start with this cavern. It is a natural formation, in a way, but it is also a convenient distance away from a major power source. There are two others like this in the area that are around this same power source: one north of here and one to the southwest. Let's see if I can explain this without sounding too technical. Again, you just don't have the vocabulary yet to completely understand. Picture an atom in your mind, a hydrogen atom. A negatively charged particle circles a nucleus. Both of these structures are made up of smaller constituent parts. For the purposes of what we are talking about, the negatively charged particle is made up of seven smaller particles, all of which contribute to its behavior. However, it can lose three of these particles and still behave like a hydrogen atom. Unlike the transfer infusion of meta-hydrogen, we are not altering the structure of the atom, we are merely adjusting it without a loss in function. We can control the direction in which they are released, and then propel them into an adjoining atom, where they simultaneously release and take the place of the same particles in that atom. Curiously, it does not matter which of the seven particles are released and replaced in order for this scheme to work. What this all means is that the energy is conducted through any available material in a direction we can specify. This energy can be collected in just about anything, but it will evaporate fairly quickly. We use casks such as the ones you are presently inside in order to store the most efficient storage solution, which, surprisingly enough, is actually a simple copper, sulfur, alcohol solution in water."

"The Brightferry estate."

"If you mean that castle at Argenteuil, then yes, that's one of the storage areas. But he's only been using Brightferry as a name for 200 years... Do you want me to stop?"

After listening to what amounted to a lecture in atomic physics—which he could keep up with but could not picture in his mind—he realized that he had forgotten about his predicament. Here he was, standing next to a likeness of his father, listening him spew out all kinds of H.G. Wells pulpish prose, and he was completely caught in it. His mind was captivated by the very thought of its possibility, if only for a few minutes.

"Is my mother actually dead?" he asked.

The father stiffened up a little. "Yes," he said with added melancholy. "And we are getting to the part where you must choose. You see, when we found humanity, it was, as you say, barely able to clothe itself. Our early energy-gathering attempts were met with fear and destruction. When we set up our storage casks, *they* split them open. When we set up our living quarters, *they* burned them down.

When we built our towers, they toppled them. Finally, we decided to leave them alone and set up on an island where they could not reach us. And there we lived for a good three thousand years. But we miscalculated our effects on the island. Our energy-gathering involves lightning. It must strike a column of conductive material to be passed down into the earth, and from there it is atomically *conveyed* to these caverns. But the continued lightning strikes destabilized the island, and it sank into the sea. So we were faced with the prospect of going back amongst the humans. We decided to do two things: one, to conceal our conductive columns beneath lightning attractors—to protect them from vandalism—and two, to help humanity become less fearful and aggressive. For the most part, our concealment worked. Of course, every few hundred years we had to dismantle our conductors in order to prevent the physical destabilization of the region, of the type that destroyed our island. Our efforts at pacifying humanity have, however, not been as effective."

Old Ezra's monologue was interrupted by the opening of the door. The sound of the latch echoed strangely around the round chamber. "All right," de Meurre said. "That's quite enough. It's time to go."

Hyim hugged his father—which surprised old Ezra—before he left.

Chapter 29

On his way back to Leah, the son tried to take in everything that the father had told him. He had to assume that it was all true; he had to try and suspend his normal sense of skepticism, which was more of an emotional response than he usually wanted to admit.

"Was it him?" Leah asked.

Hyim nodded. He still didn't know for sure, but his inclination to take the man at face value caused him comfort. His eyes darted back and forth. There was, of course, no escape from the cavern. But he had to look for any kind of opening that might present itself. If nothing else, he could get Leah away from that place if he agreed to something that their captors obviously wanted him to do.

"What he told you is true," de Meurre said, perhaps sensing Hyim's inner conflict. "But he did not tell you the whole story."

"What did he say?" Leah said.

"We talked shop," Hyim said wryly.

"Now we will present our side of the story," de Meurre said, pushing Hyim towards the other end of the cavern.

It took a little time. As they came to the edge of the cavern, Hyim noticed that the cylinders around him were not prison cells, and did not even have windows. He deduced that they must have been the energy storage containers. It did not quite make sense that there were no wires or pipes or any other conduits that led from the energy source to these cylinders. Where was that energy source, anyway?

Ptolemy was waiting for them in a kind of office. It was furnished with outdoor style tables and chairs, very informal. There was also a short slab of concrete rising from the ground about six inches. Ptolemy was on this slab, trying to be as dramatic as possible by placing himself on a stage in his own drama. "Please sit down," he

said, pointing to a wrought-iron chair.

Hyim sat while de Meurre stood guard at the only visible door.

"Your father is well, I trust?"

Hyim said nothing.

"Are you troubled by what he told you?... Do you believe it?... Have you formed an opinion about his proposal?..."

"He didn't make a proposal. You didn't give him the chance."

"Well. So much the better. Let me tell you something, young Hopewell, there is nothing I dislike more than a set of incomplete data. So I am here now to fill in the gaps for you. I will entertain questions, if you like."

Hyim gestured noncommittally.

"Excellent. Let's start at the beginning. Once upon a time, there was a race of humans who had evolved for so long and were so brutally rational that they became highly-efficient at their rationality and rationalizations. Through self-selective breeding, they created themselves, as pure and as ethnically narrow as any species of animal. They went around all day thinking, dreaming up ways of settling arguments, prolonging life, and curing disease. Utterly, utterly peaceful, over 50,000 years they eventually bred out violent aggression, over-reliance on emotion, and drastic differences in their appearance. Yes, they were very proud of themselves. But there was one thing they lacked. Energy. Over the millennia, their planet—already a poor source of electric plasma that you call lightning—had slowed down, had ceased to be a viable source for their own brand of power generation. I assume that your father has explained this part of it to you? Hmm. Yes. So they packed their bags and searched for another planet. One with suitable life-sustaining qualities, an abundance of water, and electric plasma storms. And here you are. Earth. Or, rather, Earth II. Ah, but you are now both confused and comprehending at the same time. 'Earth II'? *Why, whatever can he mean?* But you know exactly what I mean, don't you? Yes. Moving on. When this race of humans got to Earth II, they found exactly what they were looking for. Abundance of food, energy sources, and land to use for colonization. There was just one problem. The humans that were already there were just advanced enough to understand that their new neighbors were a threat, and just primitive enough to do something about it. The primitives destroyed our heroic humans' first attempts at colonization. They destroyed their energy towers wherever they were put. What to do, what to do? The primitives couldn't be killed, because our humans disdain for deprivation of human life (however undistinguished or unevolved they may be) precluded them from harming anyone. So, they came up with defenses, like the plasma shield, and the perfected masterpiece: the projected-emission particle and ether amplification generator. But even that was not enough. The primitives had to be *pacified*. So our humans did what humans have always done, they kidnapped all the females they could find and impregnated them with modified parental genetics. The material they chose, was, of course, their own. They repeated this process for three thousand years—being careful not to impregnate the same families with the same material, lest there be too much inbreeding. We still have the familial records if you would like to see them. In any event, this program of genetic dilution did not work. The primitives were now more human-like, to be sure, but instead of lessening their aggression, they were made more intelligent in their use of aggression. The primitives devised more efficient and terrible ways of killing and torturing each other, conflicts escalated into wars, and unexplained phenomenae became fodder for destructive cults. Our heroic race of humans decided to become invisible, working in the shadows, constantly pushing the primitives' society forward until such a time as they could reveal themselves without fear of wholesale reprisal."

Here, Ptolemy paused to let Hyim take it all in.

"What might your real name be?" he asked. "Your original name?"

"That's a rather simple-minded question. Names do not matter. Our people have little use for names."

"I take it your *people* arrived on this planet on some kind of ship?"

"Yes."

"Where is it?"

"We dismantled it to build our settlement."

"The one that sank into the ocean."

"Yes. I'm glad your father shared that with you. I didn't know if I should mention it or not."

"What will you do when your people are revealed to us primitives?"

"Don't forget, young Hopewell, you are not a primitive. You are one of *us*."

"According to your story, by blood, maybe. But not by culture. Your skulkery and subterfuges are not a part of my world."

"Hm. In any event, I am working to see that revealing all this to the primitives does not happen. This is the basic difference between my side and your father's side. We are working towards divesting ourselves of this planet and gathering resources to rebuild our ship and leave. We have done enough damage to this place. It's time for us to find someplace that doesn't already have inhabitants and restart our society there. However, your father's side is still hanging on to the quaint and wrongheaded notion that there will be, at some point in the future, a right time to reveal ourselves and our technology. This ignores the initial breeding program failures and the basic warlike nature of the primitives, which can never be altered. Your father thinks they can be helped, that they can be reasoned with. It's disgusting. The primitives are obsessed with death, with killing each other, with killing themselves. Death is odious and distasteful. Their violence is repugnant. Their belief system is devastatingly appalling. They are unredeemable. And we must get ourselves to a different home as soon as possible. With our current energy collection rates, I'd say in about a hundred years. So, now you know our differences, you must choose."

"You mean, make a choice between prison or ignominy?"

"Anyone can be reductionist. But no. You will not be imprisoned if you choose the other way. We're not so barbaric as that. You will be allowed to go free no matter what you choose. But there is something of which you should be aware. I have enlisted the assistance of some of your primitives. They will be watching you and reporting back to me. Personally, I don't care who you decide to help, where your loyalties lie is not really relevant to my cause. You can think what you like. But I will know what you are doing."

Hyim thought about this implicit threat and gave it no weight. "I don't get it," he said. "Why let me go free at all? Why not just keep me here indefinitely like all the others?"

"Don't you realize who you are? You are the first child to be born of two original humans in over a thousand years. You are their salvation, their hope. You are the one who will fulfill their destiny. You are the chosen one. All of their history has come down to it. If they lose you, they might try something drastic and foolish. I am trying to avoid a war."

Chapter 30

Ptolemy followed Hyim back to Leah. The walk back seemed shorter, and the people in their prison cells appeared less hopeless (although *hopeless* was not quite the way he felt about them beforehand).

"We can go," he said.

"Pardon?"

"Our hosts are allowing us to go. We'll be home in less than two weeks." He turned to de Meurre. "I take it you'll be going with us?"

"It is so," he said.

Then Hyim turned to Ptolemy: "What possible reason could you have for imprisoning these people who are not on your side? If you wish to avoid a war, this would be a good faith gesture. And it would be a damn nice thing to do, don't you think?"

"It depends on which side of the tree you are standing when it falls."

"Have you thought about how much more of a leadership figure I would be if I arrived with former captured prisoners? They would listen to me even more closely than they otherwise would have."

Ptolemy was silent. Hyim had outmaneuvered him on his own terms. It was not sitting well. The logic this man had built his life on was now towering above him to serve its purpose, instead of the other way around.

But instead of railing at him or even admitting defeat, Ptolemy merely nodded. "I was wondering if you were going to ask me that." He had not been outmaneuvered at all, but instead was only waiting for Hyim to make this move. "You may all go. Back to America, no doubt. My only purpose here was to inform you of your true legacy. That of eugenicists and meddlers. Yes, you are all free. I have no fear of your little band of geneticists. Besides, we need the space in the cells for more energy gathering." He paused, and then said: "I am not the adversary you would have me be."

"Despite killing and kidnapping."

"There has been no killing. No killing of humans, anyway. Only primitives. But those were necessary."

"I was right the first time. You are insane!"

"That's not for you to decide. And, in any case, my rhetoric has already entered your head, like a slow-growing algae. It might take a while, but you will see which ending to this story makes more sense. Ask your father how many primitives he has raped in order to 'purify' the race."

Ptolemy turned and left with a flourish. "Release the captives!" he shouted through the cavern. He turned to go, but first he flipped the glass oblong into the air at Hyim, who caught it with some difficulty. Then, as Ptolemy disappeared behind one of the cylinders, the unlocking sounds echoed back and forth along the walls and the ceiling. Then the sound of uncertain footfalls on the gravel floor. The former prisoners—including Hyim's father—made their way forward, toward Hyim and Leah, gaunt and disheveled, eyes squinting from the relatively bright light outside their cells.Spontaneously, they all stopped in a crowd in front of Hyim and Leah, as if this was an agreed-upon meeting place. They all looked at him, looked *to* him for further guidance.

"You are free," he said. "We are all free to go."

The former prisoners looked around at one another. Leah got up out of her chair and whispered to her husband, "They are looking for a leader. Lead them out."

Hyim watched the sorry crowd in its confusion. Maybe they were so used to being told what to do and where to go that they did not know how to be free. Maybe they did not believe him and thought this was all a trick.

Heavy steps came from either side of the crowd, and they cowered against each other. The guards who had been monitoring the whole scene approached. They gave everyone a passing glance and then looked away as they followed the path Ptolemy took out the back of the cavern. When the last of their footsteps' echoes were gone, Hyim put his hand up. "Follow me!" he yelled.

As they all turned to go, the forward entrance doors up ahead of them blew open in a blur of feet and fists. A blue light emanated from somewhere and sparks flew against the rock face of the cavern.

"Surrender!" came a familiar voice.

Hyim hurried up ahead to see what was going on. He found Li-Don, crouched in a boxing pose, ready to take on all comers. And behind him was Jimmy, with his emitter trained on Li-Don. They both looked up at Hyim a little sheepishly.

"We've... we've come to, uh, rescue you," Li-Don said.

"Isn't that valiant of us?" Jimmy said.

Chapter 31

Hyim, Leah, Li-Don, and Jimmy enjoyed a meal of curly macaroni out of a bowl in the middle of a table. They were on the *Esther*, headed back to America with their cargo of former prisoners. None of them was prone to seasickness any longer, and, for the most part, they enjoyed a pleasant voyage back on the small Irish passenger ship. They paid no attention to de Meurre, who was standing in one corner of the stateroom, monitoring them and the scene outside the porthole. The rest of the former prisoners were in other parts of the ship.

Hyim's father had wanted a tour of the engine room, and was busily asking questions of the personnel down there.

"The guards let their attention wander," Li-Don explained. "And I slipped out. I managed to get back to the scene where we left our friend here," he indicated Jimmy with a small nod, "by jumping onto the rails of the carriages as they rode up and down. It had been too long, however, so I went the only place I knew he would have gone. Back to the hospital."

"It's not a real hospital," Jimmy said.

"So be it. There I found him and with my impeccable sense of direction, we made our way back to that place. Our plan was to break you out..."

"Without hurting anyone," Jimmy interrupted.

"Or the equivalent. Our friend here was going to protect me with his little device as I brought you all out."

"That's quite a plan," Leah said. "But what if they had threatened to harm us if you hadn't backed down?"

"Our friend here can move quickly with that thing. We made a fine practice before we broke into the place. We managed to elude everyone as we snuck our way in, and broke the locks on the doors."

"Of course, by that time, our captors had told us that we could all go free," Leah said.

Li-Don and Jimmy looked at each other. "It was a foolproof plan," Jimmy said.

"But we were dealing with actual fools," Li-Don said. "Why did they let you go?"

"It's complicated," Hyim said. He had been silently brooding until now. "When you get down to it, all he wanted to do was tell me a story."

"You haven't yet said what it is he told you," Leah said. "I heard a part of it, but I'm afraid I didn't have a context, and I don't quite understand all of what went on."

Hyim and de Meurre exchanged a glance. Hyim still wasn't sure if his presence there was an implied threat or just a reminder of what Ptolemy had told him.

"First of all, Jimmy," he began. "He told me about the society. I assume you are a member?"

Jimmy nodded, chastened.

Hyim put his hands to his lips. Ptolemy and his father had said a lot of crazy things. But there was one thing that he could not shake out of his head. He astonished himself at being able to comprehend and assimilate both tales, but it was something Ptolemy had said that was troubling him most of all. *The Chosen One.* The phrase rang around in his head like a pealing bell. He had not the least idea what it really meant, but despite his desire not to be interested, he was deathly curious as to whether or not it was true.

"He told me about the diamond mine," Hyim began. He started with the diamond business and proceeded to tell them selected parts of Ptolemy's story: ten thousand years, another planet, energy towers, the destruction of the first experiment, long lifespans. He left out the episode on genetic modification, as well as some other less-attractive parts. When he was finished, he was met with silence.

"It's all very complicated," Hyim said finally. "But all the parts of the story fit together. I don't know what to make of it."

"You can't believe it's true," Leah said.

"I can't rule it out."

"This is all crazy," Li-Don said. "People from other planets? Secret societies? Thousand year-old people selling gemstones to Cleopatra?"

"It's the reason he let us go. He thinks I will help him."

"Why on Earth does he think you are going to help him?" Leah asked.

"He says I am one of them. He says both my father and my mother are one of them. He says... He says I am the *chosen one*."

Jimmy looked over his shoulder at de Meurre, his sudden seriousness showing on his face.

"I don't know what that means," Hyim added, half-pleading with Jimmy and de Meurre to tell him.

Li-Don put a hand on Hyim's shoulder. "I don't mean to sound offhand," he said. "But this would explain a lot of what you have been through. Your father confirms the story. I assume that our two friends here will also confirm it."

"I don't understand," Leah said. "There aren't enough stories in the world to make these stories believable."

"You, yourself were cured," de Meurre said. "Your disease is gone. It is being held at bay indefinitely."

Leah's mouth opened, then shut. She was going to say something further, but clearly his comment had trumped her argument. "Clearly that doesn't prove anything," she said. "Even if true."

209

"He said I had to choice to make," Hyim said. "Whether or not I continue the work my father has set out, or whether I help to destroy it. I've been avoiding my father because I don't want to ask him about it."

"Do *you* believe it's true?" Leah asked.

"I don't know."

Li-Don withdrew his hand. "I cannot believe in such things without proof. Belief is a hand reaching into a murky lake. There may be fish there and there may be eels. Myself, I would like to know which."

"It's just too much to take in," Hyim said. "The whole thing is too fantastic. How could it be possible?"

Li-Don cleared his throat. "My mother used to say that in order to eat something larger than your head, you must first start with the first bite. You can't be intimidated by the size of the dish in front of you. You can't take in the entirety of it at once. No one should expect you to. It's too much to ask."

Hyim looked around the room. It was true. There was too much story to take in all at once. He decided to pull out the knife of logic and cut up his doubts into smaller pieces. He stood up.

"All right," he said. He decided to address Jimmy. "The things I have seen with my own eyes I can't dispute. I believe in your technology. The *emitter* works for defensive purposes, I've seen that. And unless the good Dr. Merritt and the entire staff of the Paris Institute are all your co-conspirators and has faked Leah's disease, the *infusion* device works for curative purposes. I can accept that. And I can't explain where this technology comes from, nor can I entirely explain how it works."

"We could go over the details..." Jimmy started to say.

"Please. I'm working this out."

Jimmy stayed silent.

"All the ways my father tried to push me into a life of science.

I thought he wanted me to make a better world for mankind. But it does not stretch logic to say that he wanted me to make a better world for *his* kind also. This is circumstantial, but it is there nevertheless." Here he stopped. He faced de Meurre square on.

"How old are you?" he asked.

Ptolemy's agent sighed, still looking out the porthole. "Three-thousand five hundred and twenty."

Hyim turned to Jimmy, "And you?"

"One-thousand nine hundred and eight."

"How many people who came from your world... how many of them are there?"

"We call them *Originators*," Jimmy said. "Those humans who arrived here from Earth One. I'm not sure exactly how many there are. I think the figure is around a hundred and fifty."

"One-hundred twenty-seven," de Meurre said. "They are all over ten thousand years old. When they first arrived there were 302 of them..."

"Dear God," Leah said. "What kind of a cult have you made up for yourselves?"

Chapter 32

Jimmy looked back and forth at Leah and Li-Don. "You two are a part of this now," he said with more seriousness than ever before. "You can't reveal any of this to anyone. It is not an exaggeration to say that you are the only indigenous people in the world who know about us. I must apologize for involving you in this. The plan for you was to be a part of Hyim's life, influencing him in positive ways."

"We were part of a plan?" Leah said, affronted. "Some kind of grand scheme in Hyim's life? I can't accept that. I have free will, Mr. Primerhaven—or whatever your name is. You have no control over me."

"True enough, Leah. But we have no wish to control anyone's lives. There is only influence."

"Influence? That's absurd."

"It is a great wonder of human life that small events can change the course of history. Your father, the lamp salesman, saved his pennies and took you to a Broadway show when you were twelve. Imagine your life without having had that experience."

"Are you saying that you and your... cult... somehow arranged that?"

Jimmy hesitated. "No," he said. "But you get my meaning. A missed appointment here, a lost key there... These small experiences can change an entire life. You may have even forgotten some of these events, but they are all there. If you go back to those points, you will see that you had different outlook on life then. In effect, you were a different person."

"This cannot be true," Li-Don said. "A person's essence does not change because of outside events. The things that make us who we are and who we will become are intrinsic to our unique beings."

"I am not suggesting," Jimmy said, "that you stop being the person you have always been. But you can't deny that some experiences change a person's outlook, and that events that are beyond our control change the paths that we follow. Take this example: Your grandfather has hidden a fortune in gold on an island in the Atlantic. He stays on the island for six months, intending to return to the mainland—and to tell you about it—after that time. He also writes a letter telling you about the fortune, but not about where it is. He leaves the letter in the care of an officer on another ship headed your way. Now, imagine the possibilities. The letter—if it is delivered correctly—will arrive much sooner than your grandfather. Once you read it, you anticipate your grandfather's return so he can tell you where the fortune is and the two of you will be rich. Now imagine that your grandfather's ship is lost at sea. He never arrives, though you have been waiting for him. What happens next? The character of the person you always were determines whether or not you start looking for him, or for the fortune, or the ship that delivered the letter to you. If you are a certain type of person, you might dismiss the letter as the ravings of a senile old man. Or you might think it is a fraud, something to distract you from more immediate concerns. The point is not that you will be changed as a person, the point is that your circumstances will change, and your outlook on life will be either altered or strengthened."

"I must say again that this cannot be true. Whether or not my grandfather returns, I will still be who I am. Even if I one day find the fortune, I will not have changed as a person."

"That is where you are wrong. Humans are not endowed with immutable essences. They are the sum of their actions, which is to say *reactions*. Humans can be altered in predictable ways by presenting them with certain situations. Consider your grandfather's fortune. Let's say that your grandfather is not lost at sea, but the ship carrying the letter is. Your grandfather shows up one day without context, telling you a tale of fortune. Do you believe him? Maybe you decide to go back with him, not because you believe him, but because you wish to have an adventure or because you want to please an old man. Think of your elation when you find out the fortune is true. Or maybe you dismiss his story and then later regret it when he comes back with his fortune. Think of the bitterness your life will take from that day on. There are many possibilities."

"But you're saying you can control these events," Leah said.

"True enough. It's not an exact science, but there are predictability studies..."

"Studies?" Hyim said, coming out of his rapt attention to the conversation as it progressed.

"Many studies," de Meurre said. All eyes shifted to him, then back to Jimmy.

"It's true," Jimmy said. "The character of a person can be changed with almost a 90% accuracy in the outcome."

Leah and Li-Don dismissed this with audible exhales.

"If there is one place where your outlandish stories turn into complete fictions," Li-Don said, "It has to be here. The game is up, gentlemen. It has been an interesting mental exercise, but now, since this is affecting the outcome of our lives, I am sure we would all like the real story."

Jimmy and de Meurre exchanged another look. "This is precisely the reaction," de Meurre said, "that we have been trying to avoid all along. You are on the verge of mistaking the actions of the Originators as cruelty. Far from it. Even Ptolemy acknowledges that. You are a suspicious species, capable of great impatience and skepticism. And there is no greater piece of evidence than how you are feeling right now. You are angry, resentful, and, at bottom, afraid. Your fear will lead to violence, as it has in the past. We have left that all behind. We do not have fear, violence, cruelty. The fact that *you* do shows just how much *we* have failed. At the beginning..."

214

"All right, all right," Hyim said, his mind racing. "Accepting all this, what's next? What are your plans now? I assume I was somehow part of this plan. What does that mean?"

"Thanks to de Meurre's renegades, those like Ptolemy, all of our plans are destroyed. We must have discussions on what to do next. Folding our tents and leaving this place would have to be an option.

But when Ezra and Harriet decided to have a child..."

Passing through the air and into Hyim's mind came his mother's name, not spoken in his lifetime that he could remember. *Harriet*. He had always wanted to know more about her but was always politely rebuffed by his father.

"...it was for the good of the whole, and it was understood that this child would lead us into a new era. This child would be the one who would lead the scientific revolution on Earth Two which would pave the way for the Originators to reveal themselves. This child would make the discoveries, perform the experiments, and become the leader of the new revolution. This child would bring us out of the shadows and into the light."

It was clear that Jimmy didn't realize he had almost lifted himself out of his chair as he spoke these words, as if they were some kind of creed he had memorized years earlier. As he heard them, Hyim's mouth went dry. Once again, de Meurre turned to him: "You proved a difficult subject to control," he said. "You didn't react as predicted."

Here, he paused, maybe to gauge the room, maybe to give what he had to say a full stage. "A man given multiple traumas in his life will turn to his work and be extremely productive. Isn't that right?"

He eyed Jimmy, who wasn't responding. "Your wife there," de Meurre continued, "wasn't supposed to be your wife. The death of your mother was supposed to send you on a series of doomed affairs—or something like that. But then they found out that she was going to die of a cancerous tumor at a young age, and they

215

allowed the marriage to happen. They thought that would increase your grief and make you more productive as a scientist."

Hyim wasn't quite sure he was hearing this correctly. He looked from Jimmy to de Meurre, back and forth. "I've had it with the lot of you," he said, as he left the room. But not before he heard Jimmy say, "You are an Originator child. Nothing can change that."

Chapter 33

The narrow hallway mirrored Hyim's philosophical claustrophobia. He held onto the brass rail that ran the length of the passageway and calmed himself down.

Now he saw what de Meurre's purpose was. As an antagonist, he was determined to reveal all of the truths to him. All of the ugliness that sent him and Ptolemy and his side of the Originators to try and dismantle all that had been created. *But wait... hold on there.* This is still assuming that it is all true. But then, what was there to be gained if either one of them was lying? Surely for so many people to have carried on a dim charade this far implied some grand scheme that rivaled the one they offered.

Leah came up behind him and put her arms around his waist. "Why do these people keep saying these things?" she said.

These people were violating the law of Occam's Razor in every way but one. The explanation for all of the science-fiction insanity was beyond even some low-grade novel. The fact that the fine points of the story matched with his own experience did not matter. The simplest explanation was that these people were all—for lack of a more descriptive term—nuts: either in some form of limited mass-hysteria or religious zealotry that surpassed any other religion in the world.

"I don't have another explanation that makes any sense," Hyim said. "I have always suspected that I was somehow *different*. That there was something about myself, my person, that didn't fit with how the rest of the world worked."

"Then you can't see how their manipulations have already started to take hold of you," Leah said. "Everyone feels they are somehow *different*, as you say, at some point in their lives. There are any number of explanations for everything we've seen. If I've learned anything from you, it's that. Li-Don is right. You can't take an entire set of occurrences and overlay them onto a theory. You have to break them all down into their constituent parts and piece them through bit by bit."

It was something he tried to do. But argument was too arduous with de Meurre and Jimmy. He felt like he was making their points for them. And there was something sinister about the way they told their stories—de Meurre had a deep voice with an accent that suggested he had learned English only recently. Jimmy's eyes darted from person to person, gauging the effect his words were having.

Li-Don came out to meet them. "You seem like you want to believe them, but are having trouble with the details. I can speak for myself, and you probably know what I think. But it is not me they are interested in. You need a clear head and open eyes. Each one of them is trying to get you to do something. Regardless of their believability, this is the thing that you must keep in mind. They want something from you. Whether or not it is a reasonable thing is not for any of us to say. They have inserted themselves into your life and show no signs of retreating. They demand your service and your attention. As my father once said, 'Beware the man who does not hold an axe but does hold your attention.'"

Hyim straightened his shirt, kissed his wife, then went back into the stateroom.

"You have told me stories. Tell me stories if you must, but I want something I can see for myself. Something I can verify."

The glass oblong was sitting on top of a packing box beside the table. Hyim stared at it for a little while.

"I want to see the diamond mine," he said to Jimmy. "I want to see Molineau."

By now, Jimmy had dropped all pretense of being a fun-loving post-graduate. "I'll take you to the diamond mine," he said, then he looked over at de Meurre, who shrugged cryptically. It was a gesture that gave Hyim a little shiver.

218

Chapter 34

To a careful and cautious observer, the face of Ezra had within it the features of his son; however, it also contained the features of every other Originator. This is what Hyim was thinking as he approached his father just outside the galley.

He had made the trip (both towards his father and across the Atlantic) more times than he cared to remember. Both his father and the Atlantic were cold, windy, and unsatisfactory unless you made your own fun of it. Still, just as Jimmy had dropped his pleasant demeanor, the father had become more serious and less an object of dispassionate amusement.

"I know you have more questions," the father said.

"You have no idea."

"Answers are available. One need only ask."

"I am tired of questions and answers. I am tired of information without context. I am tired of feeling like I have been shoehorned into something that I was never prepared for..."

Hyim started to walk away, but the father joined him.

"But you *were* prepared for it."

"...and I am tired of feeling like I have been betrayed all my life by people who claimed to love me."

"You mean me."

"Of course I mean you. Evidently, I mean Mother also. I am angry at both of you. I am angry at everyone."

"Anger is not a useful state of mind."

"Oh, for pity's sake! You no longer have the right of counsel."

219

Past his father, past the starboard side of the ship, the sea began to whip up into whitecaps, the slow rolling motion of the ship signaling deteriorating weather conditions.

"I am counsel, whether you like it or not. As your elder, and, not co-incidentally, as your father."

"You know, Li-Don instructed me once in Greek drama. In school, we were told that a hero followed a story arc that included a 'tragic flaw' in his character. But apparently that is not the case at all. Those Greeks all included their *hubris* and *hamartiae*, for certain, but the downfall of the hero, in most cases, was simply a matter of academics. The real drama is what the hero chooses to do after all has been revealed. Oedipus rent his own eyes out of their sockets. Medea murdered her own children. Terrible, terrible things."

"You are who you are, Hyim. What has happened has happened. You know as well as I that as much as the people of this world solve problems with violence, *we* do not. *We* cannot. It isn't in our nature."

"You have no idea what I am capable of."

"That's where you're wrong. You have 50,000 years of selective evolution behind you. The society we built favored the pacifists among us. The violent did not live long enough to reproduce."

"Eugenics."

"That's where you're wrong. We're not monsters, Hyim. We are the good. We are the progressive. Without us, the people here would still be throwing stones at each other from their caves."

"Ptolemy said..."

"Let me tell you about Ptolemy. Even his name is an inside joke. Over 2,500 years ago, we were helping humanity set up governments, behave peacefully towards each other, and progress scientifically. It wasn't perfect. There were still vulgar wars and debauchery. But we were progressing. There were Originator children, such as yourself, who were unaware of their true ancestry, but had the capacity to help society progress. We thought they would lead the world by example. Athens. Unfortunately, they were philosophers and artists in a world shaped by violence. And not everyone thought we were progressing. Your Ptolemy was one of them. He suddenly decided that what we were trying to do was a big mistake. He wanted all of us to stop meddling in the affairs of humanity and leave for another place. The very idea was ridiculous. We had started our grand experiment and were going to see it out to the finish. We couldn't just abandon them in the middle of the process. So, Ptolemy (he called himself *Khazar* back then), decided to subvert our cause. He knew our methods of secret influence and subterfuge. He sought the most warlike and efficient race of humans he could find and caused them to become a dominant power. We didn't take him seriously. But it was Rome. Eventually, his protégés crushed our own."

"I don't want to hear any more stories. Now you're telling me that you were responsible for the Punic and Macedonian wars."

"In a way."

Somewhere, deep inside his "highly evolved" brain, Hyim felt a welling up of something. It was an oily and viscous feeling, and it felt like pure energy. He felt disgusted and energized at the same time. He left the father at the bow of this ship, and this time the father did not follow. Despite his persistent doubts about any of the stories he had been told, he felt vaguely ashamed of his perceived status. If he really was one of these people, he did not want to be a part of them any longer. He wanted to be the anonymous scholar he once had intended to be, thinking up new ways to describe the unseen micro-universes that fascinated him; toiling in obscurity at a job he truly loved.

He went back to his stateroom where Leah was waiting for him, and he spent a good deal of time in her arms. He wanted to stop thinking. He wanted to stop being who he was, or who everyone thought he might be. He, himself had not changed... or had he? During the years he thought his father was dead, he justified his obsession over the loss of his father by telling himself he was working toward some unseen goal.

He looked often into Leah's eyes, the dancing pupils that shimmered once more with life. The pain that had been a part of her life for the better part of a year was gone and would not be coming back. How was it that the people who had produced such an epic lie (or such a horrific past) were responsible for this much happiness?

Chapter 35

New York never looked so beautiful. Their voyage ended, the former prisoners milled around on the Manhattan dock patiently. Hyim waited as Ezra went around to every one of them, giving them instructions as to where to go and what to do in this foreign city—many of them did not speak English. The non-English speakers would largely go to the Lower East Side and to Brooklyn to try and fit in with other immigrants. Anyone who spoke English was to head West to places like Ohio, Colorado, and California. Money was not a problem, and neither was transportation.

Hyim and Li-Don had played a game of sorts over the last days of the voyage. With all the facetiousness they could summon they tried to speculate if there were any historical figures who might have been Originator children. Leah found their humor too dark and refused to participate. But they found there were many personages who qualified as suspects, including Plato, Jesus Christ, Thomas Aquinas, Galileo, and David Hume.

Hyim did not want to ask who they *really* were. His argumentative capacity was already full of potential truths. If proven, he might be able to accept that he should learn the entire Originator history, but as of right then, he saw no reason to inundate himself with more suspect information. He still had a curiosity, but he could subjugate it to his pride of empirical proof. He still had not told them about the genetic manipulation part of the Originator story. If that part of the story turned out to be true, he wanted to reconcile it for himself before he tried to explain it to an unwilling audience.

Leah was like a rock throughout all of this. Maybe it was her cure that made her more willing to accept the weirdness that swirled around her. She had a naturally inquisitive, skeptic mind that normally invited combative conversation with people who held irrational views, but she had not gone as far in argument as she could have. Hyim didn't know if that was a good thing or not, but it certainly made for a more civil, if not entirely polite, atmosphere.

The six of them, now, Hyim, Leah, Li-Don, Jimmy, Ezra, and de Meurre, took a gasoline-powered lorry from New York to the Canadian border, with several horses in tow for when they ran out of fuel. It was important to appear to be a normal group of people doing a normal thing.

Gathering clothes and supplies for the trip back at their house on 5th Avenue, they realized how much they had missed that place. Not to mention how much they had missed Li-Don's parents. Li-Yan and his wife knew nothing of the adventure in Paris, and no one was about to tell them anything. That left it up to Li-Don whether or not to tell his parents what happened, and he thought it best to keep them from it for their own safety. He was conflicted about it, but in the end he made the decision that would be the least dangerous for his family.

"The deepest fish survives the storm," he said.

The lorry was noisy and its engine gave off a very unpleasant odor. It was much worse than Hyim's roadster. It did not sound as if the engine was working properly. He asked to stop so he could have a look at it, but Jimmy—who was driving—did not let him.

New York faded quickly in the distance. Leah and Hyim sat with their backs to the front, facing the horses, which followed along like the tail of a kite. The scenery behind them disappeared over hills and past thick trees. The lorry stopped every few hours to stretch legs, rotate drivers, and refill the tank from gas cans; but other than that, they continued on, even through the night.

To Hyim's ears, it sounded as if a breakdown was imminent. The clunking, grinding, and sputtering sounds the lorry made were an affront to the elegant solution in physics that it represented. But despite its complaining, it had enough power to move six adults and modest luggage.

He pictured the inside of the engine, with its crude chemical reactions and miniature explosions, wasting all that energy and potential. His own roadster was at least 300% more efficient than the vehicle he was currently being jostled by. He felt a twinge of pride at this, something that didn't happen very often. Was it possible to go over 300%? He wondered. The engine would need to be completely redesigned. It was impossible to talk with the all of the racket the engine was making and all the squeaking and creaking of the chassis. He wanted to talk to Li-Don about it, but conversation was out of the question. He put his arm around Leah instead.

If only the refined petrol in the combustion chambers had a few fewer carbon atoms. Then the stability of the exhaust material could be controlled. He theorized that the exhaust material would produce a number of gaseous molecules that might be partially solid when they first were released from the explosions. These molecules could be collected in a controlled manner to produce some kind of non-reactive—if not entirely sweet-smelling—solid. Possible? Sure, why not? If the oil that came out of the ground could provide the Byzantines with a distinct advantage in naval warfare to preserve their empire and later could be used for civil purposes to enhance the freedom the country afforded them, then it was certainly possible that the fuel itself could be re-formed and controlled for its less pleasant properties. Or at least the exhaust could.

He, himself was using an oil-powered contraption to get to the location that might be able to explain—just by its existence—his own existence. At one stop, he again asked Jimmy to let him have a look at the engine. But Jimmy again refused.

"We're in the middle of nowhere," Jimmy said. "And we shouldn't stop and waste water rations while you're satisfying your curiosity."

"Though your curiosity is admirable," Ezra said. "Allow it to fester and congeal."

Later, at another point in the trip, Li-Don said, "You are about to discover your destiny. And you're worried about the efficiency of that engine."

"I'm not worried about it, per se," Hyim said. "I'm just... concerned."

"When one is taking a journey through the forest, one should look at the scenery, or the trail ahead, or take note of sticks that can be used for firewood or locate fruits that can be eaten or keep alert for large animals that could attack. One should not look at one's own feet."

"What if your feet are bleeding?"

"Pardon?"

"Your feet. What if you've stepped on something or scraped them on a rock or something else?"

"Your question reveals a preoccupation which itself suggests a fear of the destination."

Leah was uncharacteristically quiet. She smiled and moved slowly, like she was a little tipsy, but was as clearheaded as she had ever been. "You should not have fear," she said. Hyim wanted her to say more, but she only patted the bench seat next to her, asking him to sit and wait. There would soon be answers and the resources he would need in order to sort it all out. Whatever it was.

Chapter 36

They switched to horses partway through the trip, although the oil held out longer than Hyim thought it would. And that is how they arrived at Molineau, being pulled by horses.

It was a small town in the cold northern plain. Cold, despite the warm season of the year. Trees dotted and surrounded the layout of the town, which included several churches and some miscellaneous buildings, including fish markets along a relatively narrow river that went by. The buildings looked like they were made entirely of wood. The flat landscape was interrupted by thick groves of trees, and in a few places by rolling hills. But the most prominent feature was an incongruous rocky mountain that bordered the eastern edge of what might otherwise have been a valley. Other than that, the horizon was almost all grasses and weeds.

Everyone but Leah and de Meurre jumped out and started walking along with the horses. As they walked through the streets, it became apparent that there was no one in any of the houses or the markets or the churches. In fact, no one was around at all: it looked as if the entire town had migrated somewhere else and had left the structures standing.

In about half an hour they were at base of the mountain, going around it, with Ezra leading them.

As the lorry loped along, the wheels crushing grass spikes and skipping over rocks, Hyim thought of what the inner workings of the engine were doing right then. No power, no combustion. Just the wheels moving. It was the sound of the crushing grass that made him reflect on of the silence in his ears. Maybe the lack of conversation throughout the trip had made everyone loath to speak to each other. Of course, it could have been the rising tension of the purpose of the trip.

What really got him thinking was the piston inside the engine. The elegant linear movement that transferred itself to a centripetal motion might have been beautiful but for the violent explosion that caused it to move. Why did he find this mechanical solution to the problem of energy transference more interesting than the sub-atomic means described (albeit in rough terms) for the Originator energy transference? Was it the simplicity? Was it the physicality of it, the way he could hold a piston in his hands? Or was it more of his partially primitive pride, whatever made him less like his father and more like the human race?

They had made their way around the rocks of the mountain base when they came upon a strange scene. There was a wide, deep pit lined with metallic and glass chambers, about thirty of them all the way around, each large enough to contain several people. It must have been 500 feet in diameter and at least twice as deep. It was like nothing in his experience.

Li-Don muttered something in Chinese.

There was a pinpoint flash of light on one end of the pit that extended to the other side. Then a puff of smoke. Then various bits of rubble fell to the bottom.

"What is this place?" Hyim asked.

"This is your past," Ezra said. "And your future."

Someone approached them from a building on the near side of the pit. He held a white staff and wore a light green uniform. He had all the appearance of a soldier. He said something incomprehensible to Ezra, then held his hand up and shouted.

Instantly, previously unseen people came into view. They had been surrounding the small group of travelers, completely out of view. It was startling enough to give Hyim a little shiver. A part of him wanted to know how they had managed to stay out of view. How long had his party been monitored?

"Please," Ezra said to the soldier. "Speak English for the benefit of our guests."

"Guests?" the soldier said.

"James you know, I assume. And there is Mr. de Meurre from… hm… the other side. And then there is my son, his wife, and their personal secretary."

The soldier looked them over and grunted.

"Are you going to shoot us?" Leah asked.

"They don't shoot people here," de Meurre said.

"What is that rod you're holding there?" Hyim asked.

The soldier did not answer. Instead, he swiftly came up to Hyim and handed it to him. It was cold, colder than it should have been given the ambient conditions. It must have been endothermic. Which meant it there was some kind of discharge to it. Probably some kind of energy field of something or other. With these people it was always with the energy fields.

"It's harmless," Ezra said.

"Except to the one who holds it," Li-Don said.

Ezra exhaled, audibly impatient with Li-Don. "It's a defensive weapon only."

"The type of power you wield does not matter. It is still power, and its force, whatever it is, only serves to make you careless, reckless, or arrogant. Sir."

"It sounds like you've bought into the thinking from the other side."

"Sir, I've known you all my life. You have no idea how grateful I am that you saved myself and my family from hard labor, deportation, and worse. But now I have to ask myself why you have done such a thing. I can see now that you are, or at least you believe you are, someone very powerful. And very motivated to further your cause. I could ascribe to you many turning points in history, but I am still confused as to one thing. Please forgive me for asking the question, but why did you take an interest in my family? Ever since I can remember, I have wanted to ask you this question, and now I must ask if it has something to do with your cause."

Hyim spun the weapon around, looking to see if he could find a clue as to how it worked. He put a hand on Li-Don's shoulder as he handed the weapon back to the soldier.

"What about it?" he asked the father.

"You should be careful what you ask," the father said. "Be sure which answers you want to know and which you don't."

"I am asking," Li-Don said.

"I wanted you to be exactly what you are—a counsel to my son. As it has turned out."

Li-Don seemed satisfied with this explanation.

Another pinpoint flash of light crossed the pit, followed by a puff of smoke on the other side. The color of the light was the same as all of the other energy effects he had by now attributed to the Originator cause. Including that little glass oblong which was then sitting in the back of the truck in one of Hyim's travel bags.

Hyim felt exhausted; emotionally, physically, and mentally. But the way the flash of light illuminated the pit and then ended in the same kind of smoke as appeared in the glass oblong caught his attention. Caught it like a fish in a stream.

Mesmerized, he stepped forward, edging closer to the pit, as close as he could get. Then he waited, the others behind him silent. He could feel the confusion in half of them, the anticipation in the rest.

There it was again. The flash streamed across the pit in the briefest instant. Blink and it could be missed. In that flash was the secret history of himself. He realized what he had been looking for all those years. He had always thought it was his father he was trying to find. But looking inward, he realized it was the answers that his father could provide. He had always retained questions about the world he inhabited. His perceptions were askew from other people's; he always felt his brain worked differently. But he had never said anything. His father's eccentricities were usually explanation enough. At times, though, he wanted to ask the question: *How different am I?* But, of course, he never did.

Maybe by studying the way the world around him worked, he would have been able to understand the way *he* worked.

The figure who pointed the energized mining tool at the diamond pit was wearing a sophisticated suit made of a cloth-like material that had a strange sheen to it. Seeing that figure in that suit made Hyim realize just how complicated a tribe he must have come from to have created a weapon used as a tool like that—and then to have created the world around it. A world that required the use of that kind of suit. To have even thought of the need for it was incredible.

The patterns of the light flashes swirled around in his mind, and he came to a startling conclusion.

"It's all hydrogen," he said to no one in particular at first. The possibilities were fantastic. By manipulating negatively charged components in the presence of hydrogen atoms—overloading them without allowing them to deconstruct—one could produce a controllable amorphous electrical field that had not only mass, but the regular properties of a physical object. It was creation on a basic scale.

But for it to work, a stable hydrogen atom must be composed of separate particles of both a positive and a negative charge. Thomson had found negatively charged cathode electrons, but what of the positive? Hyim's theory needed a positive particle that could be positioned, based on its relationship to predictable negative particles. This would mean it would need a greater mass than the various negative particles bombarding the hydrogen atoms. *Lightning*, he thought.

"It's all hydrogen," he said, turning around to face the others. Ezra smiled.

The steely face of de Meurre also broke into a smile.

Chapter 37

The story of the mine was less impressive than it seemed. The diamonds were there, albeit in a crystalline form that was useless for international trade. But the concentrated energy—compressed-beam photons or electrons or whatever they were calling them at that time—altered their structure to make them valuable. Other than that bit of intrigue, nothing had changed in thousands of years.

After getting the history from a couple of the miners, Hyim and Leah went to the other side of the pit to be alone. Li-Don did not go with them, but he did follow them partway in order to look out for trouble.

The forest abutted the mine on that side, which made it easier to feel like they were alone, but they knew that guards were protecting that side.

"So you believe it, now?" Leah asked him.

"I can't not believe," he said. "There is no other explanation. Deep down, I wanted to believe it was true. But seeing what they have been doing here, I don't have any intellectual objections anymore."

"So you will take the infusion, now?"

He hadn't thought about that. Leah was now in the suspension state, and would remain there until it was time to take another one. He was still aging while she was staying young (even though it had only been a few weeks, it was still technically true).

"There's a lot of things I'm going to do now."

"Hy, I don't quite know how to describe to you what I'm feeling." Her eyes moistened as she looked up at him. "According

232

to the way things should have worked out, I would be dead now. But somehow, I'm not angry about that. I can sense that I should be, but all I can feel is a sense of peace."

They kissed. "I'll never let anything happen to you," he whispered in her ear.

They stood like that for a long time, long enough to notice the changing colors in the sky. It was a new world. Something had changed. There was no longer the confusion of the unknown. Like pieces of a puzzle, the events in their lives fell into a familiar pattern. Hyim let go of the bitterness towards his father. He could see the sweep of history that led everything to that moment. And then…

And then…

After accepting his identity, he didn't quite know what to do with it. But his sense of peace was so overwhelming that when— two weeks later—they arrived back at their house on 5th Avenue to see the wreckage of all his equipment scattered around their property, he was not disturbed in the least. His house was still standing, no one was killed or injured; only his laboratory had been affected. And all he could think was how grateful he was that someone had taken the time to acknowledge just how dangerous he now was. It was a new era, and he knew now there was more work to be done than even he could imagine.

END OF PART II

Part III

Prologue

Somewhere in New York, 1914

They hid in the shadows. Like all the previous times, they stood stock-still; not blinking, barely breathing. Their knives were coated with tar so they wouldn't glint in the moonlight. Their hammers were scuffed and chipped for the same reason. As they waited, their conscious minds were filled with little else than the fees they would get for this service. The people behind the money were a little strange; who knows, they might have been socialists or worse. But still, money was money. And it was a damn sight better than the fate of those wackos who volunteered for foreign armies.

They waited for activity in the house to quiet down. Lights on would be OK. Once they made their way to the third floor, it wouldn't be necessary to hide themselves any longer. Five people in the house. One, possibly two would be awake at this hour. The rest would be asleep and would not stir during the operation.

This wasn't like strike-breaking, where the object was intimidation. This was exclusively the destruction of property.

As the three-quarter moon peeked out from the clouds, they made their way towards the back door, with silent, rubber-soled shoes. The night was open and crisp. If they had not been armed with blades and pistols, they might have been testing the limits of their girlfriends' virtue on a riverbank.

The invasion was all too easy. They saw no one, were not even stopped by a locked door. It swung open at the slightest rattle of the doorknob. The five of them entered and hurried up the stairs to the third floor, following the plan given to them the night before. They no longer needed to be careful, stumbling and stomping down the hallways and up the second flight. Two of them guarded the landing while the other three burst into the top-floor room.

To their surprise, no one was there, despite the light being on. So much the better. It would be quicker and easier. They ran over to where the laboratory instruments were—metallic gray boxes with dials and readouts they had never seen before. They took out their hammers and smashed them to bits. They overturned the vats of unidentifiable sludge and smeared it all over the walls and windows. They slashed the wires with their knives. They overturned the tables and hacked until they were suitable only for kindling.

They carried on like this for a good five minutes until everything in the room was either wrecked, marred, or otherwise rendered unusable. The job done, they hurried down the stairs. A few of them thought they were home free. They thought about spending the money they had just earned: putting it on a horse, getting an automobile, taking a slow boat to Rio.

But at least two of them knew that something was wrong, that it had been too easy. Any self-respecting victim of multiple acts of vandalism wouldn't allow such things to happen so... so willingly. Doors that swing open, lights left on, rooms left unguarded. It was suspicious. It was so suspicious, in fact, that when the first one down the stairs suddenly leaped backwards into the second one, they were not entirely taken by surprise. It was startling, to be sure, to have a pileup on the stairs because someone stumbled *backwards*.

The first one stood up, shook himself off, then attempted to make his descent once again. And once again, he was pushed backwards. Not with much force, but enough to make him lose his balance and fall back onto the third and fourth steps.

"What's the matter with you?" the second one said. He brushed past the first one and attempted the same maneuver with similar results. Whatever pushed them backwards was unseen, even in the bright light of the stairwell.

"What's the problem up there?"

"What are you two clowns doing?"

They all came down to the last step, but couldn't make it to the bottom. A glass pane was stuck around the whole staircase, somehow. They could see through it, but they couldn't pass through it.

They kicked at it, punched at it, whacked at it with their weapons, but they couldn't break it. And it didn't sound like glass, either. It sounded more like thick industrial springs.

In the middle of their confused, frustrated shouts, they noticed that someone was watching them from the lower floor.

"Greetings, Vandals," he said. He was in an outmoded cream-colored vest-suit and red-striped straw hat. "I have one question for you, then I will let you go."

They recognized him as the owner of the house. The very person whose experiments they were assigned to stop. His voice sounded scratchy, like a faulty cylinder, or a wireless in a tall building. A couple of them tried to go back up the stairs, but they found that they could not, prevented by the same kind of pane as was at the bottom of the stairs.

"Just one question," the man said. "Who sent you?"

They tried in vain to whack the pane of remarkably transparent glass with their hammers, but it wouldn't even crack.

"Who sent you?" he repeated.

One of them pulled out his revolver and fired. The bullet reached the pane of glass, seemed to get through, but then dropped lifelessly to the floor on the other side. The pane was unaffected. He tried again and the same thing happened.

"Can it!" another one said, covering his ears. He pushed the gun away and put his own hammer back in his toolbelt.

"We tell you, and then you let us outta here?"

"That's the deal."

They looked at one another. "Mister, the truth is, we don't know."

"We're just getting paid for trashing your place, is all. It's nothing personal."

"Don't hurt us. We're just in it for the money."

The man on the landing thought for a minute. "How about if I offer you three times the fee from that other fellow for you guys to tell me all you know?"

They all looked at one another again. "Mister, you got a deal."

Chapter 38

The Hopewells were faced with a problem—nothing too deleterious, but inconvenient in an epic way. In ten years, Hyim had created the perfect laboratory in order to carry out his purpose. On the Lower East Side no one asked about the odd noises coming from the ten-floor walkup. At least, it appeared from the outside to be ten floors. Hyim commissioned only the façade to be built by an outside architect. The inside would be done by Originator builders.

Leah had established herself among the power brokers in New York City politics. Although technically she was estranged from her former mentor in the Roosevelt office, that seemed to make her more popular with the local Republicans. She was a suffragist who wouldn't get in anyone's face about it, or embarrass the district bosses. They liked her for her brains, but they loved her because she didn't call them on it when they used her ideas without attribution.

For ten years they were able to pass as people in that indeterminate age bracket that runs from 30 to 50. Now, however, having gone through five hydrogen infusions for their health (etc.), they were not showing the signs of age that their peers were.

At first, it was flattering. "My goodness, Leah, you still look so young for someone of 42." But after a while, it just became an annoying reminder of what was to come: the inevitable deaths of Leah and Hyim Hopewell.

In some ways it was like a real death. When Leah agreed to be a part of the Originator cause, she knew she would have to give up her identity at some point, but she never realized how devastating it would feel when she had to abandon a hard-earned position in her chosen profession. Not only that, but the adulation with which older men regarded her—which was as unfamiliar as it was

239

exhilarating—would also be gone. Her new identity would have to be dramatically different from the Leah she had become accustomed to, and no one would realize just how much she had accomplished.

By contrast, Li-Don did not feel that his participation in the Originator cause was warranted. He refused the infusions on the grounds that it upset the natural order of things. So while Hyim and Leah remained in their 35-year-old bodies, Li-Don had grown to 45. He did not once regret his decision, even while suffering through bouts of influenza, dropsy, and blinding headaches. All this, while his employers (and friends), the Hopewells, were as healthy as horses.

"Life is suffering," he said often.

On May 13, 1914, they attended the funeral of his mother, who died peacefully during the night of unknown causes (officially, it was "loss of breath"). On May 19, they attended the funeral of his father, who died of a sudden stroke (read: broken heart). That was when the first gray streak showed in Li-Don's inky-black hair. It was a signal, of sorts: time to move on to a new era of their lives. Li-Don had no family, no romantic interests that lasted for very long, and no wish to have anything other than what he had, which was a life of serving Leah and Hyim.

As for Hyim, he was not convinced that there was a need to cease the Hopewell existence. He had a plan. It was ten years in the making. His laboratories were scattered all over Manhattan, each with its own purpose and results.

One night in 1907, he found one of his labs ransacked, his experiment destroyed. He knew that Ptolemy and his standing shadow army were trying to stop him from completing his work. It was time he started preparing for intellectual battle. He began to be more secretive and consciously careful of where he went and when. He started running duplicate experiments in different labs (in case one was destroyed); he rented space in anonymous buildings, setting up phony experiments in false labs to throw off anyone who might do damage to his work; he started toying with defense mechanisms that would protect the work but not harm anyone. He had to constantly think not only about the subjects of his work, but also about their protection and the logistics of their execution.

Despite all this, he did not harbor hatred. He was sad to see that there were people who would foolishly destroy his work to prevent progress. But he did not hate the perpetrators. They were merely pawns in a larger game. And he did not hate the people who were behind it all. They were slaves to their own world-view. They were misguided, at worst, and were operating under the assumption that anything they didn't agree with should be eliminated. *Enemies.* Two opposite powers working towards a common goal, competing to get there first.

His first experiments were with gasoline. Crude oil was rapidly becoming a major commodity, and people—Americans in particular—were mad for their automobiles. Hyim tried to fuse the power of supercharged hydrogen with the combustion potential of coal tar distillates. He spent many nights with red-rimmed eyes and a dry mouth because of his hours spent watching vials and flasks. He often worked while Li-Don—who quickly became an expert on where to get materials for the experiments—slept upright in a chair in the corner.

Unfortunately, gasoline was too complex a substance to be of any use. The hydrocarbons, paraffins, olefins, sulfur compounds, and various other contaminants made it impossible to release or store *infused* energy with any reliability. He came to realize that the only practical way to utilize supercharged hydrogen was with normal hydrogen in combustion engines. It was not the answer he was hoping for.

The object of his work was to make the energy gathering technology of the Originators available to society in general, in a way that they would accept and be able to use freely. This would then be the springboard from which they could reveal themselves and their purpose to humanity. It would be in the spirit of

assistance. In the best of all possible worlds, Hyim would be able

241

to condense the lightning-rod type of energy gathering into something smaller and portable, so that individual houses or cars, or planes, or who knows what else would be able to use it anywhere at any time.

But supercharged hydrogen and its infusion into a substance that could be carried in a small container proved problematic. It worked on a large scale because the hydrogen itself needed space to transfer its sub-atomic particles around in the chamber. The smaller the chamber, the more pressure created, and the more dangerous and unstable the mix became. He would either have to create the perfect chamber or come up with an alternate hypothesis.

When he realized this, he sought out his father, who was in his new incarnation as Daniel Hedger, a Canadian timber exporter. He could not have gone back into diamond exporting so quickly because the people who he worked with would have recognized him. He and another Originator took turns working with wood and with diamonds. In another thirty years or so, it would be his turn again to be the diamond merchant.

This became very confusing to Hyim, whose own identity change was coming due.

"So, you're not Jewish any longer?"

"I never was. It's just a label. Daniel is a good Anglican Protestant. God save the King."

"Is there anything you keep from your old life?"

"Just my face. And my memory. I leave behind everything. They are only props."

"I assume you don't mean family."

"Normally, I don't have a family. I'm usually the bachelor who lives alone and no one really thinks twice about me. There is always enough money and time to set up somewhere else doing something else. Some people don't even go back into society right away; they hide out in one of the compounds. But I like people. I like being out there and keeping track of the scientific advances. But..." Here he trailed off and paused. Hyim had the good sense to wait through an uncomfortable silence. "I have only one family. Those of us who left our home to come here. Those of us who had the scientific understanding to recognize that our home was dying. Most of them stayed behind to fix the problem, but we courageous, stupid few decided to go out on our own and find another home. It takes a certain kind of person to want to sail out into the unknown in search of hospitable places. Not just to discover them but to eventually live there."

The father got a faraway look in his eye that Hyim rarely saw, if ever. "Are you ever going back?" Hyim asked.

The father turned to him, "Never. That would be to admit defeat."

Hyim sensed he had his father at a strategically weak moment. "Tell me about Harriet," he said. "I want to know."

The father took a deep breath. "Daniel Hedger has never been married. Neither was Balthazar Neiler, Henry Thompkins, Gregorio Falabri, or hardly any of them... All died much too soon of accidental causes..."

"I asked you a question..."

"I'm trying to answer. Your mother died many times, just as I did. But every so often, the Originators would have a council. One of the things we discussed at this council was procreation. Oh, sure, we all married into the local population and had children with local wives at one time or another. But there are very few pure Originator children."

"What does that matter? How could that make a difference?"

"Hm. You have a gift, Hyim. A gift that your mother and I gave you. It was supposed to help you in your dealings with the primitives. Now, it may be a burden to you, I don't know. Yours is a special case. Both yours and Leah's."

The way the father said *primitives* and *pure* gave Hyim a chill. It was almost as if he were talking about the chosen people among *goyim*.

"You are an Originator child," the father continued. "With all of the blessings and curses that comes with. Your mother found it a curse. She felt the mission was becoming stale. It was the same people making the same decisions for the same reasons. She had a choice whether to continue on with the mission. She chose to leave it to others. She stopped taking her infusions. She fully expected to watch you grow up as a primitive mother would, taking pride in her son's accomplishments."

"But she got a virus," Hyim said, suddenly understanding. "Didn't she?"

"Not a virus. She died of consumption when you were just a little one. She refused all treatment, any infusions, although, truth be told, infused super-charged hydrogen is relatively ineffective against latent infections. It is only a preventive."

Hyim knew that pregnancy was impossible while taking infusions—cell division became too slow a process for meiosis to be successful. Harriet must have gone off the infusions to have a child, then never gone back on. The ratio of living male Originators to female Originators was about nine to one, probably for just that reason.

Up until the time his father told him this, he had been reluctant to ask specifics about his mother. It was always a sore subject, but now he knew his father wasn't just mourning his loss of a wife. She had rejected the philosophy to which he had dedicated his extraordinarily long life. Hyim may never truly know what exactly happened, but he felt a new respect for the community process that produced him as an heir. Was there any love involved? Romantic love maybe, but the real love was for the Originator cause, which was rooted in a respect for the "primitive" humanity.

The Originators could have simply wiped out the native population when they arrived, but it just wasn't in their nature. It wasn't in *his* nature. It wasn't quite the heartwarming story Hyim had been hoping for, but it was a positive sign that he could be a good person and still support the cause. The only thing troubling him was the program of genetic dilution. His father would not speak about it, nor would anyone else who might have been associated with it. In his mind he conceived of it as kind of the original sin of the Originators, something for which they would have to atone for the rest of their lives. And that was a long time.

Chapter 39

In the early part of the year, Leah and Hyim saw their first motion picture. A small orchestra played lugubrious music while the images flickered on a flat screen. The process was crude and potentially dangerous. It was just a strip of film that was run over a projected lamp and through a couple of lenses. Unfortunately, the film used was made of a flammable material, a petroleum derivative that, while malleable and inexpensive, was chemically volatile.

He saw the potential in solid petroleum derivatives. The flexibility such material offered could make it a popular medium for structural support of small objects, like household items. Its use would be limited by its inherently unstable properties, however. Like the film, it would be too prone to breaking down or bursting into flames. It would not be able to withstand high temperatures.

The film stopped halfway through, got caught on something or was mis-threaded, and the heat from the projection lamp melted the frame. The effect on-screen was both beautiful and disturbing. A man and a woman, both in bold whiteface makeup, looked longingly at each other, and then a great sepia and auburn crack appeared between them, which folded back and dissolved into and away from them with horrific brown bubbling quickness, leaving nothing but the white screen and a few flecks of celluloid.

The audience gasped; many of them had probably never seen anything like this nor could they have conceived of it. Hyim hadn't thought about it all that much, but once it happened, he recognized what was going on.

The relevant chemical reaction immediately popped into his head. Ethyl chloride heats to a temperature beyond its melting point, the weak bonds of hydrogen, carbon, and chlorine atoms release their grip at such a temperature, ejecting carbon monoxide and dihydrogen chloride into the projection chamber, further increasing the temperature and leading to the film decomposing in several different ways.

The house lights came on and the master of ceremonies, who had earlier introduced the film, got up on stage tremulously, announcing that the show was over and no one would be given a refund. If they were to look at the back of their tickets they would plainly see the words "no refunds." There were shouts and hurled produce.

In the back row, Hyim and Leah sat quietly while the theater erupted in pandemonium. The kerfuffle lasted for about ten minutes before the patrons quieted down and then dispersed. A large man came up to them and asked them to leave.

"Is there any particular reason for us to leave?" Leah asked.

"The projector ain't working."

"Can't we just sit here in the peace and quiet for a while?"

"There ain't no show, lady."

""We'd just like to sit in some comfortable seats for a while," Hyim said.

"Look, *Hebe*, I told you there ain't no show. Nobody's allowed in the theater when there ain't no show."

Though Hyim admired the man's brutish persistence in the face of customer loyalty, he felt the man's epithet with its full force. It was not often he was reminded of his and his wife's religious affiliation. They didn't "look" Jewish according to the contemporary stereotypes, which seemed to consist of black beards on the men (Hyim was clean-shaven) and dark ringlet-ed hair for the women (Leah's hair was auburn). But, for some reason that had little to do with their conformation to type, this man knew or guessed that they were Jews.

They left without incident. The incendiary strip of film that had led to their ejection made Hyim more nervous than the man's boorishness. When they were a safe distance away, walking in the spring air, Leah pointed to her small nose.

"The bend in the road," she said, indicating the terrain on her face.The noise in the city had increased dramatically. Personal automobiles filled the streets. There were still some horses, but it was clear that the horse-drawn vehicles were on their way out. It was becoming more expensive to keep a horse than a car.

They ducked into a side street where there were few distractions and shared a kiss. "Your husband is smitten with you," Hyim said. "Even if you are a Jewess."

She held his face in her hands. "You shouldn't let me distract you from your work. Nor should I let you distract me from mine."

"We're both working towards the same goal. Have patience, wife. If there is anything that has changed about me it's that I can see the sweep of history that Li-Don always talks about. I'm an observer now. Not just a participant. We both are. We can afford a little distraction now and then."

"Your work is already delayed because of the attacks."

"No one can stop me," he said playfully. "No matter how much of my equipment they destroy or how often they try to sabotage my work. It is only a matter of time."

They stepped out of the side street and back onto the sidewalk.

"Time," Leah began, "doesn't mean as much as it used to. Days are not discrete elements of life, are not even markers. Day, night, day, night... It's all the same. I know we haven't really talked about this. But I see now why your Originators call other people *primitives*. It's not a function of the Originators' genetic makeup, or their snobbery; it's a function of their technology, these infusions. Regular people live out days like they are fractions of a life. Small fractions, but still significant portions. They need impatience in order to progress, or even survive. They have only a few years of life in which to accomplish what they must. It's horrible. I didn't think I would ever see it that way, but I do. Ordinary people experience things, good and bad, so much more intensely than I do now. Even after this short time of being a bastard Originator with you, I have changed so much. I have so much calm inside of me. I know I will not die. I have confidence in that. My body doesn't change as it used to, as I felt it before. Yet, I am worried that I will miss the intensity of being. Do you know what I mean?"

"I do."

"Our lives are not our own. In such a short span of life, you have to make your life your own or you'll go crazy. But we are blessed, Hy—or cursed, I suppose. We have a greater purpose now. It is not unreasonable to give your life over to the cause, because there is so much life left in you. The cause will be successful long before we die. No persistent purveyors of terror will change that. But I worry about what will happen after success. Will we have the same appreciation for life? It's preciousness and its beauty?"

Hyim didn't have an answer. He, too, felt this. Apparently, not quite as severely as Leah, who was born a *primitive*, for goodness sake. He decided he would have to stop thinking like that, in terms of *we* and *they*. They were all Originators, and they were all Primitives. It was only the technology that separated them.

As for the purveyors of terror, he was moderately successful in dealing with them so far, they had not yet been strategically organized. There had only been sporadic attacks of six or seven members on one specific target at a time. Hyim knew it was only a matter of time before they would start organizing their tactics into a strategy.

Chapter 40

Of the many inventions Hyim created from the supercharged hydrogen process, his most successful during this time was the invisible shield. It was essentially the same effect as the wrist-based emitter that produced an electro-magnetic field around something (or someone). But with a few modifications, he was able to make it behave like a solid wall of super-fast sub-atomic particles. Invisible because of the speed of the particles; solid because of their binding and repelling forces.

An object of great density and speed—such as a bullet fired from a gun—would be able to penetrate the wall, but as if it were dropped into the ocean, it would encounter so much resistance that its energy would be lost and it would be rendered harmless. This differed from the emitter in that the shield created no visible effect. It would offer protection, but that protection would not be noticeable to a casual bystander.

In terms of functionality, it was not much of an improvement. But he was able to use his newly acquired knowledge of how the emitter worked and turn that into a separate device. He had successfully defended his house from several attacks, but did not have a real understanding of who was really behind them until he constructed a kind of "cage" that blocked not only forward progress, but also retreat.

Once he perfected the cage, he went to see his father up in Molineau and proclaimed it as a victory for their side.

His father was not impressed. "Victory," he said. "Hmm. Victory is at the end of the road. One can only declare victory at the end of a war, not a battle."

Undeterred, Hyim went further: "I now know how you did it. How you destroyed your own house without damaging the adjacent houses.

You used the emitter field. It protected the walls all around."

"Don't be absurd, boy," Ezra said. "I didn't have that back then. I merely directed an explosion outward rather than sideways using a mortar. And those houses were made of stone, not wood. Really now, your profuse and profligate acceptance and evangelism of Occam's Razor should have told you as much."

His father's praise withheld, Hyim journeyed back to New York under a cloud of pessimism. But despite his protestations of not being a clever engineer nor a genius scientist, he kept finding ways to apply his own research

The emitter "cage" was a great achievement. The many gangs of vandals that had destroyed much of his early work now could be repelled. But not just that, they could be captured. And on one Summer evening, he finally got it to work. He trapped a gang of attackers by activating several emitter walls in sequence, allowing them in, then sealing them off. He then went about proposing a plan to them to reveal their employer.

"The guy's name is Franklin," one of them said. "We're meeting him tomorrow."

"Is that so?" Hyim asked from behind the wall. "Who is he?"

"We don't know. We just work for the guy. We bash your stuff around and then he gives us money."

"I think I should be there to see him myself."

"That would be dangerous."

"Don't worry about me. I've got some tricks."

They made the deal: Hyim was to accompany them to meet Franklin the next day. Hyim then gave them a choice—either they spend the night in the attic or the basement. After realizing what they had done to the attic, they decided to take their chances with the basement. It was dank and cold, but it was clean.

Other inventions were not quite as fruitful in terms of a effectiveness against the enemy, but they, too, provided some defense of the house and some comfort within it.

Li-Don helped set up the emitter walls around the perimeter of the basement so no one could escape. They then sat with Leah in the scullery, eating cheese and dried fish. Leah brought in a boule of sourdough, which they ripped apart. Li-Don had trouble grasping the edges to tear off a piece.

"These are my father's hands," he said. "Arthritic before the age of 50."

"You could fix them permanently," Hyim said.

"I understand your offer, as I always have." Li-Don's face seemed longer now, his mouth turned down more and his eyelids drooping. "It is not a question of comfort. The pain I feel is part of life; it is part of the suffering we must all endure."

"But it doesn't have to be," Leah said.

"I realize there are choices. We all choose every day whether to make our lives easier or harder. We sleep on pillows and stuffed mattresses instead of wooden boards. We eat prepared bread and aged fine cheese instead of vegetable soup or porridge. We choose like this all the time. Your cure-all is just another choice."

"You're eating the cheese," Hyim joked.

"I've made *this* choice. Happiness is fleeting, like the cheese. Like the fish. It's in our mouths for a few seconds and then it's gone. No amount of life you put into your lifespan is going to change that."

"Are you saying that death is preferable?"

"Neither is preferable. It's just the way things are. You must excuse my philosophy, I realize Mrs. Hopewell would have died without your treatment. But existence does not matter."

"But I can help this society to progress. I can give them the technology to eliminate much of the violence and evil in the world, to make life less expensive and more enjoyable."

"Laudable goals, old friend. But meaningless. You think your new power source will solve humanity's problems."

"It's almost finished…"

"Yes, yes. The fact of humanity is that any new technology is used as a weapon first, a civil benefit second. That may or may not be a result of your Originator program. But any technological introduction will have unintended consequences."

"Do you disagree with our decision?" Leah asked.

"It is not for me to agree or disagree. Things are the way they are. We can change only so much of it, and in the end what we change changes us in ways we cannot imagine. I do not understand, for example, how you can forsake your religion for this undertaking."

"What do you mean by that? How have I forsaken my religion?"

"You have let go of the will of your God. Forced his hand away, actually. As I understand your religion, your God has a date of your demise planned much ahead of time."

"But that's simply not true. There is nothing in the Torah to prevent anyone from altering their lifespan by outside means. Maybe you're thinking of the Christians who believe in pre-destination."

"No. I mean the power your God has over you. You fear death. Your God has only one power over you, and that is your fear of death and what comes afterward. Without that fear, what kind of life will you lead? I know, I know, you are good people and you would not do evil. Your God does not make distinctions between good people and evil people when he accepts them into the afterlife. But you have eliminated the one reason to believe in your God. You have eliminated the fear."

"Not entirely. We will see our end. Someday."

"It is too far off to affect you. There is too much time between now and that date—we cannot conceive, are not designed to conceive of that amount of time. Even your Originator parents will concede that."

"I don't like you having disapproved of our choice."

"There is no disapproval. There is only being and nothingness. I do not accept the gift you offer because I have no need for it.

"But we have need of you. We will lose you."

"That is a selfish feeling, and for that I am disappointed. But only for the feeling, not for the person. "Li-Don was growing more and more disconnected to their lives as he got older. It was a constant source of worry to Hyim that his longtime friend did not wish to enter into the adventure he was embarking upon. But it was especially bitter to him because it was a result of religious adherence. Li-Don't stubbornness could be attributed directly to his belief in something that would have proven inconsequential if he applied the same kind of scientific method that he did to other parts of life. Religion was inherently irrational.

"I will follow you to the end of my days," Li-Don added. "But not beyond that."

They shared a silent impassive moment together, reaching for the food in the middle of the small table.

"When you find out who is paying for the destruction of our home, what will you do then?" Leah asked, trying to change the subject.

"They've only recently been trying to get into our house," he said. "Before that it was just my labs. The truth is, I don't really know what I'm going to do. I don't suppose they can be reasoned with. Possibly bought off, but that would set a bad precedent."

"You know it's Ptolemy," Leah said. "He's the only one who has anything against you."

"I don't know that for sure."

Hammers and guns weren't Ptolemy's style. He would probably prefer to make death as painless as possible. Hyim didn't know for sure, but he thought the Originator proclivity of not inflicting violence wasn't lost to Ptolemy. Any deaths at his hands would not have been painful. Still, the destruction of property was well within his potential.

"The mere presence of de Meurre in our operation all this time makes me think it's someone else."

"You know that de Meurre is reporting all that you do back to Ptolemy," Li-Don said.

"Yes. But we're not violating any of his rules. He said he would be keeping an eye on us, we can't expect that he won't have. But his threshold for misconduct seems high, and his punishment seems different from what we have tried to accomplish."

"How can you trust him like that?" Leah asked.

"I have to think like someone who has had a plan for over a thousand years. Maybe he doesn't realize all that humanity has accomplished in the last twenty years. He's been used to a slow progression of science, and now it's sped up and perhaps sped past him."

"Or maybe," Li-Don said, "he's realized this and is nervous about your plan succeeding. If an onion does not make you cry, it may be a turnip. You have said yourself that the simplest solution is usually the correct one."

"True enough."

Chapter 41

Li-Don, of course, refused to let Hyim go to the clandestine meeting alone. But having another person there only meant there was another person to try and protect. Hyim felt safer only having to defend himself, but with another member of his team present, the danger only increased. True, Li-Don did have his own emitter, but Hyim noticed he was loath to use it when a good, swift kick felt more satisfying (which had happened more than once to a number of pickpockets on warm Manhattan evenings).

He also felt bad that Li-Don was an older man, with diminished physical capacity—although still sharp as a tack. Li-Don could handle himself with one random assailant (once, he took care of two that had threatened Leah), but more than that might be too much for him. He worried that Leah would be left alone, but Hyim's emitter walls around the house meant that she would be safe.

But, as in most things that required physical strength and coordination, Li-Don was the better driver of the two. Even when Hyim had been at the top of his game in fencing, he still did not have the strength—or was it strength of will?—to put away a match with an equal opponent.

They deactivated the emitter walls around the basement and let the enemy men out. Hands were shaken cautiously as they exited his house.

"We're all clear on what's going to happen?" he asked them.

They nodded.

They talked among themselves before they all got into a Republic Little Six sedan and departed. It was larger than most, though it looked too small to hold all of them. Hyim and Li-Don followed at a medium distance in a modified Stutz Bearcat roadster. It was very quiet in comparison to most other cars, although its size often attracted a great deal of attention.

Li-Don insisted on wearing his driving cap, as it had come to be known. It was a gingham brown and white number with a snap in the front, and he thought it made him look more distinguished. He looked younger when he had it on, if only because it hid his gray hairs.

They had to shout above the noise of the engine.

"I am still concerned," Li-Don said, "that there is no plan after this."

"Plans are not monuments, Li-Don. They are like grass huts in a fickle swamp."

"I have the distinct impression that I'm being mocked."

"Just drive, Sancho."

They followed the Little Six through the streets of lower Manhattan until they came to the Brooklyn Bridge.

"I hate driving over suspension bridges," Li-Don said. "They don't look safe."

"You live on an island. Keep going. It's a sound design."

"What?"

"I said, 'It's a sound design!' "

The scenery quickly changed from urban to rural. The trees were larger now, and the road that cut through the landscape was not paved. Hyim's danger perception told him that something wasn't quite right about this meeting. "Keep back further," he said. "There's no one else out here but us."

They kept the other car in view, though it was maybe a quarter mile away on a flat, dusty road. It abruptly stopped at a small water-pumping windmill and turned into the countryside, bumping along the grassy meadow. Li-Don stopped the car and pulled to the side of the road, into a bank of tall grass (making sure to cut his noisy engine before they cut theirs). They waited as the other car stopped next to a small grove of birch trees.

Carefully, they got out and pulled a brown and green tarp from the rear of the car and pulled it over to camouflage the car in the grass. Then they reached back into the rear of the car, pulled out a sound capture gadget that Hyim had been experimenting with, and knelt behind the car. This gadget was based on the old Renaissance design of a giant vertical dish, but was just a skeleton, with curved paddles that radiated out from the center at a steeper angle. It was much smaller than many wooden ones he had seen, although the sound reflector itself had to be mounted on an iron bar to get the proper magnetic field, so it was heavy. Plus it was amplified using stored electricity from the car, which necessitated that it be wired to the car. Hyim called it an *electric ear*, a name which made Li-Don roll his eyes at the literalness of it.

It was still too far away to hear exact words in a conversation, but it did pick up a slamming door. At one point, a couple of barn swallows flew close by and nearly deafened them both with the rustling of feathers.

Hyim found his attention wandering to the countryside itself. The beauty of the woodlands and meadows underneath a gently clouded sky made him want to cry. On a different day he might have fully imagined himself as a child again under the watchful eye of Mei-Gao, playing in the reeds, catching frogs, getting muddy by the side of a river.

"Someone's coming," Li-Don said, pointing down the road.

Another black car followed by a cloud of dust appeared on the horizon.

"Let's try to get closer," Hyim said.

They stepped and pushed their way through the six-foot grass stems, trying not to topple the electric ear or to get the cord caught anywhere. Li-Don let out more cord as they advanced forward.

"My eyes aren't as good as they used to be," Li-Don said when they got settled. "I can't tell how far away they are."

"I'd say eight hundred yards. But I still can't make out what they're saying." Hyim pulled up his spyglass and narrated the scene.

"The second car is rolling towards the first car. I think it's a Model A. Now stopped. Now everyone's getting out of the first car. I count five hats. A couple of people are getting out of the second car. They have tan suits, dark tan, light brown, I don't know. No wait, they aren't suits, they're some kind of... no, they're suits, they just have matching capes. Matching capes. How do you like that?"

"They could be tails."

"They're capes. I know the difference between tails and a cape."

"At any rate, their clothes seem hardly at issue."

"Interesting point."

The ear wasn't picking up anything definite. Although it was able to pick up sounds from miles away, it was not able to isolate them from background noises.

Hyim continued. "I can hear voices. One voice, then another, alternating. Hold on, I'm trying to fix them in position..."

The voices were scratchy, like a cylinder recording, only with more static and wind noise. "... three times what you guys... see our position... don't think we won't... got no deal..."

"Darn it," Hyim said, lowering the device. "I can't hold my hand steady for that long. This blasted thing is too heavy. I'll have to work on that."

He set it on the ground While Li-Don lifted the spyglass. "They're arguing. They're waving their hands around. Someone is pacing back and forth. One of the gentlemen with a cape is leaning over... he's produced what appears to be... Oh, no. Oh, no."

Li-Don handed the spyglass to Hyim. He saw the men in the

tan suits get back into their car hurriedly. The other men who had previously been standing next to their car were now lying on the ground. They heard the far-off popping sounds, which they took to be gunshots, delayed noises because of the distance. It was a massacre.

"Get to the car!" Hyim shouted, grabbing for the electronic ear. "They shot them! They shot them! Those stupid backward nitheads shot them!"

Chapter 42

"Are we thinking of following them?" Li-Don shouted after him, rolling up the cord while hopping through the grass.

"We have to!"

They jumped into the Stutz, throwing the tarp, the cord, and the listening device into the open rear compartment. Hyim swallowed his disgust at the senseless killings and tripped the magneto in the engine. Li-Don held onto his hat as they sped past the sedan and the lifeless figures lying on the ground.

They had lost a good two minutes on the other car, although the Stutz was a faster car.

"I don't like you driving," Li-Don shouted over the engine and the sounds of rocks hitting the inside fenders.

They couldn't see the lead car, but they did see the cloud of dust up ahead. It was arguable that they could not be seen, either.

"What's up ahead?" Hyim shouted.

"I don't know. I don't know this area." After a short pause: "Why are we following them, again?"

"We want to know who they are, or who they work for."

"Don't we already know that?"

"I'm not convinced."

"What?"

"I'm not convinced!"

The dust cloud ahead continued on. They were now at a constant distance away, maybe a little over a quarter mile. Li-Don held the spyglass up, waiting for a glimpse of the other car.

"Slow down!" he shouted suddenly. "Stop!"

Hyim calmed the engine as they rolled to a stop by the side of the road.

"They're turning now, to the right... onto a paved road. No, wait. It's not paved. OK, go. But not too fast. Our trail of dust will be visible to them now. I can see it now, it's still too far away to tell exactly what it is, but... OK, now they've stopped. One of them is getting out. He's left his cape in the car. He's pulled out something from his pocket. Uh, oh. He's looking at us. He's trying to discern who we are."

Hyim wished he had a hat.

"He is not using a lens, so I don't think he can recognize us for certain. I suggest," Li-Don said, putting the spyglass down, "we continue on this road without turning in their direction. Maybe we can convince them we're just out for a drive."

"We can outrun them if we turn back. But if we continue forward, we won't know which way to go if they decide to chase us."

They continued on without any movement from the others.

"They must know what kind of car you have. But as you said, we can outrun them."

They came up to the turn and trundled past into unknown territory. Just past the turn was a grove of trees, so they couldn't tell if the people they were following had decided to follow *them*.

"They saw us, but I don't think they know who we are," Li-Don said.

"We're just two people out for a drive."

They continued on for about ten minutes, then turned back. The car was gone from the perpendicular road when they arrived back at the thick grove of trees. With Li-Don driving, they followed the fresh tracks along the smooth but dusty road. Slowly. Slowly enough so they could see anything or anyone up ahead that might be waiting for them.

After a few minutes, they came to a rise, which dropped abruptly and turned to the left. Hyim was a little afraid that the growling of the engine would give them away, but he was confident in Li-Don's skills as a driver. He found he could not stop his mind from wandering: the leaves were different green colors in the wind, the swirling dust splayed itself across the road in front of them.

Li-Don turned the car to the left and came to a dead stop. They dared not go farther down that same road in that noisy car. It remained to be seen just how far they would have to follow the others. They hid the car in the brush by the side of the road and traveled on foot. Li-Don led the way, pointing out the tire tracks on the dusty road. The road wound through a small forest, and as it got deeper they could see less and less ahead of them.

"Maybe we should go back and get the car," Li-Don said.

"Too much noise. Not only would they be able to hear us, we wouldn't be able to hear them."

"All this assumes that the people we are pursuing have stopped near here. It's possible they are in Ohio by now."

"The probability for that is extremely low. Consider the possibilities. The most likely scenario is the one that says the two parties met here, in the middle of nowhere, to go their separate ways after the meeting. Of all the possibilities for the people we are following, the biggest variable was their intelligence. Assuming they were reasonably intelligent, they would wait somewhere to make sure they weren't followed, and to either wait out or ambush whoever it was that might be following them."

"Unless they kill the least intelligent party first."

Hyim pulled his sleeve back to reveal his emitter.

"That's slightly more comforting," Li-Don said. "Yet your patience is overwhelming. You grow potatoes with patience, corn with persistence, and roses with fear."

"Do they have potatoes in China?"

"I… I don't know. I imagine so."

"Mei-Gao was a good cook. I remember potatoes. But I don't remember cheese. Isn't that interesting? I don't think I had a piece of cheese until I was in prep school."

"We've been walking for a long time. Perhaps we should turn back."

They stopped. "I *feel* something," Hyim said. "My father has told me to trust these feelings. I don't trust him in everything else. But he's always been accurate about what I'm feeling."

"What is it? What do you feel?"

"I feel another Originator. Nearby, I think. It feels like, like a pressure inside my head, like my vision is narrowing…"

"I don't like the sound of that."

"Let's move forward," Hyim said. "We're being watched."

"I don't think I need to tell you that I am picturing dead men on the ground."

"You mean the ones back there, of course. It is revolting, it really is. The animal nature of these… people… I just can't comprehend why death is an answer to anything. The whole idea of stopping someone else's life from continuing… it's just sickening."

"I feel I must tell you that I am a little frightened."

"Don't be silly. If they wanted to kill us, we'd be dead already. We're just out for a walk in the woods."

"Just a walk in the woods. Of course."

In between their own footsteps, they could hear rustling in the brush around them that was inconsistent with the ambient wind noise. There was definitely someone following them. They continued forward, anticipating some kind of surprise attack. Hyim's muscles were tensing, something they rarely did. He pictured in his mind the actions he might take with an unknown assailant. He would turn on his heel in an instant, whip his emitter into action and cover them both with an invisible wall of security. He would have to act fast to adjust it for Li-Don's inevitable fight reflex.

He was reminded of walking along the lower platform of the *Tour Eiffel*. He had the same feeling that there was someone around him. His perception of other Originators had not been developed then—he had only felt *something* when the man—The Man on the Tower—was just upon them. The feeling had only lasted a few seconds, if that, before the attack.

He could feel that much now, and more. With each step it stayed the same distance away, watching and waiting. But waiting for what? Why not attack?

Li-Don elbowed him and nodded up the road which had opened up from the forest. Standing on a small rise at the edge of the forest, they could see maybe three miles ahead. The sedan they had been following was about five hundred feet away, stopped at a small building, alone on the prairie-like countryside.

"Go get the car," Hyim said. He expected trouble. Having Li-Don around in the presence of guns would only complicate matters, especially with a warm body skulking around in the forest around them. Splitting up was a good idea, would increase their odds of finding out just what the heck was going on.

Li-Don stared at him in disbelief.

"Please," Hyim said.

Li-Don bowed his head briefly and ran back to into the depths of the forest.

Now alone, Hyim ventured forward, toward the car and the wooden shack.

Chapter 43

Hyim did not bother to sneak up on them. He merely walked up to the building and looked through one of the windows. He stepped around it, but couldn't see anyone. As far as he could tell, the building was empty.

He went to the car and lifted the engine cover. Folding it back and holding it in place. Satisfied there were no explosives or other assorted traps attached to it, he checked around for a serial number. Maybe because the engine cover was blocking the sound waves coming from the shack, or maybe because his concentration was intensely focused on the engine itself (it's true that he may have spent too much time looking at it just to picture in his mind how it worked)—a couple of the assassins came upon him looking into the engine.

He saw the tan suits out of the corner of his eye, and he tried to remain calm. Continuing to look into the engine (he had found the serial number and committed it to memory), he traced his finger from one end of the open compartment to the other. He saw no guns.

"This is a nice machine," he said noncommittally.

"Thanks."

"What is that, a six cylinder?"

"Sure."

A hole in their formation opened on the far right side, next to the front of the sedan. He imagined diving through it and lurching behind the car as they sprayed the area with bullets.

Looking up into their faces, he did not see the traditional Originator features. They were taller, had more bone structure showing around their eyes, and thicker lips. Also, their skin was a paler white with hints of orange. These were *primitives* (he had yet to start preventing himself from using that word, but at times he could not help himself; Li-Don and Leah were both primitives, in the strict sense of the word, though both of them were perhaps converted). These particular primitives disgusted him because of their haphazard use of weaponry.

He heard the soft sound of a pistol being un-holstered from a leather belt. Casually, he pulled his hand over to the other wrist to activate the emitter. There was a short, pulsing whine as it charged up, but then was silent. And except for a spark or two that appeared around him, it was successfully invisible. He always felt great pride at having things work like this. He was sure that it showed on his face, and that it might be perceived as smugness.

"Who do you work for?"

"We work for you, pal."

"I don't follow."

"See, we're kind of a fee-for-service outfit. You pay us and we don't kill you. That way, we work in your best interests."

"What if I pay you and you still kill me?"

"You could take it up with our legal department. See Eddie, there? He's our legal department."

"Why haven't you shot me, yet?"

"You're an interesting guy."

"That's comforting."

"Hey Frankie, get a load of this. For some reason, you think we don't know who you are. We've been following you for a year and a half, you miserable dwarf."

Hyim shook his head. "Do you know how many people like you I've had to deal with? I'll admit, your boss is getting more sophisticated in his tactics, but only slightly more."

Next came the familiar gleam of steel pulled from inside a coat.

Now there were at least two guns trained on his thorax. But just as he heard the far-off rumbling of the Stutz in the forest, he felt what could only be described as a gleam of light come through him. At first, he thought his emitter had failed and he had been shot. He had always wondered what a bullet would feel like as it passed through his body, or a knife, or a sword, or something else violently painful. He had cut himself before, with a razor trying to divide a small block of limestone, had even drawn blood a few times. But the intensity of pain that the primitives felt when they were being tortured or assaulted with a weapon had interested him as much as it had repulsed him. Not knowing what that felt like, he instantly thought he was finally feeling it.

But such was not the case. There was no shot, the emitter was still working, and his person was still intact.

"Listen to the wanderer," the assassin said. "Trying to give us money to spare his life, Ain't you going to Jew me down to your gold tooth or something?"

"You have already spared my life," Hyim said. "I will ask you again. Why haven't you shot me?"

"I want to hear your views on Temperance."

The gleam must have come from somewhere else, someplace else. From the other Originator hiding in the brush? Perhaps there were technologies of which he was still not aware, but he doubted it. They only seemed to create a technology for a general purpose towards a common goal: defense, energy collection, mining. He had reviewed them all and sseen the holes in their plans. He was working trying to fill those holes.

"And now you have me trapped. What are you going to do with me?"

"Damn you, you little Christ killer."

Specifically, their energy collection scheme was admirable and elegant, but it was also too visible. The primitives were starting to explore the planet on a large scale, and these collection areas were much too large to remain secret. It was still too soon to reveal the

Originator cause—there was still too much superstition and paranoia among the primitives.

"But do you, in fact, have me trapped?"

"Huh?"

"Is there enough vitriol in your veins to kill me, when you know that if you allow me to die you will at best be unpaid? Death is an option also, I'm certain."

"Nothing says we can't pay a visit to your family."

"That leaves us with the same concerns about a war of retribution. Tell *that* to whoever it is that you work for."

They locked their eyes at him, realizing somehow that he had won the argument. *How had that happened?* showed on their faces. They understood now that he was untouchable through any means they could put to him. Or so it seemed.

Three of them tried to pummel him with their fists. But the emitter field stopped their hands in midair with an audible, flesh-meets-electricity bouncing noise. They shouted epithets and cursed as they tried to nurse their blistering hands. Guns dropped. Stones were kicked. Someone fired a shot. The nearby noise rang in Hyim's ears. But no bullet entered the field. Then another shot. And another.

Then the sight of a yellow roadster bearing down on all of them. They were firing at Li-Don who had shut off the motor and had coasted almost all the way down to them. The front grille struck one of the tan-suited men, who fell backwards in a heap of wrinkled and ripped clothing.

Li-Don then leaped out of the car and extended his foot into the throat of another, disabling him momentarily. A third came up behind him to hold his arms, but Li-Don broke out of that with a deft movement of his left leg, spun around on his heel and swatted

him square on the collarbone. He turned just in time to kick the gun out of a hand and, switching legs on the ground in a move Hyim had not realized was possible for human being to do,

269

smacked the now gun-less assassin in the nose with his heel.

It was then that Hyim noticed the four bullets lying on the ground at his feet.

"Get in the car!" Li-Don shouted, bending down to help an attacker fly by with a judo move. He set himself square and kicked one of the pistols into his hand, aiming it at the attacker, who was lying on the ground.

Hyim hurried over to the car and hunkered down in the passenger seat. There were three unconscious bodies around him and a fourth dared not move in front of Li-Don's sights.

Though the scene sickened Hyim more than he realized, he shouted at the would-be attacker, "For the last time! Who do you work for?"

"Take it easy, buddy!"

Li-Don fired at the ground next to him.

"All right! All right! He calls himself Vic. Vic something, I don't know. None of us does."

"What's in that shack?"

"There's a stairway down there that leads to a telegraph thingy. I don't know where the messages come from, but it tells us where to pick up our dough."

"So what did it tell you?"

The man looked back and forth at Li-Don and Hyim, then finally realized his situation. "There's supposed to be a general store about ten miles from here. We pick it up around back underneath a barrel of apples."

"A barrel of apples?" Li-Don said.

"Yeah, that's right, Crazy Horse. Apples. What's it to you?"

"How did you first get in contact with these people?" Li-Don asked.

The man didn't answer, looked like he was refusing to answer.

"The man with a gun asks you a question," Hyim said, "you'd better answer."

"I ain't speaking with no Injun. You can shoot me if you like, but I remember the Maine!"

Normally, Li-Don would have corrected this misapplication of American propaganda, but, as Hyim noted, such was not the time for history lessons.

"Answer *me*, then," Hyim said. "Pretend I'm asking the questions and give me the answers."

The man looked confused for a moment, then nodded briefly and eyed Li-Don suspiciously. "This guy comes up to Frankie, out of the blue..."

"Which one's Frankie?"

He pointed at one of the unconscious figures, then continued. "Like I said, out of the blue. He comes up to him and says, 'How would you like to make some dough?' So Frankie says, 'Sure'. I never saw the guy, and I don't know his name, but Frankie there says he was a little guy, like you. And he's got a funny way of looking at you. That's what Frankie says. He looks at you funny. I don't know nothing else."

"You're lying," Li-Don said.

"Is that what you think?" the man asked Hyim.

"Pretend he's me," Hyim said.

"I think you're Frankie," Li-Don said. "I think you know what he looks like, and you're terrified of him."

The man's lip started quivering. "It's not like that. It's not... The guy says his name is Carrera, OK? I don't know nothing else. I got a wife..."

Another shot from the gun rang out. It caught Hyim by surprise and gave him a knot in his stomach. "I wish you'd stop doing that," he said to Li-Don. Then he looked up again to see Li-Don on one knee, clutching his calf.

"I'm hit!" Li-Don shouted.

Chapter 44

A movement at the corner of Hyim's eye caught his attention. It was someone on the ground, fumbling a pistol in his hands. Clearly he was in extreme pain, but he was able to get an accurate shot off.

More shots. Some hit the car in places Hyim couldn't see. He slouched further down in his seat. Li-Don hobbled over as the man they were interrogating fell on his back, shot in the head.

Hyim had the presence of mind to get the car started before Li-Don had actually made it into the driver's seat. He crouched down low, watching the glass spit from the edge of the windscreen, bullets speckling it with holes. Quickly adjusting the emitter to protect both of them, in time to protect their flank as Li-Don spun the Stutz around, he tried to catch his breath as well as keep himself from getting physically sick. More bullets winged past them from the back as they sped back into the forest. Even though he knew he was protected by the emitter, he still flinched and kept low in his seat.

"How bad is it?" Hyim shouted over the engine.

"I don't know. I can barely feel it. I mean, I can barely feel my leg. Maybe you should drive."

They pulled over, careful to look behind them to see if they were being followed. When they were back on the road, Li-Don started rending his shirt to create a makeshift bandage.

"We should get to a doctor," Hyim said, glancing over at Li-Don's leg. There was an oval stain of blood on Li-Don's dark blue trousers radiating out from one ellipsis. Gravity had pulled much of it down the leg to the socks. Li-Don reached down and pulled up the pant leg to reveal a small hole on the side of his calf, messy with inky red blood. He opened a compartment and pulled out a small bottle of peppermint schnapps, which he dripped over the wound. Then he ripped a sleeve off of his shirt and tied it around the wound.

"I read about this in a history of the Crimean War," Li-Don said, trying to be cheerful. "Those stubborn Englishmen. They didn't know why more of their soldiers were dying back at camp than on the battlefield. Then this spoiled little girl faces them down and gets them to clean up the place."

"Sure," Hyim said. "Germs. Microbes. I've never studied that."

"It's particularly nasty."

After Hyim had started back onto the road, Li-Don said, "Should we be alarmed that one of your friends is still back there, hiding?"

"There isn't much we can do about that."

Leah was reading a thick book when they got back. Li-Don limped in, helped by Hyim's shoulder. The had not seen a doctor, had driven straight home. Along they way, they tried to discuss what "Carerra" might mean. They decided that Originators change their names so often it was impossible to tell who the man was talking about. It could have meant anyone or anything.

They told the tale to Leah, who got very agitated.

"Are you telling me," she said to her husband, "that you were protecting yourself but not Li-Don?"

"Wife," he started to say, to protest and defend himself, but decided against it.

"He could not," Li-Don said. "There was no warning."

"That's the trouble with all of your protective gadgets, isn't it. You have to have the presence of mind to expect danger in order for them to work."

Her remonstration over, she turned her attention to Li-Don's wound. She and one of the servants dressed the wound with ethyl alcohol and clean bandages. "You," she pointed at Li-Don. "Old man, you stay in bed. And you, husband, go get something to eat and meet me up there."

Everyone did as they were told. Hyim arrived in Li-Don's room with plums and crusty bread, and they ate lightly while telling Leah more about what happened.

"What does this mean?" she asked.

"It means," Li-Don said, "there are now more dead, and we're still in the dark."

"Why is it so important to know who you are dealing with?"

"Because," Hyim said, "if we know who it is, we will know how to stop them." Hyim turned to Li-Don. "I can't condone violence of any sort. I am grateful that you showed up when you did, and your methods did seem to lead to the appropriate ends..."

"My violent behavior was strictly defensive in nature," Li-Don said quickly. "I am proud of the way I acted, and I would do it again. You have always been a pacifist, Hyim. I have had to compensate for it. I am just glad that I was finally able to be useful in such a manner."

Leah put her hand up. "I can't stop debate," she said. "But I *can* stop this intellectual bickering. We must be focused on the important tasks. You said there was a telegraph in that shack. Who was sending the signals? Can you follow the wire back to its source?"

"We can look at a map of the wire infrastructure to see where it leads. I didn't see any wire poles, but I must admit I was not looking for them and became distracted quickly."

"Why a telegraph?" she asked. "Why not a telephone?"

"Telephones are not widespread," Li-Don said. "We were far out into the country."

"But surely the people behind all this have enough money to set up their own telephone lines."

"And telegraph lines, for that matter."

"A telephone exchange requires a switching operator," Leah said. "Maybe they didn't want to risk a third party listening in."

"Or maybe," Li-Don said, "they didn't want to reveal the sound of their voices. The inflections, the accents, the timbre."

"We need to find out who is sending those messages," Leah said. "Tell me we can do that without getting shot at."

"If we're careful," Hyim said.

"Or if we know the right people," Leah said.

The following Monday, Hyim and Leah drove into Newark, just across the river. Leah made a big show of her purple driving suit and goggles ("Just like Harriet Quimby, poor girl"), a smile on her face nearly the entire way, despite herself. Driving made her feel free of the constraints in her daily life and work. "It's not the same as being on a horse," she said. "Everyone expects women to ride horses sidesaddle. But no one expects a woman to drive a car differently. Or fly a plane differently for that matter."

When they got downtown, she used her contacts in city government to get access to the map of telegraph and telephone wires over the entire northern third of the state. The map showed the major and minor lines between metropolitan areas. Lines within cities were not shown—it was a map of rural penetration in the telephone and telegraph market. A thin web of threads spread out from metropolitan areas through the countryside and to other metropolitan areas. There were many holes and some communities and townships were bypassed altogether. Hyim remembered vividly the road they took to follow the other cars and saw it on part of the map.

"That's where we were. I'm sure of it."

"There's nothing out there, according to this. Look, here, this is your fork in the road and this is your forest. But there are no wires of any kind leading into this area, or even any planned for it."

"This means it was a private line," Hyim said. "Set up exclusively for this purpose, no doubt."

"We should go there."

"I was thinking the same thing, but it would likely be dangerous. I estimate a 70% chance of danger."

"The danger, being shot at? Because we could just go for a drive. You two apparently took the roundabout route, because it looks like it's not that far from here."

Leah made a rough map of the region, gave the map back to the clerk, and then headed out with her husband into the wilds of northern New Jersey.

Though the engine was still loud enough to drown out any other noises, it was relaxing enough. Conversation with Leah was impossible because she had such a tiny voice. He imagined what the conversation would be like. It immediately made him think of having children. For all of their technological achievements, the problem of having children still eluded the Originators. What was it Jimmy had said of sex? He found it to be *repugnant*, an animal act of uncontrolled fury. *Distasteful* might have been a better word for what he described. Hyim felt no such distaste. It made him wonder if that was a cultural distinction rather than a genetic one. He shared their revulsion towards violence—which was probably something genetic—but not towards sex. That was interesting.

The infusions they had to take to remain alive long enough to see the fruits of their long-term project made conception biologically impossible. The micro-process that caused normal cells to resist division also caused gamete cells to resist division. A fetus was not possible without such growth. And neither was cancer, or bacterial or viral infection. Curiously, hair and nails still grew, although at a slower rate. Food and water intake (and

excretion) was intact; breathing, reflexes, pulse rate, and other signs of life were still intact; and a general sense of being human was still there (something Hyim knew, but other Originators did not).

But children were out of the question. He thought of how his mother must have felt going off the infusions to become a mother. He didn't know if he could ever talk to Ezra about it.

This is what he thought of as the trees whipped by, as the lazy gnats rushed past his closed mouth and goggled eyes, engulfed by the dust behind them.

When they got to a part of the landscape he recognized, he began pointing to let Leah know which way to turn. They came to the familiar sharp turn into the forest, and Leah took that switch-backed road more slowly. With the engine popping and grinding at a lower speed, they could hear each other.

"Is this where you heard the other... the other one?" Leah asked.

"Yes. That might be more of a mystery than the one we're investigating. "They came to the lonely shack just outside the forest. Leah pulled up and stopped the engine.

Hyim got out and began locating his previous movements.

"There was a body here, and here, and here... And this is where Li-Don was shot... The car was over there." He crouched on the ground and pulled his hands up in front of him, imitating a gun. "The shot came from here, right next to the car." He visualized the angle in his mind, imagining Li-Don's back was to him.

"Get out of the dirt, Hy," Leah said. "We have work to do."

He sheepishly got up and they quietly entered the shack. Hyim didn't notice any telegraph wires outside the building. They could have been buried, or the signals could have been from radio, or the whole thing could have been a lie.

The inside of the shack was dimly lit from one window on the far side. It was empty except for a layer of dust that came up in piles here and there. It smelled like still air. He hadn't expected to find anything, but he thought there might be some kind of clue as to where the messages (if they existed) were coming from.

Leah stepped lightly, delicately over the dust, barely making a sound on the wooden floor. "Does this look like a lot of dust to you?" she asked. "With the window and door closed there shouldn't be drifts of it like this."

"There were at least five people in here two days ago. Where are their footprints?"

"Someone's trying to make it look like no one has been here in ages."

"But why scatter dust? Why not just take the whole thing down and cart it away?"

Hyim brushed aside some of the dust with his foot, then began brushing it all toward the edges of the room. Down on all fours, he swiped it around, looking for something on the bare floor. Flurries of particulates filled the air, and Leah had to step outside to get a breath.

But Hyim found what he was looking for. "There's a trap door, wife!" he yelled out the door.

He hastily flipped it open and peered inside. A spiral staircase led downward into the darkness.

"Don't do anything foolish," Leah said as he took the steps down.

Chapter 45

Hyim took down some of the dust with him, and as his eyes adjusted to the light, he saw it start to cover the dirt floor in swirls. Just as he expected, there was a telegraph in one corner, sitting on a roll-top desk like a praying mantis. He checked the rest of the room for anything that might be a trap, running his hands along the walls and scanning the area around the desk for anything. But everything was as it seemed. Curious. Why would someone go to all the trouble of sprinkling too much dust on the floor, just to hide something that could easily have been completely dismantled? Maybe it was a trap.

"Leah?" he called up.

No answer.

"Leah? LEAH!"

Still no answer.

He raced back to the stairway and climbed up, his heart pounding. How could he have been so stupid? This genius (as everyone called him) of the physics world was duped by a band of know-nothing, gun-toting, shit-loading...

Leah's head popped into the doorway above him. "What, what's the matter?"

Hyim stopped. Panic was not altogether foreign to him, but it was not something he took great pride in when it happened. He slumped on the fifth step up.

"What is it? What did you find?" Leah asked.

His chest heaved. He gradually regained his composure. "It's a telegraph, just like he said."

"Ooh. I want to see."

"No," Hyim said. "Don't come down." But, she was already half-way down the staircase. He was about to say, *It could be dangerous*, but they were past that, now. He thought of the possibility that someone could come along and close the door above them, entombing them in that little space. He met Leah on the stairway, and they squeezed past each other, Leah smiling demurely. "Naughty boy," she said.

Hyim took a lookout post halfway out of the doorway while Leah looked around. "There's some movement down here," she said. "The air isn't stagnant." Hyim heard some rustling. "The telegraph wire disappears into a hole down here. That's where the air is coming from. How are we going to follow that wire to its source if it's all underground?"

Hyim, who had not yet recovered from his earlier shock, could not think of a way. "Maybe we should find the man named Carerra."

"Or Vic. Which is it, again?"

"He said both names."

"That's leading us nowhere. We need to find a way to follow this wire back to the source."

"It can't be very far. The ground appears undisturbed." Hyim thought for a minute. "Which direction is it going into the wall?"

"West."

"So let's assume for the moment that the wire comes straight from the source..."

"...All we would need to do is head west until we find something."

"That's not entirely accurate, wife. There could be many twists and turns. Depending on how far away the source is, one degree of difference in the bend could mean a trajectory miles away from the target."

"But how could they have laid this much wire without having

dug up everything around here?

"The wire could be thirty or forty years old for all we know. And for all we know, this whole operation could have been here for that long. Or it could have been threaded from underground, leaving the surface completely undisturbed."

"Regardless, how do you follow a wire that's ten feet under the ground?"

Hyim pulled himself out of the trap door and back up into the shack. He tried to picture the line reaching from the edge of the basement out into the wilderness. It was a meadow of drying grasses and spiked flowers that disappeared into shrubbery in the distance. He pictured in his mind the snaking trail of the wire from parts unknown and thought hard about its properties. What was it about the wire that made it detectable?

"I know just what we need," he said aloud, almost to himself.

He hurried back to the Stutz to get the electronic ear. It was basically a device that detected the disturbance of the surrounding air in the form of sound waves. That would have to be modified for the detection of electrical field beneath ten or twelve feet of packed dirt (which presented its own magnetic field problems). He started bending some of the posts on the sound-catching dish to make them more receptive to magnetic fields.

His theory was that the magnetic field created by the wire would cause the iron in the posts to vibrate at specific frequencies, which could then be translated into noise from the dish. The only issue now was...

"Hy?" Leah said, emerging with a confused look on her face..

"Hmm?"

"Hy?"

"Yes. Yes. What is it?"

"I just thought you should know there's someone standing behind you."

Hyim, startled, whipped his head around. The figure was familiar, although his fedora and long coat made him look more rugged than he remembered. The face was Originator without a doubt; it was Brightferry, that man of stories and platitudes who had sent the Hopewells on their route to initiation.

"I don't think," he began, "that you should be doing what you're about to do."

Hyim blinked and looked back at Leah. His mind processed the presence of this intimidating force in their lives in a very short time, then moved on with the passive-aggressiveness of a younger relation. Hyim felt like this man was his uncle in some kind of despotic royal family and did not have the inclination to render to him the respect that a distant prince or duke might otherwise command.

"What is it," he said to Leah while turning back to Brightferry, "that we're about to be doing, my little cherry blossom?"

"We are trying to find out who has been destroying our personal property," Leah said from behind him.

Brightferry, always one for theatrics, stood above him with his leather-gloved hands folded like a woodcut of Kit Carson without the rifle. "And then?" he said.

"And then stop them," Hyim said.

"I suppose you're going to offer them cash or a bank cheque or just dazzle them with your cheap magic and hope they're afraid enough to back down."

"I'm taking this one step at a time. You can't have quail for dinner if you don't leave the kitchen."

Brightferry looked like he was refusing to smile. "Why are you trying so hard to find out? You must know who is behind all this."

"I'm not so sure. Our friend has his moments of evil, but guns for hire just isn't his style."

Hyim busied his hands with trying to convert his listening tool into an electrical tool, but Brightferry grabbed Hyim's arm.

"There's something you should know before you continue on this way..." he started to say, but trailed off, letting go of Hyim's arm. "Our friend no longer calls himself Ptolemy," he said, his tone changing. "He's having everyone call him *Cronos* now."

"You people..." Hyim said.

"It's getting to be time for the two of you to change *your* names."

"Well, that's lovely," Leah said sarcastically. "Membership in your club does come with its prices, doesn't it."

Brightferry paused and looked her directly in the eye. "The primitives are progressing rapidly in their technology, Mrs. Hopewell. I am sure you are aware of their image collection boxes?"

"You mean box cameras?"

"They are a threat to us. To all of us. The greatest defense we have is anonymity. Any of our images captured and archived can be used against us later."

"Defense from what?" Hyim said with exasperation.

"They still harbor their primeval superstitions. Our technology will appear as magic to them."

"You people. You still speak of them like they were a heterogeneous hegemony of wild asses. I'll grant you there are plenty of asses on the plains. But there are also thinkers, philosophers, engineers, poets, progressives, and scientists. Some of the most intelligent and visionary humans there ever were are on the planet right now. People like Albert Einstein, who I met some years ago..."

"Originator."

"Pardon?"

"This Einstein person. He's in our rolls. He is half Originator."

"Surely you're joking."

"He's quite famous, too, from what I gather. You realize, that should have been you. Research papers, progression of science, international acclaim. We had that and more planned for you."

"You people are supposed to stay away from us. That was the deal."Brightferry smiled. "I'm sure it was. Hmm. So you think it wasn't our friend Cronos. If it is someone else, the outcome is completely out of our control. This anonymity I speak about. It is critical to the cause. Do you understand?"

"I know what's involved."

"So you know that this is all temporary. Everything around you and your concept of it. This dusty shack will be demolished. The trees outside will die if they're not cut down first. Even that wire that you say you've found underground will eventually degrade and decompose. And the Hopewells..."

"We know what's at stake," Leah said. "It's been made perfectly clear. These... these infusions we take are like a drug that dilutes our good judgment and binds us to you. And I'm only alive because of them. Do you know what that does to me? I could have died by random chance. Lucky me, I have a disease for which there is no cure. But now, I have to make the conscious choice of searing my skin with God knows what or that random disease becomes a certainty. And you are the price I pay for wanting to save myself from that painful death."

"You see that?" Brightferry said to Hyim. "That's a human being subjected to our technology. She feels imprisoned by it because she can't accept it. And she can't accept it because she doesn't agree with its developers. Think of how the general population will look at us!"

Hyim went back to his device, bending a thin rod with his hand. "You sound like our friend," he said. "You haven't defected, have you?"

"Such things are irrelevant. This is an issue that affects both sides. If one of us is exposed, we all are. And the other side is even more concerned about this than we are. Don't forget, it's their side that wants to pack up and go on their way."

"I still don't know why you're here," Hyim said. "All you people should be back up in Molineau."

Brightferry paused, then looked toward Leah, who had emerged and was now standing indignantly amid the dust.

"Mrs. Hopewell, you've been photographed."

Chapter 46

"Is that all?" Leah fumed. "Someone took my picture?"

"Took it and published it in a newspaper," Brightferry said. "You were standing on the steps of a New York City building with your mayor and other officials. This increases our exposure unnecessarily."

"Surely images have appeared before."

"Never."

"I... I must have been in the background... This is absurd! No one is going to make the leap from that picture..." She trailed off.

Everyone was thinking the same thing now. The Hopewells would one day very soon have to disappear. Disappear and become...? Yet again, they were reminded of this, and in the harshest way. *No one is going to make the leap from that picture to one of the future selves that must be assumed.*

"I came here to remind you that the best defense is anonymity," Brightferry said. "If you discover the people behind this wire, you are jeopardizing that. Ask yourself what the greater cause is. Ask yourself what you would do if you were me. Ask yourself how rational you are being. You are allowing your emotional— primitive—side to control your actions. Your wife has no choice. She *is* a primitive. But you, you have this life as a gift from your people. No, wait. That's not quite right. It's not a *gift*. It's a *responsibility*. You asked everyone to leave you alone, and we have. But how much of your responsibility are you actually trying to fulfill? What is the technology you're working on? Defense mechanisms, listening devices, tinkering with automobiles... And for what? For your own personal satisfaction..."

"Safety. My own personal safety. Mine and my family's."

"You weren't supposed to have a family. Regardless, you asked us for your free will and we gave it to you. But you are misusing it. You must remember the cause. Integration. That is the cause. Not dominion, not servitude, not just plain survival. The cause is to bring this planet to our level, not to allow them to drag us down to theirs. This recriminatory action you pursue is a distraction from that cause."

"Are you through?"

"Quite. For now."

"Because someone is clearly orchestrating these attacks. And as long as we sit back and let them attack us, we are losing ground on any technology we might produce. Is that clear enough for you?"

"That's just a rationalization."

"You're wrong. Why is it that everyone thinks Ptolemy is behind this?"

"Cronos."

"Be that as it may. We're talking about the same strange figure. And though he is strange, he is not stupid. If he really wanted to stop me, he would have *stopped* me. He wouldn't have *discouraged* me as these people are doing. He would have put an end to everything I've tried to do. It's the difference between war and terrorism."

"But there's..."

"And one other thing," Hyim cut him off. "Why do you have this impatience now? You've been doing this for a long time, and there's never been a question of patience. Why not let me go at my own speed?"

"This planet has changed a great deal since you were born. The feudal societies are vanishing. True scientific progressiveness is sweeping the world. People can talk to one another and exchange information rapidly from place to place. The rate of change in this effect has gone up dramatically. As has the rate of danger. The primitives are getting more intelligent more rapidly than was predicted. They're just not getting smarter about it."

"I don't follow."

"In addition to warning you about exposure, I am also warning you that international tensions are high. The smallest diplomatic insult could set off a conflagration whose scope would engulf most of Europe."

"Well good riddance to the Old World."

"This is not the time for flippancy. We must mobilize and stop the primitives from destroying everything we've built."

"I suppose you've come all the way out here to tell me I have to go with you."

"You misunderstand me. I could have told you that anywhere. I came out here to save myself two trips." Brightferry started walking away. "Follow me," he said over his shoulder, "if you must know who is behind your attacks."

Hyim and Leah exchanged glances.

"It's not far. Just beyond those trees. It shouldn't take more than twenty minutes."

"What? You know? You've known all along?" Leah shouted.

"Occupational hazard," he said.

"Just tell us."

"You have to see for yourselves."

Leah shrugged and they started following him. Hyim took along his newly manipulated electronic ear, although it was essentially useless if there was no current in the telegraph wire—he hadn't yet solved that problem.

"I don't mind telling you that my in-laws are very frustrating," Leah said as they walked. "All these secrets. And not just secrets, mind you, from the rest of humanity, which I understand completely. What about the secrets from each other? Different sects, runaway factions, Byzantine plots... why must there be so much intrigue?"

They walked a while longer until they came to the shallow line of trees that separated one meadow from another. And on the other side of the trees, they saw their enemy.

It wasn't a large building by any means, it was maybe four or five stories tall. Gray stone cast a shimmer in the afternoon sun. The sign out front read "Snyder Oil Company."

"What's all this about?" Hyim asked, dumbfounded.

"This is humanity's version of the future of humanity," Brightferry answered. "Create a need within the population, then fill that need."

"I don't get it. Are you saying that Ptolemy... pardon me, *Cronos* owns this company?"

"Far from it. He has no use for companies that operate among primitives."

"I don't understand. Are you admitting that our friend has nothing to do with this?"

"Not at all. The fact is, I don't know what these people have against you, but I'm sure our friend is involved somehow."

"How can we trust you to know this is true?" Leah asked.

"A very fine question from a suspicious woman. I found out about four days ago. I was coming to visit you two to warn you about your little photography session. Little did I know that someone else had come to visit you to set fire to your storage shed. Like you, I was curious about who it was. So I followed them."

"I notice you didn't help put the fire out."

"Your gratitude is appreciated. I followed them here. For some reason, they went directly from your house to this business. Money was exchanged, then they left. They weren't very careful about any of this. They didn't check to see if they were being followed, they didn't check to see if they were being watched. Very sloppy."

"And their tactics are not very effective," Hyim said.

"On the contrary. It's a brilliant ploy. Whoever is behind this has made absolutely certain that you concentrate your efforts on engineering defense mechanisms for your personal safety, instead of on something else."

"Something else?"

"It's obvious. They're preventing you from true innovation for the integration of the races by occupying you with strategic attacks."

"That's crazy."

"It's worked, hasn't it?"

"Oh, for the love of God!" Leah said. "Have you no sense of humanity? You speak of us all like we were pieces on a chessboard."

Hyim's mind raced. Was it worth it to ask Brightferry what an oil company had to do with anything? Assume for the moment that Ptolemy... *Cronos* was somehow in the shadows of this company, controlling it or influencing it in some way. To what purpose? If he wanted to sabotage Hyim's work, there were much more effective ways. This left out altogether the fact that de Meurre was part of the agreement with the other Originators to leave his family alone unless there was a crisis. Was there a crisis? Brightferry said something about the "tensions" in the Old World. That had nothing to do with him. And even if it did, how would organizing small, tiny, *miniscule* raids against him solve anything? Probability = 3%.

Next, assume for the moment that this oil company in some way held a personal vendetta against him or his family. It's possible that Ezra made some enemies among the primitives in his work. Diamond mining, oil mining. There may have been a clash somewhere along the way. But if that was true, why the secrecy? Why didn't he just get a letter from the oil company trying to resolve some sort of inherited dispute? Since Hyim had assumed control of the diamond enterprise (or, rather had it assumed upon him), there had been no messages from anyone trying to feel him out for his attitude towards them—this is what he would have expected in any organization that was changing leadership. Probability = 8%.

Next, assume for the moment that Brightferry was lying. That the oil company had nothing to do with it. There were a number of reasons he could have had for steering them in the wrong direction. But it would be so simple to prove it wrong (and Hyim now knew how to do so). Brightferry would have known that there would be a need for proof, so his only benefit would be to momentarily distract him from something, whatever that might be. He was doing a good

enough job of distraction with the "tensions" in the Old World story, why further compound it with the suspicious narrative of following people and spying on hands exchanging money? Probability = 5%.

Thusly, assuming that the conflict was not personal, was not business, was not part of some Cronos-inspired plot, and was not just a figment of Brightferry's brain, where did that leave him?

When Cronos was Ptolemy, he had said he would be enlisting the services of primitives to make sure Hyim didn't break the rules of their agreement (or something like that). Assume the oil company was a part of this enlistment. Was it possible that this agreement contained some kind of apocalyptic scenario—of which Hyim was the instigator—that frightened the oil company primitives to the point where they took matters into their own hands? If so, clearly Ptolemy/Cronos had warned them not to kill anyone, but anything else was fair game. If true, their strategy of distracting him from the true Originator cause actually *was* working, as Brightferry had said. However, if that was true, they must know what the cause was working towards, and, by corollary, they must know exactly how they should be going about achieving the cause. If not, how would they know that building a technology bracket for defense was not a part of the cause? But, now, how was it possible that these people knew what his true purpose was, and he himself did not know? Probability = 38% and rising.

Trying to figure out what was going on should have been a zero-sum game. That is, all of the probabilities should have added up to 100. What was he missing?

"This mobilization," Hyim said. "You were coming to get us in order to join you there?"

"Join. Yes," Brightferry said. "But I won't force you. There are some things you obviously need to work out for yourselves. You have free will."

"Damn right," Leah said.

Hyim turned to her. It was the first swear word he had ever heard her say. She put her hand to her mouth as if shocked that such a thing could emerge from it.

Chapter 47

It wasn't as if he had never thought about his "higher purpose". Entire books were filled with such thoughts from rulers to poets to peasants. And it wasn't as if he wanted to abandon the "legacy" (as it was so inelegantly put) of his race. But clearly someone was waging a war of attrition with him. He could see that now. The attrition was not of troops, but his own will, his own morale. They were trying to break him down, trying to force him into a mindset of expecting what was coming next and mitigate its effects. They were trying to occupy his time with something that did not threaten them.

Some years earlier, he remembered reading about the motors inside various modes of transport. They each had their own pluses and minuses. Steam was fine for locomotives and ships because they could make up for the weight of the fuel with the power of the steam. But cars were too small to make up the difference in torque.

Electricity was fine for powering small rotors or magnetic fields in wires. But the power required by cars was too great to make it practical. So far, the only practical applicable fuel was refined oil, the major drawback being that it smelled awful. But it was inexpensive, there were yet-untapped reserves, and it was convenient. Unlike steam, there was no need to carry separate fuel, water, and a chamber for burning. Unlike electricity, there was no need for an outside source of power. It was a self-contained, highly portable material.

The real problem with petrol was the refining process. Making oil into something usable took time and chemical energy, and could only be done on a large scale in order to be economically feasible. As such, the refining made sense only for large-scale enterprises. The larger the enterprise, the better the economy of scale. Already the oil industry was experiencing growth at a geometric pace, and already the Federal government had to step in because it was growing too fast.

Hyim had never really given the matter much thought. He liked cars. He liked the sound of the engine and the wind rushing past him on a smooth road. The smell of gasoline was not altogether unpleasant (although the exhaust stank like mucky swampland). The vicarious power he could feel from the accelerator pedal gave him a sense of being one of the primitives if only for that moment when the wheels underneath him responded to his command.

It gave him pause.

The power he felt made him feel more human and less human at the same time. Although he tinkered with his engines to make them more efficient, he had never taken the time to dissect how the engines were tinkering with him, how they were making him more or less efficient. It was a kind of intoxication. He was focused on mechanical power instead of brainpower.

This was his revelation. His enemies did not want him to stop inventing or innovating or even reasoning out solutions to problems. They merely wanted him to take a different path, apply his technical knowledge and expertise in an area that not only did not threaten them, but had the potential to aid them.

He stood there on a small bluff overlooking this oil company building, taking the time to formulate what his enemy was after and why. They thought something was going on. But there was only one thing that would have caused them to wage guerilla warfare against him. If it was oil they were trying to protect, then it was him they were protecting it from. For some reason, they thought he was on a path to create an energy source that would directly compete—and then overtake—their oil resources.

This was such a simple proposition that he wondered why he hadn't thought of it before.

He looked over at Leah. He could not help thinking that she was supposed to be dead. All of his protection schemes were for her. All of his technology breakthroughs were done so that she would be safe. It was technology that was keeping her alive. He wondered: if she *had* died, would he be on a different course? Was that what his father had planned for him?

"You must remember," Brightferry said. "You have free will."

Free will. Free will. In an instant, Hyim had the answer. He grabbed Leah's hand and headed back to the Stutz. "Start without me," he said to Brightferry. Then he took his wife and they marched, drove, and stormed back in to their house in Manhattan.

"That didn't take long," Li-Don said, greeting them from the top of the stairs.

"We're back in business," Hyim said.

It was a simple process, really. The power generated by the various emitters around his house was produced not through some mechanical process, but through a thermodynamic process at a sub-atomic level. The actual power produced in terms of watts was not very much, but the effect was larger than the measurable power.

By combining three emitters aligned at 120° angles to one another, he was able to create a mechanical rotation force that could drive anything that was able to translate rotary power. It was a solution that had been staring at him all along, but he had refused to see it because he was not defining the problem. The binding and repelling action of these sub-nuclear particles worked not only as a solid in a defined plane of space; it also worked as an artificial force which, when applied to other emitter fields, enhanced the forces to such a degree that they caused the emitter devices themselves to undergo physical motion. This process was curiously cumulative. That is, the incremental changes in the energy of the particles—because of the peculiar nature of the field—made the total mechanical energy increase over time. The only way to keep a constant speed was to slowly and gradually power down the emitters, something which had to be done from a remote location. He also had to design a new type of rotor mechanism that he could mount the emitters onto, so it wouldn't overheat.

295

It took him a month of eighteen-hour days to get the process correct and manageable, and another two weeks to fit his car with his new power generator. He worked in a decrepit-looking shack about a mile from his house, hoping that the look of it would deter any would-be saboteurs. He was suspicious because no one had been back to try and stop him any longer. When he was satisfied with the way his apparatus worked in the car, he brought Leah and Li-Don to the site.

"What are you going to call it?" Li-Don asked.

"You name it this time."

"It appears to me to use simple mechanical centripetal force. And yet the energy involved comes from the supercharging of hydrogen atoms."

"If I understand this correctly," Leah said, "it works because you've created a perfectly insulated chamber in which you increase the energy."

"Yes, that's right. The three fields overlap one another causing both unlimited friction and thermal insulation."

"This is Jimmy's coffee cup," she said. "In a perfectly insulated chamber, you can control the way substances behave. Do you remember?"

Hyim had to admit that he hadn't remembered that conversation.

"It was your dissertation. He was just taking it to its logical extreme."

"This sounds like it should mean something," Li-Don said.

Chapter 48

The meeting was scheduled for 11:00 AM, local time in the underground chamber at *Place du Trône* near Reuilly. It was a crisp summer morning on the ship going over to Bretagne. A few clouds floated overhead mixing with the steam exhaust from the ship's funnels. They were already several weeks late, but Jimmy— who stayed in Canada—said the meeting would be going on for months, until tensions had subsided.

Hyim arranged to have the Stutz shipped over as well, so he could demonstrate his invention. He wasn't sure what it meant just then, but he knew it would be something no one had tried before. If they had, things might be different even then.

"It is interesting," Li-Don observed, "that you decided to create the one thing your enemies were trying to prevent you from creating."

"I don't know that for sure. It's only an 82% probability."

Hyim felt a twinge—just a twinge—of panic. Not panic, exactly. It was more like anticipation of dread. He would be seeing his father again. There were still so many unresolved issues between them, not the least of which related to his identity. There were other problems also. His mother, dying needlessly for some unknown purpose; the eugenics plan for the human race, and exactly how that was carried out (it was something he never mentioned to Leah or Li-Don, fearing their disapproval would taint his own investigation); and the exact reasons for the Originator migration to this particular world. They were questions he did not want to ask. They were parts of conversations that had already taken decades to work themselves out, with little progress.

He had a renewed sense of *destiny*, whatever that meant. He still didn't feel comfortable with that label. He was sure that his invention of the *centripetal hydrostatic field emission generator* and its application to a native primitive machine would be received enthusiastically by all sides (he rejected Li-Don's moniker of the *Hopewell Drive*—if for no other reason than *Hopewell* was an ephemeral name).

Being on a ship meant time spent doing nothing. Jimmy was right. If people knew it were possible to make such a trip in a week, they would expect nothing less. So Hyim, Leah, and Li-Don had that week to be apart from the rest of the world, to enjoy each other's company, and to catch up on reading. But it wasn't the same to be on a ship like that anymore. In their minds was the still fresh taste of the tragedy of an immense ocean liner that went down in the north Atlantic almost two years earlier. The crew made sure everyone knew where the lifeboats were, and everyone was assigned a life jacket. The Titanic had been billed as unsinkable, but its representation of technological progress was hindered by the primitives' inability to wield that power correctly. It was very discouraging for the cause, because it was more proof that they were unprepared for the Originators.

About halfway through the trip, the engines of their ship changed their pitch abruptly. It was in the middle of dinner, and the patrons felt it in their chairs and heard it in the jingling of silverware and spilled drinks. There was a short lurch to port, then a continuous mechanical whine from below deck. The ambient noise got louder as people started to speculate about what was going on.

"We're turning," Li-Don said. "This ship is heading in a different direction."

"I can feel it, too," Hyim said. "We're turning back."

Someone from another table overheard him. "Turning back? Are you sure?"

"The rudder has moved 12 degrees and the left engine has slowed down. We will be heading back towards New York in about twenty minutes."

"Oh my. How could you possibly know that?"

"I can tell by the sounds and by the motion of the deck."

Leah pulled on his arm. "Why would we be heading back home?"

"It's a problem either with the ship or with the destination."

"Maybe we've run out of gruyère," Li-Don said, smiling. Then he lowered his voice a little. "Perhaps France has gone to war," he said.

People around them gasped. Li-Don realized he hadn't lowered his voice enough. "I wasn't serious," he said to them. But the concern on his face showed. He leaned in towards Hyim and lowered his voice more. "Perhaps your friends have failed in their mission."

"Honestly," Leah said. "It could be nothing more than an iceberg. For goodness sakes. The two of you are such pessimists."

But Li-Don's words clearly struck a chord with everyone in the room, especially Hyim. It wasn't so farfetched an idea that the ship's radio operator could receive a message that France had declared war. The Hapsburgs had just declared war on Serbia as they were leaving. But surely France would let the matter rest in the Balkans. That region had seen its share of troubles.

"I'm going to find out what's going on," Hyim said, getting up.

"No," Leah said. "The two of you stay here and finish dinner. Reconnaissance is a job best left to a woman." Then she delicately placed her napkin on her chair and strode out of the room.

His wife's grace and self-assurance gave Hyim a picture of her in his mind as a sexual object of desire. He watched her leave, as did many of the men in the room. Her diminutive feminine form in her dinner dress had much the same effect on all of them. But it

only served to remind Hyim of his diminished sexual appetites. Leah had felt it, too. It was one of the physical effects that started with the infusions. He had not discussed it with other Originators, and it was the most distressing. He and Leah had discussed it a little, but only to the extent that they felt it in the same way. It distressed him greatly that he rarely longed for his wife just because she was there. It was usually some show of femininity that made him want to take her to bed, and then only occasionally. Her perpetual youth only made this more poignantly ironic. Leah did not discuss when she felt this way about him. More correctly, he had never brought it up.

He guessed it had something to do with the production of gametes, and probably with the cells of the blood, or maybe it was some autonomic nervous system depression.

The dining room was not an appropriate location to show such intimate appreciation, however. Hyim ordered two desserts, an *aperitíf*, and coffee, trying to delay having to leave the room. Other patrons had already left, and the immediate area around them had cleared.

The appetite for food had suffered no ill effects. And, in fact, tastes seemed to grow more and more refined—or perhaps *subtle* was a better word. Food that seemed much too salty or heavy with spice for Li-Don to find palatable was exquisite to Leah and Hyim. (Although, to be fair, Li-Don had always preferred plain potatoes, noodles, rice, and boiled poultry). Hyim ordered a cherry cinnamon pastry and a *glacée á menthe* that reminded him of the effect that Hungarian peppers had on his tongue.

Li-Don, who had nothing but Turkish coffee, eyed him throughout the latter part of the meal like someone watching a precocious child learning to play Mozart on the piano. "The taste of honey belies its own sweetness," he said.

"I'm not sure I know what that means."

"Wordsworth said that we can only appreciate music after it is over. He likens it to a castle whose grandeur we cannot comprehend while we are inside. We must see it from the outside to place it in context with our experience."

"Are you saying that I eat with no subtlety?"

"I am saying that you are so far inside your trifle that you can no longer see the room you are in, nor the meal you have just finished."

"I could argue that this is still part of the meal."

"This only proves my point. You cannot hope to make sense of the meal while you are eating it."

"'Make sense of the meal?' What the devil are you talking about?"

"Forgive me, sir, but I do not think you have a comprehension of how you affect your own experience of the food." Li-Don picked up the end of his cane, maybe unconsciously, and used it as a gesture of emphasis.

"This conversation has suddenly become something other than dessert."

"This conversation has never been about dessert. Listen to some advice from a lifelong friend of yours." He leaned in closer and lowered his voice once more, trying this time not to alarm the few others left in the room. "Leah must remain in her youth in order to survive, in order to beat the disease that will lie perpetually dormant. What is the reason you have chosen to remain this age? And what is the reason you choose to tell yourself? They are not necessarily the same thing."

From anyone else, this would have come as an insult, a direct attack on who he was and his life choices. But coming from Li-Don, he took it seriously. And he was in the mood for a discussion (or *argument*, as Leah would have described it).

"I have the work," Hyim said. "My knowledge. My work is predicated on the knowledge and experience I have gained through my years as a researcher and engineer. There is no one able to do the same work I am doing."

"So you are saying there is also no one who is able to understand the work you are doing, nor capable of taking up where you may leave off should you become incapacitated in some way.

Is it that you are a poor record keeper, a bad teacher, or simply have no faith in those who may come after you?"

"I'll grant you, there is some selfishness in this. But it's only because I want to see the outcomes. I want to be there when the integration starts. I want to see the faces of children who are cured of their ills because of the technology I helped create. It may take years or centuries. Who knows? But that will be my satisfaction."

"You speak of outcomes, yet your actions are that of a man who is merely treading water. Only recently have you begun to explore the possibilities of Originator technology out in the world. And even that only after a crisis moment."

"Are you suggesting that I lack the will for this undertaking?"

"Certainly not. I have seen your stubbornness, even in the face of logic. I am suggesting that you lack *imagination*. You have the intellect of a minor deity compared to the people around you— myself included, I must admit—but what you are blessed with in technical and syllogistic skill, you make up for with a dearth of creativity. Even after all that I have tried to inform you about political realities, you still do not see the broader scope of what is possible."

"I am always learning from you, Li-Don."

"That's very kind, but hardly my point. From what I have seen of your friends—your race, if you like—they are inherently un-creative. They are plodders. They seek to improve the way things work incrementally. They are afraid of dramatic change, yet it is what they have sought all their lives."

"This is what they have learned from history."

"This I understand. Dramatic change is usually violent and met with resistance. From what you have told me, this is their understanding of humanity and why they decided to undergo their grand experiment. However, I am not talking of the limits of pacifism in this way, nor am I talking of the moral disgust I find myself in when I think about what they have tried to accomplish. I am talking about the causes and effects of your decisions. Your own personal decisions."

Li-Don was becoming increasingly belligerent and accusatory. While it was true that Hyim had been focused on other technologies that were not directly a part of the cause, he believed he could still defend himself on moral grounds.

"I am a patient man," he said, giving ground to Li-Don's intellectual broadside. "It wasn't always this way. When I met Leah—shortly afterwards, I mean—I was desperate to marry her. I made the mistake very young of having in my mind a picture of what kind of woman I wanted for a wife. And there she was. I was seventeen. I had my whole life ahead of me, and yet here was this girl—the perfect girl. And still, she is my every imagining of what an ideal woman is. I was impatient to marry her. I am impatient to be with her when she isn't here. I'm sure she would give you a different story..."

"She does."

Hyim laughed. "Yes. I'm positive she does. But the impatience I feel is strictly on this level. I don't even know if you could classify it correctly when you put it next to everything else. Maybe this is the real reason I gave myself for joining her in psuedo-immortality."

"That's honest, at least."

Leah came back into the galley with an ashen look on her face.

"What is it?" Hyim asked, standing. "What's going on?"

"You were right, Li-Don. France is at war. With Germany."

"Well, that explains that."

"No," Leah said as if in a daze. "You don't understand. I spoke with the radio operators. The whole continent is at war. Germany, Russia, England, France, Belgium, Austria-Hungary..."

There was a short silence. "No one knew how it started," Leah said.

"What have they done?" Li-Don asked no one.

Chapter 49

Hyim's hands shook as he removed the emission generator from the Stutz. The power of an emitter lay in its handling of sub-hydrogen particles. Bohr had proved as much with his paper on the structure of atoms. They were little orbital systems, shells within shells like little Russian dolls.

But that model did not answer Hyim's questions about the true workings of emitters. While it was true that the supercharging of hydrogen atoms was merely the overloading of electrons to an intact hydrogen nucleus, that did not fully explain the raw power that was generated from an emitter's containment chamber.

Jimmy and de Meurre sat behind him in his third-floor studio, watching him examine the emitter and talking to one another. Hyim tried to convince himself that he was alone.

"Your oil companies aren't very active today," Jimmy said.

"I don't know how many times I'm going to have to tell you that we have no oil companies," de Meurre said. "I don't know where you get these ideas."

"Thy face is a blank page. I can't tell when you're lying."

"Imagine for the moment that we did have an oil company or two, and we did send these small unprofessional soldiers to pillage one of your storage warehouses. Look how simple it was for you to find out who was behind that. It would be just as simple to connect them to us."

"True. Simple. But, you had not figured on us being one step ahead of you—that is, two steps forward, three back, then four forward."

"Your analogy is specious..."

"Would you two just can it?" Hyim shouted. "The world is at war, and you are responsible. The two of you and everything you represent."

"You give us too much credit and too little faith," de Meurre said. "There is too much randomness in the world for us to be able to accomplish anything anymore. As the world population has increased, the influence we are able to exert has become diluted to the point where we are no longer relevant."

"So says the man who is giving up," Jimmy said. "Don't listen to him. I'll admit, there was a time when we had the world in our hands, so to speak. It's more difficult now, and there are fewer opportunities for real societal change. But we're not at *zero* like my counterpart here would say."

"Point-oh-one is still greater than zero, it's true."

"I've had it," Hyim said. "You two can debate this all you want. I'm getting out of here."

Hyim left by way of the stairs, and joined his wife in the sitting room. She was reading a newspaper. Hyim felt a more defined sadness than he had ever experienced—it was the kind of hopelessness he remembered as a young child watching his mother in pain.

Leah was strangely calm. Sitting there, with her dress falling in decorative, playful cascades down to the floor and a newspaper that wasn't rattling in her hands, she appeared much like a painting. The focus on her face was of someone who has something to say, but was waiting for the right circumstance or else would remain silent.

"Don't mind me," she said. "I'm just the mistress of the house."

He sat down in the plush chair next to her, exhaling loudly. "I'm troubled, wife."

"*Troubled?!* The world's on fire. Myself, I'm *outraged* that those two miscreants are even in my home. I don't care if technically they *are* family."

Hyim felt like an old man. He glanced over at his beautiful wife with her *petite* nose and pursed lips and wondered what he ever did to deserve her. And what did the world do to deserve such acrimony within itself?

"It's not hopeless, is it?" Hyim asked, somewhat offhandedly and blindly.

"The Earth, you mean? Why, of course it's hopeless. There's no doing anything. Look at the way these barbarians have interpreted their own history. They have the temerity to think they are the masters of their own destiny. They somehow feel they are independent from everything else, not a part of anything larger than themselves. Those... those cavemen! Whacking each other with ever larger sticks. If only they were somehow less aggressive... What do you think? How could we accomplish that?"

He knew her display wasn't directed at him, although it was meant for him to hear.

"Pull yourself together," she suddenly growled at him. "You want to give up now, go right ahead. Those primitives surely aren't worth it, are they? As much as I hate to admit this, you have to finish what your fathers and uncles and cousins have started. You. You have to clean up this mess. You. They have repeatedly told you that you are the chosen one. Do you know what it means for a *Jew* to be *chosen*?"

"I don't want that burden!" he shouted at her.

"You have it whether you want it or not, husband. Whether or not either one of us likes it."

"You're asking me to validate all the mistakes they've made."

"First of all, I'm not asking. I don't really care, to tell you the truth. Second of all, it's not about validating the mistakes, it's about fixing them. You have a purpose. It's all laid out for you."

"I don't want a path laid out for me. I want my own path."

"So lay it out! Resisting only wastes time. I don't like it any more than you do, you know that. But if you give up now, there is truly no hope. You say you don't want this burden. That's the problem, isn't it? If you think of it as a *burden*, it will weigh on you until you do something about it. And if you do nothing, it will weigh on you for the rest of your life... I guess that's perilously close to forever, now, isn't it?"

Leah was still calm. She had not raised her voice or even sounded a note of vitriol, and yet it seemed to rise into a crescendo when she spoke. Her measured tone was unnervingly effective.

"The primitives are revolting, sire," she said. "What shall you do? Shall you sit in your garden and sing a lovely tune? Shall you vacate to Versailles?"

"I'm not a king," he said. "I'm just a man. I didn't ask to be given charges or the reins to some kind of economic empire."

"You never had to ask."

"If there was a way for me to get away from all of this, to get out of all of this, I would take it."

"Fine, then. Go with de Meurre back to his Platonic cavemen and bury your head in the stars. Where is the man I married? Lost in his laboratory." At this, she raised her voice. "You don't like the way the world works? Change it, you bloody simpering unidirectional coward!"

She pulled the section of newspaper she was reading over her face to hide her quiet sobs. If he'd ever wondered what she thought of him, he had no doubt now. He crossed his legs and sat back into the plush of the chair, turning away from her.

"Oh, *zisaske!*" she whispered. "I'm sorry. I'm so sorry." She got up from her chair and kneeled at his feet. "I hate it," she said. "I hate what it does to you. I hate what it does to me. I hate what it's been doing to *them*. All of them."

Hyim put his hand on his wife's head and mussed up her hair a little. "*Bubela*," he said. "You're right, of course."

"No... No..." "Yes, it's true." He cleared his throat and shifted in his chair so that Leah's hand was now over one knee. "I've been holing myself up. Walling myself off. I've been striving towards

307

omfort, security. I've allowed us to become defensive and reactive. You knew me once."

"You had initiative."

"I did. If not ambition. There was always a plan. And now... It seems I am merely making the tree more comfortable after the bear has chased me into it." He recalled the escape from the Brightferry estate. "Complacency," he said. "That's the fault of too much patience. Too much watching and waiting. It's the same as giving up in this case. My father had a plan, then he became complacent. The world has moved slowly since it started."

"But now it's speeding up," Li-Don said, appearing in the doorway behind them. He made his way into the center of the room as gracefully as a man with three legs can. He had recently purchased a shimmering cherry-wood cane with a whalebone handle and a brass tip. It was a present to himself for their aborted trip abroad. He had not intended to use it until they got there, and then only for the special occasion of unveiling the Hopewell drive—as he insisted upon calling it. Now he used it as an everyday conversation tool the way some people used cigarettes. It emphasized a point by being a natural gesture.

"I agree with Leah," he said.

"How long have you been standing there?" Hyim asked.

"Long enough. Long enough to know that it's time for the two of you to disappear. You must retreat for the moment, regroup, and start a new offensive; or else retire altogether from the fight."

"That's remarkably Sun-Tzu of you," Hyim said.

"I will help you accomplish any goal you set, for the rest of my days. By now, you should know that. You should also know that

you can trust me. So trust me when I say that there will never be a better time for the Hopewells to vanish than right now, when these wars are in their early stages and chaos is gripping Europe."

"What do you suggest?"

END OF PART III

~ The Originators ~

Part IV

Prologue

The Azores, 1934

Fichelson took a sip of his tea on the veranda of his monstrous home overlooking the ocean and the port of Praia. To be fair, just about every home overlooked the ocean on those tiny spots of land in the middle of the Atlantic. But this house was the largest on San Miguel, having been completed some years before for an ungodly sum of money.

The Earl Grey was bitter. George had allowed the water to boil too long again. The lemon wedge did not help.

Fichelson shouted for George, who did not respond. He shouted again, then made an ungainly attempt to stand up in his bathrobe and tossed the teacup across the stone tiles that separated the civilized world from the wild tropical forest. It shattered and scattered shards of porcelain and tea leaves.

George is new, he thought. *Give him time, and he'll get it right.*

The noise awoke the sparkling blond from her restless sleep. She was naked except for the silk *chinois* top sheet she was curled in.

"Béarnard?" she said with a voice graveled from sleep.

"It's all right," he said. It was just the stress. Everything had been going brilliantly for so long, he was perpetually nervous now. It hadn't always been that way. He used to be a top lieutenant in a vast army until he figured out how to play all sides against one another for his own gain. He hadn't realized all the things that could be accomplished with just the right amount of currency.

Money was the secret to everything, he realized. Power, prestige, women.

Oh, yes, the women. He didn't need to seek them out; they found him. They funneled what they could from him and then someone got bored with someone and there was a separation. He thought he would get tired of it, but that hadn't happened so far.

And now, his days were so tortuously pleasant, so filled with the ecstatic delicacies of everyday living, that he had to wonder when it would all end. Maybe this was the ultimate price that had to be paid for so comfortable a life.

That meeting with all of those unpleasant oil men seemed so long ago—a lifetime, assuming that could be measured accurately. They had seen the object, and he could tell they coveted it. What would they do to get it—or to keep it out of the hands of the competition—beyond the obscene sums of money they had already been giving him?

After fretting about his tea and kissing his female companion on the small of the back—which made her giggle—he shuffled over to grab a fig and a glass of clear juice from a small table on the terrace and sat down in a padded wicker *chaise*.

The woman came out to see where he was. She had slipped on a sheer nightshirt, unbuttoned in the front, without regard to her nakedness in front of him and the view of the sea. The ocean gave way to the land in slow-moving white streaks. The industrial noises from the airstrip being built at Lajes, some ways to the north, could occasionally be heard, but not today. Then the view gave way to the woman, blocking it.

"You did not tell me you played the coronet," she said. Her swallowing accent from western France—just south of Brittany, he thought—was irresistible. God, but he loved young nubile French women. He did not quite hear what she had said, such was his content at being in that spot. He loved hearing her talk; he loved Portuguese cuisine and immature coconut water; he loved the view of the ocean from a far distance. And all these things he now had in the palm of his hand. He let it wash over him.

She had brought out the black canvas, wood, and leather case with a handle. It was shaped roughly like a stiff doctor's bag with a bell shape at one end. The sight of it brought him back to reality.

"Where did you find that?" he asked suspiciously.

"In the back of your closet. I was looking for a shirt of yours to put on."

He smiled. "That was a long time ago," he said.

"Why don't you play something for me?" she pleaded.

"I don't use that thing anymore. It's a part of my past. The breath is gone, anyway. And besides, I have everything I need, right here."

"So you don't want to share it with me?" she pouted.

"There's nothing to share. My skills have dwindled over the years. I don't need it, though, do I?"

"But you've been playing it, haven't you?"

He got angry. "I just told you I haven't. Not for many years."

She withdrew. "I... I just mean you have taken it out of your case."

"No I haven't, you silly, stupid girl." He got up and grabbed the case from her. Instantly, the emotional shock spread through him like tiny icicles in his nervous system. The case was empty. His legs became weak. How long had it been empty? He opened the case to find... nothing.

"Where is it?" he demanded. His panic was rising quickly. The instrument was the source of his power, but not just his power. It was a source of tremendous power for anyone who knew how to use it. "Where did you put it? *Crasseuse souillon! Puteresse!*"

She gasped as he grabbed her by the back of her neck, making her short fluffy hair shudder. Suddenly he wanted to snap that pretty neck, although he knew that would be impossible. "Where is it!"

"*Caisse vide*," she said in a voice tiny with fright and physical pressure. "I found it empty."

In an instant, he knew it was true. His apology tactic towards her flashed through his mind; then he moved on to bigger things. There were only a few people left alive in the world who knew about the *coronet*. But when was it taken? He let the girl go. "Go to the bedroom and stay there!" he snarled at her. She did as she was told.

He opened the case a second time and brushed the insides with his hand. He rebuked himself for becoming lazy, and worst of all, *complacent*.

Chapter 50

Danzig, 1934

Since the Battle of Warsaw, where the Poles pushed back a counter-attacking Soviet force in 1920, many expatriate Poles had made their way back to the motherland. Rebecca Hathaway was no exception. Polish by birth, she had grown up in America, married an American industrialist, and became a generous donor to Polish humanitarian causes.

This was the woman on the other side of the desk from Bronislaw Pieracki, the Polish Minister of the Interior. He had heard of her good will and profligate intentions, and was very deferential towards her. His office was not the largest in Warsaw, nor was it very ornate or impressive. He wanted to meet her in a more suitable environment for such a woman, a standing government office in the Grand Hotel on the Baltic shores of Danzig.

She was younger than he expected. He had heard of her generosity towards Poland that ran back at least fifteen years. Her maiden name was Nadzieja, but the records of her family from the Bialystok District were lost in a fire. All that he could gather was that she maintained a residence near Ustka.

She was very pretty and had an elegant demeanor, in a New World kind of way. Her small nose reminded him of certain Prussian ladies he had known, but those eyes were definitely up-country Slavic farm girl. How the daughter of a rural lands immigrant manage to seduce a wealthy American businessman was startling, to say the least. The fact that he was a Jew certainly must have helped.

Such things he thought before he actually saw her in person. And then the vague stirring deep within his fifty-year-old eros told him all he needed to know. He sat down behind his rented desk as quickly as decorum would allow. They exchanged stilted pleasantries, not

altogether uncomfortable, but with an air of anticipation.

"To what do I owe this immense pleasure?" he said, coughing.

The humidity was high that summer day, all the windows were open to let an intermittent Scandinavian breeze lightly cool the building. He was sweating through his shirt and socks, but the woman appeared distinctly comfortable despite her dark-colored woolen jacket and calf-length dress.

"I have an offer for you," she said.

His pace quickened. "I am anxious to hear it."

"I offer Poland the future."

He blinked. *What did she say?*

"I am involved with an energy company that is looking for a manufacturing venue."

"Um... energy manufacturing? I don't understand. not to be discourteous, madam, but we have our own oil exploration, as I am sure you are well aware."

"Oil is distasteful, *Pan* Pieracki. It is messy, difficult to refine, and has a foul odor. What I am offering is nothing like that."

"Electricity? Some sort of electrical power?"

"Precisely."

"Forgive me, madam, but electricity requires messy, stinky oil and coal."

"The future of electricity is neither oil nor coal." She pulled a small glass box out of her oversized handbag and placed it on his desk. From what he could tell, it was the type of clear glass presentation case that an heirloom egg timer would be kept in. And then, suddenly, it flashed. At first, he thought he imagined it. It was quick, like a lamp being flipped on and off in an instant. But in the place of the flash was a bluish gas cloud floating in the chamber, drifting and dissipating like exploding ordinance.

"A cute toy," he said.

"It's no toy," she replied. "This is a supercharged hydrogen reaction. This is a miniscule portion of the electrical power that a generator the size of this desk can produce."

Pieracki grinned patronizingly.

Rebecca stood up for a moment and removed her jacket. Watching her struggle against her own sleeves was a thing of beauty. It revealed a sleeveless blouse. She, too, was sweating. No... a lady like that *perspired*. His mouth went dry as she unbuttoned the top button on her neck and sat back down. She fanned her face with her small hands.

Collecting himself, he noticed that she also wore two cream-colored armbands on each arm, above the elbows. He recalled the pictures he had seen of the National Socialists in Germany, with their armbands and odd Scandinavian whirligig star. Hers had no such symbols, but he became more wary of her nonetheless. Was this the secret of the National Socialists, the backing of a wealthy Polish woman? The idea seemed preposterous, but stranger things were true. He decided on a gambit.

"Hathaway," he mused. "That's not a Jewish name."

She seemed caught off-guard. "We're Americans, sir. The Jewish Diaspora goes far and wide.

"You women and your odd fashions," he said, trying to sound genial. "What are those things?"

"Oh, please, *Pan* Pieracki. Never ask a woman about her scars."

"Scars? Oh, my poor *sheynah madel*. I am sorry for thinking the things I am thinking."

He protested, but she coquettishly pulled down one of the bands to reveal a roundish healed-over scar. It looked like

316

something an ice-pick might have done. It made her more mysterious and desperately attractive. He found himself at her mercy as she described the process of the little glass of hydrogen something or other.

"I will take this to my government," he said. "I will, of course, make no promises. But, uh... I will fight for this. We will probably ask you for relevant studies, research, independently verifiable science, and so forth."

"Of course," she said. She retrieved her strange egg-timer case and stood up. They shook damp hands, and she took her leave, smiling at him over her shoulder.

He left the hotel in a kind of dream state, picturing Rebecca Hathaway trying to get out of her jacket. His driver took him back to Warsaw that night. He left the windows down until they got farther inland. Arguably the richest woman in Poland had just offered him an opportunity to not only expand his country's infrastructure—if it worked—but also the opportunity to work closely with her on the project. That brought a warm satisfaction to his lips, and he planned to offer it also to his wife that night.

When they reached the city, it was late. The sun was still up, but it was low and most workers had gone home already. He ordered his driver to stop at the Interior Ministry, where he wanted to get some detailed information on the oil wells in *Beskidy Zachodnie*. There was some sort of land dispute with Romania in Carpathians, but that wasn't as combustive as the sort of dispute there was with the dirty Cossacks. Oil was just a commodity, but nationalism was a cultural problem.

He waved to the guards as they let him in the door. The building itself was always a more quiet, eerie place when it was empty. A few secretaries were bustling about. He smiled and winked at them as they passed by, and was unsure if they saw him. The records office was on the third floor. The stairway, with its stark wooden steps surrounded by decorative stone, was chilly and quiet—a welcome change from the damp heat of the morning. Keeping such a stairway between the street and the records was a deliberate attempt to discourage such research and keep everything as stable as possible.

It was impossible to keep things stable. There were too many people with too many interests. It was hard enough keeping track of what was going on within the borders—he couldn't imagine having to monitor the situation in the world. The records office, such as it was, didn't have the transparent preciseness of the Prussian office; nor was it quite as willy-nilly as the mess that was Galizien.

He spent the better part of the evening shuffling back and forth between deeds, mineral rights, and bi-national agreements. Satisfied with what he found, he stuffed some papers into an expanding folder and headed back downstairs. There was no one around except the guards at the door.

He told his driver to take him home. The road was rough from lack of civic attention. There were other pressing matters. He sifted through the folder to find something, but it was too dark. He pulled a flashlight from the seat compartment below to get a better look. As he bent down to retrieve it, he heard a shot. An instant later, he heard broken glass, the buzzing air around him. Some shouts in what sounded like Ukranian. Then the night air was filled with the peppered sounds of gunfire.

Chapter 51

Nánjīng Dà Túshā , 1934

Jian Ziwei didn't think of himself as an important member of his family. He was the third son of a minor diplomat, fourth child overall, who had no wish to serve in any government capacity. His older brothers had joined the Kuomintang against the Japanese and the Communists, and he could feel the pressure from his family, especially his mother, to join also. Local merchants and tradesmen made a little bit of money, but soldiers in the National Revolutionary Forces kept their families in silks and gilt-rimmed houses. His mother was noticeably envious of her neighbors. Jian's older brothers had not yet sent any money or goods home, and she was becoming anxious.

Jian wanted no such life as the military life, or even the conservative life of a diplomat. He foolishly imagined himself as a scholar of antiquity. He was interested in the islands of Taiwan and Hainan, especially the Gaoshan people of Taiwan, who had been living there for centuries.

He explained all this to his cousin who had arrived from America a few weeks before. His cousin was a sixtyish man with gray streaks in his short hair just above his ears on either side. Although his jowls hung like an older gentleman, he had a youthful appearance and usually wore a cracked smile of almost perfect teeth, something Jian had not seen in an older man before. He walked with a slight limp and held a cane. Sometimes he leaned on it, but Jian thought it was just an affectation.

His cousin, Donald, had never been to China before. He did not speak Mandarin or any other of the Asian languages. Only English. Jian—as well as many other middle sons—learned many foreign languages. None was as satisfying as English, however. The

319

Christian missionaries were only too happy to teach English to Confucians if the Christian Bible were involved.

It was a peculiar time for a foreigner who did not speak the language to arrive. The country was on the brink of civil war. Though, to be fair, it didn't seem like it in that spot of China.

They were walking along a dirt path that wound around a plowed field of onion seedlings. Cousin Donald tapped his cane on a rock. "So this is China," he said.

A noisy crowd of chickens was following them, waiting for either one of them to drop crumbs of something or other.

Jian ate a small orange, dropping the peels and the pith as they walked. Combined with the smell of the tiny onion plants, it made him think of his grandmother's pork rolls.

"It's a lot like Canada," Cousin Donald said.

"Canada," Jian repeated. He had heard of the place. Many Chinese went there when the American immigration quotas had been filled. It was spoken of as an endless series of plains and forested mountains. At 22, Jian was becoming restless with his own country when there were so many tales about this land of the eagles and bears across the Pacific.

"I understand the Communists have been surrounded," Cousin Donald said.

"I do not know of the happenings. You may have more luck with others in town."

"Your brothers, have you heard from them?"

"Not in a while."

Jian offered an orange wedge to Cousin Donald, who politely refused.

"Do you know why I am here?" Cousin Donald asked.

"You have never been to China," Jian said. "You wanted to meet family."

"That's true in a way. But I have come for another purpose."

"*Purpose?*"

"*Reason.* Another reason."

"I know what *purpose* means, cousin. But, forgive me, please. I'm being impudent to an elder."

"An elder, yes. I understand you are familiar with the professors at the University of Nanking."

"I know a few, it is true."

"I want to see someone in the sciences department. Someone involved with the physics of molecules."

"I confess I do not know if such a person exists."

Without breaking stride or losing composure, Cousin Donald reached back with his cane and whacked Jian in the back of the left knee. It was a calculated blow, which sent him to kneel in a cry of shock and pain. The remains of his orange fell in a dirt-covered pile to the ground. Cousin Donald walked ahead of him without turning back. Jian got up and continued to walk despite the sharp ache in his upper leg and the connecting tendons.

"I want to see someone in the sciences department. Someone involved with the physics of molecules."

Jian clenched his teeth and pulled his fingers into fists. He was backed into a corner now. He couldn't refuse to answer even if he wanted to. Through closed teeth, he said, "His name is Sochu."

"Interesting," Cousin Donald said. "You will take me there."

"You must not tell my family about this."

"Then we are both sworn to secrecy. Such things do not concern me, anyway. I am here to talk about atoms, not how you spend your leisure time."

They walked for a little while longer. "The University is over ten miles away from here," Jian said.

"We're not going to walk there."

"You would like to take my family's donkey cart?"

"I do not need transportation."

"I am confused, cousin. Is there something I can help with?"

"You already have. Just tell Sochu that I want to see him. He will see me."

A sharp blue streak of panic gripped Jian, and his vision narrowed. Sochu was very dear to him. This unknown cousin was suddenly a threat, but one he could do nothing about.

"What should I tell him this is about?"

Cousin Donald stopped, tapped his cane once, and turned to the young man. "Hydrogen," he said.

Three days later, on the morning that Sochu was to arrive at the house where Cousin Donald was staying, there was an explosion in the sciences building at the university. The shockwave could be felt for miles. Sochu did not arrive.

Chapter 52

Washington, D.C., 1934

Howard Leigh felt the stiff leather rims of his shoe tongue digging into the tops of his feet. He had never had a more uncomfortable pair of shoes in his life. Some genius city planner had put the new Justice Department building right between the Capitol and the White House, a good mile and a half. Cummings didn't want him to use any cars. He still didn't trust Hoover. No one trusted Hoover. But still, it wouldn't have been such an unpleasant walk if his shoes had been made for the trip.

The walk was nice in the spring, when it was in between the two mythological extremes of weather: Frozen and Melting. It was just at the twilight of the melting period, Indian Summer. He would be sweating through his woolen socks by the time he reached the Capitol building. He could already feel the sweat from his palms seep into the cardboard box he was carrying.

The sergeant-at-arms at the top of the steps asked him where he was going.

"Senator Nye's office."

"I'll give you some advice, kid," the sergeant said. "Don't go directly there. Take the back way. Republicans don't like it when young Irish kids like you pass by their offices."

Leigh didn't know if that was supposed to be a joke. His mother was Hungarian and his father was a "Damn Portagee" from Connecticut. Did he look Irish? He didn't know. Still, not wanting any trouble, he took the roundabout way.

Senator Nye's office wasn't far from the back stairs. But those stairs were killing his feet. He sat down just outside in the hallway with the box next to him. He fought an impulse to look through the documents in it. He just glanced at a title under the lid, *Senate Committee on Public Lands and Surveys Report on the Extraction, Manufacture, and Storage of Petroleum for the Purpose of Wartime Surplus and Munitions Manufacture*. He did not envy the man who would have to read that report.

He went in to see the secretary after catching his breath and having a cigarette.

"Senator Nye says to go right in," she said.

"Yes, ma'am."

He opened the inner door and put the box in front of him as he entered. The edge of the box caught the outside pocket on the jacket of a man who had been standing too near the entry, and the pocket ripped. Leigh was horrified. That suit must have cost a hundred dollars.

"Geez, I'm sorry, mister," he said quickly.

The man whose suit would now need stitches, simply chuckled. "It's all right, young man," he said. He was a small man, medium complexion, with dark hair and a non-descript face whose only memorable feature was an impish smile. He had the air of being older than he looked, which was not much older than Howard.

"These things happen," he said with that smile.

Howard set the box down on the edge of Nye's desk.

Senator Nye sat back and put his hand over his wide-set face. He had the face of a terrier in a world of bulldogs. "Oh, Howard, for God's sake," he said. "You klutz. I must apologize for the pages they send down here."

"It's nothing, really," said the man. "It's all my fault for standing by the door." He extended his hand towards Leigh. "Howard, is it? My name's Hathaway. You can call me Joe."

They shook hands.

Senator Nye motioned for Howard to sit down. "Listen, Joe, Howard here is one of the sharpest tacks on the carpet. Never gets drunk, do you Howard?"

"No sir."

"That's my boy. It's all right, Joe. Go on with your story."

Hathaway stood still as he talked. "I was saying that oil is not a winning strategy. There's only so much of it in the ground."

"You can't tell that to an American, Joe. Those wildcatters get more than the thrill of getting rich. I've seen it. They talk about drilling rigs like they're looking for the goddamn Holy Grail. And when their cup runneth over, it's the thrill of the gambler that they feel, not that of the entrepreneur. It's like a powerful magnet that only attracts other things that are magnetic. You can have the most powerful magnet in the world and you still won't get an apple to move an inch."

"I'm not sure I catch your meaning, Senator."

"I'm saying there's a certain... mentality to being a wildcatter. You know what I mean. It's the thrill of getting the Ace of Spades in a poker hand. I mean that the oil industry will always attract that sort. And there's nothing you or I can do about it."

"But there *is* something we can do about it, Senator. Our economy is fast becoming dependent on petroleum."

"It's true, as I've said all along. But you can't tell me there's a better alternative out there."

"Oh, but there is, Senator. Hydrogen. It's combustible, it's plentiful, the byproducts are harmless—and don't smell bad, and it can be gathered cheaply and easily."

"Isn't that what they use in those German balloons?" Howard asked. He had been following along but didn't know if he should be involved in the conversation or not. The Senator had told him to sit down, so maybe... But you could never be sure.

"That's right. The Graf Zeppelins. But that's for lift, not power."

"Those things are deathtraps," Nye said. "You can't tell me hydrogen isn't unstable. I've seen it burning. Damn stuff goes up like a Roman candle."

"As does petroleum," Hathaway said. "But we have contingencies for that. And there have been many more storage problems with oil than with hydrogen."

"That's only because we've had to store so damn much of it. Listen, Joe, I've had a hatred for oil just as much as the next guy. More, in fact. The trusts we busted back in aught-six just made more of 'em. It's a damn shame is what it is. And I've been trying to run these guys out on a rail since I got here. But the simple fact is, we don't have the stomach for this kind of thing. You want to talk about Teapot Dome? Those guys spent, what, six months in jail? Oil is a moneyed interest that can't be fought. Trust me."

"What if I told you that there is a successful oil replacement that could be available for free?"

Senator Nye laughed—in a way that reminded Howard of a butcher hacking at a hambone—then whistled through his teeth. "Do you know, Joe, what's in this box that I had Howard bring over for me? It's reports that I sponsored about the oil industry after Teapot. Damn scary stuff. But they'll never see the light of day. If they ever knew what was in these things, they'd burn this whole town down just to get at 'em. The corruption in this place is too thick and too tightly wound to do anything about. But that's something altogether. You're looking in the wrong place if you want some kind of power over this market. My advice? Start your own energy company with *your* cockamamie ideas to compete with all of *their* cockamamie ideas. That's the capitalist impulse that this country was founded on."

"If I'm hearing you correctly," Hathaway said. "You're telling me that I can't kill the beast, so I should starve it."

"That's a very interesting analogy. Damn incisive, if you ask me." He put this hand to his chin.

"Howard, what do you think? We've been dealing with a

different beast here, one who has the ear of Roosevelt the Younger. This beast has a thirst for war and conflict. How do we starve that beast?"

Howard froze. His mind raced. Senator Nye, unlike other senators he had done errands for, often asked his subordinate staff to give him some of their opinions, and encouraged discussion. But actually doing so was frightening.

"Stop all war?" he said tentatively.

Senator Nye laughed in that hacking kind of way. "Stop war. Stop war. That's funny. That's goddamn hilarious is what that is. Nevertheless, my boy, that's where you and I agree. Hand that box to Mr. Hathaway here. It's OK, I trust him. He's not from North Dakota, but he's still one of the good guys. Do me a favor, would you? Mark the box in big, black letters 'Senator Nye's War Medals.' That'll get 'em if they're curious."

Howard took a Waterman fountain pen and wrote on the side of the box.

"Mr. Hathaway," Nye continued. "I apologize that I was not able to help in any substantive way. I'm afraid you've come along at the wrong time in history."

"How do you mean?"

Nye had clearly been winding up the meeting, but this Mr. Hathaway was now introducing—or, rather, expanding—a tangential topic. Howard felt nervous for him.

"Well, you know, I just mean that these oil bastards are already entrenched. They got the cars, the ships, the planes, the factories, the power companies. Hell, they've even got middle America with their lamp fuel. As I understand it, there's even an industrial solid based on the black stuff. What's that called, Howard?"

"Polyvinyl chloride," he said, happy he was asked something he knew. "They just discovered a clear type of it too, that's going to take the place of burlap, polyvinylidene chloride. It's like paper, only you can see right through it, and it's a hundred times as strong."

"Imagine that. That's what you're up against, Joe. They've got us all by the balls, and we're just happy they don't squeeze. You should have gotten to them during Roosevelt the Elder. But we were just young punks then, eh, Joe? I wish you luck." Senator Nye put this hand up and then out, ending the meeting abruptly but as courteously as possible.

Howard put the pen back on Senator Nye's desk and handed the box to Hathaway. "You need any help with that down the stairs?"

"No thank you, young man. I can manage."

"Remember that name, Howard—Julius "Joe" H. Hathaway. This guy's going to be a millionaire while the rest of us suckers toil in obscurity."

After Hathaway left, they worked all afternoon on a report about the munitions industry, or "racket" as Senator Nye called it.

Later that evening, as Howard was trying to hail a cab in front of the Capitol, a black sedan pulled up instead. The door opened and a burly man in a coat and a bushy tie motioned to him. "You Leigh?"

Howard didn't know what to say.

"You Leigh?" the man repeated.

"I... I... Sure, I guess."

"Well, even if you ain't, get in the damn car."

Howard did as he was told. His law career flashed before his eyes. His applications to Columbia and George Washington had not yet been responded to—it was late for response. He was thinking about taking a year away from school altogether to see the world anyway. If they didn't respond by the end of November, the decision would be made for him.

Those guys in the sedan looked like movie-time gangsters. One guy even had Edward G. Robinson's loosely chewed cigar in the corner of his mouth. They were all dressed nicely and with nice hats. There were a total of four of them, three in the back facing him and one next to him.

"Gentlemen," Howard said, petrified. "What can I do for you?"

The Robinson-type spoke up. "We're just going for a little drive is all."

They even spoke like movie-time gangsters. Howard would have

laughed to himself if he weren't so terrified. He would have been enjoying the warm late-summer evening if he didn't have the feeling he was going to die.

The car pulled away, and now there was a certainty of no escape. He watched the familiar landmarks pass by the windows and turned back to Robinson.

"Do you know who I am?"

Howard shook his head.

"That's good."

"What do you want?" Howard asked, the panic shaking his voice as he looked from hoodlum to hoodlum.

"We're just going for a drive. Just enjoy the night air."

Howard clammed up. He couldn't help thinking that he could be walking up the steps to Margie Wiggham's two-bedroom in Fairfax, ringing her bell and asking if she wanted to go for a walk and maybe an ice cream. She was one of the reasons he didn't really want to see the world just yet. Maybe in a year or two with Margie and her Clara Bow eyes and Myrna Loy hair by his side.

For now, that would have to wait.

When they got out of the city limits, Robinson leaned forward. "We understand you work with Gerald Nye,"

"That's right."

"And you were in his office today with another guy. The name of that guy?"

"Hathaway. Say, what is this...?"

Howard was interrupted by a fist to his jaw. It was a sharp pain followed by a rattling ache that spread down his neck. His mouth was bleeding. It tasted like undercooked English sausages. He had never been hit before, had never been in a position to expect it. He hung his head down, holding his jaw. He wondered if it was broken, and if this is how Paul Muni felt when he was socked.

"It's important that you know what your place is in this transaction. I ask the questions. Then you answer the questions. Got it?"

Howard nodded weakly.

"This Hathaway character... Have you ever seen him before?"

Howard shook his head. The shaking made his jaw hurt worse.

"Do you know who he is?"

"No. I don't know who anybody is."

One of the other guys in the car reached into his jacket. Howard braced himself. He had seen enough movies to know what was coming out of the jacket. Instead, the guy showed him a newspaper clipping. It was a grainy picture on yellowed newsprint of man with a hat pulled down over his eyes and a woman with her hand over her face. There were some other people in the background. It looked like just outside a restaurant in a big city somewhere.

"Is this the guy?"

"I can't tell. No, really. I can't tell with the hat and the newspaper pictures being so terrible. I swear. I can't tell."

The other guys all looked at each other. "I believe you," Robinson said. "What kind of a character is this guy?"

"I... I'm not sure. I think he's in energy or something. That's what they were discussing."

"What kind of energy?"

"Hydrogen something or other. You know, like zeppelins."

"Like zeppelins, he says. German stuff. These guys got something going on with the Germans?"

"No. No. Nothing like that. They were just talking about the uses for hydrogen. Theoretical."

At the word *hydrogen*, Robinson's eyes narrowed and his neck stiffened. "We know he left with a box. What was in it?"

Howard brought his hand up to his face, partly because he thought he would be hit again. "The senator asked me to mislabel it. It was full of reports."

"Reports, eh? What kind of reports?"

"I'm not sure exactly. It's true. That's the truth. Don't hurt me!"

"What do you think was in them?"

"Some kind of geological surveys from the Department of Justice, maybe. I don't know for sure exactly."

Howard looked up at the man who hit him. "He's lying," the man said.

"OK," Robinson said, leaning back. "I'm going to give you a chance to tell me everything you know. But Lindy here, he has one job in life. You know what his one job is?"

"To hit people?"

"That's right, Howard. You're a smart guy. Now be smart and tell me everything you know."

"It ain't much. Like I said, I've never seen the guy before." Howard gauged his options. Until this moment, he had held back *oil* as a mental reservation. He had also held back the munitions industry report that Senator Nye was working on, but that was common knowledge. Then again, what could these people possibly have to do with oil?

"It's true, I don't know for sure what the reports were. I saw one of the titles by accident. Something about a land survey for petroleum products during wartime. That's all I know, honest to God."

"Lindy?" Robinson asked.

"He's saying the same thing, but now he looks truthful," Lindy replied with an arched eyebrow. He and Robinson exchanged looks.

"I tell you what we're going to do now," Robinson said. "I think you know what kind of people we are. I think you know what we're capable of. And I think you know that the only reason you're still able to speak through your mouth is that we want you to do something for us. Let's see exactly how smart you are. What do you think we want from you?"

Howard couldn't speak—he had a lump in his throat the size of a golf ball.

"That's right," Robinson continued. "We want you to let us know whenever this Hathaway guy shows up at the Senator's office, and we want to know what they talk about. You can make a good life for yourself here; that Wiggham girl is a looker."

"What do you...?" Howard started to say. He felt another blow to the other side of his face. It wasn't as hard, more like a slap, but its intention was the same. "All I want is to give you a job. A side job. One for which you'll be well compensated."

Chapter 53

Somewhere in Maryland, 1934

Julius Hathaway stepped out of his 1932 Duesenberg SSJ, then calmly walked around the entire length of the car and opened the door for his wife, Rebecca, who stepped out with somewhat less flourish than her stylish hat and dress demanded. They walked slowly down the sidewalk to a small café where an elderly Chinese gentleman awaited them.

"A pleasant voyage, I trust," Julius said to Donald.

"China is nothing like I expected," he said. His sixty-ish face was more expressive than it used to be—with wrinkled brows and sagging cheeks, any small change in his countenance was exaggerated. "I don't know quite what I expected. Maybe I had always pictured the mythical land my parents told me about. Most of them are farmers, up to their knees in mud."

As he recalled his trip, he tapped his cane more often than usual.

"There was an explosion," he said finally, after recounting more of the food and hospitality. "China is in revolution. There is violence all over that part of the world. But I can't help thinking I was responsible for his death. The man I went to see was killed shortly before I was to see him."

"You can't think that way," Rebecca said. "The same thing happened to me in Poland. It was reported as assassination by Ukranian radicals. How can I not think I was responsible? And yet, it's not how we're supposed to think."

"You want to talk about ipsedixitisms?" Donald said, which caught Julius by surprise and made him laugh. It was a word he had not heard since a college course on 19th century ethics. Donald

(*Li-Don*) was always full of surprises.

"It seems," Julius said, "that Asia is too unstable, Europe is too selfish, and America is too bureaucratic. I tried to get our government involved, but even the most sympathetic senator isn't recommending that we go that route."

"After fifteen years," Rebecca said, "I can't believe we've exhausted every avenue. Corporations, universities, governments... Either they don't want to listen or they are prevented from listening. You know, I really thought my home country would have been a perfect crucible. An example for the world. Had it not been at such a confusing time in history..." Rebecca didn't finish her sentence.

It made them all think of their lost time at Molineau. For five years, they had stayed out of society, making everyone believe the Hopewells had perished in a boating accident off the coast of Nantucket Island. Li-Don had made a show of the arrangements, including selling the house. The hardest part was for Leah, knowing her brothers and sisters would think, would *have* to think that she was dead.

When she married that handsome, mysterious scientist, her mother told her that she was no longer just her own person, that she was now someone else's person also. She was in the marriage for love, and she was a wife and a lover first. "You don't choose your family," her mother told her. "But you choose your husband. Back in the mother country, there were marriages where you didn't choose *mishpacha!* We should all be so lucky to choose our family."

Rebecca made her choice and she hadn't regretted it, but that didn't mean she didn't have regrets.

When the Hopewells were resurrected as the Hathaways (Li-Don's literalist joke: because Hyim "Hath A Way"), they required not just a new identity but a new history. Julius could no longer claim to be a graduate of Harvard. But Princeton, that could be arranged. No fewer than four faculty members were Originators— university professors became the desired option for progressing society forward, even more so than political figures or individual scientists (but it was difficult to get used to *the Orange and the Black*). And out of the post-war era Julius Hathaway was reborn as a junior partner at a railcar manufacturer. Later, his mysterious foreign wife Rebecca showed up. During and after the Great Depression, Julius used her family's money to buy that company and many others.

But now they had spent so many years building up their identities, perfecting their approach (and the technology), it was difficult to admit having been defeated. None of the government they approached could carry out their ideas. Julius did not take it badly. After all, the patience required to be semi-immortal gave him a long-term perspective. However, he did feel bad for Li-Don—*Donald*, he kept having to remind himself. It was now likely that he would not live to see the new era.

"We have been clumsy," Rebecca said finally. "Just like your friends. We've been using a blunt instrument for something that requires a delicate touch. Your senator, you said he was sympathetic, but that there was no support in Congress for introducing hydrogen as a fuel."

"He said I should start a hydrogen energy company to compete with the oil interests."

Donald—*Li-Don*—lifted his head from his coffee. "Is that possible?"

"It would not be possible to compete using current technology. And it would be impossible to use our own technology to start something new."

"There would be too many questions we couldn't answer," Rebecca said. (Somehow Hyim found it easier to think of his wife as *Rebecca* than his best friend as *Donald*.)

"What about a research foundation?" Donald asked.

"That would require too much scrutiny also. I've had people ask me too many questions about our companies as it is. It's been a struggle to keep my picture out of the papers; I can't imagine having to worry even more about exposure."

"Maybe next time you can assume the identity of someone more anonymous."

"Next time," Rebecca said wistfully. "God, I don't know if I can keep doing this without cracking up. It was hard enough renouncing my family. This life I've built up, I don't feel like it's real. I feel like I'm playing a part in a play. I know it's going to end, but I don't know when. I feel like I'm losing my identity, myself. It's slipping away."

Julius picked up his wife's hand and kissed it. "This is larger than either of us," he said.

"You could fund existing hydrogen research," Donald said. "Find out who is doing it and help them. Deuterium research, maybe?"

"Deuterium doesn't interest me."

"That hardly matters."

"Deuterium is merely the addition of a neutron. It serves no purpose in the supercharging of hydrogen. It is, in fact, the wrong path to take entirely. I don't know how to deal with that line of research."

"Perhaps that is the problem."

"I'm doing my *own* research. They're just feeling around in the dark, trying to get a sense of what that world is."

"As you were once. You were able to assimilate it quickly. You are centuries ahead of the rest of the world. Do you take it to them to assimilate, or do you let them come to it on their own?"

"I confess, I don't know. Neither approach seems satisfactory."

"What is the nature of your reluctance? Are you still so driven by ego that you assume no one would be able to follow your research. *Leah* can follow your research."

"Please don't use that name," Rebecca said. "I'm having a hard enough time."

Donald nodded.

"My wife believes in me," Julius said. "That can hardly be said of anyone else, even if they knew what I was trying to accomplish."

There were a few moments of silence as they all sipped coffee and nibbled on some kind of fried seafood.

"The other side," Rebecca said. "It looks like they might be killing people. People that we tried to make contact with. That's not like them, is it?"

"It depends on who you mean by *the other side*," Julius said.

"They've lost control," Donald interrupted. "It's the pattern. I remember all those years ago, your friend said he would be recruiting *primitives* to do his dirty work. I propose that your friend has lost control of his own police force."

"That's rather a grand leap," Rebecca said.

"But it does explain some of their tactics," Julius said. "Our friend would not set off an explosion at a University just because our Mr. Lee here wanted to have a conversation. Our friend has shown that he will allow conversations and even research. I have not heard one word of caution from de Meurre through this whole time. And you never know—your assassinated minister might be the victim of a real attempt."

"What a terrible thought. I can't decide which is worse."

Donald sipped his coffee and then tapped his cane. "A family of hedgehogs," he said, "is worried because the littlest one is dying of a disease. The only chance for a cure is to travel to the land of the voles and beg them for it. The three eldest hedgehogs set off on the dangerous journey to the voles. The first day, one of them is stalked and set upon by a wolf, who kills him and carries him away. The other two become despondent at the loss, but they press on. On the second day, one of the remaining hedgehogs gets too close to a riverbank, which gives way and sends him tumbling into the torrent, carried off to a watery death. The remaining hedgehog is now doubly despondent, but presses on.

"He finally arrives, alone, at the land of the voles. He tells them of his situation, how his littlest brother is dying, and how his companions were killed on the journey for the cure."

Here, Donald stopped and took another sip, then didn't go on.

"Well?" Rebecca asked incredulously. "What happened?"

"There are two endings to the story. The first ending is that the voles inform the hedgehog that they have no such cure, and that the hedgehogs should verify their information before embarking on such a journey. Hm."

Julius and Rebecca exchanged glances.

"The second ending is that the remaining hedgehog never makes it as far as the land of the voles. He is so downhearted at losing his two brothers that he cannot go on. He never moves from the riverbank. Instead, he curls up into a ball out of grief and remains that way until he dies of starvation."

"That's not fair," Julius said. "You went on with the original story to a point where the second ending was impossible."

"Did I really? Or was it just your impression that there was a clear divergence between the two endings?"

"They're both horrible endings," Rebecca said. "But at least the first ending adds dignity to the surviving brother."

"The point of both endings is that you must focus on the goal while appreciating the journey. It is not enough to do something in a crisis; you must do the right thing."

"But what is the point of having two endings?" Rebecca asked.

"You must not confuse a story with an object lesson. There are no hedgehogs; there is only the idea of the quest, and there are many ways that things can go wrong. Your identification with the hedgehogs in the story serves as a warning that there are paths which should not be taken without knowing what is on them. Grief, obsession, joy, satisfaction, anger, vengeance, pleasure, pain—these are all valid human feelings, but they are distractions."

"You sound like you're trying to convince yourself of that as well as us," Julius ribbed.

Donald tapped his cane. "Making fun of the old Chinese man is just another distraction."

There was another pause as they all reflected. "This is like Jeremiah," Rebecca said. "Persevering despite punishments. He was given the choice whether or not to leave his home and be safe or stay and face persecution. He chose to stay to try and save his people."

Why, after all this time, after all these years, had Julius' wife suddenly brought up something from the Bible? He wondered. He said nothing aloud, but watched her sidelong as she spoke. They had been married almost fifty years and she never failed to surprise him when it was least expected. "His friends kidnapped him and took him anyway," Donald said. "But the analogy is valid. "Julius didn't know what they were talking about.

Chapter 54

Somewhere in Pennsylvania, 1934

Taking Donald's theory to its most logical extreme, Julius and Rebecca decided to do a little reconnaissance. Espionage was not unknown to them, though they had never carried out an operation quite like this one. The had to enlist help for their operation, and Julius could think of no one sneakier or more shifty than his one-time Harvard Colleague and fellow Freecobbler, James H. Primerhaven.

"I've reinvented myself for the 20th century," he said. "You can call me Thessalonica G. Scattershot."

As Julius and Rebecca stood there in the lobby of an anonymous hotel with their mouths open, he said, "Just kidding. Call me Wendell. Wendell Afton, banker from Framingham, Mass." He shook both their hands. "What seems to be the trouble?"

"We're organizing a production of sorts," Julius said.

"No kidding?"

"We're interested in some covert operations. There's a building we want to break into."

"That's not legal."

"Hence our interest in you," Rebecca said.

Wendell smirked at her.

"It's in rural New Jersey, about twenty miles north of Flemington..."

"Snyder Oil?"

"That's right."

"I'm surprised you people haven't gotten around to doing this until now."

"It's an offensive move in a tactically defensive battle. I've never really gone on the offensive. It's kind of exciting."

"Whoa, there, Hannibal. Have you thought this through? This kind of thing is dangerous. Reckless. I... I don't think I know you anymore."

"We need your expertise at being a distraction," Julius said, "While we get in there and find out what they know. We should also find out what our friends on the other side of the hydrogen atom are up to."

"Find one, find the other."

"I don't think so. We have a theory that our friends enlisted the help of these oil people to stop us from reaching our goal."

"But now," Rebecca said, "Someone's gone native. How did Donald put it? They've 'lost control.'"

"What about our contact with the other side?" Julius asked. "How is de Meurre? Has he assumed a new name we should know about?"

"He hasn't changed his name in over 500 years. He's never chosen to be public, as far as I can tell. But you have to remember, I'm a junior member of this club. I was born in, how do they say it?—4 B.C. I'm still younger than you are in biological terms, and I'm much younger than most of us in actual terms."

"Did you say 4 BC?" Rebecca asked, "Husband, isn't that when they say Christ was born?"

"I don't follow that sort of thing," Julius said.

"Well I do. And I want to know."

"I don't know what to tell you," Wendell said. "I was raised in Spain until I was 16 or 17. Or was it 18? We didn't really follow the time there. Wrong place, wrong time. Sorry. But you know who was in Judea at the time? You should speak to Sylwyn.

He might know something about it."

"Brightferry?"

"Mmm. Yes."

"He never changes his name either?"

"He always arrives claiming to be the descendant of the previous Brightferry. Different strategies, I suppose. Though, I must say, when I first met him, his name was Bruteferros, or something like that. Then at one point it was Brinyfarre, I think. I imagine it will continue to evolve."

"Honestly!" Rebecca exclaimed. It made other people around them in the hotel lobby look over at them. They decided to take a walk outdoors to finish their conversation.

"What's to talk over with this operation?" Wendell said when they were outside. "You fire up one of those funny gadgets of yours and everything becomes easier."

Julius stared hard at him. "As you may recall, I don't make offensive *gadgets*, I make passive defense *devices*. In any case, leave that part of it to us."

At midnight, the four of them arrived at the edge of the forest behind the Snyder Oil building. Wendell was ready to create a scene on the other side, distracting the guards—who were suspiciously armed. According to the newspapers, the company was worried about union retribution for a lockout at one of their facilities in Harrisburg. But whatever the reason, they were the main impediment to getting inside.

Donald was the lookout, with binoculars and the electronic ear. He set up in a position just inside the forest. He had a pin-light and a small wireless radio clicker, which they would use for speechless communication. The low light (and Donald's failing eyesight) made the binoculars almost useless, but he could see flashlights as they moved.

The way in was remarkably clear. Julius and Rebecca stationed themselves on the dark side of a tree near the back entrance, which was not guarded by anyone. When the disturbance came from the other side of the building, Julius couldn't believe his ears. He could have sworn he heard an angry mob trying to storm the gates. But being on the other side of the building, it was unverifiable. He saw the pin-point light from Donald flash three times, and then he and Rebecca ran towards the back entrance.

He pulled out a neat little (so he thought) fountain-pen style skeleton key. The emitter field sensed the contours of the bearings in the lock and created a pseudo-solid shape in the slot. When he had invented this little wonder, he was trying for something that would be able to manipulate a switch or a lever from a distance, such as through a window, but that was beyond his grasp. The closed-in shape of a keyhole, however, was perfect for the field because it utilized the atoms in every surface of the keyhole. They were inside in no time, having locked the door behind them.

For a moment, while they were planning this break-in, Julius thought about the implications of his actions. He was now breaking the law in an overt way, something he had never done before. Not only that, he was involving his wife. And although she was only too eager to take this adventure seriously, his reservations were the same as they always were: how could he defend her if the situation called for it? He had confidence in his emitter that would be able to protect both of them. But he had to admit that it was not exactly battle-tested. It worked in specific situations, such as entrapment of the enemy and protection from bullets. In both cases, part of its defense was the fright it put into the enemy, not because of what it did, but because of the subject's lack of exposure to this type of technology. It worked because they were frightened of its "magic."

But if the enemies he was dealing with now had any knowledge of Originator technology or methods, they would not be as affected by it. It's possible they would have a plan for dealing with such things. Counter-actions that would render the emitters useless, somehow. He had to admit that he couldn't see how that would be possible, but that didn't mean it wasn't.

"Husband," Rebecca whispered, shaking his arm. "Where are you? We have work to do."

Julius shook himself back into reality and followed Rebecca down a hallway. "Remember, we have four hours," she said.

They crept up the metal stairway to the second floor. There was no way of knowing if someone else was in the building. All the lights were off, but still—it was not unheard of for employees to sleep at their offices, whether because they had lost their homes in the Crash or because they had demands on them from their employers that didn't allow them to leave for any length of time.

They began searching room by room. Based on the layout of the building, the number of floors, and the size of the rooms, he estimated that there were 88 rooms. Surely some spaces were larger than others, however, and Li-Don (sorry, *Donald*) would have been better able to estimate the number.

The first few were nothing but empty offices, some in-built space for expansion of the company in this location. Eventually, though, they found themselves bogged down in poorly organized offices and files.In each room that had a window, they tacked up a section of thick black cloth, so they could light a lamp without anyone on the outside seeing it. It was a decidedly low-tech solution, but it was successful. They passed in and out of various offices, supply rooms, and closets for the better part of two hours before they found something interesting on the fifth floor.

Rebecca slipped open a large, wide drawer of a thick metal filing cabinet while Julius scanned the desk for anything. He heard her gasp. She handed him a sheet of paper that resembled the type of merchandise transfer forms his father dealt with for diamonds. The numbers (and handwriting) were sufficiently obscure so as to be indecipherable, but one element was very clear at the top—it was their old address on 5th Avenue in Manhattan. It sent a very tiny shiver down Julius' spine.

They began reading from the stack of papers that cabinet held. They were non-descript invoices, bills of lading, and all manner of receipts that were filed under 5th Avenue. About halfway through the stack, Julius saw some writing in the margin of one of the invoices, in pencil and printed in schoolhouse script. The address was circled and a line went from it to the note: *suspected of Communist activities*. After that note in the stack, the addresses changed to ones they didn't recognize.

"Did someone misfile these?" Julius asked. "Or did they leave it here for ready reference in case of an emergency?"

"The name on the desk is Victor Carreri," she said. "Does that mean anything to you?"

Julius' mind scattered itself for a memory of that name. "It does sound familiar," he said. He ran back through every minor memory he had. It was getting tougher to access those memories. There were so many of them. Each one was like a clear painting, with its foregrounds, middle-grounds, and backgrounds. But the museum that housed them was so vast that it took a while to get through all of it. It suddenly occurred to him that massive amounts of memory power must be required for someone who lives for 10,000 and more years. How did that amount of memory affect someone?

"That's close to the name Li-Don got from those people outside the shack. At gunpoint, I might add. *Donald*."

"From twenty years ago? And he's still in this same pitiful little office?"

"Look at the rest of these papers; I can't find anything beyond 1915. What about in that stack?"

Rebecca quickly rifled through the stack. "Here's one from February, 1916. That's all that's here. This one is some kind of shipping manifest. I can't read this man's handwriting, but it appears as if some kind of package of documents arrived and was sent back."

"Does it say where?"

"There's some sort of complicated address. I can't make it out. The first letter is a D or an A or an O or something else entirely.

It's a short word, but it could be anything."

They searched a while longer, but didn't find anything else. The 1916 document was intriguing for a number of reasons. The fact that it was in that building suggested more than its contents. They had another floor to search.

Brightferry was right. The enemy was sloppy.

"They think we're Communists," Rebecca said on the stairwell.

"Or they're using that as a rationalization. It's likely they don't know who we are, just that we're some kind of threat."

Julius' legs felt tired. The stairs were not built with comfort in mind. They reached the top and started down the hallway, just as on the previous floors. But there was something different on that level. Julius felt a glow within him. It was a similar feeling—the eyes in the back of his head feeling—to when another Originator was nearby. Only this was different. For some reason, he could not *sense* another person nearby. But there was a thing, an object of some kind that was... it was... was it singing?

In the darkness of the hallway, Julius saw his way past the first few offices to a storage closet. "In here," he said to Rebecca, who was still at the top of the stairway.

"What's in there?"

"I don't know. But it's in here."

"You're not making any sense."

"I can't explain. Do I really need to make sense, after all this? Hand me the key."

She gave him the artificial key, and he opened the door. "I can feel it. It's... It's... you can't hear it?"

"Not a bit."

Rebecca lit the lamp and they ventured inside. There was no danger of the light being spotted from outside because it was an enclosed room within the building. There was a definite harmonic humming coming from somewhere. It wasn't a large closet, but it was big enough to feel like it was a different space from the hallway. And it was small enough to awaken his feelings of claustrophobia. He felt around in the dark for Rebecca's hand and squeezed it.He stopped searching when he saw a metal trunk with slotted wooden trim. It was padlocked shut. He quickly unlocked it and flipped up the lid. Rebecca moved closer, holding the lamp over their heads to illuminate it.

The noise he was hearing now wasn't loud or shrill, as he feared it might sound when he got closer to it. Instead, it was a more of a mid-tone drone with harmonic overtones, pulsating yet constant, much like a sitar. He pulled away some wrinkled rags and used tarps, tossing them to the ground like a child unwrapping a present. There, in the bottom of the trunk was a familiar object that he had never seen before.

"Is that a bugle?" Rebecca said.

"I have no idea. But I feel it. Like it knows what I'm thinking. And I feel... I... don't know what I feel. My God. Now I know what the Christians talk about with their Holy Grail. This... object is completely at peace and yet I feel it has enormous power..."

This curving and curving and curving object seemed to draw him inward, focused his vision on it, and it glowed and kept singing to him. Gold, brass, copper, platinum; whatever it was made of, it was cool and smooth to the touch. As his fingers brushed against the foreign metal of the bell and the valves, he immediately knew it was the source of something awesome. He lifted it out of the trunk and held it like a Dixieland jazz player while the clarinetist is soloing. The pipes that ended in a trumpet bell wrapped in on themselves—there was no beginning to it (no mouthpiece, to carry that metaphor). There were four coils, parallel to each other, with one valve plunger on the third coil and the bell arriving out of the fourth coil. The first and second coils were in each other's mouths like a Mobius strip.

"This is Originator technology," he said. "But I didn't see anything like this in the files."

347

"Are we thinking of taking it?"

"We are. I have to take this to my father. He must know what this is and why it's here."

"Maybe it's here for a reason."

"Maybe, but that's unlikely. Something with this much power must have a great importance. Either good or bad. I'm thinking it should either be on a pedestal or behind glass in a museum somewhere..."

"Or else in a Tartarus prison, locked away forever."

They decided to leave right then, having found not quite what they came for, but something else more intriguing. Rebecca blew out the lamp, and Julius wrapped the bugle in the black cloth, tying it tight with a piece of twine.

They crept across the floor as quietly as their shoes would allow toward the stairwell. Slowly, Julius opened the door, and then...

And then...

The noise they heard coming up the stairwell, echoing and clanking up the shaft, was the sound of footfalls on the metal steps. The noises were determined and methodical, but the echoes made them chaotic and frantic.

"Oh, God," Rebecca said. "Somehow I don't think that's Jimmy's sound generator."

"Wendell's," Julius corrected her.

It was dark, but he sensed she made a face at him. "Is there another way down?" she asked.

"I don't think so."

They ran toward the other end of the hallway and hid in one of the rooms they hadn't searched. It was very dark. Through the window, the gibbous moon was obscured by clouds. Behind the silence they could hear the footsteps. It was unclear whether or not they were on the sixth floor yet, but they reverberated through the entire empty building.

"Shouldn't we be closer to the stairway?" Rebecca asked in a whisper.

"They would check those first."

"So are we thinking that it's better to have them delay finding us that have them find us at the outset?"

"We don't even know who *they* are."

"I think it's pretty clear. It's always the same people who seem to show up wherever we are."

Julius tried not to think about what had happened to Wendell and Donald, if anything. The lighted radio receiver had not lit up. Donald was supposed to send a signal on that receiver if there was any trouble. In that case, the best he could expect was that it had failed somehow. "If we know who they are, we might be able to think of a way to elude them." Julius sensed something ominous, something he was holding back from his wife. It was something he recognized from deep within the buried past. The sensation gripped him like a hand at his throat. Without saying anything and without first preparing for it, he activated his emitter to surround both of them with the protective field.

While the field was around them (something Rebecca implicitly understood as a sign of impending danger), they managed to quietly crawl behind a metal shelf on one end of the room and surround themselves with boxes full of something that was heavy and solid, probably paper or books. They now had a clear view of the door through the spaces between the boxes, but were obscured by the contents of the room.

It was ten minutes of sheer fright and unbearable anticipation. Julius felt them getting closer. Three of them burst into the room, shining lights and stomping all around in their heavy shoes.

Then the familiar figure of a man who had been in their lives before. Julius did not need to see his face, that face was burned into his memory for all time. The Man on the Tower. Again, it was something beyond his physical senses. Again, he hadn't felt this in many years. And again, they were all playing the same parts. It was the same scene as their odyssey on a cargo ship; the same players in the same roles.

The Man on the Tower stood by the window, his silhouette shifting and turning as he lifted his nose in the air and pointed it around the room, then looked out the window into the night..

"They were here," he said. "But they left abruptly."

Julius wondered if the emitter field blocked the smell or his sense of being an Originator. It made sense in some ways. But it didn't make sense in others.

"And they've taken it with them," the man added, almost in a whisper. "I've traveled half-way around the world to get it back from the idiots who stole it from me. And now someone else has stolen it again."

Chapter 55

Molineau, 1934

Julius' decision to form an economy based on hydrogen energy production was in part an objective, detached experiment. Part of it, however, was his reaction to handling the object which Ezra had called a long unintelligible name in the Originator's original language, which involved sounds unfamiliar to the ears of others.

Ezra had affected a short beard. It had taken thirty years to achieve five-o'clock shadow, but for him it seemed worth it. He displayed it with a little pride while he spoke.

"I didn't think there were any more of these," Ezra said thoughtfully. He held it out in his hands, and to Julius it seemed to vibrate. "Where did you say you found it?"

"In a nondescript trunk on the top floor of an oil company building."

Julius was nervous. The object had a strange effect on him, simultaneously demanding attention and making him excruciatingly aware of his surroundings: the sharp, crisp bite of the Canadian air that reached into the small cabin; the radiating warmth and confusion from Leah (that is, *Rebecca*) behind him; and the general sense of dread coming from the world all around their enclave.

"This means our friend had it all along. I'll be damned."

"What is it?"

Ezra handed it back to him. "Can you feel that?" he asked.

Julius nodded gravely. He could feel the vibrations pass through his bones.

"Funny how names stick sometimes," Ezra said.

"You were the one who called these little wrist gadgets *emitters*. We never had a name for them before. But this... this magnificent God-awful thing had a name all right. This was our first attempt to control the power of the supercharged hydrogen atom (again, son, your word). These pipes and chambers hold the reaction. The bell magnifies it. *Merveilleux!* Naturally, we made hundreds of these and used them in our first major attempt at a colony. They powered everything from our transportation to our cooling housings. Industrial machinery, cooking, building materials... But we miscalculated. The energy they stored and produced was unpredictable." His voice became more introspective and almost a whisper. "We had all the materials, all the will, an unlimited energy source, an unlimited catalyst supply... This *thing*. I wish I had never laid eyes on it."

His voice went back to normal. "Gathering lighting for our energy supply is damaging enough to the local geostructure. But couple it with the multiplicity of output from these gadgets, and it was too much for the colony. When our island sank into the sea, these gadgets went with it. At a certain depth in the ocean, they overloaded themselves on various concentrated hydrogen isotopes in seawater and were destroyed. The resulting series of pressure waves caused a chain reaction of instability in the oceans. We were not able to specifically confirm it, but one hypothesis had tsunamis on every coastal area around the globe."

Julius was beyond disbelief. His ability to comprehend the utterly preposterous and fantastic tales presented to him had grown to such a degree that he no longer held any suspicion of being lied to. It simply did not matter.

"And this one?" he asked.

"I really have no idea. Anything is possible, I suppose. In any event, we discovered what was wrong with them and came up with smaller, more manageable gadgets. The kinetic power was too raw, too close to the source. We had to further process it to keep it under control. The vibrations you feel are the actual reactions

352

happening right next to your fingertips. It's quite exhilarating."

Unlike the case of the emitters, which were his only exposure to this technology so far, the raw power from this object was palpable.

He was surprised that Rebecca and Donald couldn't feel it. Ezra was surprised too. He couldn't fathom the experience of *not* feeling it.

Instead, he recounted how they had found the *object* and were almost caught. He played up the dramatic angle and played down Jimmy's (that is to say, *Wendell's*) role.

"It was very similar to an incident that happened before," he said when he was through. "We were on a ship, in a secret compartment in the hold, trying not to breathe. That same person came through, with his nose in the air, like he was a bloodhound smelling us. He was fatter, though he had not aged. One of our friends, no doubt. It was the same scene. That man's face haunts me all my days. I only know him as the Man on the Tower. And I have still not reconciled who he is or what his role might be in all of this."

"It is a persistently curious phenomenon," Ezra said. "Patterns. If you live long enough you will begin to see patterns. Situations repeat themselves. It's not because the universe is an ordered place, mind you. It's because we are slow to change, and we react similarly in similar situations. Throughout history. We make the same mistakes. Though we may be different people and assume different *roles*, as you say; though we may make different choices and have different friends; at bottom we are still the same set of actions, thoughts, reactions, and mysteries. We can't help it."

And that was the moment Julius decided to form his company. Donald's original idea involved a foundation that would give grants for hydrogen-related research. But Julius was worried that the current tack was toward neutron-based hydrogen research instead of the more fruitful electron- and sub-atomic-based research. Creating his own company would let him control its direction. But as to the product or service it would provide, he did not have an answer. He left it as a research-only institution and did not give it a name. (Donald persisted in calling it the *Hopewell Enterprise*).

As Originators around the world had to leave their lives behind and disappear, he recruited them to work at the Hopewell Enterprise in the upper Mohawk Valley in New York. It was the scene of many electrical storms throughout the year and could be relied upon to provide the most wild and raw form of electricity.

Within a year, he was able to duplicate a version of the Originator object. In one of his more Donald-like jokes, he made it look like a French horn.

Chapter 56

Somewhere over the Atlantic Ocean, 1937

Jareich was sweating. It was almost 10 degrees Fahrenheit outside the cabin, but inside it was a sweltering 70. He was used to the cold winters that Pommern brought in from the Baltic sea. He would have been much more comfortable if he had been in the superstructure rather than at a dinner table with eight strangers. All in good time.

The constant rumble of the engines made some of the other guests nervous, but Jareich found them soothing. They reminded him of the railroad near his house when he was a child; the constant sounds of machinery, of a world power growing stronger with each trainload.

He hated America, as all good Germans did. It was their treachery in the Great War that led to Germany's destruction and humiliation. But some things couldn't be helped. He couldn't exactly refuse a mission. If the Führer tells you to travel to Belgium and bed the Queen, then that's what you do. All things considered, a trip to New Jersey wasn't that bad a proposition.

His coffee rippled in its cup. He refused all attempts at small talk, barely managed a smile, just enough to show politeness or mild disinterest. Too much interaction. Even with other Germans. He disliked people. People in general were a stubbornly uninteresting lot. There was the girl in Presburg, but even she repeated herself too often when there was a lull in the conversation. It was just so difficult and tiring to be with her. With the lot of them. To Hell with them all.

A short lurch to starboard. An otherwise smooth trip interrupted occasionally by the buffeting winds. He did not like airplanes or airships, did not even like being on the top floors of buildings. When he was a small child, his parents took him to see what was then the tallest building in the world, a ten-story office building in Chicago. He was terrified. Its elevators were nightmarishly small and had a fetid odor he later learned was lubricating grease. It was just another reason to hate America.

And now that his military career was nearly finished, after having been a prisoner of war to the English (of all nations) in the Great War and survived Weimar looting around Salzburg, it might be a fitting end to serve the only truly great leader Germany ever had. Now in his fifties, Jareich was tired of struggling through the Jew-caused depression, tired of mollifying his harping wife and children, was just tired of being a ten-year captain when snot-nosed kids half his age were colonels already. Maybe that's what they sensed in him when they sent him on this mission.

He got up from the table when land came into view . There was a general commotion around the cabin as people stood up and went to the windows to see it for themselves. This, despite the warnings not to make any sudden movements lest the balance become unwieldy. He took the opportunity to slip out of view and into the undersized galley. There was a small door in the bulkhead that reminded him of the U-boats he had toured in dry-dock. Making sure he could not be seen, he unlocked it and passed through.

This was an unauthorized area, but he had his military credentials with him. One flash of those would send any little Bayern guard shaking in his shoes. The low drone of the engines was punctuated by his metallic footsteps. His shoes were fitted with metal plates so he wouldn't generate static electricity, which would be deadly and premature.

Right where it was on the blueprints, he found the access corridor to the superstructure. As he stepped through, the temperature changed to a modest cold, maybe 40 degrees with no wind. That felt better. He paced up and down the catwalks examining the hydrogen tanks. The landing apparatus at Lakehurst was portside, so that would have to be where the incendiary should be. Plausibility was the key. It was plausible for the latent electrical charge in the air itself to react with the mooring and the hydrogen at the same time.

There was just one thing that Jareich didn't understand. He never questioned his Führer's intentions, of course, but he did wonder why there was an underground hydrogen production facility around Erz, when there were above-ground facilities that worked just as well. And there were others being planned. He allowed himself these questions only because he would not be returning from this mission.

He found the location aft and portside, just in front of the tailfins; that would make the best show. It would briefly illuminate the coat of arms on each of the fins, and then, hopefully, cause the entire airship to disintegrate within seconds.

He did not understand how destroying one of the flagships of the zeppelin fleet would benefit the Reich, but he realized it was beyond his comprehension, and that was enough. The fact that it was in America was curious. Why America, of all places? Why not Poland or Sweden? Or even Palestine? The destruction of the Hindenburg would certainly prove to the rest of the world that hydrogen-based airships were a menace and should be discontinued. What, then, to do with all that excess hydrogen production being planned?

He let his question hang. The engines of the great ship slowed through a gentle rocking motion that became a little more violent. He fought to keep his footing on the thin-railed catwalk. Then the engines revved up again and the nose came up. They were turning around for another try at a landing. It took about an hour, more or less. Perhaps it was raining. The wait was almost unbearable. He drew upon his training to think of easier things, more regimented things; things with definite times, like songs he knew, or poems he had memorized—certain passages of *The Magic Flute*.

Then he felt the descent once again. The engines whipped into reverse. The familiar tug of men and ropes on the ground. He took solace in knowing that he was a player in the grand scheme of things. After years of ignominy and anonymity, he was about to be martyred for a cause. He counted to three hundred, then lit his fuse.

For his part, he did not want to be killed in the initial explosion; he wanted to see it happen, and then he would content himself with being engulfed in the ensuing conflagration.

As the fuse trickled its way to its destination, he wondered if America was the enemy. It was certainly a land where the dregs of the rest of the world came to be regarded as something other than what they were. All of the citizens of Europe and greater Europe who could not hack it in the motherland slogged their way across the ocean to pretend that their lives would be worth more in a different place. Disgusting.

If nothing else, America would have the distinction of having two of the greatest ships in the history of mankind, the Titanic and the Hindenburg, destroyed as they made their way towards its shores. Even if he would not live to see the humiliation America would endure for this disaster, he was comforted by the thought that there would be humiliation.

END OF PART IV

Part V

Prologue

In the Summer of 1948, something curious happened. The state of Israel was born in the violence of the moment. Zionists attacked British targets until Britain completely pulled out. Some Arab Palestinians, having refused to share any land with Jews, despite a UN mandate, were legally expelled from some parcels by the new Israeli government. Hyim discovered that even Jews have their violence when the cause was sufficient. It was instructive. There are things worth fighting for, yet he still could not fight—and he still could not see that the world was getting any more tolerant. If anything, this half century had more killings than all previous centuries combined. And yet, he knew Jews survived in all ages, and still remain with their hands tied behind them in a twilight of immortality. This fact may have increased the enmity of the world toward them.

Richard and Anne Wallace sat in their dining room after dinner was finished. They sipped tea until they could discuss the article in the newspaper that sat between them on the table. The article described a war that was breaking out in the Middle East, and the two of them had adopted very different views of it. Richard, in particular, did not understand his wife's view.

"Are you ready to discuss it?" she asked.

Richard looked up at her. Though her soft features were still distracting after many years of marriage, he tried to focus on the argument. Her small, soft hands that gripped the teacup did make him think of other things, but there was a fundamental disagreement between them that had to be aired. Otherwise there would be misunderstanding, and that was worse than enmity.

"How can I argue with someone so beautiful?" he said.

"Put your libido in the icebox for the moment."

Richard regarded the picture on one of the inside pages of the newspaper. It was a picture of some Israelis holding up the flag of the new country. They had only been *Israeli* for a short time, but they already looked proud. Pride in nationalism.

Anne countered this argument immediately. "It's not nationalism. If it were nationalism, they would have to have had a nation in order to be proud of. Jews are a diaspora, my dear. They are an ethnic people without a nation. Descendants of other Jews scattered to the four winds by Rome and Persia two thousand years ago. This is pride in ethnicity. They finally have a place to call home."

Richard conceded the point, though he felt it was a semantic one. "The conflict," he said. "Its validity, however strong that may be, will always be suspect because of the arbitrariness of how it was drawn."

"Are you blaming the British?" she asked.

"Why not?"

"The British are not responsible for centuries of antipathy. And this fighting has been going on for over twenty years. The only difference is, there is a national army instead of a series of small militia."

"Why must they all kill one another? That doesn't hold legitimacy."

"Britain administered that territory, and they decided who to invite. Israel is the ancestral land of the Jews. It only makes sense that they would return."

"But after two thousand years? They are only returning to an area that may not have any identifiably historical attributes. Their own families do not have legal claims there, just a UN mandate,

which is based on an outdated, useless book based on an oral
history with no real basis."

"Really, now, husband. That outdated, useless book is what has
kept them all connected to their ancestors. Their families—my
family, yes, husband, *my* family, as you may forget—chose to keep
their traditions alive. This outdated, useless book told them—us—
how to do that."

"Other races melted into their surrounding cultures. What's so
special about yours?"

"Have you read that outdated, useless book?"

Again, Richard had to concede the point. They again stared at
the article on the table in between them, separating them. Though
he conceded the point, he refused to be moved.

Molineaux, 1968

My Dearest Ezra:

Forgive a man who, if not older than you, at least feels older than you do. I am dictating this to my secretary, having lost the use of my right hand and most of my sight. The occasion of this letter coincides with my 100th birthday, which may not sound as impressive to you as it does to myself. I, at least, feel all of my 100 years and have forgotten many of them. This, I am told, is not the case for your kind. I could not imagine being able to remember as many details of a life that has lasted far longer.

But this is not what I am writing to you about. Nor is it about my 100th birthday. I would like to submit what will likely prove to be my final and only report on your experiment to produce an heir and savior. I believe I have stated before that you saved the lives of myself and my family, for which I am eternally grateful. Of course, not eternally grateful; although you may feel the gratitude for an eternity or two, I will not always be there to give it. Be that as it may, I do not feel it is beyond my place to point out failure and foolishness where I see it.

Your cause, for all it is worth, is a noble one, as far as I can tell and as far as I can believe it to be true. Your kind probably did the right thing by trying to tame this world. As an outside viewer, I can see that many things have gone wrong since then. This world that you have sought to create has turned around and corrupted you. If there was an original intention to sincerely help us—meaning we primitives—gain the insight into the universe that you had already gained, it has been lost amid political infighting, decadence, and general lassitude. As your son says, there is a point where patience becomes an excuse for inaction. And this is the real point of my letter to you. I feel it is necessary to point out that your creation of a savior took the same route as your creation of a world. That is, you had a theory about how things would work... No, wait. Theory is not the right word. Theory implies some kind of scientific endeavor. You had expectations of how things would work. And

363

all your subsequent actions were based on these expectations, despite the prevailing and persistent data.

I have a story for you. A man goes into town to buy a cow for his family to eat. But he does not have enough money to buy the cow. He has enough money to buy chickens or pigs or sheep. But he wants a cow. So he works for the rancher until he has enough to buy the cow and take it to his family. When he gets home to his house, his family is dead of starvation. Had he bought the chickens, the pigs, or the sheep, his family would have been saved. But he wanted a cow and did not see any other way.

I submit to you that your actions, although understandable and logically justifiable in every way, are nevertheless wrong. And in the face of a persistent and previously unseen enemy, you have continued to make the wrong choices. Myself, I am not smart enough to go farther than that. But you are. Your convictions lack inspiration, your logic lacks reason, and your reasons lack purpose.

The son you sought to create no longer feels his destiny, whatever it might have been. I have no wish to berate you for mistakes you have made. We all plough our own fields, and the son is primarily responsible for the son's despair. I only point out that it was you who created the despair that he willingly jumped into.

The destruction of humanity on that field in New Jersey was merely the spark that burned down his life's work. The fact is, his life's work was flammable in and of itself, and any spark would have sent it up. But I submit that it is you and your kind which helped pour the butane.

I have known your son for all his life. I have seen him at his best and at his worst. Too many of those times at either extreme, he was thinking of you. The proverbial lost boy searching for his father. Though he may outlive us all (literally), I do not think he will be capable of understanding who or what you are. I, myself, do not, but I am not that smart.

Yours, Donald

Chapter 57

New York, Sometime in the Near Future

Life for them at Molineau was reminiscent of a university setting. Much of the time there was spent doing research, playing out hypotheses, and observing computer models. It was meant to be a way station between lives back in American society, but recent events had caused it be more research focused. The mood of placidity and studiousness had not changed, but it was tinged with sadness and growing alarm. They were accepted by the other members, but it was always understood that they (and especially she) were apart from the rest of them. They were living symbols of past failures and current troubles.

Their forays in and out of society in America had given them a sense of belonging, for however short their stays were. It was tremendously easy to wander in and out of housing developments, apartment buildings, various jobs around the country; different lives, different societal postures to take. They watched as automobiles became cars, planes became jets, petrol became gasoline, and computers became PCs.

By 1937, he had already realized how late it was to try and change the economy of oil. Suppliers created demand by furnishing lifestyles based on it—the falseness of the way it sprang up around the country was astonishing. Within twenty years, industry was awash in it. It spilled over and coated the ground like varnish, hiding the imperfections behind a shiny veneer.

What was worse, the other side forgot about him. All that trouble they took earlier to divert his attention, to throw him off course, to keep him from learning his destiny. It had all worked. They won. And now he was irrelevant. Worse than irrelevant, he was now a living example of just how severely they had succeeded. He got the girl, the grail, put the bad guys in jail, and he still lost. Now they paid no more attention to him. None of them:

Richard and Anne Wallace

George and Julia Kornbluth

Martin and Wendy Helton

It was a typically hot and humid day in Manhattan. The room was packed with mourners and well-wishers. On one side, Chaim and his wife Leah, family friends, sat in the front row, with many of their Family scattered around the next several rows. On the other side, over a hundred people, half of them middle-aged Chinese women, sat dabbing their cheeks with tissues.

Wei Donald Lee's actual birthdate was a mystery to most people in the room. He claimed to be a hundred and fifteen in the weeks before he died, but many did not believe he was that old. His stories were colorful, and though they were hardly believable, they had the ring of truth. He told stories about being present at the dedication of the Eiffel Tower, which would have made him at least a hundred and thirty. He told stories about being the first Chinese graduate of Harvard, and on the boxing team no less; the records of neither could be found.

Chaim looked behind him, then peered around the room from behind his wife's shoulder. He made a note of all the women seated on the other side of the aisle. He knew that Donald was a confirmed bachelor, but he didn't know just how confirmed. The thought made him smile. Cause of death was listed as "natural," but it was only human nature to wonder.

Just two days ago they had been talking to one another. Donald was blind, deaf in one ear, had trouble speaking, and could not move around without a high-tech wheelchair. Yet he still was able to make fun of Chaim's new haircut. Their friendship was a mystery to outsiders. They constantly picked on each other's philosophies, made fun of one another, and argued about food. Their last conversation centered around whether it was cruel and unusual to make the yeast in beer die for its cause. Donald argued only half-jokingly that it was the worst kind of slavery. Causing the yeast-serf to do all the micro-chemical reactions for you, and then killing it. Worst of all—the result was a drink for decadent recreation.

"Chaim," Donald said in his voice, now like wet gravel. "It is not long for me. But you will continue. I want you to remember something. A wolf will hunt many rabbits in his lifetime. The wolf's survival depends on the rabbit. The rabbit must be allowed to reproduce in order to provide sustenance to the wolf. There is a balance. If there is an artificial increase in the number of rabbits, wolves become lazy because the hunt is so easy. The amount of rabbit food goes down, and then there are fewer rabbits. The lazy wolves then find it is not so easy to hunt and must get off their asses. It is their responsibility. But hold on. If there is an artificial increase in the number of wolves, they require more rabbits. The rabbit population goes down and many wolves starve. Listen to me. There comes a point at which the number of wolves is so large that the rabbits can be wiped out in one generation. Then there are no more rabbits, and soon there will be no more wolves. You must ask yourself every day how your actions affect the numbers of wolves and rabbits."

"Wolves also eat squirrels."

"Your impertinence will not be welcome in the next life."

They laughed at each other and then had dessert. Four hours later, in the middle of the night, Donald died in his sleep.

Five years previous, Chaim had chosen that name for himself and Leah had chosen her own name. It was well past time where they could use their own names. But there was something of a finality in the way they were chosen. After decades of dallying with the reality of the world, they were finally beginning to come to terms with just how quickly things had gotten away from them.

The immediate aftermath of World War II seemed to present the perfect opportunity for re-establishing an Originator plan.

Jubilation over the end of conflict seemed to give humanity a new purpose of peace. It didn't last. War was so destructive that the paranoia over further potential war was just as destructive for any alteration in society. Change, though inevitable, was controlled. Instead of new, revolutionary ideas popping up in the minds of many, as was promised by the industrial revolution, the old ideas were maintained and built upon. Maintain and build. That's what the rest of the century was about. Maintain and build. The only truly new idea was communism, and even this was warped in implementation.

Hydrogen research virtually ceased during the war. Research itself was changed forever. Instead of individual breakthroughs, new paradigms, and individual innovation that produced fundamental change, research was concentrated on those areas that would provide the most immediate opportunities for cash. Additionally, most innovations were directed at the new paranoia.

Chaim saw a long, slow slide into complacency over the promise of technology. He was surprised to find himself technologically suspicious. Maybe it was because he disagreed with the direction of the technology. It was hopelessly on the wrong track across the board.

He and Leah dropped in on society from time to time, but only to observe. They were no longer in the business of trying to help. He had made the decision to cut Originator losses. They would no longer try to alter the primitives' lives. They could move in and out of society as they wished, having been practiced at it for so long. But they couldn't interfere with any direction that history would take. They were released from their mission.

Chaim took his name as a symbolic gesture of life in general. *Life* as opposed to just living. It was his way of acknowledging his humanity.

After the funeral, he and Leah sat in the library of their 5th Avenue condominium. There was a music stand in the middle of the room with sheet music of Bach's cantatas for trumpet opened to a random page. Neither of them played. It was an original edition from 1665 bound in acetate and a combination of formaldehyde and varnish. Anyone who accidentally discovered the Originator grail would assume it was some kind of classical instrument. A priceless musical antique paired with a priceless music manuscript.

Chaim had it in his hands. Inactivated, it still gave off a dull hum and glow. He pondered it, turning it over in his hands. It was the ultimate legacy of his people. A lost relic of a lost civilization. The home world, Earth I, was surely dead by now. Other colonizers might have done better on other worlds. Or worse. There was no way of knowing. For all their technological progress, their focus was on energy collection, not communication. There was no way to communicate between colonies because all effective technological progress had by then only encompassed the surrounding few light years. Between galaxies was impossible.

On a computer, the astronomical team at Molineau had finally charted where, exactly, Earth I had existed. Then they tracked the migration to Earth II. The original records were lost in the Gulf of Mexico thousands of years ago. It was a sad commentary on how far they had come just to get to this point.

Chaim tried to picture the early days, when towers of conductive material were erected all over the globe, only to be toppled by the primitive tribes as signs of defiance. Then, after the isolated island fell into the sea, they constructed false monuments hiding their conductors: Cairo, Burubudur, Cuzco, Babel, Crete, Moab, Paris, Mid Manhattan.

That was the extent of the plan. Everything else was an on-the-fly decision. Chaim held the grail like a trumpet player at rest. He sat back in his brushed leather chair and felt the waves of energy run through his bones.

Of everything they had lost from the previous generations of selves, Leah missed the complexity of the clothing. She had fallen in love with that green and pink dress from the *Exposition Universelle* all those years ago. It had been a long time since she had fallen in love with a piece of clothing like that.

"Donald would have made fun of me for being so female," she observed. "I don't care. I was born a Victorian Jew at a time we were called *Jewess*."

She had on black pants and a light blue turtleneck sweater. But she did notice that Chaim looked one hundred percent better in his jeans and button down shirt than that silly vest suit he used to wear.

He put the trumpet back in its case, then in the safe behind the potted patio palm. He set it next to their infusion devices, which were tucked away in black round cases that resembled film canisters. Their biennial infusion was due in a couple of months.

"I don't see the point anymore," he said. "What good is immortality if the future is so bleak?"

"There isn't a certainty that you will always fail. The coin flip for winning and losing isn't a zero-sum game. Heads, you win; tails, you flip again."

"How can we just keep on going with no hope for success? I don't understand what makes you so optimistic."

"I'm not optimistic," she said. "I've seen too much for that. But I have faith."

"I don't understand your faith."

It was the same conversation they had been having since the late 1940s. Chaim, the strict rational vs. Leah, the emotive.

"I'm tired of watching just how quickly the world is disintegrating," he said.

"If only your impatience could be tempered by humility," she said, playing Donald's part. "It's not your fault."

"I failed my destiny," he said. "I'm tired of saying that. I'm tired of thinking it. I'm just tired of playing a part in a scheme I had no part in creating. I used to be a person. We both used to be regular people. Don't you miss being in the world instead of looking down upon it?"

"The god lowers himself to be among his subjects."

"I'm serious. I've had the responsibility for this planet given to me by the real gods. And I fumbled it. I don't want it anymore. Let it be handled by someone else. Let things happen as they will. This planet isn't a bonsai, for God's sake. Clip here; clip there; wire this; anchor that. Catch its shape and exaggerate it. This planet is a weed—runaway growth and cruelty, ignorance and bliss. I'm done. I'm done worrying about it. I'm done feeling responsible."

"What are you saying?"

"I'm ready. It's time to pack it in. I want to go to a baseball game without having to worry about being televised. I want to read a paper without having to wonder if some disaster could have been prevented or was actually caused by a member of my extended family."

"That will never happen. You'll never be off your guard, and you'll never get over where you came from. That's true for all of us, all of them. Part of being human is containing all of the tragedies of the past and living your own life."

"*Bubela*, I believe you're making my point for me. We can't possibly forget, but we can move on. I think it's time we were human again."

Chapter 58

Following one of the numerous pieces of Donald's advice, they ceased moving into society as public or even semi-public figures. They didn't own a high-profile company or have political posts. Chaim was, of all things, a diamond broker. Leah found time to be a professional liaison between business and government. Chaim and Leah Onward were anonymous.

They were visited occasionally by Originators. The Onwards had a lot of relatives. All of Leah's immediate family had died. It had been very hard on her, but she'd borne it for the cause. Now the cause was dead, and she finally visited their graves.

When the time came to use the infusion devices, they kept them in the safe. Their decision was greeted with mild disgust at Molineau, but no one tried to stop them (short of Ezra's disapproving stare and silent treatment). Immediately, Leah saw a doctor for her growing tumor. Medicine had come a long way, and it was probable she would survive and even be able to have children. It was done. Their part in the Originator cause was to die with them.

During one of these visits to the hospital, Chaim, unable to stay in the waiting room for an extended period of time, crossed the street and started walking. It was the middle of the day. He stopped in at a small Kosher deli. He no longer wished to *act* like a Jew. Being human meant *being*, not *acting*.

He sat by himself and ordered a pastrami sandwich. He almost ordered a ham & pickle sandwich before catching himself. He was no longer an Originator *Marrano*, he was a Jew. This thought sent a tremble down his spine. It was at no time more real than when he almost ordered that sandwich. He thought of the many things he would be required to do now, like attend Temple and... and raise pigeons or some such. He couldn't remember what all the requirements were. It had been such a long time since he had learned all that, and there were many memories taking up space in his head.

Before his lunch arrived, an older gentleman came up to him. "Excuse me," he said. "You look troubled."

Chaim did not know what to say. He simply stared up at the man. He had the craggy features and drooping nose of his wife's relatives.

"You just came from the hospital, didn't you?"

"How did you know that?" Chaim was instantly on his guard.

"Your expression is downcast. Your actions are nervous. You are alone on a Wednesday and you are not in business clothing. Forgive me for imposing my own personal stereotype on the worried husband... or son? or brother?"

"Who are you working for?"

"Working for? That's a strange question. I work for all mankind. I sense you're in some kind of conflict. I could see it when you came in. Do you mind if I sit down?"

"Do I have a choice?"

"Your anger is misplaced, but understandable."

"Where will you be dragging me off to, today?"

"Pardon? We don't operate that way, young man. This is all voluntary. If you want me to go, I will. But you can't escape God."

"God? What does God have to... Hold on, you're a rabbi."

"Guilty. Now tell me, what's your name?"

"Chaim."

The rabbi laughed. "That's a good name for a Jew. I assume you are a Jew. But this is New York; you can never tell."

"I was a better one a long time ago."

"There is no good and bad to this. Just a degree of commitment. You don't see me with my skullcap on all day long. You ever see *On the Waterfront?*"

"I've been down there."

"No. It's a movie. There's this Catholic priest played by that guy with the schnozzle the size of Poughkeepsie. He's a tough old bastard. Smokes, drinks, gambles. At least, I think that was him. Anyways, he's successful because he's one of them. One of the workers, not one of those holier-than-thou schmucks. That's what I'm doing. You don't see me with the hair and with the long beard and with the always looking at my feet. Except on Saturdays. Flying yarmulkes and all that."

"That's very impressive."

"Impressive isn't what I was going for."

The waitress brought Chaim his sandwich and Dr. Brown's soda. The mustard was in a small dish on the side of his plate. The smell wasn't as strong as he was used to. It made him wonder if the mustard was weak or if his senses had been weakened.

"That's the best pastrami sandwich in ten city blocks. My name is Fesenden. Everybody calls me Rabbi Fez. I think it's some sort of joke."

"Fez is an old Muslim state in North Africa."

"Something like that. But..." he trailed off with a gesture of his hand. "I sense you want to talk about the loved one in the hospital."

"My wife. She has a tumor."

"I'm sorry. I see now why the lines on your forehead are dancing."

"The doctor says she'll be fine."

"But she's going through a lot of pain right now."

"It's inevitable. There's the surgery and then the radiation treatments."

"For the best. But let's talk about you. You are having personal troubles with God."

Chaim looked up from his sandwich. "What makes you say that?"

"It's my business to see these things."

"I don't know that there's any trouble I have with God. God seems irrelevant."

"Them's fighting words. But, as it happens, I don't disagree."

"You don't?"

"Irrelevant is such a pejorative term. But if you mean that He has left us to our own devices, you're right. Take that sandwich you're holding. It's spicy beef, right? So take that beef out of there and put in some ham, or lobster and bacon, or some *treyf* like that. What happens? Nothing is what happens. You have free will. God gives you the brains to choose a lifestyle. He has His reasons, but what does He know, really?"

"You have to excuse me if I say that I've never heard this kind of argument before."

"I didn't realize we were arguing."

"No. What I mean is, you don't sound like any rabbi I've ever known." Chaim set his sandwich down.

"Well... What do those other guys know, anyways? People are too attuned to their religions, if you ask me. People want to know what their God wants of them, but they think they already know. That's the trouble with people."

"That's not what I meant," Chaim said. "I wasn't talking about my religion. I was talking about life in general. People do things for the sake of something they can't see, can't detect, can't perceive in any way. They destroy things based on a distant rumor. They kill people based on their interpretation of some story that is irrational to begin with. And for what? I don't like the term *free will*. Like you say, we have free will. But that also implies that something or someone gave it to us. Do animals have free will? Giraffes? Trees? Phytoplankton?"

"Hold on there. Let's stick to people, can we? Of course the stories are irrational. You think being so sensible is sensible? Let's run around and declare there is no God. That we are accidents of history. That's fine. But then what? It's not just about God, you know. Science teaches us that there will always be things we can't know. Is that God? You people and your theories.

I tell you, there is more in the human heart than just blood. People who can feel it, feel it here. They are people who believe that there is something larger than themselves. Is that a good thing?"

"Of course that's a good thing. But why does that thing have to be your God? There is plenty in the universe that is larger than ourselves. We can be awed by the expansion of space, by the multitude of planets and stars..."

"What! All of a sudden He's *my* God? Listen, Mr. Chaim, from where I'm sitting, your problem is with being a Jew. You don't want to follow the rules, hah, who am I to stop you from abandoning them? The God that I believe in lays down the law for reasons that I may not understand—although I'd like to think that I understand a lot. Maybe not all, but I'm OK with that. Let me tell you something. My ancestors, and yours too, came from a place on the map. Then there was a place on the map no longer, and we dispersed. We were completely disconnected from each other. But we kept the traditions.

For thousands of years, through empires that rose and fell. We were thrown out of some of the best houses in Europe. We had to keep ourselves secret. We practiced our traditions out of the view of the world. We pretended to be Christian and Muslim and Protestant, and sometimes we were out in the open. But we survived. Through sheer will. Stubbornness. Refusal to assimilate in that manner. If God is as irrelevant as you say... well, what? Your God, my God... forget God for a minute. Stubbornness is what binds us together as Jews. Ritual lets us know what kind of fathers we had. Look around at the *goyim* who don't know their families from just a few generations back. We know where we come from. We weren't the smartest people, not the best warriors in battle. We certainly don't have the looks—although, if I may say so, you're a handsome guy, I mean in general... What I mean is, we don't have anything going for us except our difficult and crotchety constitutions. That's what Nietzsche was talking about. Will to power. You think about that. My parents' and my grandparents' generation had people come here from Italy, Germany, Poland, Czechoslovakia, Hungary... you get the picture.

You know what they did to their kids? They didn't teach them the old languages. Learn English, they said. Be an American, they said. But, despite leaving their languages behind in the cupboards of their mother countries, they insisted... no, they *demanded* that the Hebrew traditions be followed. Just in case they were someday brought together back into a common community. No mother country. Just the idea of one. You think about that."

"But now there is a mother country."

"Now there is a mother country. Yes, that's true. But, what? How many Jews you think identify themselves as Israelis? Hm? That's what I thought. We went forth. We multiplied. And now there are millions of us. But the world grew around us, and it grew out of religious states. Israel is a state based on our people. But we transcend religion. Do you know what I'm saying? As a Jew, you have your beliefs and you have your God and you have your Bible. But more than anything you have your experiences. We share the experience of ritual, of secrets, of cynicism. Tell me something, Mr. Chaim. Have you been to this mother country?"

"Once," Chaim said, lying. This extraordinary man sitting across the table from him was accusing him of something. He didn't appear to be insincere, but you never could tell. He really missed having Donald around. A part of him was missing, and it was this part—the side of him that constantly wanted debate, argument, intellectual discourse. Donald had been an enthusiastic foil, constantly challenging him to defend himself, think differently, assess his choices and interpret his actions. To the end.

He lied now, not because there was an impression he wanted to create, as had been the case before. His entire life was a lie, his reason for being was to continue a lie. But this lie was something else entirely. He felt ashamed for some reason. Raised half-heartedly to be a half-hearted Jew, he was all too quick to abandon that persona for others of a more *satisfactory*, less *painful* lifestyle. He was ashamed to admit that he did not know what it meant to be a Jew. Leah had often talked to him about such things, and he usually followed her in their observances. But he was just going through the motions, disdaining the underlying rationale for them.

He quickly recovered from his lie to make it seem less egregious. "It was a stopover in Tel Aviv on a flight to Nairobi." Which, while not true, was possible. Were it not for a lack of first-class seating, he and Leah might have taken that flight. As it was, they took a flight that stopped in Cairo instead.

"As a Jew, it is your duty to go there. But a person of the world, as I sense you are, also has a duty to leave and forge your place in the world outside. With a country, recognized by most of the rest of the world, we now have a home. But it is understandable to feel that *home* is a relative term. We've been away so long that it is an alien place for most of us. I went there six years ago. I did the whole thing. The wailing wall, the Dome... I even saw Golgotha, for what that's worth. All that stuff. Eh... I have to say. It didn't feel much like a home to me. It's interesting, but if this is the chosen land, I say choose me out. People are killing each other over the right to live in this place? But spirituality cannot be debated on these terms. I can do my work in a nicer place. I can make some kind of religious excuse like my God has asked me to do my work here. But the fact is, I like it here better. I like being around people from other parts of the world, listening to different languages, accents, the way people think. Stories. People tell better stories about their native countries when they're away from them. New York is just the best place in the world for things like that. If God wants to talk to me and tell me I'm in the wrong place for this stuff, let Him do it. But I haven't heard from Him, so I've got my sanity to think about."

Rabbi Fez grabbed a lump of pastrami from Chaim's plate, dipped it in the mustard and took a bite.

"But that's just me," he added.

"You've got a definite sense of who you are."

"It only seems like it, because I'm such an opinionated S.O.B. But if it helps, sure, why not. I know who I am. You, you've got a lot to get through. Your wife and whatever it is that is weighing on you." He got up to leave and handed Chaim a card. "I apologize that I must philosophize and run. Give me a call if you want to chat. I have many more opinions and views that I can foist upon you. Bah, I'm no diplomat, am I? Don't think of me as a barge carrying you from one place to another. I'm just a tugboat trying to push you."

"Thank you for the conversation."

"My pleasure. Please call. There's more where that came from."

Chapter 59

Having lived almost a hundred and forty years, having been all over the globe, Chaim was almost surprised he had never made it to Palestine (now, *Israel*). Had he been consciously avoiding it? Or was it simply a case where he never had the chance?

Leah was excited about the trip all the way from the air terminal at JFK to the rental car counter in Tel Aviv. In their hotel room, she was in an emotional state, having been through two series of treatments; they were still unsure they would ever have children. She wore a blue kerchief tied around her head to help her feel less freakish about her hairlessness. Her oncologist advised her not to go but in the end didn't object too strongly and gave her the name of another doctor in Yafo. Chaim and Leah Onward were in Israel.

"I don't know if I'm supposed to go through the conversion," Chaim kept saying to her. My mother wasn't really Jewish..."

"You were bar mitzvah-ed weren't you?"

"Sure. I did all that."

"Then don't worry about it."

After lamenting that there were no good cheeseburgers in Tel Aviv, they decided to take the tour to Jerusalem. Rabbi Fez was right, this place didn't feel like home. Not for either of them. Leah was disappointed. She had been raised to believe that this was the land of return for all Jews of the world. But it didn't feel real. It didn't have an authentic feel. It seemed like they were in some kind of Jewish theme park.

The trip didn't feel real. It had been so long since they had gone anywhere that wasn't related to one kind of business or another. They were just sightseers. Maybe when they saw the

Wailing Wall they would feel different.

Leah leaned her head on Chaim's shoulder as they rode the bus to Jerusalem. It was a small bus, more like a converted van. But air-conditioned, thank God. That was one of the most welcome inventions Chaim had seen in the previous century.

About halfway through the trip, the ride became rougher, and the bus abruptly slowed down. The driver's voice came over the loudspeaker. "Ladies and gentlemen," he said. "We have experienced a small problem with one of the wheels. It is my belief that a tire has gone flat. We should be delayed no more than twenty minutes while we try and fix the problem."

Chaim glanced out the window. They appeared to be between towns on a highway in the chaparral. No trees were taller than five feet. It made the poles that held the power lines appear that much more artificial. The driver stepped off the bus with a plastic box that held tools for the tire.

Almost immediately, the bus started shaking, The passengers heard popping sounds from outside the cabin. There were about forty of them, and there was now a commotion at the front. A man in a green army-style uniform stepped on board, brandishing a machine gun. He had on a cloth cap with large flaps in the back and the sides, and his face was covered with a scarf of some kind. He shouted something in a foreign language.

Chaim prevented Leah from raising her head, and they kept still. Another man climbed onto the bus, dressed similarly but with a white cloth hat and bandana. He walked up and down the aisle. He pointed at people at random, saying, "You, off the vehicle!" in an Arabic accent. The people got up, hurried and prodded by the machine gun, and stumbled down the steps.

He paced up and down the length of the bus a couple of times, pointing out more and more people, until finally it was just Chaim and Leah. He shouted something and then three other gunman jumped on the bus. One of them got into the driver's seat and they drove off, leaving the rest of the passengers stranded.

"Where are you taking us?" Chaim asked.

The man with the white hat smacked him quickly with the back of his hand and shouted something. Leah fell off his shoulder as his head snapped back. The reddening pain came later.

"Be quiet and we won't kill anyone."

Chaim looked around the bus and assessed his options. There was no obvious means of escape. Behind them about four or five rows back was an exit and behind that was the emergency exit. It would be impossible for them to escape without a major diversion. Oh, to have Li-Don in a situation like this!

Then again, they no longer carried their emitters with them. Protection from others in the family had seemed no longer necessary. Their entry into the maelstrom of humanity meant they would be governed by its fate now; no longer by a fate of their own making. He thought of the many times he had been with death before. His father, his mother, his wife, himself, and just recently his best friend. He looked at it rationally. If death was to come, he would do what he could to stop it, but in the end, if it was meant to be, he would give way. If they were to die on that bus, so be it.

He looked over at Leah, who looked back at him in fright and an almost weary sense of dread. It was a look that said *What have we gotten ourselves into this time?* More patterns.

For about an hour, they drove roughly northward through desolate wilderness. The jagged hills framed a salty white and yellow landscape. Chaim thought he saw the outline of a city through the front window. On a straightaway towards the city, the bus began to slow down. A grinding noise coming from underneath the cabin startled them, then the engine whined and finally died.

The driver smacked the wheel and shouted something at it. Both side doors burst open. Chaim and Leah ducked down and held each other—they heard the clicking of gunmetal in preparation for firing, but the shots didn't come. Chaim wondered if they were being hijacked again.

From behind the seat and underneath the windows, they couldn't tell much of what was going on. There were some threatening noises, and shouts in different languages. There was the unmistakable sound of violent anxiety in them. Then the guns started firing. They covered their ears, but the noise was too loud to drown out entirely. The popping was constant and then trailed off as the hijackers reloaded. But instead of more popping, there was the sound of metallic boots on the steps of the bus. Many, many boots. They dared not poke their heads up, but they were curious.

A man dressed in light green, army-style fatigues and sunglasses stood over them. "You'll want to come with me."

Chaim looked up at him, still holding on to Leah's shoulders. "If it's all the same to you, we'd like to go home now."

"What makes you think you're going home?"

Chapter 60

Chaim and Leah were put into a modified RV that had pulled alongside the tour bus.

"What's going to happen to the other tourists?" Chaim asked an anonymous soldier.

"I wouldn't be worrying about that if I were you."

As he held Leah, who had already been weary because of the treatments, he felt her totally give way to their situation. All tension went out of her body. She was resigned to whatever happened. Chaim felt resigned too. It was strangely peaceful and satisfying. Fighting against an unseen enemy for so long; fighting against himself, his father, his ancestors, the planet in general. Fighting against being who he was, and being discovered.

It felt so familiar, being taken under armed guard to see someone. Patterns repeating themselves. How else to acquire information from members of a secret society but by kidnapping them when they least expected it. Chaim recognized the tactics of the other side—the dramatic entrance, the impressive presentation, the power of just the face and the voice.

The RV drove for a while farther north, then turned off the highway onto a dirt road that became secluded with cliffs and trees. He guessed they were heading towards Haifa or maybe Nazareth, but he couldn't be sure. He had only seen those cities on a map. They stopped by a river, brakes squeaking in protest, as if they hadn't been attended to in a while. A small yacht was idling at a private dock, waiting for them.

They were welcomed on board heartily by Cronos. "So nice to see a familiar face," he said.

Chaim and Leah said nothing. Cronos had to have known the utter chaos he had brought into their lives. And yet he had been responsible for keeping Leah from death.

"I want you to know that I mean you no harm," Cronos went on. "I never have. I should tell you that you've become easier to get at in recent years. I prefer the good old days when even entire teams of mercenaries would not be able to get to you. It was more of a challenge. But I have some good news for you, what *should* come as good news anyway."

The boat sped off as they took their seats on deck. Chaim noticed that there were no guns anymore. Or were they hidden? The people dressed in fatigues were now relaxed, and there was no air of threat any longer.

"You've done us proud," Cronos said when they were well underway downriver, to the west, towards the Mediterranean. "I asked you not to interfere and you haven't. For that I am eternally grateful. I know there is nothing I can offer that you will accept, but here is something you can't resist. I'm giving you the entire world. By the look on your face, I can tell you are skeptical. But I assure you that the Earth is now yours to play with as you please. I have heard rumors that you have decided to commit intellectual suicide. Are those rumors true? No matter. Regardless of your state of mind, the inheritance will now pass to you, unobstructed any further by me or my operatives."

"I don't know what your game is, and I don't care. Just leave us alone."

"You are not understanding me. This is most unfortunate. I must say, you tried so hard to defeat me without really knowing how or why you were trying. For someone with so many handicaps and so much personnel and firepower against him, I'd say you did quite well. In any event, you did not slow us down, and we have now completed our mission (which was a good deal easier than the mission that was chosen for you)."

"What mission?"

"To leave this planet alone. To allow the primitives to continue to evolve on their own. Your influence lasted up until, what, sixty or seventy years ago? And just look at the progress they've made since then. I can only imagine what this place will look like in a hundred years."

"What are you talking about now?"

The rumbling of the boat's engines intensified the silence between remarks.

"How can you not have seen this? I knew we were working in secret, but our aim was only to keep our plans from the primitives. I had no idea that you had no idea. We are leaving this place; we've acknowledged the failures here and we're moving on. We've finally collected enough energy to get off of this stinking rock. This is why I brought you here. To tell you that we're leaving. This planet has been an interesting experiment, but it's time to let it go. We'll be leaving within the week. I won't tell you where we're going, but I *will* tell you that we don't have a fixed destination. We have enough power to last us a good long time, though, so I'm not worried. It's only a matter of maintaining your speed once you get out beyond the gravity of a star."

"You're really leaving?" Leah asked. Her voice was clear and definite. Chaim was surprised to hear her voice.

"Our time has come, young one."

"I'm staring into the face of the man who has both saved my life and made my life a living Hell. I'm wondering if he did one just to do the other."

"There are a great many questions in the universe. We can't always know everything. You can assume many things. Such as one event following another. But also you can't always assume that events that follow one another were planned that way. Like lightning that strikes a tree which causes the tree to fall over. You can't assume that the intent of the lightning was to kill the tree or even to hit the tree. *It happens.* That's all one can say."

"I'll tell you what I can assume," Chaim said. "You planted that rabbi to send me to Israel."

"Hold on there, son. He is no more of my army that he is of yours. But you must remember that people are malleable. Let's just say it wasn't a coincidence that the most talkative and persuasive rabbi in The Bronx somehow ended up in a Manhattan Delicatessen. But there does not need to be a network of conspirators in order for a conspiracy to exist. That meeting was my last gift to you as someone who truly understands the nature of persuasion."

"How did you find the sanity to maintain this collective conspiracy of yours, keeping it separate from the rest of them?"

Cronos smacked his lips. "It's easy to use the word *them*, isn't it? Calling these people *them* must make it easier to stomach what you're doing. But I'm not the sole cause of your perceived troubles. The collective conspiracy is just as menacing as your own. And yet, neither of us is a particularly circumspect person. I've told you everything I was going to do, and I've done it. You have done the same, only you failed. A noble failure, to be sure, but a disappointment nonetheless. Those Palestinian mercenaries who hijacked your tour bus... We freed you from them. You must know by now that there are no coincidences. Your true tormentor hired them. He's a good deal sloppier than I am. Myself, I made you fearful and suspicious. But him, that free radical of selfish wiggery, he made you bleed."

"One of your generals gone amok?"

"Hardly. He's one of yours. I do wish you people would talk to each other once in a while. Ah! But here's our stop. You can do as you wish. No more subterfuge. Travel the world and tell your story. Publicize the shame and the betrayal. It's of no matter to me. As I said, the Earth is yours."

The boat slowed down; the engines reversed. Chaim and Leah were showed off the boat—they stumbled onto the land; the boat never actually stopped moving—and were thrown the keys to a car that sat at the top of a ridge about a thousand feet away. The boat sped off again, fading into the landscape.

"We'll never see each other or the like of each other, again," Cronos shouted from the prow. "*Shalom*, my good man. *Adieu!*"

Later that week, infrared images taken by the Mexican Army appeared to show odd lighted objects passing through the atmosphere and then disappearing. Many scientists explained it as the dispersal of petroleum vapor in the atmosphere, a phenomenon which the Mexican oil industry was known to cause from time to time.

Chapter 61

Hardly. He's one of yours.

Chaim's father was ecstatic over the news that Cronos and his cronies had left (as ecstatic as he ever got). He thought this was the perfect time to resume their cause and find a new way to integrate themselves.

But Chaim refused. As the acknowledged leader of the remaining Originators, he still had the final say. Chaim knew integration was impossible, perhaps less so than in earlier times. Ezra disagreed, but his global vision was not as acute as it used to be. He had not been among humans in a number of years and had only observed society from his high perch. He also claimed that he didn't know what enemy Cronos was talking about.

"As if there were some sort of rogue element on our side? Preposterous. They were the cause of all our troubles. They were the ones who had the special knowledge of our side and blocked it at every turn. They exploited our mutual desire to remain hidden in order to sabotage our cause. What are you afraid of now?"

Chaim and his father were corresponding over the Internet using a VPN chat. His father couldn't see, for example, Chaim's bemused grin at his father's attempt at rhetoric. Or the fact that Chaim's plaid shirt was hanging out of his jeans. Or Leah's fuzzy head of short strawberry-blonde hair.

Chaim typed a reply. "Consider your cause in a different light. This world you set in motion now has a momentum of its own. No scientist in his dreamy wondering of experimentation would ever think something like that was going to happen. Integrate if you like, but don't put the burden of your alternate hypothesis of the Genesis epic onto the world. Regardless of truth, these people have mythologies of themselves that are too powerful to play with. To address your question, I'm afraid of reactionary forces. Not from our friends, who are no longer with us, but from humanity in general."

Ezra had never been aggressive about taking the plan forward, but this new development had made him bolder. Almost impatient. It was unsettling.

They had begun having short chats like this a few years earlier. It was much easier to have a conversation with him when he wasn't in the room. There were no interruptions, no blurted out profanities, no knee-jerk vocal or facial reactions to one another. Writing a conversation was much more civil, like it had been in the old days, when a letter took weeks to arrive at its destination and correspondence was more thought out.

"Your fear is simply a manifestation," Ezra wrote, "of your deep desire for anonymity, which is itself a masked desire for death. The guilt you hold is for your entire race, but it is misplaced because you are not the cause. You can't believe that your failure is yours alone."

Chaim didn't quite know where Ezra was going with that ending to the message. It was an incomplete thought, and not very well-reasoned either. That was unsettling also.

The chat program indicated that Ezra had broken the connection. It wasn't the first time that he had left in the middle of a thought, but it was an odd thought to leave on. There were a few incomplete accusations in the air.

"He's responding erratically," Chaim said to his wife.

"He must be preoccupied with practicing being sensitive and caring."

"His arguments are incomplete. His accusations are contradictory and poorly constructed."

"Nothing's stopping you from going up there."

"Except my better judgment."

The drive up was uneventful. Crossing the border into Canada had become tedious because of the increased terror warnings, but there were no problems.

Leah stayed behind to keep an appointment with her oncologist. The preliminary results of her treatment were promising, and there was hope they would be able to have children. Chaim suspected that part of the reason for the number of tests they were running was her unique physiology. But he had no proof.

Driving in his refurbished 1968 Avanti (originally Donald's car), he came up to the hill in the middle of the forest around evening, but the characteristic glow coming from behind it was absent. As he drove up to the front gate, he sensed something was wrong. The place was deserted, the gate locked with a chain and several padlocks. That was not unusual. But there was no one at the gate to meet him. *That* was unusual. A small sign on the fence in small official-looking letters read, "Closed for Refurbishment".

He took a look beyond the fence and tried to see something that he recognized through the trees, the shape of the buildings or the hardhats of workers. But there were only trees guarding the unusually dark background.

Logically, having the mine go dark would indicate some kind of crisis. Probably precipitated by the departure of one half of the Originator population. Perhaps there was a power vacuum, causing some kind of civil war. Or maybe it had been discovered by an outside group and had to shut down as a precaution. He was always waiting for that day, but the mine was located in such a desolate part of the wilderness that it had not been a problem, so far.

The instinct to lightly rub his wrist where the emitter was located survived even his mortality decision. And there it was. He may have lost hope in the mission, but he was no fool. Protection was protection. He flexed his hands, then pulled a pair of leather gloves out from under the seat and took a bolt cutter out of the trunk—from underneath the spare. He cut two of the links from the locked chain clean in half and unwound it from the gate. Then he swung open the two sides and drove through. Though he tried to be careful, at this point, he was a little pissed off. He now felt annoyance and irritation that he should somehow end up here.

He tried to understand what he had learned and when. But there was so much. What was the pattern? He had in his head the hundreds of physical formulae of distinct chemical and particle reactions. He could find the patterns through the reactions. Yet he couldn't seem to find the pattern of behavior of many people. Least of all his father. Without any empirical evidence, and the will the collect it, he had to devise theories, many of which turned out to be wrong.

Driving through the dense forest to get to the main office building at the edge of the mine pit was normally not an unpleasant experience. The eerie feeling he got winding his way across the partially paved road now however, was not just because of the darkness of twilight. He *sensed* that something was wrong. But, having come this far, and having had the partial expectation of finding something amiss, he now had an obligation to take the situation as it came.

He didn't know exactly when he realized it was a trap. Maybe when he first arrived to the darkened operation. Maybe when he turned the corner to find broken windows and strewn metal parts of the building around the edge of the pit. Whatever it was, he had to face it.

Cronos had been prescient about that other antagonist, who was now standing in the middle of the road with an unknown weapon pointed directly at Chaim's forehead.

Chapter 62

From *Introduction to Sub-Atomic HyperActivation*, by Chaim Onward

The means by which true plasma weapons can annihilate the structure of matter does not violate the conservation laws of physics. Just because the atom is dismantled does not automatically mean that the nuclear force is unleashed. There are hundreds of forces hidden within each atom: binding, repelling, attracting, pushing, pulling... even indirect influence through mechanisms we don't quite understand yet. The point is, we can control which known force is affected and apply our strength to that force. For example, the repelling force can be strengthened through the ejection of plasma from crystallized carbon oxides, such as corundum exposed to hyperactivated hydrogen. The resulting hyperkinetic ball of positrons and half-positrons can activate the repelling force in any object in its path, thereby causing atoms to split apart along the natural repellance cracks. The resulting dispersal of particles mimics the effects of photosynthetic oxidation or, more accurately, vaporization. Applying directional force to this ball can turn it into a useful industrial cutting tool, or a devastating weapon.

Chaim threw himself down on the bench front seat as a violent ball of energy tore through the windshield and back window of his car, sizzling and crackling as it passed over him, electrifying the air inside the car much as lightning does on a dry day.

Another ball shot out of the radio on his dash, carving a cylinder of nothingness from the nose of the car to the back bumper. He dove out the passenger side door and flipped on his emitter all in one motion, just as he hit the ground, avoiding the third volley that effortlessly burrowed its way from the left headlight to the right taillight.

The emitter popped and crackled, reacting to the free quarks in the air. He crawled backwards, away from the car. A round ball of energy flew through the frame of the open door as if it weren't there and headed directly for him. The contact of the plasma ball to the emitter field was anti-climactic, although the relief he felt wasn't. The emitter field seemed to swallow it up, briefly changing color—to purple, of all things—then returning to its former state of transparency.

He was hit with several more volleys that lit up his general area. He could feel the air-borne electricity even from within the field, but it was harmless enough. He stood up, almost defiantly, and tried to let his eyes adjust to the darkness to see who was shooting at him. Of course, he knew who it was. Who else could it have been? The Man on the Tower, having failed to kill him numerous other times, was trying again. He came closer, walking forward, firing more rounds at him. Chaim felt each impact as it was absorbed by the field. It was a sensation like a buzzing cloud of mosquitoes, where every spot on the skin felt on guard for a sting that never came.

The lights in the facility began blinking on their sulfur yellow. The Man on the Tower came into view as Chaim backed up into the dull glow of a safety lamp by the edge of the pit. His face was screwed into a scowl, with one eye almost closed and his teeth edged together. It was the face that had haunted him all his life. It was quite possible that he had massacred the entire population of the mine. This weird weapon, bastardizing the Originator technology for breaking apart and fusing carbon deposits into precious gems, would not have been expected and could have caught a number of employees without any defenses.

It was something Chaim refused to believe (although, intellectually, he still allowed for the possibility).

"The best we can hope for is a stalemate!" Chaim shouted.

He received no reply. The figure came closer, walking briskly and firing with each step, seeming frustrated at the lack of progress.

"You can't harm me with this or any other weapon!" Chaim's voice was drowned out by the violent flashes and sizzles of the plasma balls.

It passed through his mind that it was irrational for this man to try to kill him now, after having for so many years not done so.

"Is there something about this situation you don't understand?" Chaim shouted between shots. As expected there was no reasoning with this man.

He had thought about this moment many times. Not just seeing him face to face, but staring him down with their lives in the balance.

"Are you Originator?"

Nothing. He had the right homogeneous facial features to be one. It was a question meant as a diplomatic gesture rather than true information gathering. However, information was going to be hard to come by, so he might as well have asked.

The firing slowed. The other man's face became more impassive. He seemed genuinely confused by his weapon's weaknesses. He stared at it for a short time and whacked it with the heel of his palm. He fired again with no effect.

Chaim repeated his question: "Are you Originator?"

The other man glared at him, then threw down the weapon and walked off. Chaim rushed over and allowed the emitter field to pass over it. He picked it up at his feet. It was white and red, shaped like half of an airplane, with one wing and one horizontal stabilizer. He couldn't find a trigger or an activation switch. There must be some kind of rotation or push action. He wasn't paying much attention to what the other man's hands were doing to make it fire. He also didn't want to accidentally set it off while it was within the field.

The man came back with a different weapon, a photon beam cutter used for the mining operation. He was very calm about it. The beam passed across the emitter field, but not through, altering its red color but nothing more. He was getting more frustrated. He switched off the beam and threw the second weapon down. Then he approached Chaim and his field.

The Man on the Tower reached out with a finger and lightly touched the field. He drew back his hand. It would have felt like a combination of hot steam and a small electric shock. Chaim was filled with disgust and pity.

"You're not that smart," the man said suddenly. It was odd hearing that voice he associated with terror and hatred speaking directly to him. "You're still here. Why are you still here?"

"I have many failings," Chaim said. "One of them is curiosity."

The other man sighed, then blew air through his teeth as he looked into the distance.

"Are you Originator?" Chaim asked once more.

"What does that matter?"

The man picked up a rock about the size of a golf ball and threw it directly at Chaim. The emitter field slowed it down as it passed through, and then let it fall to the ground.

"Why don't you just fucking die?" the Man said, putting a hand to his forehead. "Things would be better if you were dead. But you don't die. You never do."

That question had been on Chaim's rational mind for many years. "So you *were* trying to kill me," he said. He felt a strange sense of relief that he had discovered the answer. The mystery surrounding that question had plagued him for so long, he hadn't realized how much finding the answer would mean to him.

"You just keep going," the Man added.

Chaim's mind cleared quickly. He dropped the weapon. He had been asking the wrong question. This was a different intellect than he was used to. "Why are you still alive?" he asked.

The Man on the Tower looked at him with a sour expression. "You think I don't know who you are? You think I haven't been thinking about you every day for the last hundred and fifty years?"

Chaim looked around again and tried to suppress his anguish at the destruction. He wanted to know where the mine personnel was, where his father was, Jimmy... he wondered if de Meurre had left with the rest of them on that side.

"You Goddamn intellectual! You pacifist snob! Where were you when the world was at war! Hiding in your academic hole, wringing your hands at the state of things. You want to know who I am? I'm a soldier. I fought with the British at Ypres. I fought with the Americans in Sicily. While you sucked on your toes and pulled the blankets over your head, I was trying to help stabilize the world. Not by whispering in the ears of bureaucrats, but by firing guns at evil. You and your kind don't have any idea what it takes to keep things on the right course."

Chaim was dumbfounded. It had not once entered into his mind that this terrorist thought he was benefiting mankind.

"That's right. You've been fucking things up since you were born. You perfumed lily! You don't fight for what's right. You know what needs to be done, but you can't do it. Well, I can. I'm not interested in your experiments, your superior technology. You're so afraid of being persecuted that you can't see just how much your machines will help the world. You choose to see only the bad, and you ignore the good. Only you have the right answer, is that it? And those poor peons down there just won't accept it. They won't accept your rule. Look at you. The Philosopher King. You think and sleep and think some more, and you can't hear the barbarians outside laying waste to your kingdom. Don't you read what humanity has written? Watch its plays? Listen to its music? Madness is everywhere, but so is sanity. Violence is necessary to maintain the balance."

"Are you Originator?" Chaim repeated, unable to argue.

The other man threw up his hands. "Is that all you want to know? Faced with your nemesis, is that your question to him? Son of a bitch! You already know the answer. But since you're so interested, and since we have all this time on our hands, let's have a conversation. Let's just put down our weapons and talk and maybe we'll become friends, fight side by side against the evils of this world. Is that it? You still want to play psychological games with me, don't you? All right. Let's fight by your rules. Look at me, look into my face, my eyes, the shape of my chin. We both know we come from the same ancestors. The same direct ancestors. Let's have this out, shall we? In the interests of warfare. Because I'm ashamed to say we share parents.

You father was my father, your mother was my mother. But don't for a second think that we're brothers. We're no more brothers than a frog and a bear. I was born in the human year 1430. They wanted me to lead them into the promised land. Much later, of course. We were Tuscans. Medici footmen."

From behind him, Chaim heard a noise. It was a tentative step of someone trying to get to his feet. He turned around to see Old Ezra, dusting himself off. He had a few bruises and some scorch marks along his neck. Hyim noticed that Ezra was missing his shield of protection, the emitter.

"But something went wrong," Old Ezra said, steadying himself. "The child displayed some aberrant tendencies. He was quick to temper. He fought with the servants. Eventually, he joined the infantry. It was an old-fashioned genetic mutation. The aggression we had spent thousands of years trying to weed out of our race had shown up."

"So they abandoned me. They left me without my infusions and refused to help when I was stricken with the Black Death. Then, a knock at the door. A doctor in a crow's beak mask administered the infusion for me. Ptolemy saved my life. He saw what they were trying to do to me, and he helped. He made me see how wrong they were, how damaging and destructive their experiment was. How, by insinuation and passive sabotage, they were waging ideological warfare by proxy."

"You're wrong," Ezra said. "Our only purpose was to create a peaceful world."

"It wasn't up to you to create, was it? Father. Only gods can create on absolute terms. You failed to account for what you call mutations, like me. You never accounted for me. It's the way of all things. You can't breed out aggression like you can blond hair. It's a part of our evolutionary past. It's a survival strategy from our reptilian ancestors. No matter how many of those you create," here he pointed at Chaim, "you're always going to get one of these," here he pointed at himself.

He turned back to Chaim. "And you. what shall we do with you? After years of Rousseau and Voltaire and Spinoza and Schopenhauer and Hume, they thought they had a handle on what it took to pursue their endgame. That's you. You're the Golden Child. You are the living embodiment of everything that disappointed them about me. The idealist pragmatist; the theoretical engineer; the academic industrialist; the socialist businessman. The Philosopher King. But as it turns out, you're nothing but a selfish coward. We would all be better off if I were in charge."

"And wage war against the primitives?" Ezra asked.

"If that's what it takes."

"If that's what it takes for what?" Chaim said. Having followed the argument, he was now ready to take it on.

"For assimilation, of course. For the veil to be lifted; to live our lives without secrecy. We're all after the same thing."

"To live as the aristocracy, in other words."

"If that's what it takes."

"Did you learn nothing from the past hundred years? True power is given, not assumed."

"True power is seized through sheer force of will. I've stayed under your veil of secrecy up until now because it suited me. The primitives are too stupid to understand who we are and will just misunderstand our motives. That much I agree with. But show me the primitive who would not be awed by this technology, either through superstition or curiosity or envy or through scientific inquiry. If I wouldn't be an emperor, I would at least be a celebrity, and if not a celebrity, then extremely wealthy."

"And *you* accuse *me* of being selfish?"

The Man on the Tower picked up another rock and hurled it in utter chaotic frustration. It sailed over Ezra's head. Clearly, the five hundred-odd years on this Earth had not given him maturity. It was quite likely he had gone through most of his life as a hedonist. This would naturally cause him to identify with anyone who opposed his father and react with suspicion and violence towards anyone who was on Ezra's side. And maybe feel a little jealous of a younger brother?

"All I want is for all of you to go away. You should have been on Ptolemy's ship."

Why did he keep saying *Ptolemy*? He'd changed his name a long time ago. Was it possible that this man had dropped out of sight just as he did? Not only out of sight, but out of contact. News of name changes usually spread quickly throughout the Originator world. He must have been cut off entirely by both sides. Ptolemy would only have cut him off if he'd become a danger.

"What is the cause?" Chaim asked.

"The *cause*. Didn't we cover this?"

"What is the cause, soldier!"

"To... to be accepted, of course."

"Wrong!"

"Wrong? What are you...?"

"What is the cause?"

"What do you mean, *wrong*?"

"What is the cause?"

"Why do you keep asking me that?"

"What is the cause, soldier?" Chaim got to his feet. He felt the power rise within him. It was like holding the grail. He approached the Man on the Tower, weapon still in hand.

"Stop it! Stop it!"

Chaim deactivated his emitter. He stood there, facing his assassin. He could have forced him to do any number of things. He could have fired a plasma ball through his brain cavity and watched his lifeless body fall. He could have handed the weapon over and hoped for the best. None of his choices were satisfactory.

Then he remembered something. He had been repeating his question because he had nothing else he could do. The fact that it was working to defuse the situation was as complete a shock to him as he could have imagined.

He remembered Donald's story about rabbits and wolves. He found he didn't know which one he was, or which one anyone else was. But he felt the weight of the story and its need for balance.

Chapter 63

*Enemies. Balance. Progress. We all feed off of each other.
We're nothing but characters in a morality tale. That's the trouble
with being immortal, we don't give future generations any lessons.
All the choices we make are without fear of death. We are all
rabbits, we are all wolves. Not in an individual sense, but in a
collective sense. Just as no wolf lives forever and yet the race lives
on; no rabbit lives forever and yet the race lives on. Is this the
secret? The collective memory, made up of stories and cautionary
tales does not serve to give us lessons; it is merely the residue of
being a species that has existed for thousands of years. At each
other's throats, educating our young about the enemy, whatever
that enemy might be. All the residue of a time when fear was a
legitimate response to other people. Evil seems like such a familiar
and comfortable concept. And we are suspicious of good news.
Why is that? Why do we tend to form communities when we are
threatened by a common enemy and yet we are at each other's
throats when we are faced with a common good? Does the greed
for the good blind us all to each other? What is greed? Is it merely
the logical extension of the fear of having nothing, or is there a
true desire to possess more than we need? Or is it simple envy and
the fear that we could have done better if only something were
different? If only something were different...*

"The cause is to make a better world," Chaim said. "We left
our Earth because it was dying. We came here to start again and
make it a better place than the one we left. That is the cause."

The other man's face fell.

"Join us," Chaim said. He could feel behind him Ezra's face
turn upside down with protest. "You've been alone for so long.
You need us. You need me. You said it yourself. You're a man of

action. You have the ambition I lack. And now I realize that I need you. You are what I have been missing. I've been imagining the day when I confronted you. Almost my entire life, now. I couldn't imagine how it would happen. What could I do, take revenge? Punish you? Imprison you? These are abstractions to me. The power I feel, the power I wield comes not from violence or force of will, it comes from the logic of community. And I have the context you lack. I have the legitimacy. I have the patience and strength you do not."

"I have strength."

"Physical strength. But you lack the will to use it correctly. Ask yourself why you want me dead."

"You're in the way."

"Am I? I would not have had the chance to be truly in the way had you done nothing. I would have probably extended and expanded the technology base of the world had you left me alone. I might have won a Nobel prize or two for my research. The only reason I was in your way is because you put me there. You're more haphazard than our parents were. And worse, you know this already and you haven't changed. To kill me makes no logical sense. With me dead you would not be able to achieve your goals. Instead, you killed my wife, which turned out worse, didn't it? She is dead to her family, to the world. She can never be herself again. For that I will never forgive you. But given the choice between revenge and clemency, I choose clemency. Now, ask yourself why you want me dead."

The Man on the Tower fell to his knees and began sobbing. "You pompous bastard! They stole my inheritance and handed it to you, and you squandered it! You didn't know what you had, and you threw it away!"

"That was *after* you intervened."

"I... I was working on it... I needed time for it to work... I needed more time. But they became impatient. They had always been patient, and suddenly the rules changed. You changed the rules! If you were dead, they would have turned back to me. I had a plan. I was working on a plan. You have no idea. You never had any idea."

"Pull yourself together, man! If you're going to help, it's going to have to be at arm's length. So I need you to be able to keep it together while you're working alone. Do you have doubts?"

"Yes..."

"Good. That will keep you alive. Are you able to help?"

The Man on the Tower quietly cried.

"Are you able to help, brother?"

His name, Fichelson, was not known, though he claimed not to have acted with secrecy most of the time. Since the First World War, he had been hiding out in the old Portuguese colony of the Azores. He had decided a long time ago that the Originator cause was irrelevant and sought to preserve his lifestyle of being a rich playboy. Everything and everyone who wished to change this was an enemy to be destroyed.

Deep down, however, as he confessed, he still had a self-destructive desire to be the one true savior of the Originators. His exile gave him the anger he needed to stay alive and exact revenge. To his dismay, revenge was hard to come by. He was born with a "throwback mutation" which caused him to accept violence and death as necessary and desirable in most cases. But his rage was undirected and in some cases uncontrollable.

As they traveled back to New York in Ezra's car, Fichelson told his tale. Chaim could not decide if he wanted to tell Leah who this man was. It might be enough to know that he had become interested again in the future fortunes of the Originators. As a brother, he might be accepted more readily by everyone; as an operative, he would be more useful; and as an ally, he would be more controllable. As an enemy he was effective. It was unnerving enough to have this man sitting within a few feet of him. Contrite? Maybe. But there would never be the trust necessary to maintain a command structure with him in it. He would have to be viewed as family.

Chaim was still unsure whether he should reveal all to his wife when they arrived at the apartment. No one had been killed in Fichelson's rampage, but it was disturbing enough behavior to make anyone question his future actions.

"Pleased to make your acquaintance," Leah said carefully. "It's just like my father-in-law to fail to mention another son. Tell me, what have you been doing with yourself?"

"He's been hiding out," Chaim said. "He's been a target."

"As have we," she reminded him.

Leah's hostility towards his father made his choice clear. She could not be told. At least not for the time being.

Chapter 64

Somewhere in Qatar

Sheik Nasir Al Akkali arrived in his custom-made Maserati limousine. It was strange meeting in such a public place. Usually, important conversations took place in more secrecy. But these people were playing a different gambit. Ever since the towers came down in New York, all kinds of Americans wanted his help of one kind or another. Just one of the benefits of not being one of those wild-eyed wackos who tried to stir up trouble in inappropriate places.

But before then? Nothing. They were all just content with purchasing his Saudi oil and his Iraqi potash. Now he was a celebrity. How many moderate sheiks were there who could claim friendly relations from both the Middle East and the West? He could count them on one hand.

He had never been to this part of Qatar. Not that it was in a bad location, it was just a little... middle class for his taste. There were Westernized touches all around the hotel, including the columns that reminded him of certain parts of Cairo. He had never really been outside of the general Middle East area. There was that one time in Odessa, but that was long ago and not so far from home. Not like his son, enrolled at Stanford in California. Asim was a world traveler compared to his father. He had learned English at the University of Cairo, had almost gone into diplomacy before he came to his senses and went into the family business.

His receiving party was composed of four men and a woman. The men all looked remarkably alike, same height and general appearance. The woman was shorter, but not by much. She was shockingly pale and dressed in acceptably loose light-colored clothing— her hands did not show.

Sheik Nasir was pleased.

They all sat down at a Western style conference table in one of

those rooms where the walls move to accommodate different-sized committees. The carpet was a dull green with a strange pattern of yellow and white rectangles. The green reminded him of a Saudi flag he had seen flying in a slum outside Riyadh once, discolored from years of smoke and sand. Desecration by neglect.

"All right," he said after a silence when they sat down. "You don't want any of my coffee, I am sure of that. And I don't want any of your cola. So tell me why I am here."

"Good afternoon, Sheik Nasir. My name is Chaim Onward. Now, I know what you're thinking. *Chaim.* You've heard that before, I presume. What's a Jew doing in this part of the world talking to an important man such as yourself?"

"These things cross one's mind."

"I'm here for both our benefit."

"Once a merchant always a merchant."

"I want to help you by putting you out of business."

The old Saudi stopped moving entirely, focusing his attention on this strange man. He slowly pulled off his sunglasses, bringing the room into a slightly better focus with more colors than he had often been used to. "I have been threatened by better minds than you," he said.

"There's no threat here. There will be no violence. Violence solves nothing, as I'm sure you're aware. All it serves to do is block commerce."

"Please continue," Sheik Nasir said, nodding. "What is my retirement plan?"

"I have in my possession a technology which will make oil burning obsolete..."

Nasir put up his hand and brushed it. "Please. I have heard such tales of energy sources. They have a habit of, shall we say, not materializing."

"This is already done. All we have to do is put it in place. Once we do, everything in the oil industry will be altered forever. I'm only here as a courtesy. You have a reputation for being fair, so I am, in a sense, coming to you in hopes that you will accept this in the spirit of peace I offer it."

"So, this process of yours that will put me out of my business. Say it works. Say it is wildly successful beyond dreaming. What is my concern with this, apart from my immediate poverty?"

"Oil will still be useful. Plastics, lubricants, pharmaceuticals. You can even extract the proteins and use it as a food source (which we may consider subsidizing if you ask nicely). The point here is that your oil, anyone's oil will not be used for power. I don't need to emphasize to you that this will cause its value to plummet. Possibly your potash business will become more valuable; who can say?"

"You must understand that I am naturally suspicious of apocalyptic scenarios like this."

"I know this is an interruption of the natural course of oil production. At current rates, in thirty or forty years, maybe fifty or sixty—seventy if you're lucky—the wells will start to dry up and the value will skyrocket. Soon after, the flow of crude will be a mere trickle. The industry might hang on for another fifty years or so, but let's be reasonable. Oil companies are already taking steps to be known as *power* companies. There will be alternative technologies. It's just a matter of time. Take away power production and you'll be in business for over two hundred years. At less than ten percent of current profits. But I'm offering you now the opportunity to be a part of our operation. Nothing can take the place of your oil empire, but we can guarantee you a better return than the default scheme."

Nasir chuckled. "And this is your offer? You won't bankrupt me if I become your poodle? What would you have me do, go around on a speaking tour to 'talk up' your technology?"

"If you don't mind."

"That's crazy. It's foolishness. I am dismissing you. I am sorry I wasted my time listening to your drivel. There is no reason for me to listen to you at all." He stood up as if to leave.

"And yet you came."

"Your reputation suggested something more substantial. The article about your company in *The Economist* was interesting. Myself, I preferred the missive in *The New Yorker*. But they say your process is theoretical. Are you asking me to risk my future on a theory?"

"No. You are risking the future of your *country*."

Nasir waved his hand at them again. "You Americans. I just learned the other day a funny little word. *Hubris*. Do you know what it means? Arrogance. Self-righteousness. Hubris before the fall? This is what America is. The rest of the world is just waiting for the day when you stumble and break apart into bite-sized pieces."

"Rhetorician, speak to thyself."

Sheik Nasir got up and left quickly, before he had a chance to listen to any more useless argument. He had missed his son-in-law's polo match for this meeting. Now he had nothing to show for it. Ah, but not quite true. He had the knowledge that he would not be flushing his family's future down the toilet on another energy scheme. He had survived many such encounters with crackpots and idealistic dreamers. There was no reason to feel bad about something that was not a loss.

He had heard of this Chaim going to other important people all over the region, looking to make deals with just the shifting winds to back him up. As far as he could tell, there was no one willing to help. The Jew should have known better than to enter into a meeting with just a theory—he needed an application, a demonstration of the power. It was bad enough that he was wasting the time of so many important people.

And yet, what did this funny little man have up his sleeve? He should have known that his request was at best an oddity and would go nowhere. As an Arab potentate, he had heard most of the details before the meeting, and yet—as the little man said, himself—he had gone. Why had he gone? To see for himself? Now he was more curious than ever. It went exactly according to plan, and exactly like all the other meetings he had heard about. And yet...

"Turn the car around!" he bellowed to his driver.

He caught the other party in the lobby of the hotel. "What's your game?" he said to Chaim with no warning.

"There's no game. I'm putting you out of business. What happens after that is up to you."

"I'm not interested in how you will be bankrupting me. I want to know what your strategy is. What your purpose is in coming here. You must have known everyone talks to everyone else. Why did you give me a failing pitch? It is the silliest and the least credible of any I have heard in a long time. So tell me, why does a famous, wealthy Hebrew man such as yourself, come to me for a partnership?"

"It's all about forgiveness."

"I'm sorry, what? What did you say? *Forgiveness*?"

"Killing is a commodity around your neighborhood. I think there are those among you who have a great deal to do with that."

"What are you on about?"

"Oh, I know terrorism is merely a tool. Money makes the world go around, and all that. I wonder how many of *them* have a problem with being funded by the oil money you take from the West."

"You mistake me for some of my more unorthodox brethren."

"We know you're not involved," Chaim said. "But *you* know who is. And that puts you in a dangerous position. For both sides and yourself."

"Both *sides*? What's going on? Who are you people?"

"Don't be alarmed. Like we said, we're here to help."

One of Chaim's associates spoke, "At this very moment, we are making arrangements for your transition to this new economy. Your name is being put on partial ownership papers of the company, and your welcome collaboration with us is being distributed and broadcast as part of a goodwill gesture."

"Goodwill? There is no such collaboration. What are you talking about? Why are you trying to ruin me?"

"We're not trying to ruin you, we're trying to save you. There will be a market collapse once we make our announcement."

The sheik straightened up, looked at each member of the other party quickly. They were either sun-crazy, bluffing a con on him, or...

"You're a very powerful man," Chaim added. "And you also happen to be the man most likely to build a following if you choose to lead."

Nasir looked around at the people in the lobby. Someone rang a bell for the concierge. Chaim stepped closer, which made Nasir's guards nervous.

"It is not enough to help your country by being a wheel in its machinery. It is not enough to be a critic of policy decisions. I know who you are, *Shaykh*. More than you realize. You are an intelligent man and you disagree with a lot that is happening in your country. In fact, you abhor some of your friends' ways of thinking and carrying out their agendas. But you lack the will to stop them. You do not fear death, but you fear for the life of your son, your only son. Tell me I'm wrong."

The funny little man was not wrong. How could he know such things?

"Antagonism fuels misunderstanding, and back again," Chaim continued. "Soon people forget their differences to the point where they don't matter, and hate becomes a religion in itself. *Shaykh*, we are all people of the Book."

Nasir, mouth ajar just a little, nodded slightly. His greatest fear was that the people who murdered with impunity, in the name of Allah, would anger his God so much that his entire country would suffer. In the end, he knew that he would cooperate with this Western cipher—not because he represented an additional source of cash or because he believed in the energy scheme or because he was being threatened. In that moment, he knew that he would cooperate because, in his heart, he was a patriot.

Chapter 65

Stockholm, Sweden

Of the three letters in his suit pocket, folded back in their envelopes. Chaim relished the last one most of all. It was what he came to realize as "standard" anonymous hate mail. It called him various epithets that were more amusing than they were damaging. It tickled him every time he thought about it. Not so much because it was funny—it was unintentionally hilarious—but because it was so full of ignorant vitriol and so much the product of a darkened mind ruled by irrationality that he had to crack a smile. Such absurdities were not few and far between in this created world, but they were rarely so amusing.

The other two letters were from his devoted wife, Leah, who asked him not to read it until after his speech was over; and from Fichelson, his erstwhile brother, about the status of their operations in the Middle East. He had long since proven his loyalty, and was routinely given specific missions. All the parts of the plan were in place. Chaim disliked the drama that so many other Originators preferred. He had to be talked into all of this.

Leah was seated in the gallery with the journalists. She waved a small kiss at him, which he could hardly see.

He could not help but think of Donald, Li-Don, who had advised him to be a less public a figure if he couldn't handle the publicity. Nothing could be more public than having fifty television cameras pointed at your nose, ready to record your best and your worst moments. Not everyone on the planet was watching, of course. Most likely, the actual number was far less than one percent of the world's population. But the cameras were there, and eventually enough people would see the tape.

He was introduced by the ambassador from the U.S. and then

413

took his place at the podium. He had been debating with himself (as both himself and Li-Don) whether or not to open with a joke. He decided against it. He had to remember to speak slowly, as the organizers told him, to allow for translation.

"My fellow citizens," he began. "Citizens of every nation in this golden world of ours, in this little place at the edge of the future; Leaders of the world and leaders of our industrial infrastructure."

There are moments in every nation's history when she must stop and assess the progress she has made and decide whether or not the foreseeable future is desirable or not. In these times, there are often unseen and unconsidered choices. Choices that are hidden because of the ease with which we continue on. When times are good, when we are well-fed, when we all have work to do and are paid fairly for it—these are the times to assess our choices. Because in times of sorrow and famine, there are often difficult choices or none at all.

I say this not just because the company that I founded works toward a better future for all, but because I, myself, have a selfish motive for bringing this to the world's attention.

Among other things, I am a Jew. It is through no small act of faith that I have remained so. It is very easy to stop being a Jew. It is very tempting to completely assimilate into a greater society and become a part of it, as so many other ethnic groups have.

Indeed, it is difficult for the nations of the world to live in the presence of the Jews. We are irritating and most uncomfortable, not unlike a pebble in the shoe of Western Civilization.

The Jews embarrass the world with their actions, which are beyond the imaginable. They have become moral strangers since the day their forefather Abraham introduced the world to high ethical standards and to the fear of Heaven. They brought the world the Ten Commandments, which many nations prefer to defy.

They violated the rules of history by staying alive, totally at odds with common sense and historical evidence.

They outlived all their former enslavers and antagonists, including vast empires such as the Romans and the Greeks. They angered the world with their return to their homeland after 2000 years of exile and after the murder of six million of their brothers and sisters. They aggravated mankind by building, in the wink of an eye, a democratic State which others were not able to create in even hundreds of years. They built living monuments such as the duty to be holy and the privilege to serve one's fellow man. They had parts in every human progressive endeavor, whether in science, medicine, psychology or any other discipline, totally out of proportion to their actual numbers.

Jews taught the world not to accept the world as it is but to transform it. Jews introduced the world to one God, yet only a minority wanted to draw the moral consequences. The Bible was their gift, and from this tradition sprang the *Savior*.

Do the nations of the world realize that they would have been lost without the Jews? Within the conscience of Western civilization, the concepts first articulated by the Jews reside. But these ideas are suppressed at the same time they are followed. It is too embarrassing to admit that the existence of this small band of zealots and heretics remind them of the possibility of a higher purpose. It is too much to handle, and their rules are too difficult to follow in this age of technologically assisted narcissism and decadence.

415

I am reminded of a joke I was told once by someone who did not know I was a Jew. I will not attempt to deliver it for a punch line. My colleagues and friends will tell you that my humor is far too dry and obscure to sustain a good joke. But the gist of the joke is that Israel occupies the only contiguous stretch of arable land in the Middle East that does not contain oil. What kind of a joke is God telling us that our adversaries have inherited, seemingly by accident, the single most important and valuable commodity of the modern world? But surely it is not an accident. Surely there is a reason for this.

I speak to you not just as a Jew, but also as a human being. We are all prone to stumbling, backsliding, dallying, growing fat and lazy with our own success. We are a world awash in currency, yet there are millions who are dying for lack of resources. I am not the first to point this out. Nor do I advocate the redistribution of wealth through socialism. I, too, believe in the marketplace. But I also believe in the triumph of ideas over brute force.

The Jews have a oil-free homeland in an oil-rich area of the world. I believe we are meant not to rely on just this one resource for our survival. Oil is a slave in our economy, but it is also a master. Israel has an economy based not on one resource, but on individual achievement.

And it is here where I wish to continue my original point. Just as the Jews in this world maintained their identity through the centuries, my kind and myself have done the same. I am referring to science and the exploration of the physical properties of forces.

Most of you here are familiar with my work, as I imagine most people watching this remotely are familiar with the motivation of world harmony behind my work. The goal of a renewable, reliable, powerful, and clean energy source is now within our grasp. The application for this energy source is limitless. I would like to take this opportunity to announce to the world that my hydrogen supercharging process will be available to any group, any organization, any world body, and any individual who wants it, free of charge. This has been my goal.

[murmurs in the crowd]

As you know, my foundation is funded by private donations. My family's trade was diamonds up until a few years ago, when I discovered that diamonds cut into cross-cubic crystals would intensify the lab results I was getting with just glass tubes.

At this very moment, we are conducting tests of a prototype vehicle, using the drive process that I engineered, which will revolutionize the way people travel. We are testing self-propelled drills that will look for potable water endlessly. We are testing artificial heart valves which will last far beyond the lifespan of the person using it. And, most importantly, we are testing the viability of large scale power plants using this process to provide clean electricity to the existing grid, with the potential to supplant the current pollution-producing energy sources we now use.

[shots heard in the gallery. screams from the audience. general confusion.]

Please, ladies and gentlemen, do not be afraid. My assassins will be dealt with in a fair manner. I am frequently the target of such attempts. No, really, it's all right. Please sit down. We are quite safe in this building. I am frequently the target of assassination attempts. In the last five years alone I have been the target of numerous plots. As you can plainly tell, they have all failed.

[nervous laughter among those still seated]

Who these assassins are is anyone's guess, but I ask you to ask yourselves who would be hurt the most if my technology were ever to reach the hands of the consumer. Don't say it out loud. We wouldn't want to offend anyone.

I have been called many names and have had many things thrown at me. There is a large number of people who will find that they will no longer be needed in their present line of work, and they will doubtless blame me. But I see a new industry, one that is predicated on clean energy in all areas where energy is required: transportation, information systems, civil engineering and government, computers and small electronics. The adaptation of my technology to every single piece of equipment that now uses any sort of power will be a cottage industry of its own. And when that is through with, we can start progressing as a society without fear that we were doing the irreversible environmental harm to our planet.

Our world will not be perfect by then, I assure you. I am a utopian, but I am also a realist. But in this way, I hope to spend my time on this planet breathing air, drinking water, and enjoying the landscape free of harmful particulates. We will not be free from all the tyrannies that men have devised, but we will be free of this particular one.

[anonymous messenger enters and whispers to Chaim at the podium]

I have an announcement to make. The Swedish police have apprehended the suspects in my assassination attempt. We may know shortly who they are or who they are working for. In the meantime, I urge you to look around at your lives. See all the objects and processes that currently use some form of electricity, or that require power of some kind in order to operate. Then imagine their operation with this new power machine and without the traditional forms of power—nuclear, coal fire, natural gas, solar, wind, thermal, waterfall. Then ask me for a sample machine. I will give it to you to try out your own solution. If you like, you can patent your implementation and sell it to others

who think it's a good idea. I do not claim any ownership of the process, nor of the engines themselves. I am already wealthy beyond imaginings and only wish to help our civilization transition to this new era.

Thank you.

Please follow the instructions of the police commissioner on how to exit this building safely.

Chapter 66

Mecca, Saudi Arabia

The craft was not that difficult to steer, even in the high-altitude winds. The controls took some getting used to, however, and Fichelson was not an accomplished pilot to begin with. He made his descent carefully. The silence of the craft was eerie. Though the gyroscopic fantail mechanism was rotating at a speed of xx revolutions per second, the emitter capsule that surrounded it kept the noise down. The Gravometric pressure generated by the fantail was apparently unaffected by the emitter field, something Chaim was at a loss to explain, but was more than willing to exploit.

Chaim had not liked this idea. It was one thing to put the world on notice that a new era in energy was upon them. It was quite another to bring about social revolution through ideas. But Fichelson had wanted to do it. This was his show.

It was close to noon and the sky was clear. He could see the xx below—with something less than the teeming mass of humanity he had expected. That might come in the next few days.

The craft descended out of the sky. He was not altogether confident in his ability to speak French, Pushtun, Farsi, and Arabic, but he was able enough to say what he felt he had to say.

Heads looked up. Hands pointed. Knees hit the ground. Mouths shouted. This object had descended from nowhere out of the sky. The message that came from this object repeated in different languages:

"PEOPLE OF ISLAM.

I AM A MAN WHO SHARES YOUR FAITH IN GOD.

I AM HERE ON A MISSION FROM MY CONSCIENCE.
WE ARE ALL PARTICIPANTS IN THIS WORLD,
FROM EVERY BACKGROUND, EVERY LANGUAGE,
EVERY MOTHER, EVERY NATION, EVERY BELIEF.
WE ARE ALL BELIEVERS AND WE ARE ALL INFIDELS.
WE SHARE THE SAME EARTH, THE SAME SKY,
 THE SAME AIR, THE SAME WATER. FROM MY GOD,
WHO SAYS
THOU SHALT NOT KILL,
THOU SHALT NOT STEAL,
THOU SHALT NOT COVET,
I HAVE CHOSEN TO SPEAK THIS MESSAGE.
THERE IS A POWER WITHIN US THAT DOES NOT
LEAVE US EVEN WHEN WE BREAK OUR
COMMANDMENTS. THAT POWER IS LOVE.
BUT LOVE WITHOUT DUTY IS MEANINGLESS.
OUR DUTY IS TO SEEK WAYS THAT DEATH
IS NOT A THREAT, BUT A NATURAL THING.
DO NOT BELIEVE FALSE DOCTRINE. I AM NOT HERE
TO PREACH, BUT TO WARN.
FALSE DOCTRINE WILL ARISE
LIKE THE OIL FROM THE GROUND.
DO NOT BELIEVE ME
BECAUSE YOU ARE LOOKING UP AT ME.
ASK QUESTIONS. READ THE QU'RAN.
IT IS NOT FORBIDDEN.

WE ARE ALL PEOPLE OF THE BOOK.

I CLAIM NOTHING.

 I AM JUST A MAN ON A COMPLICATED FLYING

MACHINE.

BELIEVE ME BECAUSE YOU BELIEVE IN YOUR

 HEART THAT YOU AGREE.

THAT IS ALL.

AMEN."

Around the world, news coverage got hold of the story. Special dispensation from the Saudi government was granted to three networks in order to cover him by television as he repeated his speech daily for the entire length of Ramadan—as long as they did not record individual faces of those in the crowd.

Commentators seemed doubtful as to whether or not the message amounted to anything. Was this a new prophet or just some wacko with a new toy? Debates raged in the usual places. Television coverage of the improbable event repeated itself over and over again. Scattered reports of other similar sightings in places like Jerusalem, Vatican City, Canterbury, Salt Lake City, Rio de Janeiro, Kyoto, and Katmandu were also reported. These reports were not as reliable and the events, as indicated by eyewitness accounts, only lasted one or two days, so television coverage was not possible.

After a while, the event made its way into the middle of the front page in newspapers, and finally completely out of it. It was supplanted by a different news event, and then people largely remembered it as if they had seen it in a movie once. In the years to come, it would be commemorated in This Day in History specials.

Chaim turned off the TV set in his hotel room. It was coming to the time when another infusion was necessary for him. Just this one lie, he thought. This one untruth hidden from the public until such time as it was impossible to hide. He would no longer actively hide, though. Maybe when he was a 200-year-old man with the face of his mid-thirties he might have to answer the inevitable question. But not today.

Today, he would seek the comfort of his wife, whose time for infusion was also almost due. But she wouldn't take it. You have to make a deliberate decision to have a child, there are no accidents.

He felt his wife's belly. She would lose almost a year of her life for this child. But the decision was made. They had always wanted children. He felt a kick and the two parents smiled at each other. Leah was smarter than he was, he knew. She would know how to handle it all.

~ Charles Schwartz ~

Epilogue

Manhattan

The Son faced the Father across the divide of the private table at Carlisle's on 6th. The father lit a cigar, though it was not allowed in the restaurant. The son nervously tapped his coffee cup and fumbled around in his inside jacket pocket. Another attempt on his life had been made just that morning by two people with machine guns who drove by his apartment building. The car was a white Mercedes sedan with no license plates and blackened windows.

He was not particularly nervous from this encounter—it was not unexpected, as similar attempts had been made since he set up his company some five years earlier. Each time, some kind of token was left at the scene, a coin or a card or a small piece of cloth. The only thing they had in common was the picture of a bugle. It became the icon of his assassination.

He wondered when they would realize that simple bullets would not work and would try something else.

There were several bills in Congress to either outlaw his technology as "polluting" because of its abnormal heat generation capacity or relegate it to limbo with perpetual study. These impediments to progress, too, he knew would happen.

Fichelson was back at the office, trying to think of ways he could be useful. Leah was at the doctor's office, making sure the baby was OK. Jimmy was somewhere in Scandinavia, studying new areas that could be used for building large-scale energy collectors. (The less he knew about what Jimmy was doing or where he was, the more secure he felt.)

It was just the Father and the Son.

After the soup came, and they each salted it before tasting, the son gathered up his strength and spoke.

"Leah and Jacob are doing fine, if you were going to ask."

"I was."

"Of course you were."

The son pulled out the glass oblong from his pocket. It was in mid-cycle, with the bluish cast already fading from the haze.

"This was clever," he said.

"How so?" The unflappable father.

"It got me thinking about perpetual energy production."

"Did it?"

"And about closed vs. open systems."

"Is that a fact?"

"And about lightning."

"Really? How marvelous."

The son smiled. His father, the *deus ex machina* in his life. It was all a play in which he was supposed to act the hero.

Then he straightened up, turned the glass oblong on its side, and set both hands on the table, crossed arms in front of him. He was about to ask the question that he had been afraid to ask, not necessarily because he did not want to know the answer, but because he did not want to face the proposition implied by the question. There were many other questions he had not yet asked, whether out of necessity or expedience, fear or shame, practicality or emotional stability. But this was the one question he had yet to fully run through his head.

When he asked the question, the father stopped eating his soup, set the spoon down and folded his arms on the table in almost exactly the same way as the son.

"To answer that," he said. "We have to go back to when your mother and I met."

THE END

GLOSSARY ON FOLLOWING PAGES

GLOSSARY FOR "*THE ORIGINATORS*"

Some of these words are simplistic, but they are roughly in order of where they appear in the manuscript.

Champ de Mars - Location of the Eiffel Tower in Paris.

Mathematikai és Természettudományi Értesítõ - Title of an applied mathematics journal in Hungarian

monde á deux - "The world made up of just the two of us"

Exposition Universelle - Universal Exposition

Dôme Centrale - Central Dome

Galerie des Machines - Gallery of the Machines

Cochinchine - modern day Vietnam & possibly parts of Cambodia

Palais Archépiscopal - Arch Episcopal church (palace)
"On n'a pas besoin de medecìn" - "I don't need a doctor"

"Message pour Monsieur Hopewell" - Message for Mr. Hopewell

"Un télégramme" - A telegram

GLOSSARY FOR "THE ORIGINATORS" continued

"Tant pis. Cela ne fait rien." - "Too bad. That doesn't mean anything" or "That has no effect on me."

"Monsieur Brightferry ne fait qu'aller et venir" - "Mr. Brightferry will be with you shortly."

au courant - trendy; styled with the times

spoorweg - railroad (Dutch)

"On doit quitter! Quittez maintenant!" - "You must leave! Leave now!"

Pourquoi? - Why?

chemin de fer – railroad

mascaret - a tidal force wave in a river

adieu - goodbye (usually "goodbye forever" = "Until God"; this is opposed to: au revoir = "until we see each other again"; or: a tout a l'heure = "see you later")

Maison de Sacré Coeur - Boarding house at Sacré Coeur

hôpital – hospital

Comme ci, comme ça - OK; (literally: "like this, like that")

GLOSSARY FOR "THE ORIGINATORS" continued

egoiste – arrogant

Café Soufflot - (just a name; Soufflot means a kind of breathing)

Je m'excuse - Pardon me

As-tu dit Madame Curie? - Did you say Madame Curie?

Ah, bon? - "Is that a fact?" or "Really?"

porportionale – proportional

liebling - my child (German)

departement – department

C'est la vie - That's life; that's the way it goes.

demitasse - half of a cup (half a cup of coffee because it's usually so strong)

molécules – molecules

mélange – mixture

Promenade - leisurely walk

déjeuner – lunch

GLOSSARY FOR "THE ORIGINATORS" continued

Jardin des Plantes (The Garden of Plants, really just a name)

Arrêtez - stop!

Allons - Let's go!

Place du Trône - (just a name)

aperitíf - small glass of liqueur before or after a meal

glacée á menthe - mint ice cream

chinois - type of very fine cloth material

Crasseuse souillon! Puteresse! - "Stupid bitch! Worthless whore!"

Caisse vide - "The case is empty"

Merveilleux! - Marvelous!!

Merveilleux! - Marvelous!!

~ END ~

~ Charles Schwartz ~

BLANK PAGE

BLANK PAGE

~ Charles Schwartz ~

www.ingramcontent.com/pod-product-compliance
Lightning Source LLC
Chambersburg PA
CBHW060806030726
47503CB00002B/363